THE LAST OF THE HUSBANDMEN

THE LAST OF THE
HUSBANDMEN

A NOVEL OF FARMING LIFE

Gene Logsdon

OHIO UNIVERSITY PRESS

ATHENS, OHIO

Ohio University Press, Athens, Ohio 45701
www.ohio.edu/oupress
© 2008 by Gene Logsdon

Ohio University Press books are printed on acid-free paper ∞ ™

15 14 13 12 11 10 09 08   5 4 3 2 1

Excerpts from "At a Country Funeral" by Wendell Berry
from *Collected Poems* (North Point Press, 1987), © Wendell Berry

Library of Congress Cataloging-in-Publication Data
Logsdon, Gene.
  The last of the husbandmen : a novel of farming life / Gene Logsdon.
    p. cm.
  ISBN-13: 978-0-8214-1785-0 (hc : acid-free paper)
  ISBN-10: 0-8214-1785-1 (hc : acid-free paper)
  ISBN-13: 978-0-8214-1786-7 (pbk : acid-free paper)
  ISBN-10: 0-8214-1786-X (pbk : acid-free paper)
  1. Farm life—Fiction. 2. Farmers—Fiction. 3. Rural families—Fiction.
  4. Ohio—Rural conditions—Fiction. I. Title.
  PS3562.O453L37 2008
  813'.54—dc22
                                                    2007041293

For the farmers and villagers of Wyandot County, Ohio,

with great affection

ACKNOWLEDGMENTS

My thanks to David Sanders, Gillian Berchowitz, and all the people at Ohio University Press for their enduring and understanding support in publishing my books. I am also indebted to the people of my home grounds, who have in so many ways inspired this novel. They will have fun, I think, trying to separate fact from fiction but will ultimately be stumped because although some anecdotes and details are true to life, the characters are all made up, and what happens to them is entirely fictional except in the broad sense that they represent the way real farmers and villagers have lived in this area in the twentieth century and even to this day.

O N E

Had Ben Bump been able to foresee what would happen to him before the day was over, he surely wouldn't have dozed off as he cultivated corn with the horses, Bell and Florie. Dozing off would have seemed impossible anyway, as he tried to master the operation of the two-row cultivator. The horses had to be kept walking straight down between the rows of corn without much guidance while he focused his attention on the two gangs of shovels that hung from the high frame of the cultivator, one over each of the two rows being weeded. Enthroned on the iron seat between the tall, skinny iron wheels, with his feet in the steel stirrups of the two gangs, he knew he looked very much like a sulky driver in a harness race at the fair. But that was as far as the similarity went. As the horses plodded ahead, Ben used his feet in the stirrups to push the gangs toward or away from the corn row a bit, as conditions demanded, to accommodate a stalk not quite in line with the others, or to make up for a slightly wayward pull of the horses, or to hold the shovels down in the harder yellow clay on the knolls that occasionally swelled above the black, low ground that dominated the field. If he managed to operate the shovels just right, they not only plowed out the weeds between the rows, but rolled dirt into the row, burying sprouting weeds there where the shovels could not reach. He could give each hill of corn a bit of the personal attention of hand-hoeing, but with more speed. Speed was everything. Economy depended on how fast a person could learn the knack of using the forward motion of the cultivator to help him guide the shovels in and out rather than relying only on his muscles, and how long one could endure the labor. In this case, Ben's legs would finally cramp up enough so that he had to stop the horses, hop off the cultivator, and stamp out the pain from his legs.

Although at sixteen Ben had already developed the muscle-knotted frame of a young farmer, his legs and shoulders ached badly after he had cultivated only eight rows across the field. The blessed fact that kept him going was that this particular day was the Fourth of July. His father, Nat, always took the afternoon off to celebrate the holiday, saying the weather was too hot in the fields for the horses.

The cramps gradually subsided. He became a part of the un-thinking machine, automatically moving the gangs with his feet while his hands kept an attentive hold on the horses' reins and worked the levers that lifted and lowered the shovels out of and into the soil when he turned at the end of the rows. After a while, he could do it with his mind on Roman candles and skyrockets. He slipped gradually into the kind of reverie that made long days in the field pass, if not quickly, at least rather pleasantly for a person of pensive character. After only two years on their new farm, the Bumps were beginning to achieve the kind of success that good land and wise farming bring. For Ben, the first farm, in swampy Killdeer, and the awful tension of his father making moonshine to get enough cash to buy a better farm, remained only as a childhood nightmare.

He daydreamed now about his favorite subject: how he would manage some day to buy his own farm, hopefully without resorting to bootleg whiskey, and how he would turn it into an absolutely calendar-perfect homestead, a white house with a gleaming, standing-seam metal roof, red barns with white trim, a main hay barn with cows and horses stabled underneath the mows, a sheep shed to the rear, a separate pig barn, and a chicken house with an orchard close by. Like the self-sufficient old farms, it would have a big cypress-wood water tank, insulated with sawdust, kept full of water by a windmill beside it, the water flowing underground through pipes by gravity (no need for pumps) to the horse trough and to tanks outside the sheep shed and cow stable. With wood for fuel to heat the house, his farm would be able to continue operation even if the electricity that had come to the county a year earlier failed. From his father, Nat, he had inherited an innate distrust of those poles marching down the country roads. Nat at first had refused to "get connected." The "electric," as he called it, would make them dependent on the outside world for survival. But when everyone else's "missus" had it in the house, who could be so heartless as to refuse his own wife the comforts of electric power?

Ben would divide his tilled land in the traditional manner, into eight fields of ten acres each, three every year in corn, one in wheat, one in oats, and three in hay and temporary pasture, all rotated from year to year, with another ten acres in permanent pasture through which would run a clear, spring-fed creek. There would also be a ten-acre woodlot westward of the buildings to cut the cold of winter winds and provide firewood and lumber. Part of the woodlot would be a catalpa grove for a steady supply of fenceposts.

Tiring of that reverie, he turned his attention to the corn he was cultivating. The rows had a mathematical exactitude as well as botanical beauty that appealed to him. Three or four kernels were planted to a hill, in hopes that at least one or two would survive the rigors of germination and early growth—"one for the cutworm, one for the crow, one for the drouth, and one to grow," Nat would say, echoing ancient farm lore not unlike what he had heard as a boy in Austria, made over to apply to New World maize. The hills were forty inches apart both ways to allow space enough for a horse to pass through during weed cultivation. A skilled farmer's hills lined up both lengthwise and crosswise, which meant that they lined up on a 45-degree angle as well, forming a sort of diamond pattern if one looked diagonally across the field. The whole affair resulted in numerical detail that Ben found intriguing. It took 144 hills to make a shock. Every 25 shocks marked an acre of land. Ben amused himself with the numbers, multiplying 144 times 25 in his head like Nat had taught him to do, first 144 by 20, then by 5, and adding the two figures together. Every acre therefore held 3,600 hills of corn, or roughly 36,000 in a 10-acre field like the one he was cultivating. That meant 144,000 kernels were necessary to plant the field, at 4 kernels per hill. If 2 plants survived in every hill and assuming 1 ear of corn per stalk, that would be 72,000 ears per acre, or 103,000 if 3 plants each with an ear grew per hill. Counting 50 kernels per row on an 18-row ear, that was 900 kernels per ear times 72,000 ears, which came out to 648 plus five zeros— 64,800,000 kernels per acre at 2 ears per hill, or 92,700,000 at 3 ears per hill. But if all 3 of those ears in a hill could be 14 inches long and 20 rows of kernels around, like one ear he had found in the last field of open-pollinated corn his father had grown, that would be at least 60 kernels per row times 20 rows, or 1,200 kernels per ear. Twelve hundred kernels per ear times 103,000 ears per acre—and here he had to focus all his mental strength on the multiplication—that would be 100,000 times 1,200, or 12 with seven zeros (120,000,000) plus 3,000 times 1,200, or 36 and five zeros (3,600,000), which two figures added together made 123,600,000 kernels per acre. That would be a lot of corn. He decided that he would count the kernels in a pound of corn when he got a chance, multiply by 60, about the number of pounds in a bushel of corn, and find out how many bushels 123,600,000 kernels amounted to.

Although Ben was not yet aware of it, this kind of mathematical exactitude was a reflection of the cultural attitudes that shaped the landscape around him. His father's fields, like all the others in the area, were either square or rectangular, hardly ever more than fifteen acres each, all marked off by arrow-straight roads and fence lines issuing out at right angles from each other, whether the land surface was gently rolling, as most of it was, or fell away to short but steeper slopes where streams and small rivers cut their valleys through the leveler land. Along with the homesteads of red barns full of livestock and white houses full of people dotting the landscape about every 160 acres along the roads, the result was an almost park-like beauty, a prim, civilized neatness joined to a varied landscape of well-defined woodlots, meadows, grain fields, and hay lands, all demarcated by brushy fencerows, the whole pattern breaking up what would otherwise have been the monotony of rather flat surfaces. It would be forty years yet before this land would be cleared of fences, pastures, and woodlots into vast, almost unending fields of corn and soybeans dotted with faded, deteriorating barns, each a monument to the dying down of husbandry.

Laid out in 1785 by the Ohio Company of Massachusetts, whose officials in New England had never set foot on the land, most of the Midwestern countryside was divided into square 640-acre sections—"checkerboard square" country, as the Ralston Purina company so aptly characterized it. The one-lane township and county roads followed the section lines, accentuating the checkerboard image in reality as effectively as the drawn lines did on the survey maps. Farm fields thus followed the unbending rigidity of the roads, or so farmers tried to make them do, and the mentality of straightforwardness seeped even into language. Reliable people kept everything "squared away" and always made a "square deal." The untrustworthy were "crooked" or "ran around in circles." Most farmers, like Ben's father, Nat, so dearly loved the idea of severe straightness that they took great pride in keeping their corn rows absolutely straight even over rounded hills and side slopes, which required consummate skill. When Nat mowed a hay field, he took great pains to keep his corners absolutely square as he mowed. If one paid close attention to every detail of guiding the horses and maneuvering the mower, such a square corner of still-standing hay was possible, but where tractors had replaced horses in hay-mowing, but still pulled the horse mowers, which had not been designed for them, a precise right-angle corner was extremely difficult, if not impossible. As a result, so amusing to Ben, *very* particular farmers, like Adrian Farnold, would drive through a corner as they mowed, instead of turning right directly into the standing hay, and make a wide sashay out into the already cut portion of the field, turning left and coming completely around so as to engage the uncut hay again at *exactly* a right angle. Doing that at every corner added considerably to the time required to mow a field, but that was of no matter. One must remain, at all costs, "square with the world."

Another result of the idolatry of the straight line was that often a flat, cultivated field next to, say, a creek valley might have, at the corner nearest the valley, a short but rather steep, erosive slope falling away toward the stream. Such slopes would normally be in permanent pasture, as most such rolling land next to creeks was kept, but in order to finish out the field in a perfect square or rectangle, the sloping corner had to be part of the cultivated field so as not to disturb the mindset of rectilinear perfection. Nasty gullies ran down these little slopes after spring cultivation and over the years washed away the topsoil. Crops finally would hardly grow there, but the farmer invariably refused to take the slope, often only a portion of an acre, out of cultivation by running a fence along the rim of the slope. Doing that would mean abandoning the right angle of the fence corner at the bottom of the slope and running a little stretch of fence at an angle (horrors) along the top of the slope. Such a fence would have saved the slope from erosion, but would not be "square with the world."

If a person knew in which direction the sun rose or fell, it was impossible to get lost driving the country roads of Ben's farm country. Take any east-west road westward, and the traveler would eventually reach the Mississippi River, unless a town got in the way. At every mile, the east-west road intersected perpendicularly with a north-south road, so it was easy to keep track of mileage as well as direction. From an airplane, the traveler could count the parallel roads as the plane flew over them and know not only the mileage traversed, but, with the aid of a watch, the speed at which he was flying. When a road less traveled by did not sport a bridge to cross intervening streams, one had only to take the nearest intersecting road a mile right or left to find one headed in the right direction that did have a bridge crossing.

This pattern of land settlement led to anomalies whose proper explanations were unknown to the farmers who were bound by it.

Covering a round object exactly with square, flat two-dimensional shapes is geometrically impossible, as all mapmakers know. Thus, checkerboard squares of land won't quite fit on the curved landscape of the earth. To compensate for stubbornly trying to bend mathematical ideal to natural reality, every few miles the very straightforward country roads had little jogs built into them, veering perhaps twenty feet to left or right before continuing on course. There was one such jog in the road near the Bump homestead. When Ben asked his father the reason for it, Nat said there must have been a big tree in the way, so the road builders dodged it rather than cut it down.

His mind came back to the present in delicious anticipation, to the events that would occur in the afternoon and evening. His father's real reason for stopping work on July 4 was not compassion for the horses but passion for fireworks. Nat loved explosions. He would unroll his old muzzle-loader out of the greasy rags he kept it in and show Ben how he could still strike a match with a musket ball at twenty paces. And this year maybe Ben would be able to do it too. Nat would then make a cannon out of a short length of plumbing pipe, put a slug of black powder in it, and shoot off lighted sparklers stuck down the barrel—a sort of homemade skyrocket. He also made sure there were Roman candles on hand and did not get a bit perturbed if Ben and Nan, his sister two years younger, starting shooting at each other with them. To Nat, a life of perfect safety was not worth living.

Then that night the whole family would go to the park in Gowler with the rest of the neighborhood to gasp in wonder over real skyrockets and pinwheels. Last year his friend Emmet Gowler, a year older, had tossed a cherry bomb into the outhouse pit through the rear hatch just as Lester Cordrey sat down over the hole. When the next to the stalks straightened them up enough to pass muster at a cursory glance. But the telltale furrows left by the cultivator shovels plainly told the story. Until he could get all the rows cultivated properly, wiping out the signs of his negligence, Ben's sin would be plainly visible.

Back to the cultivator he ran, and back to work, urging the horses up and down the rows as fast as he dared push them. By noon, when he could see his mother, Dorothy, in the yard waving him home for dinner with a white towel, there was only another hour's work left to obscure the trail of shame. Ben found himself wishing that his father would tell him to keep on cultivating that afternoon, Fourth or no Fourth.

The conversation at the Bump table that day took a peculiar turn.

"Awful hot out there today, ain't it?" Nat remarked.

"Oh, not so bad, really, Dad. It was a lot hotter yesterday."

His father looked at him sharply. "Well, I say it's too hot for the horses, and we should lax off a little this after'."

"But it's supposed to rain, Dad. Be good to finish up the field. Only have an hour or so left. If it rains, that corn will be too tall to cultivate by the time the field dries out again."

Even Dorothy and Nan looked at him unbelievingly now. On any other day, his and his father's remarks would have been exactly reversed.

"Boy, it must *really* be hot out there," Nan said sarcastically. "Must have addled your brain."

Ben gave her a withering look and she said no more. He had promised that she could go with him and Emmet that evening, and she didn't want him to change his mind.

Ben knew he had to switch tactics or his father would suspect something. "I sure would hate to miss shooting off Old Blunderbuss, cherry bomb exploded, Lester had popped off the seat and out door so fast that he could not get his pants pulled up, being unwilling to come to a full stop in his pursuit of the pranksters. "The Lord shall smite the firstborn male of every family in Gowler!" he boomed when he finally got himself properly dressed. No one in the neighborhood was willing to pronounce Cordrey either a genius or an idiot, and it was likely, as Pinky, the general store proprietor, said, that he was a little of both, but not enough of either to find his place in life.

From daydreaming, Ben dozed off into real sleep without knowing it. Bell and Florie, sensing the reins going slack, angled off slightly from the row. Feeling no correction from Ben's hands on the reins, they angled a little more and learned, within a hundred feet or so, that they could head directly for the barn without objection from their young driver. Diagonally across the field they plodded, Ben nodding in the driver's seat, the cultivator plowing out a lane of corn as it went.

The horses stopped when they came to the fence, and Ben pitched forward off his seat. Wakefulness came abruptly but realization only slowly. In anguish he looked back at the trail he had blazed through the foot-tall corn. Oh, boy. He was in for it now. He tied the reins to a fencepost and walked back along the sad wake of destruction his wayward cultivator had left. As quickly as he could, he set the uprooted corn plants back in place and stomped dirt around them. If the plants died, maybe the wireworms would get blamed. With one eye turned up the road toward the barn, from where his avenging father would approach if he came to the field, Ben worked his way back to the point where he had fallen asleep. Fortunately, many of the stalks that the shovels had hit were only partially uprooted. One well-placed sock of his heel into the dirt though," he said, as if reconsidering his earlier eagerness to return to the field.

"We'll get her out soon as we've et, and see how many matches the ol' gal will light this year," Nat said.

"Emmet says he'd like to see Old Blunderbuss in action," Ben continued smoothly, "and he can't get here until after two o'clock. I left the cultivator back in the field, and the gate opened, and the horses still harnessed, so I'll just go back and finish up."

Ben thought he saw Nan's expression quicken a bit at the mention of Emmet's name, but he was in no position to tease her now.

He managed to finish the field and wipe out his errant tracks while his father was busy polishing and tuning up Old Blunderbuss. With a sigh of relief, Ben drove the horses and cultivator out of the field, closed the gate, and headed homeward down the road, whistling. So intent was he on thinking about the good time he planned to have that night that he hardly noticed the sound of a car approaching from the rear until it drew alongside. He turned his head to see that the car was occupied by his long-time nemeses, Billy Burks and his brother Buck, hanging out the windows, leering at him. Wayne Gitchell, who was driving, was also smiling wickedly. Ben smelled trouble. The Burkses and Gitchell went to Surrey High School, where they had become, in the tight little world of high school life, the sworn enemies of Emmet Gowler. They disliked Emmet not only because he was a "rich kid" but because he was a traitor to his school, running with the Gowler Village bunch instead of staying home in Surrey. But they feared his fiery temperament, too, and preferred to pick on his younger friend, Ben, when occasion arose. Like now.

One of the Burkses—Ben would recall later that it was Billy— swung his arm, which had been hidden below the car window, and a giant red popper firecracker dropped from his hand, the fuse already half burned down. The firecracker hit the road, took two little hops, and rolled underneath the horses. The car roared on past, its occupants howling in glee, and a split second later the firecracker exploded.

On her own, Florie might have only reared in sudden fright and settled down again, but Bell was of a different temperament. He bolted straight up into the air and showed no interest at all in coming back to earth. He seemed to fly forward on wings, like the Fleet-Wing horse on the gas station signs that so fascinated Ben when he was younger. Before he could react fast enough and haul back on the reins, the two horses were off down the road in a full-scale runaway, ears flat back against their heads, blind with fear, their eyes rolled under until only the whites showed, the cultivator careening along behind them.

"Whoa, Bell, whoa!" Ben screamed, his voice breaking ludicrously from the high soprano of boyhood to the huskier bass of puberty. With his feet in the cultivator stirrups, Ben could brace himself and haul back on the reins with mighty strength, but he might as well have been trying to pull an oak tree out of the ground. The horses pounded on down the road, weaving from side to side, oblivious of the iron bits twisting cruelly at the corners of their mouths. Frozen in terror, Ben could think to do nothing except continue to pull back on the reins with all his might, the way a car driver, heading into a skid, continues to jam the brake pedal insanely into the floor. As always, no matter how dire the circumstances, a part of Ben's brain was observing the whole affair as if from outside himself, telling him that he really did look like a sulky rider coming down the homestretch, or a Roman charioteer going into battle. What if he met a car? Ben began to whimper, then wail, the wail turning into a sort of Shawnee death chant. And then in his fear, a most inexplicable image appeared in his mind: a mason jar of very clear liquid bobbing up out of water that a little boy was swimming in. The boy was trying desperately to grab and hold the jar out of sight beneath the surface. What in the——

The horses were approaching the house now, still at breakneck speed. The wheel of the cultivator caught the mailbox post and snapped it like a matchstick. Then suddenly there was his father, running out the driveway, brandishing Old Blunderbuss and yelling wildly: "Jump off, jump off!"

For a second, Nat seemed to debate in his mind whether or not to shoot one of the horses as they tore past him, but the team, still creatures of habit even in their panic, swerved into the driveway, and Nat had to dive out of the way, still yelling at Ben: "Get your ass off of there!"

Ben was trying to do just that, but that strange vision of the mason jar bobbing up out of water kept getting in the way of action. It seemed to him that he could move only by infinitesimally small accretions, like a snail. The horses were heading straight for the barn, showing no sign of slowing, and Ben remembered his father saying that a runaway horse was capable of galloping at breakneck speed into anything in its way. Is that where the word "breakneck" came from? Focusing all his concentration on his hands, Ben now managed to ignore the bobbing mason jar in his head and unwrap the reins from around his wrists. Now he managed to let go of the reins. Relieved of them, but still feeling as if he were in slow motion, he flung himself backwards out of the seat and onto the ground. Seconds later, the horses, not so blind after all, swerved to avoid the barn and the cultivator slammed sideways against the barn wall. As Bell tried to crash through the closed gate at the end of the barn,

Florie quit on him. She planted her feet, sat on her haunches, and dragged Bell to a shuddering halt. A shattered piece of the gate ended up dangling ludicrously around Bell's neck like a wooden necklace. He glared at Nat out of the corner of his eye with a malevolence nearly as murderous as the fire in the farmer's eyes.

Nat swore in German and slowly leveled the gun, lining up the sights on Bell's rolling left eyeball.

"Weren't their fault!" wailed Ben, still on the ground. "That goddamn Billy Burks threw a firecracker under them."

Nat lowered the gun and contemplated that bit of news. "I oughta shoot him anyway," he muttered finally. "Maybe I shoot a couple of Burks boys vhile I'm at it. And who the hell said it was all right for you to start cussin' like that? God almighty, what's the world comin' to?" He glared at Ben for a long moment, getting his sanity and his breath back. "Next time those horses do that, get 'em going in a circle. Pull on only *one* rein, dummkopf. Sometimes that'll stop 'em."

Ben told his mother what happened when she came running, pale as a full moon, from the house. He rehashed it when Emmet arrived, embellishing the details a little to make it look like he had remained calm and cool throughout the ordeal.

Emmet reacted more angrily than any of the Bumps, who had, with the exception of Nan, calmed down by the time he arrived. Emmet knew Nat would not go to the sheriff—he'd had enough of the Law in the moonshine days. He would grumble, but the peasant caution bred into him by centuries of European condescension and by immigrant poverty would in the end prevent him from retaliating. Emmet doubted that Ben would act either, partly because of his retiring nature and partly because, being two years younger than the Burkses, he probably felt a little cowed by them.

Not so Emmet. The long-suffering peasantry in the cultural genes of the Bumps was as foreign to his gentrified, Anglo-Saxon freeholder heritage as West Indies voodooism would be. Gowler Village was named after his great-great-grandfather. The Gowlers had ruled the village from the beginning, and by God, Emmet meant to keep up the tradition. His combative mind, conscious of the fact that the Burkses went after Ben to get at him, ached for an excuse to do battle. Not the least of the advantages that might be gained was the admiration of Nan. Though he still pretended to ignore her, she was beginning to grow out of childhood, and her sausage-shaped, wheat-colored curls, hanging almost to her shoulders, drew from deep inside him a keening that he could neither articulate nor understand.

"Did you buy your Roman candles yet, Mr. Bump?" he asked abruptly.

"Yup. But it's too early to shoot 'em off. I got to fetch some nails and fix the gate, and then we'll shoot Old Blunderbuss."

Ben was eyeing Emmet, knowing there was a plot brewing in his friend's mind. Nan watched Emmet too, wondering why she had to be only fourteen, too young for Emmet to take notice of.

After Nat had gone to repair the gate, Emmet spoke again.

"It's time those townies learned a lesson." He used the word "townie" deliberately because, living most of the time in Surrey with his mother, he was often considered by the farm boys a townie himself, even though he spent every free moment possible at his grandfather Gowler's farm mansion in Gowler. "I've got a bunch of firecrackers. You've got Roman candles. If the Burkses think a runaway is so funny, let's see how hard they'll laugh with a car full of exploding firecrackers and Roman candles up their asses."

Ben looked baleful. "How you gonna manage that?"

"I got a plan."

"I'm comin' too," Nan said.

"No, you might get hurt."

"I'M COMIN' TOO," she repeated, a statement of fact, not a request or suggestion.

"I think maybe she should," Emmet said, keeping his purposes alive on all fronts. "We might need all the firepower we can get." He beckoned them both into a huddle. "Now here's what we're gonna do."

Nat had calmed down enough so that by the third try he lit a match at twenty paces with Old Blunderbuss. Then he did it a second time to prove it wasn't luck. Both Ben and Emmet failed, their minds perhaps too much focused on something else. Nan struck her match with her first try and strutted like a turkey. But the pleased look on her face had little to do with her marksmanship except as evidence that she was plenty old enough to be going out with Emmet Gowler that night. Dorothy wouldn't shoot the old rifle. Guns only annoyed her. She sometimes wondered if Nat were raising their children to be outlaws, and she might have wondered even more so had she known what they were about to do.

On 364 evenings of the year, the streets of Gowler were as somnolent and slow-footed as a village of the Middle Ages. The only sure proof that it belonged to the twentieth century was the Sportsman cannonballing down the tracks on its way from Toledo to Columbus, passing through the village at 9:03 p.m., at which time the porch sitters and the group gathered in front of the general store would all set their watches and go to bed.

About five hundred people lived in Gowler, and twice that many in the flat farmland around it. This flat land was, geographically and botanically, something of a contrary curiosity, reflecting the people who lived there. It marked the farthest extension eastward of what scientists called the Prairie Peninsula, part of the prairie that predominated in Iowa and stretched back through Illinois and Indiana into Ohio. Instead of the dense forestlands more typical of Ohio, the prairie remnants around Gowler had been treeless in pioneer times, referred to then as the Sandusky Plains or later, more locally, as the Killdeer Plains, after the bird that commonly thrived there. The soil was heavy and nearly impermeable, home to tallgrass vegetation that could endure being flooded in springtime and then survive in the droughts of late summer. Trees grew only where occasionally the land rose gently above the flats to allow for better drainage. These rises were called by early settlers "oak islands" in the expanse of grass. Gowler sat on one such island.

As the wetland prairie was drained for crops, it also made the land hospitable to trees, and so the contrariness of the landscape. Instead of the axe invading the forests in pioneer times, trees began to invade the drained farm fields. By the time Ben's father, and many others, had tried and failed to farm the Killdeer Plains after only rudimentary drainage, woodland gained a foothold. The old differentiation between prairie and woodland began to disappear. For younger people like Ben, who liked to hunt raccoons in Killdeer, the land seemed as much forest as prairie, or more so.

Much to the consternation of Emmet's grandmother, Odelia, and the few other well-read inhabitants of Gowler, most people in and around town soundly rejected this scientific explanation for the treeless plains. They maintained that Indians had burned off the tallgrass prairie every year in massive ring hunts, in which wild animals would be driven inside an ever-shrinking ring of flames, where they were easier to kill. Tree seedlings would be burned off in the process. This was a fact, too, as old historical accounts proved. So the debate was joined. Scientists could assert that the treeless plains were there before the ring hunts, were in fact the reason that the ring hunts came into vogue, but to people of a more literal persuasion, the fire as the cause of the treelessness made more sense. "They're the kind who believe that the world is only four thousand years old and was created in six days because the Bible says so," Grandmother Gowler would complain. "And you might as well argue with a fencepost."

The town itself displayed a kind of anomaly too, only of an economic kind rather than a natural one. The several large brick mansions dated from the peak agrarian years of the late 1800s, when farming really was a profitable business. Some of them were already showing signs of neglect. Interspersed among them were humbler houses, sided in wooden clapboards, sometimes over the original logs, with metal, standing-seam roofs, mostly in good shape, showing a slowly growing lower-middle-class prosperity. Lawns were generally well kept, and the whole was neatly remindful of a New England village. Indeed, George McPherson, who operated the egg market business in town, had decided to settle in Gowler in the 1930s because it reminded him of his home village in New Hampshire.

The railroad cut through the middle of town, north to south. The main street, running east and west and actually the only street in parts of the little town, was lined with shops which together reminded the traveler from more urban areas of a mock frontier town set up as backdrop for a Western movie. The places of business provided in plain and practical "henhouse architecture," as Emmet's grandfather Gowler liked to call it, the usual necessities: gas station, bakery, grocery and general store, doctor's office, several café-type restaurants, bank and post office. The public school and a Methodist church stood across the road from each other at the west end; the Gowler mansion on the east edge. On the north side, where the railroad entered the village (actually, the railroad preceded the town), stood a clay tile factory, recently closed, and a stockyard, which would also close as husbandry declined in the area. On the south side, where the railroad exited the town, rose an imposing grain elevator and flour mill. Other than the grain elevator, the brick church and school, and the building housing both the bank and general store, which had been a hotel in grander times, the rest of the business block, so to speak, seemed perched on the edge of the road ready to take flight for more profitable climes should the need arise.

However humdrum the town appeared most of the time, it went a little crazy on the evening of the Fourth. From all around the countryside, rednecked, white-browed farmers and their families drove or walked into town to sit in the grass of Clewis Park and watch a fireworks display that Pinky, the general store owner, who financed most of it, said was the best one in northern Ohio. Even Ironia Gowler Stone came home for it, all the way from New York City. She was the widow of the wealthy clothing merchant who had come to Gowler in 1880 to buy wool from David Gowler, known far and wide as the Wool King of the World, and had gotten his daughter in the deal. She held herself erect and alert, yielding nothing to her advancing age, radiating a regal air. Her pale skin appeared to possess not so much the delicacy of bone china as the brittle hardness of crackled ironstone. Given her spirit, she might have driven cattle to Baltimore on horseback with her father if the Victorian era had allowed it. Instead she escaped by becoming a businesswoman, both taking over her husband's company at his death and overseeing the Gowler fortune. The real reason she came to Gowler every summer was to perform her self-appointed duty: to go over the family's financial situation to make sure the farm records were in order and the profits still coming in. Floyd and his banker brother, Cyrus, allowed her this power because they could not disallow her.

"My God, I came out here to get away from the din of New York," she complained in her haughty way, as she sat with Emmet's mother and grandmother on the front porch of the Gowler home, where they would be able to see the skyrockets. "But the town's so crowded with clattering machines, a person can't think."

"Not like the good old days of horses," Grandmother Gowler said, trying to be agreeable.

"Hummph," replied Ironia. "The good old days were terrible. The whole of New York thirty years ago smelled like a livery stable. Those city slickers had the nerve to call me a hayseed, but their streets had more horseshit on them than our barnyard back here did even in March."

Emmet edged past his elders and out the door without being seen. His mother had given him permission to take the Packard, and he was afraid that if she saw him and had time to think the matter over, she might change her mind. And he would never get away if Great-Aunt Ironia started telling about how Indians still roamed the swamps of Killdeer when she was born near the now-vanished Bowsherville, and how she was absolutely the only person alive in the whole wide world who as a child watched hunters and Indians drinking liquor in a pioneer saloon in Ohio and then rose to the top of New York's high society.

He piloted the long black Packard carefully out the driveway and tooled to the general store as fast as traffic would allow. Ben and Nan were waiting. The rolled-up blanket Nan carried, purportedly to sit on during the fireworks display, concealed a bundle of Roman candles. Emmet's pockets bulged with firecrackers.

"Get in," Emmet commanded, as he eased up to the loading dock in front of the store. Nan wanted ever so much to ride in front with Emmet, but Ben beat her to it.

"Where you going?" Ben asked, eyes widening in wonder as he inspected the grand interior of the car. He sank back into the seat, and it embraced him like an overstuffed velour couch, which is what it was. Nan, in her turn, fingered the curtains on the windows.

"Going to find the Burks boys," Emmet answered. "I expect they will be riding with Wayne, smarting off in his daddy's '37 Ford. We'll find 'em."

Sure enough, they had to cruise out of town only as far as Swamp Poodle Field, a name no one knew the origin of, to spot Gitchell and the Burks boys ahead of them. Emmet tailed them the mile into Linner. Gitchell pulled up in front of the Blue Room, one of two saloons still remaining from the seven that had reigned over the tiny village right after Prohibition was lifted. The Blue Room was half grocery store and half saloon, and neither half had been painted blue for thirty years. Partly because it combined beer with groceries, the Blue Room was not considered as sinful as the Corner Pocket across the street, which was devoted entirely to the evils of liquor and pool, the devil's own sport. Respectable people could go into the Blue Room and not raise an eyebrow. There was no pool table there, and a customer could be buying only food, although the chances of that were slim. Ben could never understand why pool was wicked and croquet innocent. In croquet it was even okay to cheat if you could get away with it, which was never true in pool.

"They're probably going to try to get beer," Emmet said. "Close those window curtains back there, Nan, and both of you lay low. I want them to think I'm alone."

That done, Emmet oozed the Packard up on the right side of the Ford and stared into it as if viewing the inside of a garbage can. The trio in the Ford stared back with equal disdain.

"I'm surprised that bucket of bolts got this far outta Surrey without breakin' down," Emmet said.

"It'll be around a long time after that antique you're drivin' dies," Gitchell replied, never at a loss for words.

"Don't get up too close behind me," Emmet returned, "I'll suck you up the exhaust and spit you out through the fan blade."

"No chance of us ever being behind you," Gitchell snorted.

By way of answer and challenge, Emmet gunned the Packard back out onto the road to Gowler. Once he made sure that Gitchell was following him, he turned on Churchfield Road and headed into Killdeer, just fast enough to keep Gitchell from overtaking him. He knew the Packard could attain ninety miles an hour, because he had done it. Turning again on one of the lonely dirt roads through the swampland, where autos rarely traveled, he raced along until cattails proclaimed oozing swamp water just off the roadside. Then he slowed down and let Gitchell pass in a hail of laughter and clatter of loose stones. "Peee-uuuu, Packard!" Buck Burks shouted out his open window.

Then Emmet pushed the accelerator to the floor, and all twelve cylinders hummed like a swarm of angry hornets. Emmet, not daring to take his eyes off the road, pulled a pack of firecrackers out of his pocket and tossed it to Ben. "Get a match ready. When I pull alongside, I'll yell, and you light the fuse while Nan jerks that curtain back and opens the window. Chuck the crackers right into their laps."

Ben's fingers trembled as he tore the cellophane from the pack and located the main fuse to which each firecracker's individual fuse was attached. But he faltered. Both cars were rolling along now at a dangerously high speed. What if Gitchell lost control?

"I don't think we ought to do this," he mumbled.

"Get ready!" Emmet cried, pulling abreast of the Ford. "Light the fuse."

"We better not . . ."

Nan was in her element now, let all men beware, and all women too. She snatched the firecrackers from Ben, turned down the window, ripped back the curtain, and raked a match across the metal of the window frame. With her puckish little face stuck out of the car, nose to nose with a surprised Billy Burks, she yelled:

"You think it's so funny to throw firecrackers under horses. See how funny you think this is!"

"Now!" roared Emmet.

The firecrackers, fuse smoking, landed on the floor in front of Billy Burks. He jumped in surprise, banging his head on the ceiling as he tried to escape the danger in front of him. The firecrackers began exploding in machine-gun staccato. The Burks boys leaped from side to side in the car, hopped from back seat to front, howling in fear, wildly trying to avoid the explosions, while Gitchell, hunched over the steering wheel, tried to get the car stopped before a firecracker went down his neck inside his shirt. As one cracker after another exploded, it would send the pack hopping into the air again, until the car rattled like a popcorn popper full of hot corn.

Emmet had immediately slowed down after Nan had thrown the firecrackers, and he watched with great satisfaction as the Gitchell car weaved back and forth, then slid into the ditch as it came to a stop, landing softly in a stand of cattails. He brought the Packard quickly alongside the Ford, slammed on the brakes, burrowing quickly into Nan's blanket and grabbing a Roman candle in each hand.

"Light 'em," he commanded. By now Ben had passed beyond his natural caution into a robotic state of mind where neither emotion nor rationality held sway. He dutifully lit the Roman candles in Emmet's hands. He lit the ones Nan thrust in his face. He burned his fingers on the dying match, struck another, and lit himself a whole fistful of candles.

Emmet was already out of the car, standing on his side of the Packard, pouring Roman candle bursts of fire into the still-open window of the Ford. Gitchell and the Burks boys then made a strategic mistake. Instead of simply rolling the window closed, they attempted to escape the car, only to be bombarded by the combined fire from both Emmet and Nan. The hapless trio tumbled back inside their car and tried to escape on the ditch side, only to find themselves knee-deep in swamp water. As they staggered around the car to dry land, Ben met them, two flaming Roman candles in each hand, driving them back into the cattails.

All the while Emmet was yelling like a crazed banshee. "Careful out there, boys, that swamp's full of rattlers!"

Dodging Roman candle bursts and several more packs of exploding firecrackers, Buck Burks lost his balance and fell into the black swamp soup. His brother tripped on him and fell too, while Gitchell cowered in the cattails, begging for mercy and promising vengeance in turn.

Emmet started the Packard and Nan piled in. Ben, fully aroused now, had a final word before he too jumped in the car: "And if you can't get that pile of junk out of the swamp, get a horse."

On the way back to Gowler, Ben marveled about how he had turned as wild and angry as his sister. He was the one who was supposed to remain responsible at all costs, as his mother had taught him. To his surprise, he was pleased with himself, no matter that he might actually have burned the Burkses with the fireworks. Nor did he feel guilt when he realized that if Gitchell had lost complete control of the car, someone might have gotten hurt badly. After all, what they had done to him could have killed him in the runaway. From now on he would have to live with one eye over his shoulder, waiting for the enemy to strike back, but he would do so proudly like Emmet would.

Emmet and Nan did not give the possibility of injury any thought at all. They were recklessly radiant with delight over the success of their attack, retelling each detail to each other and howling gleefully in turn. It was not until they reached Gowler that they both realized that Nan had snuggled close against Emmet, a warmth passing between their bodies that was more than the hot July night or the frenzy of the Roman candle fight. They fell silent then, a little embarrassed. But neither made any attempt to move apart.

In the park, the crowd waited for the Sportsman to come through, signaling enough darkness to start the festivities. Lieutenant Governor Arnold Clewis spoke with soaring bombast about the glory of America: "We are the most powerful nation in history, and you, the thirty million farm people of America, are the BACKBONE OF THIS GREAT NATION." Cheers of approval thundered from the little park. "Prosperity is RIGHT AROUND THE CORNER. With modern technology, WE CAN FARM MORE LAND, raise more food, and receive the just rewards of our labor for WIPING OUT HUNGER in the world."

More cheers. Nan and Emmet lolled on Nan's blanket, bored with the speech, waiting for the fireworks to begin, wondering if Gitchell had gotten his car out of the swamp yet. Only Ben listened, or half listened, and only one sentence registered in his consciousness. "We can farm more land."

"Did you hear that?" he asked.

"Hear what?" Emmet replied.

"With tractors we'll be able to farm more land."

"And so? That's what we're doing, isn't it?"

"Well, if everyone is going to farm more land, where is it going to come from? Will there be any left for me?"

"Oh, for cryin' out loud. There's enough land for everyone who wants some."

"Easy enough for you to say," Ben replied, but was glad that the applause of the crowd as the lieutenant governor once more promised that prosperity was just around the corner drowned out his remark. Between the two boys there was always the Gowler wealth.

"What did you say?" Emmet asked.

"Nothing."

As the lieutenant governor bowed off the lectern, the first skyrocket cut a slit of light through the dark sky and opened into a bower full of blossoming flashes. For the time, Ben forgot the disturbing thought that had so disingenuously insinuated itself upon him—that it was mathematically impossible for every farmer to get more land.

Every burst of rocket flashes brought a rippling sigh of wonder from the crowd. Could the world produce anything more radiantly beautiful than a skyrocket?

"You're really something with a Roman candle, Nan," Emmet said, between the bursts of light. Nan glowed like a firefly in the dark. Emmet became aware of her leg against his again, and looked around to see if anyone else noticed.

"You can watch the skyrockets explode by their reflection in the pool," he said, referring to the Victorian reflecting pool in the park that agrarian practicality had made extra large so children could frolic in it. "Easier on your neck."

The mason jars suddenly came back into Ben's mind. He turned to Nan. "*That's* what I was remembering!" he exploded. "Remember the day when we hid the Fruit Juice in that pond so the revenue officer wouldn't find it, and the jars started floating to the surface? That's what I thought of when the horses ran away. The runaway must have made me as scared as I was that day. Oh, wow."

Nan remembered. How could they ever forget? In those days, Dorothy would drive them to the park and they would swim while she read, and customer after customer would pull up to their car, take a jar or two of moonshine from it, and leave money, never a word spoken. But the Bumps always referred to it as the Fruit Juice, as if not naming it somehow avoided some of their guilty feeling about it.

"What I remember is Emmet riding Pony across the park to warn us that the revenuers were coming," Nan said sweetly. They all laughed. After Emmet's timely warning, they had transferred all the jars of the Fruit Juice into the pond, and the two children had splashed around in the water to keep the jars hidden from sight until the sheriff and the revenue officer had searched the car and left. Now they told the whole story to each other again, laughing. But it had been a harrowing adventure, not at all funny. Their father would have gone to jail if the moonshine had been discovered. Nat had forbidden them to speak of it again, and they had not, until this night. It was after that narrow escape that he quit bootlegging and used the money he had made to buy a good farm several miles from the hardscrabble place he had settled on when he immigrated from Austria, thinking the unyielding blackjack clay of Killdeer was good farmland.

"Until tonight, that was the most exciting day of my life," Nan said. She smiled in the darkness. "We must live in the most exciting place in the whole world."

In her diary that night, she concluded the day's doings with the remark that appeared at the end of nearly every entry: "Boy, did we have fun."

T W O

There was too much clamor afflicting his usually placid life to suit Ben Bump. He did not like school in the first place, and now a senior, having gathered unto himself all the trappings of twelve years of trivial schoolday matters, he liked it even less. One more year and he could settle into the ordered serenity of farm life, where everything fitted, if not smoothly together, at least in a natural harmony of planting, growth, and harvest. He loved the tranquility that sometimes enveloped farming: the quiet of big barns, the soft sound of horses munching hay, dawn in the pasture field full of sleeping sheep, a moon over the cow stable, cutting firewood in the solitude of the forest. Now in late November, husking corn would have been enough not-so-tranquil activity for him, but his mind was afire with apprehension over the Thanksgiving weekend football game in which he would play that afternoon. By Gowler standards, he was good at playing the game. That was why he had let himself be drawn onto the high school football team without making any particular commitment to what that decision might eventually lead to. With him and the stout Farnold boys playing, the school had enjoyed a winning season, and everyone dreamed that this was the year that the Gowler Cornhuskers would finally beat the larger school, the Surrey Rams.

As if that were not enough clamorous activity, Floyd Gowler was having a barn dance the next week, preceded, fittingly enough, by a cornhusking contest. Ben shivered, not just from the November cold, but in nervous anticipation of taking part in all three activities. It was almost too much to bear.

"You comin' to the game?" he asked his father working beside him, shucking the ears out of the jumble of bundles between them, tossing the husked ears into a central pile.

Nat shook his head. "Too cold to go out in weather like this."

Ben laughed, and his father, seeing the inconsistency in his remark, added: "Well, too cold to watch boys buttin' heads instead of doing something worthwhile." He stopped to watch his son. "If you're gonna win the cornhusking contest, you gotta husk faster than that. Rake that hook across the base of that ear like you mean it. Grab the top of the husk with the other hand all in one motion. Ear's gotta *pop* out of the husk."

Both he and Ben wore the traditional husking hook over the palms of their right hands. The hook was a simple enough affair, as all good tools are, a piece of leather covering the palm and buckled over the back of the hand. A steel hook was riveted to the leather, on the palm side. "And remember: I think Floyd's got that new strain of DeKalb that husks easy. Shake every bundle first. Some of the ears might drop out already shucked." Ben was not sure whether Nat was serious or was making a joke out of the DeKalb salesman's claim.

They set the bundles of cornstalks, relieved of their corn, over the pile of husked ears to protect them from the weather, and then tied the bundles into a fodder shock. Usually three or four corn shocks were husked out into one pile, and so the resulting fodder shock was much larger than the original shocks. To tie the fodder shock, Nat stood next to it and whirled a rope, to which an iron cinch was attached, over his head until it was moving in an ever-widening circle above him like a lariat in the hands of a cowboy. Then, with a practiced whip of his arm, he directed the rope around the shock in such a manner that the cinch end swung all the way around and back to his waiting hand. Slipping the other end of the rope through the cinch, he drew the noose tight around the shock. Meanwhile Ben pulled a strand from the sash of twines he carried looped under his belt, tucked one end under the rope tight against the shock, and walked around the shock, paying out the twine until he had come full circle to the twine end stuck in the rope. Then he pulled both ends together and tied them. Nat released the rope noose and they were on to the next shock to be husked. Through the winter, the fodder shocks would be fed one by one to the livestock, and the corn picked up and hauled to the crib.

Husking corn out in the field in cold weather was not one of Ben's favorite jobs. What made the job acceptable was the anticipation of sitting later by a warm stove with a belly full of food. He almost liked hard, uncomfortable physical work for that reason: respite was so enjoyable. "Husking in the old days was fun," Nat was saying. "The corn bundles were gathered into the barns and the young people went from barn to barn in the evenings, husking. A lot more comfortable in the barns with the animals keeping the air warmer. If you husked a red ear, which happened fairly often in those days before hybrid corn, you got to kiss your sweetheart."

Ben did not reply. What would he do in those circumstances? He did not have a sweetheart to kiss. He could not seem to attract the attention of the girls at school who interested him. He could not bring himself to lean against the school hall walls like the other boys did, their hands in their pockets, thrusting their bulging crotches outward for the girls to pretend not to see, big he-man stuff without enough brains, in Ben's estimation, to stuff rags in ratholes. That girls were attracted by such bullishness appalled him. He once asked Nan why some girls could be fooled so easily: "Idiots attract idiots," she replied.

Nan was just then walking across the field, as if the thought of her had conjured up her presence. "Time to eat," she said when she got close enough. "You gotta hurry, Ben. You're supposed to be at school in an hour." She appeared peevish.

"What's got your goat?" Ben asked her.

"It's not fair."

"What's not fair?"

"Why can't I play football, too? Why do boys get to have all the fun? I can run faster than you can."

By game time at 2:00 p.m., Ben's gut had wound itself as tight and jagged as a newly stretched strand of barbed wire. Emmet, a year out of school and in a constant bicker with his mother because he would not go to college, had somehow wangled the position of assistant coach for the team. But he was no help in calming Ben's nerves.

"You gotta watch that Billy Burks, Ben. He's out to get you, you know. He's a slippery bastard and quick as Ex-Lax."

Franklin Farnold, who played fullback on offense and middle linebacker on defense because, as everyone said, he was built like a brick shithouse, was more reassuring. "Surrey's a bunch of marshmallows," he said.

"Then how come they're seven and one for the season?" Ben replied, feeling his stomach congealing into a stone. Sports would be his death, he feared. He loved to play them, but he hated the stress of competition.

"I wish I could be back in the field husking corn," he said plaintively.

"That's why you are a true-blue Cornhusker," Emmet said affectionately. "You are the only person in the whole county who'd rather husk corn than play football. Maybe in the whole state. Maybe in the whole world."

Ben paused in his struggle to get into his shoulder pads. "*That's* why Surrey is called the Rams," he exclaimed.

"What brought that on?" Emmet asked, accustomed to his friend's habitual leap over several thought processes to a conclusion that seemed to have no bearing on the topic being discussed.

"Well, we're the Cornhuskers because we husk corn and Surrey is the Rams because we also raise lots of sheep around here. History explains everything."

"Wrong history. We're the Cornhuskers because we copied the name from Nebraska," said Emmet.

"Actually, Gowler should be the Rams," Ben observed, not listening. "On account your grandfather Gowler was the Wool King of the World."

Franklin rolled his eyes. "That's a little thar-thetched."

Ben and Emmet giggled at their friend's way with words. Franklin's tongue had never learned how to negotiate the letter "f." He looked now from one to the other, puzzled. "If somebody gave you two guys each a wit, you'd still add up to only a halfwit."

And then they ran out with the team, roaring vengeance against Surrey, Franklin shouting, "Thight, Thight, Thight!" until all the players joined him. "Thight, Thight, Thight."

The field behind the school, which also served as the ball diamond and otherwise general playground area, was part of the park land that Lieutenant Governor Clewis had donated to the village. The field was barely big enough for a regulation gridiron, not that anybody really worried about that. What they worried about, at least Della Gowler, Emmet's grandmother, was that an end run too often ended up in their precious shrubbery. "It's not good for the *Taxus* and the *Euonymus* and the *Pinis*," Grandma was saying at that very moment to Larry Luvre, the science teacher, along the sidelines.

Ben, overhearing her as he passed on the way to the field, shook his head in wonder. Della Gowler didn't care about the game. She cared about the playing field, which would be around a long time after any game. That amused him so much that he smiled his way right out to his position on the field, took the opening kickoff, and streaked untouched, straight down the field for a touchdown. In the roar of cheering, Della Gowler was worriedly examining the *Taxus* that a Surrey player had trampled when he overran Ben in the act of trying to tackle him. Even in the excitement, Ben noticed her. He nudged Emmet, who was pounding on him, and nodded toward her. "She's worried that trampling the shrubbery is not good for the *Pinis*," he said with fake solemnity. Emmet shook his head. He could just never know what Ben would say next.

Nan had managed to work her way right up next to Emmet and was screaming over the touchdown and staring at him. He screamed and stared back at her. Only gradually did the two realize that after the cheering had died, they were still staring at one another.

The opening play proved to be a fluke. Gowler could not even execute the point after touchdown against their bigger opponents. For the whole first half, the two teams battled grimly up and down the field, while Grandma stood in front of the *Taxus* as if to protect it, and grumbled about the game ruining the *Poa protensis*, which everyone else thought was mere grass. Whenever an Upper Surrey runner tore up through the line, there was always a brick shithouse waiting to block the way, and the few times a runner got past Franklin, Ben was there to stop him. The score remained 6 to 0.

Halftime lasted five minutes because with night coming early now, there would otherwise not be enough time to finish the game before dark. Time enough, however, for Pinky Ghent to share a drink of hard cider, which he called "My Precious," with Gowler fans around him. "It's not really cider," he confided to Floyd Gowler. "It's applejack, several times faster on the draw."

Billy Burks blindsided Ben shortly into the second half. While Ben rolled in agony on the ground, Billy stood over him and growled, "That's called the Roman candle leg-buster block."

Emmet appeared to be having a seizure on the sidelines. "Clipping! Clipping!" he screamed, but I. P. I. Perg, who umpired baseball in the summer and refereed football and basketball in the winter, had not seen the disputed block and now merely stared at Emmet from behind his grizzled beard. At the height of Emmet's fury, nose to nose with him, I. P. I. winked. That was his time-tested way of dealing with angry coaches and players. A wink. Sometimes a second or third wink. "By the third wink," he liked to explain, "even the angriest guy in the world will just kinda break down into a total fluster-butt." Sure enough, after the third wink, Emmet rolled his eyes heavenward in a fit of helpless exasperation and then started laughing insanely. There was no one on earth like the Immortal Pig Iron Perg, a name he had earned as a boy because he went up and down the streets of Surrey, collecting junk iron in his little red wagon and selling it.

"I'm gonna break you in two and score field goals with both pieces," Franklin said to Billy Burks as play resumed.

"Very funny," Billy spat back at him. "Here's something funnier. We're coming up the middle on the next play and run right over you, you sawed-off Killdeer hilligun."

Billy faked a handoff to his fullback and charged up through the middle of the line. Two blockers ahead of him bounced off Franklin like ping-pong balls off concrete. Now it was just Franklin against Billy. They collided like two stags in rutting season. Billy's legs buckled and he collapsed into a heap. "That thunny enough for you?" Franklin bellowed down at him. "Or do you want some more thun?"

But the heavier weight and greater depth of Upper Surrey's team slowly wore the Gowler players down, and midway through the fourth quarter, Billy Burks, revived after a long rest on the bench, slipped past Ben, as Emmet had foreseen, and scored. With the extra point, the score was 7 to 6. "Strange," observed Pinky Ghent, taking another swig of His Precious. "That's the same score by which Jack Mogan once got elected marshal of Gowler."

It was not the year for Gowler to beat its archrival after all, as Surrey held on to its one-point lead. Ben, Emmet, and Franklin sat in the locker room long after everyone else had left, moaning through every play.

"We aren't ever going to beat them," Ben said sorrowfully. "I was born to be a second fiddle."

"We'll beat them in softball next year, I promise," Emmet said. "We'll win the softball league, and that's what counts."

"Thuck it all," Franklin said. "I'm goin' coon huntin'."

It was mostly because his new corn shredder had broken down that Floyd Gowler had decided to hold the cornhusking contest. He had been pleased with the machine, which snapped the ears off the stalks and conveyed them into a wagon while it blew the fodder into the barn loft. It husked out the ears as fast as a separator threshed wheat and oats, ending the long, grueling hand-husked corn harvest on the Gowler farms. But with hardly thirty shocks left to run through the shredder, the bearing on the main drive shaft froze up, twisting the shaft so badly that a new one had to be ordered and installed. That could take all winter, so, adapting to the situation as he always did, Floyd was inspired to hold the husking contest. He had his hired hands haul the last shocks into the big barn's main floor, out of the weather, where the contest would be held. It occurred to him that this was a chance, too, for someone from Gowler to beat the state record held by Noble Roodman of Surrey. Roodman had achieved the record in 1937 by shucking out thirty-three bushels and thirty-six pounds in thirty minutes, a little bit more than a bushel a minute. There was no way anyone was going to beat that figure outright, Floyd figured, but maybe he could cheat a little, holding only ten-minute contests instead of the usual half-hour ones, and then multiplying the ten-minute amount by three to arrive at a projected figure for half an hour. Some of the local lads might be able to keep up Roodman's pace for ten minutes.

Though the night was fairly cold, the main floor of the barn, insulated by mows of hay above and warmed by the body heat of cows and horses from below, was comfortable enough. If the older people needed more warmth, they could stand around the bonfire in the barnyard, where a young roasting pig was slowly turning on a spit. More fortification could be obtained from the barrel of His Precious just inside the barn door.

Most of the families sauntering into the barn sharecropped Gowler land, which was another reason Floyd had decided to hold the event. Keep the morale up. Renew the feeling of friendliness and cooperation between landlord and sharecropper. Sometimes that was all the profit there was in a harvest. Dick Farnold, who was there to do the fiddling for the dance, said he could make more money playing in a band on Saturday night than he could husking corn all week.

Present were some townspeople, especially those connected with the school and churches. But the bulk of the crowd were farmers: the Chafers, Remps, Nyers, Gelbos, Caceys—all twenty of Floyd Gowler's renters, along with neighbors who owned their land or at least owned it with the bank: the Bumps, Farnolds, Dalls, Einharts, Mottrells, Cughes, some 150 people altogether, counting children. Though these people were generally reserved to a fault in public, His Precious made them nervy enough now to approach Ben and congratulate him on his touchdown in the game with Surrey, and generally embarrass him with praise.

"If you play football at Ohio State, think how it will reflect on Gowler," Coach Rakid said, although he was really thinking how it would help him get a job at a bigger school.

"A person of your scholastic ability should get off the farm and make something of himself," admonished Larry Luvre, the science teacher, not one to let sports get the upper hand.

"With your intelligence, you would make a fine priest," said Father O'Brien, representing God with the pomposity merited by such a grave responsibility.

Ben looked for a place to hide. He wondered if Mr. Luvre and the Reverend O'Brien realized that what they said was a slur on all the people in the barn. As his father said, both the teacher and the reverend would starve to death if forced to make their way as farmers.

Floyd Gowler was in his glory. Most of the other men wore new bib overalls, blue chambray shirts, and denim jackets, but Floyd had decked himself out in black shirt and trousers with white stitching around the pockets, a black, wide-brimmed Stetson, and a sheepskin coat that his grandfather had worn driving sheep and cattle on the trail. He looked, in Grandma Gowler's words, "like the crooked mayor in a Gene Autry show."

The women all wore woolen shirtwaist dresses and heavy stockings. Woolen coats and hand-knitted head scarves completed their outfits. Little girls wore leggings under their dresses. Many of their dresses were cut and sewn from feed sacks purposefully made of cotton cloth adorned with pastel flower prints so they could be recycled this way.

Out of the general din of complaints about farm prices, the crowd prepared itself for the husking contest. Some twenty of the men, mostly the younger ones, buckled on their hooks, fidgeted on nervous feet, poked at each other self-consciously, stole glances at the girls in the crowd, made sly observations about the phallic suggestiveness of large ears of corn. Nan was begging her mother to allow her to enter the contest. No success. Not "ladylike." A platform scales was rolled to the middle of the floor with a wooden potato crate on it that held approximately fifteen bushels. From the wagonload of bundles at the rear of the main floor, a shock was set up next to the scales. The first husker stepped up beside the shock. The crowd pressed around. Children climbed into the haylofts above to get a good view. Floyd himself acted as timekeeper. Pinky Ghent manned the scales.

The first contestant was Jake Lavendar. "The man with the fastest hands in Gowler," bellowed Floyd, "and I don't necessarily mean only with corn." The men laughed and the women pretended to be offended. "Are you ready, Jake? Get set." Floyd studied his watch. "Go!"

Lavendar leaped at the shock, jerked the twine apart, and grabbed a bundle from the shock in such a way that the other bundles fell in an orderly manner, all butts facing the same direction, at his feet. Then he knelt to the task, his fingers flying over, under, and into each bundle, left hand seeking out the ears, one after another, right hand slashing across each ear's base with the hook, left fingers stripping the husk down, right fingers simultaneously slipping inside the husk to snap the ear off the stalk by bending it between thumb and forefinger of the left hand, and then tossing the ear into the potato crate while the left hand grabbed for another ear. To beat Roodman's record, the husking rate would have to exceed a bushel per minute, as everyone knew, and for several minutes it appeared that Lavendar just might do it.

"Time's up!" roared Floyd.

Pinky slid the top weight of the scales forward along the scales bar, then tapped it back until the bar balanced.

danced over the bundles on their own, without any conscious com-
munication with his brain, like the fingers of a harpist over strings.
He watched his hands now as if they belonged to someone else.
Would he beat Lavendar? Could he beat Noble Roodman?

"Time's up!" he heard Floyd bellow, and then the crowd broke
into cheers even lustier than those which had accompanied his
touchdown. Pinky was holding up a card with the number 698.2
on it. Ben had won the contest, had come within an ear or two of
husking a bushel a minute. Emmet was pounding his back; Jake
Lavendar was shaking his hand in disappointment. Nan wanted to
hug her brother but knew he'd melt with embarrassment if she did.
Instead, knowing her brother, she pushed a slab of savory roast
pork into his mouth.

The floor was cleared, Dick Farnold tuned up his fiddle, the
dancers formed their sets. Ben, too shy to dance, slipped back into
the shadows of an empty feed room before Nell Cughes or Margie
Dall could drag him onto the floor. Emmet, emboldened by His
Precious, marched, full of resolution, across the floor to where
Nan was standing.

"I've been wanting to do this for two years," he said, loud enough
for everyone nearby to hear including Nan's mother. "May I have
the next dance? In fact, may I have all the dances?"

Nan giggled at his exaggerated air of chivalry. Instead of answer-
ing, she took his hand and led him to the group of dancers. Floyd
Gowler pretended not to see, but there was a pleased look on his
face. His wife, he noted, did not look so pleased, nor did Mrs.
Bump, for that matter, but all in God's good time. He liked Nan.
She was full of piss and vinegar.

As he swirled Nan through the dances and promenaded her
"back home," Emmet felt his heart and mind opening to a love

"Keep your thumb off that scales," someone in the crowd joked. "This ain't down at your store."

"Six hunnert seventy-eight pounds," Pinky called out, writing the figure down on his pad, while Jake bowed in mock-grandeur to the cheering crowd. With ear corn calculated at seventy pounds per bushel, that meant about 9.7 bushels in ten minutes. Could anyone beat such speed?

The husked bundles were laid aside and a new shock made for the next contestant. But husker after husker failed to beat Lavendar's score. Emmet, less experienced than the others, and only consenting to be in the contest at all to please his grandfather, didn't come close, but when he husked an ear slightly tinted red, he stuck it quickly inside his shirt so no one would notice it.

Ben hung back, characteristically, to the end, dreading his stint in the limelight almost as much as he had keenly anticipated it the day before. "Go on," Nat said, sidling up behind him. "You can win it, I know. If you can score touchdowns, you can husk corn fast. All da same thing."

Ben's hands flew to the task, though he was so nervous his fingers fumbled the first four ears. He figured that would cost him the contest. But then the glare of the crowd passed from his mind's eye, and he became enveloped in a world all his own, so quiet and serene that he felt like he was husking in a kind of slow motion. He heard the ears methodically and regularly thud into the weighing crate, but the sound seemed far away. When he did look up at all, it was to see Nan kneeling in front of him, pounding the floor, urging him on. Over the roar of the crowd she screamed into his ear: "Remember the Fruit Juice!" That was their battle cry for rising above all odds, and once more he felt the terrible fear as that mason jar floated toward the surface of the park pond. His hands now made exquisite because he had held it back so long. "I've got a surprise for you," he shouted in Nan's ear as they passed each other on an allemande left. When they had worked their way through the set and were back together again, he teased her more softly. "You'll never guess what it is." And then they were off again into another dance:

> *Chase that rabbit, chase that coon*
> *Chase that gal around the room.*
> *Allemande left with your left hand*
> *Right to your partner's, and a right, left grand,*
> *Swing all eight a-comin' round straight*
> *And take her home, boys, don't be late.*

Out of breath, they finally sat down against the wall on the fodder bundles left from the husking.

"What's the surprise?" Nan asked as they gasped for breath.

"I don't think I can show it to you right here," Emmet said, faking mystery.

"Why not?"

"Because."

"Because why?"

"Just because."

He led her outside, out of the light of the barn and the eye of the crowd. Then he pulled the red ear of corn from under his shirt.

"Surprise!"

"That's just a dumb old ear of corn," Nan scoffed.

"No, take a closer look. Over here where the light hits it."

"Well. It's red. So what?"

"Whaddya mean, so what?"

Nan, suddenly remembering the tradition, broke into a big smile. Instead of saying anything, she stood on her toes, threw her arms around Emmet, and kissed him, square on the lips.

Abruptly the music stopped in the barn, the silence arresting them in their embrace. Standing in the doorway, the light streaming out from the barn silhouetting him sharply, was the strange figure of a haggard man who might have been masquerading as Father Time ushering out the old year. His hand was raised to catch the attention of the crowd. Wild-eyed, long-haired, clad in sheepskin coat and leather leggings, he waited, hand still aloft, for silence.

"I haven't seen Miser Meincer since we lived on that place in Killdeer," Nan whispered. "I always liked him. He would bring me honey from wild hives."

"He gives me the creeps," Emmet said.

"He's all right, really. Just that he's a hermit."

In a loud, quavering voice that reverberated through the entire barn, the strange man intoned: "It just came over the radio. The Japs have bombed us. They've bombed Pearl Harbor. Now there'll be hell to pay."

People looked at each other. Some broke for their cars and switched on the radios. Others gathered round the cars in little knots, listening to the fateful news. There had been talk of war for so long, but here in the isolation and seeming safety of the countryside, the omens of its coming had seemed improbable and far away. Now the static-riddled voices on the radio, tense with apprehension, brought home the cruel reality of it.

People talked in low voices. Dick Farnold put away his fiddle. Dorothy motioned to Nan to follow her to the car. Normally Nan would have protested, would no doubt have protested more vigorously than ever before, now with Emmet in her embrace. But the ominous war news stopped her. She squeezed Emmet's hand and followed her mother. Motors started. Headlights flashed. The crowd moved out, down the road, headed home.

Floyd Gowler stood finally alone in the light of his open barn door, filled with grave foreboding. He could remember the last war.

For a while after Emmet joined the navy, he and Nan exchanged letters often. But for Emmet, there was a hesitancy in his approach that was out of character. He knew that Gowler society considered it a bit odd and perhaps improper for a young man several years out of high school to attempt a relationship with a girl still in school. Letters could indicate an interest even more serious than dating, and in Gowler there were few secrets. Letters arriving at the post office would be noted and commented upon. Normally this would not have bothered him, but with Nan, whom he had for so long considered more like a kid sister, his usual amusement over society's little games failed him. So he answered Nan's letters with more circumspection than he by nature would have shown, almost as if the postal workers were reading what he wrote. Then he felt guilty because he was being so cautious and wondered if he really was serious about her.

Nan, on the other hand, knew her heart and did not care one little plop of chicken dirt, as she put it, what people thought. But without encouragement from Emmet, she too did not express her deepest love. What they wrote was more like the frank communication between close friends.

"I wish sometimes that I had just secretly joined the army," Emmet wrote, "instead of letting Mother make a big deal out of it and getting Congressman Maxley to wangle a commission for me in the navy just to prove she's got money and influence."

To which Nan replied, "If money and influence improve the odds of you coming home alive, it's okay by me."

"Well, joining the navy was the easy way out," Emmet wrote back. "I didn't have to wait to be drafted. I felt I had to leave home for a while. Mother is bent on me marrying Betty Torman, as you know. The Tormans got money, that's what that's all about. When I say I want to be a farmer, the whole family, except Gramps of course, starts fidgeting."

"I don't know why," Nan suggested in her next letter. "The richest people around here are farmers."

Most of the time, she tried to remain noncommittal about Emmet's mother, but Betty Torman was too much to resist.

"Everyone came to the Last Day picnic at school. It was warm and sunny and the woods behind the park were full of violets and wild phlox. Even the farmers stopped spring work long enough to come, some driving horses, some tractors. I felt a little sad about the school year being over, even though I hate school. To cheer myself up I started imitating those stuck-up town girls from Upper Surrey. I played Betty Torman, you know, real ootsy-dootsy-like. I said to Fern Merick, 'Fern, you *must* quit milking cows. Your hands are getting big and ugly.' Everybody got a kick out of that because Fern has the tiniest hands in school and she's the only one that does milk regularly."

After graduation, Nan tried to press Emmet for surer signs of commitment than his letters had thus far revealed. "Now that I'm out of school, I don't know what to do. I'm supposed to find a husband but all the possibilities are off to the war. But it looks like Ben is going to the army and then I'll be busy enough helping Dad on the farm."

Emmet did not take her lead. He did not write that the only future plan he could think of was marrying her and farming with Gramps. The longer he did not write it, and the more heavily he became involved in navy life, the less sure he was of that plan. His letters came less frequently and were shorter, even after he got back from a training stint on an aircraft carrier and had plenty of time on his hands stationed at a naval base in Florida. He began to think of Gowler and home as a quaint and isolated fairyland far removed from the grim world he had to cope with. He began to understand that he should not be encouraging Nan toward a future he might never live to see.

Home on furlough, he went directly to the Bump homestead but could not bring himself to rush up and hug her right in front of the rest of the family. He talked awkwardly, referring to his life as a navy pilot as if it were something that the Bumps would be unable to comprehend. Nan stared at him, sensing a different Emmet. Just as he was about to ask her to go with him into Gowler for a milkshake, Ben drew him away to the barn, where they talked with great animation. War talk. Ben felt guilty because of his farm deferment.

"You would go crazy in the armed forces," Emmet said. "You've never seen money and supplies wasted like the military does. Did you know you can cool beer by setting the bottles under a can of dripping high-octane gas? The evaporation does it."

Ben thought his friend was only trying to make him feel better. "I've got to go," he said sorrowfully. "I can see the accusation in people's eyes. They think I'm a coward."

Although Emmet kept looking over Ben's shoulder at Nan as she pretended to be busy around the barn, he did not know how to extricate himself to go to her. He kept looking at his watch, too. He was supposed to be back at his mother's right now. He walked toward Nan, and Ben, finally understanding, retreated into the barn.

"Nan, we need to talk," Emmet said lamely. "I've got only a three-day pass and Mother has every minute planned, as you might expect." He rolled his eyes. "I have to humor her. She's all alone. I'll try to come back here tomorrow. Maybe we can go out?"

Maybe? No maybe about it. What was wrong with him? Her eyes said as much.

Emmet suddenly knew he could not put off any longer what he had to tell her. He took her hands and pulled her to him. "Nan, dearest, I will be going into combat very soon. Flying a torpedo plane." He hoped she understood how risky that was without him saying it. No, he hoped she didn't know. "Life in the military is not human, not like anything you and I living here in Gowler could ever imagine. I have to be different out there, have to be someone I'm not. I just . . . I just feel I dare not love you too much right now."

He embraced her then because he could not stop from doing so. He could feel her body shudder against him and then he turned away quickly and strode toward his car. He was afraid to look back at her. Was it the possibility of death or his doubts about his love that was driving him? Nan haltingly followed a few steps, her hand still stretched out to him, then falling to her side as she stopped. A great rush of sorrow and realization washed over her. Emmet was no longer sure of his mind.

But Nat was sure of his. When Ben told him he was going to join the army, his father's face wrinkled up like a corn leaf in a drought. "I need you here," he growled.

"I can't bear to go but I can't bear to stay," Ben said. "I doubt I can get my deferment extended anyway. Nan will have to take my place."

Nat started to answer, then turned away. "Damn war," he muttered.

The anger in his voice did not make sense to Ben until next day. They were at the grain elevator in Gowler inspecting the new storage silo that the Gowlers were building to hold the outpouring of corn and soybeans that the government was urging farmers to grow. In its shadow the farmers lounged, trying not to exhibit the quivering delight that wormed through their minds at the predictions of $2.50 corn and $5.00 soybeans. Without thinking, Dob Hornley remarked that he had already made more money from the war prices than he had in the whole five years preceding it. "Who says war's so bad?" he remarked.

Nat walked over to him, rage visibly building on his face. He grabbed the hapless Hornley by the shirt front and lifted him into the air, the knuckles of his fist grinding into Hornley's chin and pushing the man's head back until his eyes rolled white in their sockets.

"You never been in war, you son of a bitch, or have a son going in or you wouldn't say that," he growled. "By God, if I had a gun I'd give you a taste of just how good war is when the bullets are parting your hair." Ben paled as his father shoved Hornley against the grain elevator wall and stalked off to his truck.

Driving home, Nat's hands trembled on the steering wheel. "You're wondering why I got so mad," he finally said. "I never talked to you about being in the last war." He paused to emphasize what was to come. "*On the German side.*" He let that sink in. "I mowed down Americans with my machine gun. Either that or get killed. I still see their faces in my dreams. I didn't want to fight no damn war. They chained us to our machine guns to keep us from running away." He was silent, his lips quivering and then he repeated almost in a scream: "*They chained us to our guns.* My brother went insane. We were just shepherd boys. The loudest noise we'd ever heard before that was lambs crying for their mothers."

Ben had never gone against his father's wishes and feared arguing with him. "I've got to go," he said simply. He bolstered himself with the eternal conviction of youth: others would die, never I. But he would wait to be drafted. Draftees went straight into the infantry, but they had only to stay in active service for two years instead of three for those who enlisted.

The work of the farm went on, as it always must, through the seasons, nature unconcerned by so ordinary an event as humans killing each other. But the quickening pace of technology, which the war brought with it, was bringing as much change to the way food was produced as the way battles were fought. Grain and livestock prices began to rise along with the general cost of living. Ambitious farmers responded by plowing up every acre they could wheedle out of absentee landlords, retiring farmers, and each other. Soybeans, hardly known before 1940, suddenly became a cash crop more lucrative than corn, and Floyd Gowler discovered that the oriental plant would grow well enough, at current prices, to make money even on the blue-black jackwax of Killdeer. "By God, I'm going to make some money from these old sheep pastures yet," he muttered to himself. He bought two more tractors and began tearing up every acre in Killdeer that dried out enough by the middle of June to plant.

Miser Meincer stood at the edge of the swampland, his bony fingers twisting his beard in agitation. Was it not enough that the farmers were plowing up all the good land? Did they have to plow even the poor? He retreated into the deepest recesses of Killdeer, to his last secret oak island, where he could commune with the shadowy forms of the Wyandots and Delawares that he claimed to see moving silently through the woods. He knew how they must have felt a hundred years ago, when the white man, crazy with greed for land, shipped them to Kansas and took their farms away from them.

Even Nat Bump was bitten by the expansion bug. He had talked Sarah Jane Lively, a spinster who lived in Columbus, into letting him farm the three hundred acres she owned but had never set foot on. She had inherited it by mere happenstance of family ties and held on to it, following her wealthy family's constant admonition: "Land is the best investment. Never sell it." When Nat learned that the poor sharecropper who had farmed it was going to work in a factory, he made his move.

Nat's acquisition miffed Adrian Farnold, who thought Sarah Jane should have rented the farm to him, "seeing as how," he explained, "that it was his mother's uncle who had worked for the Lively family in the old days when Nat Bump was still in Austria." And now, after the incident at the grain elevator, there was talk that Nat might be a German sympathizer.

The economic competition became savage. Floyd Gowler's more ambitious tenants, like the Remps and Chafers, kept farming for him but found other land to buy or rent. Floyd was tempted to buy too, in which case he could have run up the price beyond what the Remps and Chafers could pay. He decided against it. In truth, he already had more land than he could handle properly, and he wanted to cultivate the good will of his tenants.

But among farmers generally, there was a loss of brotherhood. "The Lord ain't makin' no more land," Nat said grimly, echoing the favorite rationalization. "It's every man for himself." He said it again on May 10, 1943, facing the agonizing decision that had followed on the decision to rent more land.

"Bring me the crosscut," he ordered Ben, as he straddled the horse tongue of the corn planter. Even though most other field work he now did with tractors, he had continued to do the planting with the horses. But now, with eighty acres of corn and soybeans to plant, horses were just too slow, and rain was threatening. As everyone else was doing, he would shorten the long tongue on his horse-drawn planter so he could hitch it handily to the tractor drawbar. Horses were just too slow. He jerked the crosscut across the wooden tongue with such vehemence that Ben on the other end could hardly keep in rhythm. Nat growled, but not at Ben. In cutting off the horse tongue, he knew he was cutting himself loose from the old ways. Something in him feared that change. But what choice did he have in the race to see who could farm the most land? To hell with it. He kept on sawing.

Dorothy liked the idea even less. "You'd make more money just improving the land we own and farming it well, Nat Bump," she scolded. "In the long run, building up the dairy herd would be more profitable than running all over God's creation growing soybeans." Nat sniffed. Why milk cows twelve months a year if you could make the same money tractor farming eight months?

That fall, Nat brought $3,000 in cash home from the bank after "settlin' up" and threw the bills into the air in the living room so that they fluttered down like autumn leaves. It was as if he were saying, "So there, Dorothy Bump, your mister knows what he's doing." She was too awed and excited, however, to see anything more in the money than the joy of having it, their first surplus cash from farming except for the Fruit Juice days. Ben and Nan watched, open-mouthed, as their parents danced a jig around the room. Neither son nor daughter could appreciate the potential freedom that the cash represented to their parents. All they could think about was the war. Nan waited for news from Emmet, who was now "somewhere in the South Pacific." Ben would be headed for Fort Knox in Kentucky in two weeks.

Nat did buy Dorothy a new washing machine, but he used most of the money to "gear up for high production," a phrase he learned from a farm magazine. He bought another tractor and equipment designed to operate at faster speeds than the converted horse machinery could maintain. The latter he pulled back into the woods or gave away as junk iron for the "war effort." Dorothy said nothing. She did not want to cloud the vision of prosperity that shone in his eyes.

Ben left the farm with a heavy heart, trying not to let the other inductees see the tears that pressed out from under his closed eyelids as the Greyhound rolled on through the night to Fort Knox, Kentucky. He had no interest in their excitement and listened with disgust to snatches of their braggadocio.

"I'm gonna screw every girl in Kentucky."

"I hope I get sent to the South Pacific. Women don't wear no clothes down there."

"My cousin says the way to get along in the army is never volunteer for anything."

"My brother says never to call a rifle a gun. If you do, you have to parade in front of everyone with a rifle in your hand and your cock out. You have to say over and over again, pointing from one to the other: 'This is my rifle, this is my gun. This is for killin' and this is for fun.'"

"In the army a bed is a fart sack."

Would he be able to endure two years of that? Ben wondered. He began right then the mind game that would comfort him for the next two years. As the bus rolled southward, he picked out a specific little part of the farm back home—the fence line on the eleven-acre field in this case—and walked it in memory. He recollected the condition of each corner post, the precise position of the elder-berry clumps on the south side, and whether or not the post with the bluebird hole in it was the third or fourth one from the south-west corner. Then he reviewed the crop rotation for the field: last year corn, this year wheat, next year oats, the year after that clover and timothy hay, and then maybe a cutting of timothy before going back to corn. He would be back again for the hay harvest in that field. Concentrating on that fact, he could shut out the present.

At Fort Knox, he wrote home whenever time permitted, and his letters at least helped Nan endure the lack of news from Emmet. She noted, with some amusement, or a feeling as close to amuse-ment as she could muster under the circumstances, a side to her brother she had not discerned before. Ben had a lot more to say in writing than he had expressed verbally around the farm. Inside his quiet, retiring exterior was a coldly calculating spirit more stub-born than even his father's, a sharp contrariness he could express with surprising articulation.

December 12: "I despise everything about the army. I've decided that my sense of patriotism doesn't go much farther than the bor-ders of our farm and certainly not beyond our country. I don't care who owns the Pacific Islands or who runs Poland and Yugoslavia. Those are not my marbles."

January 22: "Most of the guys are okay once you know them. I made a friend even. He gets the *Farm Journal* and we practically memorize every issue and talk farming while the others run on and on and on about getting drunk and chasing girls. But some-times I think I just might try getting drunk and chasing girls."

March 4: "I'm sorry I had no time to write to you these past weeks. I have been totally taken up with staying in radio school where they put me after the first tests. I thought sure I would flunk out. Everyone else in the class seemed to have previous experience. But while we were sitting in the classroom, I could hear soldiers marching almost continuously past the windows. All I could see through the windows were bayonets, row after row of them marching by. I can almost stand to think about getting shot with a bullet, but a bayonet going into my belly is too much for me. I am a coward, I guess. I knew that if I flunked out of radio school, I would be in those marching ranks, headed overseas to die with a bayonet sticking in me. So I studied night and day and what I didn't understand, I memorized. I made myself a little model of a Morse code sender and I practiced on it, sometimes all night. I did not want to die with a bayonet sticking in my belly. I'd fall asleep tapping away at that Morse code and wake back up still tapping. I passed. Six of us got picked for more radio training."

August 14: "Now you can see I have a new address. I am in an advanced class for radio communication. Decoding and stuff I can't talk about. I am still studying night and day because I do not want a bayonet stuck in my belly."

October 4: "So now I survived the cut again and six of us from this class are taking still more training. I am learning a whole lot of stuff that no farmer or anyone else needs to know, about electronic espionage. But at least now we are being treated as if we are almost human."

Meanwhile, Nan waited anxiously for a letter from Emmet. Earlier in the year, he had sent a terse note. He was back at the training base in Florida recovering from "combat fatigue." He thought for the rest of war he would be training new pilots and "preparing them for hell." That was all. Nan was torn between relief that he was still alive and panic over what "combat fatigue" might mean.

The day came when she knew, as the mailman pulled up to the mailbox where she, as usual, waited, that there was a letter from Emmet. The mailman's face was radiant. She snatched it from him, not even saying thanks, and turned abruptly away, walking down the road away from the mailbox, wishing to be alone, afraid to open the letter. Finally she tore savagely at the envelope, and with a great stone of dread in the pit of her stomach, she read, the very brevity of the letter a foreboding:

Dearest Nan,

Yes, that is the first time I have written that word, dearest. And it will be the last time, though you will always be dearest to me. I have been in a great turmoil and loneliness since combat and watching Japanese sailors drown after I helped torpedo and sink their ships. And seeing those Jap kamikaze pilots dive their planes into our ships. Do you know they are locked into their cockpits and the wheels of their planes drop off when they take off. That's what we're told. They have no choice but to die "gloriously" for their country. Human beings are all crazy.

What I have to say I know you will not understand. I don't either. I met a nice girl, a nurse, while I was convalescing from what was really a nervous breakdown. I was so mad about the war I refused to speak for six weeks. She got me to talking again and made me feel sane again in this loony bin, and I guess I fell in love with her. My mother is having fits. She had such a nice wedding planned for me and Betty Torman. But after what I've been through, family fits bother me no more than a mosquito bite. You will probably hate me, I know, but I am playing the cards dealt to me just like I did in combat and that's why I am still alive. If you were here, you might understand better. A person does what a person has to do to keep from dying or going insane.

But I will always remember you as the happiest part of my growing up. I may never come back to Ohio because the pain of seeing you would be too much to bear.

Your old friend,

Em

Old friend, she snorted, even as tears welled up in her eyes. Old friend. "Emmet, you stupid, stupid boy," she screamed to the lowering black clouds of November. And then she ran on down the road, away from the house, throwing the letter into the ditch, stopping, going back and picking it up again, running, running blindly along the roadside, noting, in spite of her great preoccupation with Emmet's message, the details of the familiar scene she was passing, as if her mind, to avoid disintegration, had to anchor itself in the commonplaces of her life: the bittersweet growing in the brushy fencerow that hid the fields so well from the road that in summer she could drive the tractor there with her blouse off and no one could see; the wild grapes now dried to raisins on their vines and which the cardinals were eating; the hickory tree that generations of farmers who had owned this land had not cut down because the nuts cracked out as easily as pecans into whole halves; the abandoned quail nest in the deep grass of the ditch, in which she had counted sixteen eggs that spring; the catalpa tree—an escapee from a catalpa grove grown for fenceposts—that had a hole in it where a flicker nested every spring. She came finally, still running, to the Gowler Road, and stopped, surprised that she had gone so far. She toyed with the idea of walking on, across the Gowler farmlands and into Killdeer, to sink down into the depths of the swamps and drown herself.

But then, when she did not think she could stand to live another second, a kind of miracle occurred. She saw walking toward her a familiar figure. Through her tears she recognized who it was, but at first her mind refused to accept the sight. It could not be. She must be dreaming. She almost hoped she was dreaming, because that would mean Emmet's letter was a dream too.

"Ben! *Ben!*" She ran toward him, hurling herself into his arms, still not believing he could really be there, but prepared to embrace any hallucination that would erase the reality of Emmet's letter.

Ben smiled at her, puzzled by her teary face and her unabashed hug. He was trying to remember if she had ever hugged him before. Both of them said the same thing at the same time.

"What are you doing here?"

Nan repeated the question before Ben could.

"I got a pass to come home for Thanksgiving," he said. "My captain insisted that I go on leave." The inexplicable wonder of his good fortune was obvious in his voice. "It's a very long story. I came on the train and thought I'd just walk home from the station and surprise everyone."

Nan began to sob again as she held the letter out for him. He read it, stared in shock at Nan, read it again, put his arm around her shoulders, and eased her down with him to a sitting position in the ditch. For a long time, they both sat there, staring into the hedge-like fencerow, saying nothing, waiting for Nan's sobs to subside.

"Why can't girls go to war too?" she finally said. "Then I could have taken care of him."

"War is no place for women. It's no place for men either."

"Haw. I can shoot better than you or Em."

Ben could only look at her, amazed as always at her belligerence, and shake his head. "They won't let women in combat ever. That might mean not enough babies to fill the ranks of the next army."

Later with the whole family gathered around the table, eager to know the miracle of Ben's homecoming, Nan sobbed her way through Emmet's letter again.

"You two were never meant to be together, child," Dorothy said, trying to remain detached and unemotional.

"I'm going to lay down and not move until I die," Nan said, resolutely.

"No, you aren't, young lady," Dorothy replied. "Only rich people can afford to feel sorry for themselves. You will keep on going like the rest of us and work the pain away."

Nan ran to her room. But before long she returned, unable to resist the urge to hear the remarkable events that Ben was relating in the kitchen. The angry cunning behind his story stunned his parents and Nan. He had always seemed so shy and acquiescent. Now he had grown hard, the dark side of the husbandman rising up in him, the husbandman who can be patient and kind to animals right up until the moment he kills and butchers them.

"I worked hard to pass all those tests to become a radio operator," he explained. "I made all the cuts. The officers called me in and congratulated me on my accomplishment. But that's when I learned that to do what I'd been trained to do, I now had to become an officer and go to officers' training school and enlist for three more years. My pay would go up from $50 to $200 a month. That was a really great raise. I said I would do all the work they wanted me to do, double shifts, anything, but I would not stay in the army one hour longer than I had to." He paused, sipped on his coffee, continued.

"The officers' attitude changed immediately. I was no longer their good old buddy. I'd either reenlist or it was straight to the infantry and overseas for me. I didn't have to think long on my decision. Even risking a bayonet in the belly was better than three more years in the army.

"So I was outta there. They put my records in a big envelope, sealed it, and sent me off to Camp Atterbury, where I understood I would soon ship out to Europe." He paused again, trying to find the right words to describe what he did next.

"I don't know that I was ever so mad in my whole life. I had earned my radio position. And now because I wouldn't reenlist, it didn't matter. They'd make me do what I was trained for, I figured, but without the increase in pay. I was traveling by bus to Atterbury, and the way things worked out I had to stay overnight in a hotel in Memphis. In the middle of the night I thought of a way to strike back at them. I carefully melted the wax on the envelope containing my records and removed all information pertaining to my radio training and resealed the envelope. I was going to make sure they would not make me do two-hundred-dollar-a-month work for fifty dollars a month."

Nat broke right out laughing. Dorothy could not repress a smile. As she had said many years ago when Ben thought of hiding the jars of the Fruit Juice in the pond right under the sheriff's nose, she repeated: "Ben Bump, you could go far in this life."

"I don't want to go far. I just want to stay home."

Then he resumed his story. The most remarkable part was yet to come.

"At Atterbury, they found out I could type and so they put me in charge of doing the paperwork for mustering out returning veterans. I'd learned to type while I was learning radio. Not very good at it, but good enough. As it turned out, I could do the work much faster than anyone had done it before and I cleared up the logjam of paperwork that had been getting the captain in trouble. I guess it sounds braggy, but you know something? All that work out there that everyone finds hard to do is really much easier than good farming. He was so pleased he started treating me like I was his long-lost son. I was supposed to be on my way to Europe, but he got this mysterious air about him. Said he had figured out a way to keep me working for him for the duration of the war but that part of the scheme required that I had to go home for Thanksgiving. He had a pass for me. Didn't make any sense at all. 'Don't ask stupid questions, soldier,' he said. 'Get the hell outta here and let me handle this.' So here I am."

Nat pounded the table in joyful amazement and Dorothy scurried around getting supper, tears of happiness in her eyes. God did exist no matter what Nat said.

But the climax of this strange day was yet to come. After supper, to celebrate the homecoming and to cheer Nan up, Ben suggested that he take her to the movie in Surrey. Dorothy thought that a fine idea for the same reason, and besides she almost always bought a ticket for the "Bank Nite" movie every Wednesday. She rarely went to see it, but she hoped to win the drawing afterwards. Nat loved to remind her that this was gambling, something she claimed to disapprove of, but she ignored him. Fifty cents out of the egg money was a mere pittance and someday she'd win the hundred-dollar jackpot. She pressed the ticket money into Nan's hand and hurried them out the door, ignoring protests that she should come to the picture show too. They did not ask their father because he would never go. He said real life was all the excitement he could stand.

By the time Ben and Nan reached the theater, even Nan was smiling a bit, but her spirit sank again when she saw Betty Torman and Wayne Gitchell waiting in line to buy tickets. Wayne could not forget, especially when he was drunk, the night that Emmet ran him off the road in Killdeer, and it was evident that tonight he had been drinking.

"Well, here comes Killdeer," he said, loud enough for everyone in line to hear. "Hey, they got shoes on. Bet they had rattlesnake steaks for supper."

Nothing might have come of the remark, which the Bumps pretended not to hear, but Betty Torman added: "Does anyone smell pig? I smell pig."

"A fox smells her own hole first," Nan said. Having lost Emmet, she did not care what she said to anyone, anywhere.

About that time the two Burks boys, also home on leave and dressed nattily in army uniforms, approached the ticket booth. Seeing their friend, Wayne, they pushed into line behind him and ahead of the Bumps. Billy, perhaps accidentally, perhaps not, nudged Nan off balance.

"Excuse me," she said hotly and wedged her way back in front of the Burkses.

"You watch your step, Killdeer," Wayne said to her but with his eyes on Ben. "I've been saving a place in line for Billy and Buck. They're soldiers and you better respect them. If you clodhoppers don't like it, get yourselves back to Gowler."

Ben rolled his eyes and sighed. If only Emmet were here, he'd take command of the situation and put Gitchell in his place.

"I hear you lost your boyfriend," Betty Torman said sweetly to Nan. Nan tried not to show surprise that Torman already knew, but she turned red and Ben shivered. When Nan turned red, look out.

"At least I had a boyfriend. I didn't have to run around with a jackass like Wayne Gitchell," she replied.

Tense silence. Finally Gitchell spoke, still eying Ben. "Feisty little bitch, ain't she. I bet she'd put up a helluva fight in the backseat of a car, too."

Nan turned to see Ben's face turn as hard and white as a sauerkraut crock. When he did not respond, Nan figured that he was just going to back off as he usually did, the shy and retiring husbandman. She did not know her history. She did not know that shy and retiring husbandmen have been known to revolt against oppression with pitchforks drawn.

Moreover, Ben was not the shy innocent soul he had been when he left home. The army had taken care of that. He had held his peace while he was herded naked, like an animal, through his physical exam in the army; had held his peace in boot camp, when he was forced to charge up an empty hill with fixed bayonet on his rifle, while an officer screamed, "Kill! Kill! Kill!" He had even shown no outward sign of his growing boldness when, after he had driven himself to the brink of physical and mental collapse to stay in radio school, he had been rejected because he would not accept more time in the army. But this was too much. He did not intend to stand idly by and watch the village bully ridicule his sister. There was a war that he was willing to fight, and it started right here in Surrey.

He stepped up to Gitchell and the Burkses with an air of resignation that they misinterpreted as timid hesitancy. Ben noticed, again with the peculiar detached drollness that always insinuated itself in him in the most critical moments, the fittingness of the background: a life-sized poster of his boyhood hero, Gene Autry, with drawn guns blazing away almost directly at Gitchell and the Burkses. "I want you two guys to go to the back of the line," he said to the Burks boys, forcing his voice to speak without tremor. "And Wayne, I want you to apologize to my sister for what you said and for calling us clodhoppers. I'm here to tell you this is 1944 and I don't ever want to hear that word used in reference to farmers in Surrey again."

Gitchell, not tipped off by the new tone in Ben's voice, screwed open his mouth to say "clodhopper" once more, but before the last syllable was out, Ben's fist slammed into his jaw. Gitchell fell back but Ben stayed right in his face, fists pumping. He had learned that from what a sergeant had said after surviving a barroom fight unscathed. "If you're gonna attack a guy, don't fool around. Hit him fast and then keep hammering away until he goes down. Before he can collect himself. Don't give the son of a bitch a chance to git organized. That's the secret of blitzkrieg."

The line of people broke to get out of the way, girls screaming, a boy yelling, but no one moving to stop the fight. Like windmills, Ben's arms continued to whirl, his fists working over Gitchell's body with punishing force. The Burkses, taken aback, and lapsing into their characteristic cowardice, could only stare dumbly at the fight. The hapless Gitchell, unable to escape Ben's pounding fists by backpedaling, turned and ran. Or tried to. But with his first terrified step, he lunged headlong into the Gene Autry sign propped in the middle of the sidewalk, then stumbled and fell down, almost as if, Nan would say later in great glee, Gene Autry had shot him. While Ben continued to pummel his hapless adversary out into the street, the Burkses finally came to their wits enough to remember that they outnumbered Ben. They started to come to Gitchell's aid.

But Nan was waiting. Spit-snarling like a cougar, she drew herself up until she looked to the Burkses as tall as the Statue of Liberty, or at least the Gene Autry sign, and pointed a finger directly into Billy Burks's left eye. "Billy, if you take one more step, so help me God I will scratch your eyeballs out of your head and roll them down the sidewalk."

The Burkses stopped, unprepared for so unlikely a threat. They could only grin at her in confusion, like a dog that's been embarrassed.

Clarissa Jones in the ticket booth had reached for the phone to call the police, but now her arm seemed paralyzed in midair as she watched a diminutive human wildcat hold two hulking hound dogs at bay with sheer fearlessness.

Betty Torman fainted and slid to the sidewalk.

Gene Autry, teetering from the collision with Gitchell, righted himself and continued to blaze away in the general direction of villainy.

Torman's swoon stopped the fight as quickly as it had started. The Burks boys knelt beside her and clumsily tried to revive her. Gitchell was still going up the street as fast as his wobbly legs could carry him, unaware, if he cared at all, of his date's distress. She blinked, propped herself into a sitting position, and began to cry. Ben stared at the pavement in embarrassment. Wearing a sneer that her face could scarcely contain, Nan said: "Why, Miss Torman, I fear you may have wet your pants." And then she stepped up to the ticket window. "Two, please. No, make that three. Mom wants one for Bank Nite." And then, marshaling her brother ahead of her, she walked triumphantly into the theater.

With Ben back in Camp Atterbury, Nan was left to deal with the gossip about what had happened in front of the Dorral Theater, which was being widely referred to as the Fight at the OK Dorral. Descriptions of the fight, based mainly on the versions of Betty Torman and the Burks boys (Gitchell, in his humiliation, remained silent), took on the grandeur of epic tragedy.

"It was horrible. Lasted maybe an hour. The Bump boy beat the livin' hell out of Wayne Gitchell and two soldier boys, and no one tried to stop him."

"How could that be, three on one?"

"Well, you know that Killdeer trash. Mighty rough customers."

"Their women don't take no backseat either. The Bump girl kicked Betty Torman ass-over-applecart right out into the middle of the street."

"And when Clarissa in the ticket booth tried to call the police, the Bump bitch jumped her and said if she touched the phone she'd claw her eyes out."

"It's time to keep those Killdeer hoodlums out of our town."

"You know they were bootleggers back during the Depression. Probably got connections with the Mob."

"You know their old man fought for the Germans in World War I."

The part of the story that claimed two soldiers had been beaten up ultimately became the dominant theme. Ben had not been in uniform, and no one mentioned that he was also a soldier home on leave. The notion that he had thrashed two men in uniform fit in neatly with the local theory about his father being a Nazi sympathizer. The old man probably encouraged his boy to beat up on American soldiers.

Nat was torn between a secret pride in his children and his anguish over the trouble he feared was coming. Since Ben was absent, he vented his worries on Nan.

"But we didn't start the fight," Nan argued with him. "They did."

"Ben swung first. You said so yourself. How many times have I told you we can't afford to make trouble," Nat replied. "When you're an immigrant and a poor dumb farmer to boot, you gotta use your wits, not your fists."

"We gotta stand up for our rights. And I'm not an immigrant," Nan shot back at him. Unlike her brother, she had never been afraid to dispute her father. "And I ain't no dumb farmer, either."

"You should be ashamed of yourself acting like a hussy," Dorothy scolded. "And 'ain't' is not a word. If you don't want to be called a dumb farmer, don't talk like one."

Nan glared at her mother. Just like her to try to act like those fancy Gowler women even at a time like this. "Ben was outnumbered. I had to do something. If all three had jumped him, he'd have gotten hurt. You oughta be glad I did."

Silence. Finally Nat smiled ruefully and deliberately leaned back into his half English. "Yah. The hell of it is, I *am* glad."

Sheriff Mogan saw that he was going to have to put his foot down before the fight became a community problem. He would have ignored it altogether, having heard from Clarissa at the ticket office what had really happened. But since the disturbance had taken place in Surrey, it actually came under the jurisdiction of the town's chief of police, who, Mogan knew, would try to do something about it and screw up the delicate balance of local pride and prejudice that gave villages that aura of peacefulness that big-city fantasy attributed to them. So the sheriff had followed his usual procedure. He told Chief Truman that the sheriff was ruler over the whole county, so he would handle the case because the Bump boy lived outside of town. And for Truman to stay the hell out of the way. Truman as usual, was relieved to hear this. He liked being police chief in Surrey only when the town was living according to the urban fantasy.

Mogan got Wayne Gitchell to admit that he had provoked the fight, then declared to one and all, in the barbershop from where he knew his words would go forth to all of his kingdom, that Ben Bump and the Burkses were in the army and he, the sheriff, was by God not going to arrest anyone away from home defending their country for anything so insignificant as disturbing the peace. And anyway, Bump hadn't so much as touched the Burks boys, but only Wayne Gitchell, who ought to be horsewhipped on general principle. And as for the Tormans, they had just better settle their hash before someone looked into why their daughter's traffic tickets always got dismissed.

Normally that would have ended the matter, except for Nat Bump's rumored connection with the Germans. The gossip had escalated into a theory that he was actually a spy. Even Nat found that amusing. "What da hell would I spy on around here that would benefit da Germans," he remarked, more and more relying on Old World accent just to spite his detractors. His logic was so unassailable that the spy theory faded in popularity.

But Wayne Gitchell and his friends were not so easily discouraged. Sitting in the Bloody Bucket saloon in Surrey, growing bolder with each beer, they discussed how they might make life miserable for Ben Bump when he came home again. It was bad enough to be humiliated by a redneck farmer, but a farmer from Killdeer to boot, and on top of that, the Bumps were Catholic, or supposed to be.

Dob Hornley, who had been listening, turned from the bar to stare at them, perhaps sympathetically, perhaps drunkenly, perhaps both. He was remembering how Nat had slammed him against the grain elevator wall.

"Things like this wouldn't happen when I was your age," he said thickly. "The KKK would take care of it."

"The what?"

"The Ku Klux Klan. They kept the niggers outta this county. Catholics and furriners learned to stay in line or they might get their barns burnt down. Need a little of that kind of education now."

"You were in the Ku Klux Klan? You really went around with a white hood over your head and burned crosses in people's yards?" Even Wayne Gitchell found that hard to believe. Everyone said that Dob Hornley was all shit and wind.

"I'm not sayin' I was in it or I wasn't in it. Just sayin' we need for true Americans to take a firmer stand today."

Gitchell and his friends glanced at each other. "What you got in mind, Dob?" he asked.

Something woke Nat Bump up shortly after he had gone to bed, a noise not part of a farm at night. A car door slamming? A motor suddenly accelerating? A muffled voice? Light flickered in the window. He jumped up and looked out. A fire burned in the front yard, and as his sleepy eyes slowly focused, he realized it was a burning cross.

"Gott in Himmel," he muttered.

"What's wrong?" Dorothy asked from bed, and then, seeing the flickering in the window herself, rushed to see.

"What in the world is that?" she asked, genuinely puzzled.

"It's what I've feared ever since this godforsaken war started," he said.

He jumped into his boots and ran out the back door. The burning cross probably meant the perpetrators did not intend to burn the barn, but he could not be sure. As he jumped off the back porch, headed for the barn, a hooded figure clad in white confronted him from the shadows. Two other similar figures emerged at the edge of the porch light. KKK, all right, even if their outfits were ludicrously makeshift, Nat noted. Sheets draped over them with slits for eyes and arms and gathered at the waist by belts. He stopped and waited for them to speak. Only the one in front carried a gun. Looked like a .22-caliber rifle to Nat. Whoever these characters were, they didn't know much about gun combat. If he got a little closer to them, he could probably take one slug while he wrenched the gun away from the slimy bastard. But maybe the others had guns under their bedsheets.

"Nat Bump, we are here to test your loyalty to America," the rifle-toting figure finally spoke, but in a high, queer tone, obviously an attempt to disguise his voice. One of the other figures stepped forward, drawing an American flag out from under the folds of his sheet. He, if indeed it was a he, unfurled the flag and laid it on the ground. It appeared obvious from the way his hands trembled and the hesitancy with which he moved that he was at least as scared as Nat was. The third figure fidgeted nervously in the background. Nat decided that only the leader was of any real concern.

"You will kneel down and kiss this flag," the high, fake voice ordered. And then he raised the rifle menacingly.

Nat thought fast. If he were alone, he would have called the man's bluff, would have told him he would kiss no man's flag nor no man's ass. But there was Nan and Dorothy to think of. If these idiots got the better of him, no telling what they might do to them.

"Why are you doing this to me?" he asked, hoping to find some leeway in their intentions.

"Just do what you're told, you goddamn Nazi spy."

"If I kiss your flag and prove I'm a loyal American, are you going to leave us alone?"

In answer, the ghostly figure levered the bolt action on his rifle, and slid a bullet into the chamber.

Nat slowly knelt. If he had known that his assailant did not have the gun ready to fire, he might have taught him something about what war was really like. Too late now. But his knee barely touched the ground when suddenly the whole immediate area around him was bathed with light and a high, thin voice was speaking, this time from the porch.

"Drop that gun and step back."

Nat turned his head sharply. Gott in Himmel. It was Nan. She had a coon-hunter's spotlight strapped to her forehead and both hands gripped his shotgun. Gott in Himmel, she was going to get them all killed.

Before the stunned Ku Kluxers could decide whether to obey her or shoot her, she fired. The shotgun pellets blasted into the dirt not an inch away from the foremost figure's right foot, kicking mud up on his white gown.

"By God, I said drop it, or by God, I'll shoot your legs right out from under you next time." Nan's voice was firmer now and full of deadly resolve. Nat was fairly certain she would do it too, but what happened next was something he would never have anticipated.

"Better do what she says, or this little incident is going to precipitate your entrance into hell," said another female voice out of the darkness at the corner of the house. Gott in Himmel, it was Dorothy! Nan almost laughed, despite the terror that gripped her. She was sure her mother was trying to model her words after some novel she had read. But what was really funny, or what would seem funny later on, was that Dorothy was brandishing Old Blunderbuss, which she did not even know how to load.

The Ku Kluxer, confused, lowered his rifle slightly. That was all Nat needed. He sprang from his kneeling position, grabbed the gun barrel with his left hand, and kicked his would-be assailant brutally in the crotch. Before the other two could think to attack or flee, Nat trained the rifle on them while their comrade rolled in agony on the ground.

"Help him up and git," he spat. "Git, and I'll make no more of this."

"No," said the squeaky voice on the porch. "I got four more shells in this shotgun and I aim to start using them unless you take those stupid sheets off. I wanna see who you yellabellies are."

The would-be Ku Kluxers meekly loosened the belts holding the sheets tight around them and pulled their disguises up and off their heads. Wayne Gitchell and Henry Remp. The other, older one looked like Dob Hornley, though she wasn't sure.

"Just what I expected," Nan said derisively. "You no-good skunks."

"Don't shoot, Nan. Please don't shoot," Gitchell pleaded. "We was just funnin'. We don't mean no harm."

Nat did not even notice who was speaking because his eyes were riveted on the older man. Rage was welling up in him and with it, his true self, not the apologetic immigrant image he so often projected.

"Dob Hornley, you bastard. I never much liked you, but I never thought you could stoop this low. If I was wearin' work shoes, I'd kick you to death right now."

"No, no," Dorothy said, coming down off the porch.

"Just tell me why," Nat said, paying no attention to his wife. "How could you do this? And bringin' these youngsters into it. You know me, Dob Hornley. We've neighbored. We've had our differences but we've worked together. How in the hell could you do this?"

Hornley had quit groaning, but he only stared sullenly at the ground.

"*Now* you can git," Nan said, gesturing with the shotgun.

"No, I think not," Nat snapped. A tone crept into his voice more sinister than his threats of violence. "I got a better idea. You wanna hide behind your goddamn bedsheets. Well, I'm gonna give you reason for wearin' em."

Hornley looked quizzically at him.

"Put your sheets back on."

"Whaaat?" Dob protested.

Nat squeezed the trigger and a rifle bullet whizzed past Hornley's head close enough that he could almost smell it. "Oh, God, Nat. Don't shoot me."

"Put your goddamn bedsheets back on."

All three did as commanded.

"Now take your pants off. Underwear too."

Wayne Gitchell's eyes were about to bulge right out of his eye slits. Hornley began to shake. What the hell was Bump up to?

"Take your pants off or so help me I'm gonna start shooting," Nat growled.

He waited as the three men slid their pants and underwear down their legs into piles on the ground under their sheets. Nat then turned to Nan. "Get some binder twine and tie their hands behind their backs. And ankles together." She moved to obey, afraid now that her father had lost his mind. Tying men's ankles together when she knew that under their sheets they were naked as jaybirds all the way up the gazoo made her fear she was going to start laughing hysterically. What if one of them had the piss scared out of him? She tied the knots of the twine so tightly that she knew they would have to be cut loose.

"Now back the truck up here," Nat ordered her. In the meantime he continued to glare at Dob Hornley with a malevolence that sobered the man out of his considerable intoxication.

"What you gonna do to us?" Dob whimpered. He had decided that Nat planned to throw them in the river and drown them.

Nat set the rifle down and threw each of the men in turn into the back of the pickup, like he would sacks of potatoes.

"Drive, Nan. We're going to Surrey. To the courthouse lawn."

Nat perched on the pickup hood, facing the bed, the rifle across his lap. Dorothy jumped into the cab beside Nan. Whatever was going to happen, she had to make sure Nat didn't kill anyone. Nan was wide-eyed. Whatever was her father up to?

Saturday night in Surrey was the peak of the week's social activities, excepting of course Sunday morning church. Country folk came into town for miles around to do their trading early, and then to mingle and visit. The streets became so jammed with people that car traffic was all but impossible, giving the streets a carnival-like atmosphere. Still, the merchants had begun to worry. Saturday night sales were decreasing slightly every year lately. Some thought it was the war and the lack of young men to lure the young women to town. Hard to say. Times were changing.

The courthouse lawn, at the very center of downtown, was, as usual, full of loungers. Throngs crossed and recrossed at the stoplight where Main Street and Surrey Avenue intersected in front of the courthouse, all looking for friends and acquaintances with which to trade news. Humpbacked Beenie Thrattle had his two-wheeled popcorn cart set strategically next to the curb at the intersection, where the smell of the corn could waft over both the street throngs and the courthouse lawn loungers. Della Gowler, always the schoolteacher, often sighed about how tragic it was that there was no Pieter Brueghel to paint Saturday nights in Surrey.

Nan stopped the truck in front of the ornate sculpted horse trough in front of the courthouse lawn, as Nat had directed her. He jumped down off the truck, threw Dob's rifle in the trough, opened the tailgate of his truck, and dragged the three men out, propping them up on their feet. He opened his pocketknife and prodded them toward the courthouse. Gitchell was sobbing openly. He thought Nat was going to stab him. In single file, the three robed men shuffled inch by inch in their binder twine shackles up the sidewalk toward the two sinister black Civil War cannons that flanked the main door. It was the last dance of the KKK in Jergin County. By now the crowds of people were beginning to gather round the strange scene. Most had never seen real Ku Kluxers in full regalia, but they had heard plenty. Most of them did not like what they had heard. Now they pressed tightly around the strange procession and fell silent.

In front of the cannons, Nat stopped the shuffle and turned to the silent crowd. "These sonsabitches were burning a cross in my yard," he shouted. "Don't you all want to know who the cowards are?"

No one answered, but the crowd pressed closer. Of course they wanted to know. Nat was not a familiar figure to them, and they assumed he must be some kind of law officer.

"Don't you all want to know the kind of rats who go around at night trying to scare people they don't like?" Nat asked again and then turned to the shrouded figures, one of whom appeared to be weeping. "Take your goddamn bedsheets off and show these people who you are!" he roared. He stepped behind them and slashed the twines that held their hands.

None of them moved to comply. The one who was crying bowed abjectly and covered his head with his hands. Another tried to loosen the twine around his ankles, but the knots were too tight.

"You mean you don't have the guts to take off your Halloween suits and show these people who you are?" Nat roared again. And with that, he grabbed the sheet over Dob Hornley, pulled it free from his body in one mighty sweep, and cast it aside. Hornley stooped to the ground, trying to pull his shirt down far enough to cover his genitals. The crowd, at first falling back in shock, began to titter. Gitchell and Remp, in panic, their ankles still tied, tried to hop away as if in a sack race. They stumbled and fell, their bare butts exposed to the crowd. Gitchell sobbed, but Henry Remp was silent, his face gone dark and murderous. The Bumps would pay for this; he'd make sure of that. Titters from the crowd became a ripple of laughter and then a roar as people pressed in to get a better look. In the confusion, Nat slipped away, jumped in his truck beside Dorothy, and said to Nan, still at the wheel, "Drive!" Even Dorothy was having a difficult time not smiling as Dob Horn-ley hopped madly across the courthouse lawn, trying unsuccessfully to hold his shirt down over his privates with one hand, while, with his other, trying to grab his bedsheet uniform, which a nasty little boy was dragging enticingly in front of him.

SEVEN

The army had convinced Ben of one thing: he never wanted to live anywhere again except in the fields of home. For a while after his return, he would hardly leave the farm, content to walk alone along the creek or through the woods or over the fields, like some latter-day Thoreau, while the revulsion against society that had festered in him after the violent and rootless life of the army slowly healed. Without Emmet around, and without a special girl to come home to, he felt alienated from local social life. He did the work that Nat told him to do, mostly in silence. In the evenings he read farm magazines or Jack London novels or listened to the Sons of the Pioneers sing on the radio. As he said, dryly, when a worried Nat suggested that he might enjoy the New Year's party the Elks were sponsoring in Surrey: "I prefer the company of cows."

But by spring 1946 his soul began to stir with a renewed zest for life. As much as he loved his parents, and even though he got along better with Nat than others his age did with their fathers, Ben yearned for his own place. Farming for someone else, even a father, was work without the satisfaction of ownership or decision making. Farming for oneself, on the other hand, would be more play than work, he felt, no matter how brutal the job. He was also feeling the loneliness of the single man. In desperation, he dated Nell

Cughes, who was still trying to win his favor. He didn't even like her. Halfway through a movie they went to, he let his hand fall slyly against her leg, and she yielded so quickly that she alarmed him. He was saved when the projector malfunctioned and sent the image on the screen shuddering in disarray. By the time things were back to normal, he had thought better of his impulse. On the other hand, Margie Dall, the only girl he was sort of attracted to, turned down his offer of a date. That so injured his pride that he did not ask her again. Most girls were not interested in becoming farm wives. The postwar restlessness infusing society considered the life of a farmer's wife only dull. Beyond the humdrum of Gowler lay the Promised Land, a world of unimaginable excitement.

In March, Ben stopped by Floyd Gowler's farm. The old man was feeding his hogs—the few he still kept "out of habit," he said. He had forsaken all other livestock in favor of cash grain farming, except his beloved flock of sheep.

"Well, it's a pleasure to see you, Ben, my boy," he said in his customary ornate way, "You're a sight for sore eyes."

"You shouldn't carry heavy loads like that," Ben said, catching up with Floyd as he staggered across the hog lot with a hundred-pound sack of milled corn and oats over his shoulder. Ben tried to take the sack from him, but the old man pulled away. "I don't need no guardeen yet," he snorted.

"You should get your hired men to do that."

"Oh, time I get them wound up, the hogs'd starve to death," he said. Having arrived at the self-feeder, he lifted the lid with his free hand, let the sack plop, open end down, into the feeder, and then stuck out his hand. "How the hell are you, anyhow? Sure is good to have you back home."

"It's good to be back, Mr. Gowler."

They small-talked the weather and market prices awhile, but it was obvious both of them had something more on their minds. It was Floyd who got down to business first.

"You heard anything from Emmet?" he asked, squinting at Ben.

"Well, not since, not since—"

"Not since he got hitched," Floyd completed the sentence. He spoke in a way, had not Ben already known, that indicated he was not entirely in agreement with the marriage. The old man waited a bit and then asked, trying to sound nonchalant, "Think he'll come back home?"

"I expect she'll have something to say about that," Ben said.

Floyd nodded silently. He had hoped Ben would know something he didn't. He wanted more than anything for Emmet to come home and take over his farm empire. And so did Ben, missing Emmet's companionship. But now the whole thing was doubly difficult for both of them to contemplate because of Nan, who was still openly unreconciled to Emmet's marriage. How could Emmet, married to someone else other than her, live in the same community with Nan?

But there was something else on Ben's mind. He cleared his throat, wanting to get down to a proposition over which he was not so powerless.

"I was wondering, Mr. Gowler, how you might be inclined to reply if I were to ask you if I could rent that thirty-acre field above Swamp Poodle, the one that sets kind of by itself there along Old Sawmill Road?"

Of all his thousands of acres, that field, somewhat above the level of most of the Killdeer Plains and so better drained, was some of Floyd's best land, and they both knew that the other knew it.

"What you have in mind?" Floyd asked.

"I need to make myself some extra money towards getting my own place. I have in mind farming it on the half with you. Putting it to corn."

"You can't really make any money grain farmin' on the half, you know," Floyd said, softly, almost guiltily.

"Well, I don't know any other way to start, and the grain prices are pretty good right now. Dad'll let me use his machinery when he can spare it in return for my working for him. So I won't have much overhead." He stared levelly at Floyd. "And Lord knows I can do better than that stump jumper you got farming it now."

Floyd laughed. "By God, I like you, Bumps. I bet your Dad don't even know you're over here askin' me, does he?"

"No, sir."

"He'd try to rent it himself if he could work up enough humility to ask," Floyd said, laughing again. He paused then, and lifted the sack so that its contents poured into the feeder. "Well, mind you, if Emmet comes home, I'll have to have that land back but I'll go halves with you for this year anyway. I supply the land, you supply the equipment and labor, and we'll divide the other expenses. Okay?"

"I'm much obliged," said Ben, sticking out his hand for the confirming shake, trying hard not to show his elation. "You won't regret it."

Nat tried to match his son's excitement when Ben told him the news. He noticed the new snap in his son's eyes and was glad, but his fatherly possessiveness was hard to conceal. He had hoped that Ben would stay with him on the farm, and it was difficult to adjust immediately to this first act of independence. But his good sense quickly came to the fore. Better to have Ben in the neighborhood than not at all. Nat would play the cards dealt him as cool as possible, like he always did. He bought more seed corn than he needed and then told Ben, "You know, I miscalculated on my seed corn and bought too much. There's enough left to plant your thirty acres. Lord knows, I don't pay you enough as it is."

When Nan heard what Ben was doing, she reached a decision that had long been on her mind. The very next day, when she got home from her clerk's job at the courthouse and everyone was waiting on her so supper could begin, she made a formal announcement—as formal as it was in her character to manage.

"I've had it with the courthouse," she said. "I quit."

"You just be thankful for that clerk job," her mother said. "It's a nice, secure, well-paying job and it could lead right up the ladder to being the recorder or something."

"I *quit!*" Nan said. "It's so boring I will die up there."

"Oh, you will come to like it eventually," Dorothy said, setting the potatoes on the table. "I don't want to hear any more of this foolish talk."

"Mother, I. Have. Quit. Q-u-i-t."

"You mean already? Oh, no. You didn't really," Dorothy said.

"Yep."

They glared at each other. Why, Dorothy thought, had she married into such belligerent blood. But she could be belligerent too. "Well, don't think you can just lounge around here. You've got to pay for your keep, just like everyone else."

"I'm going to be a farmer," she said.

Dorothy's jaw dropped. "What do you mean, you're going to be a farmer?"

"I mean I'm going to be a farmer. If Ben can work here and rent some land, why can't I? I can drive a tractor just as well as he can."

"It wouldn't be seemly."

"Oh, crap."

"Don't you talk to me that way, young woman. What you should be doing is thinking about marrying one of those young farmers who keep asking you out. Then you'd get all the farmin' any woman could rightly handle."

"I'm never going to get married, I've told you. I hate men and I hate courthouses, and I hate people who try to run my life." And off she stomped up the stairs, slamming the door to her bedroom. Ben, accustomed to his sister's flurries, grinned. Nat, who usually would not tolerate such backtalk, was strangely silent.

"A lot of help you are," Dorothy said to him.

"Now, Mutter, don't be too hard on her."

"Don't you 'Mutter' me. You're up to something, aren't you?"

Nat did not reply.

A little later, Nan, hearing Ben tell that Floyd had asked about Emmet, and how Floyd had not known any more than they did, decided that her curiosity was greater than her anger, and she came back to the table, trying to ignore her mother.

"So you want to farm," Nat said to her.

She looked at him, not knowing what to expect.

"Yes."

"Then farm you shall, but you will work every day as long as Ben does excepting those times when your mother needs you in the house. Okay?"

"Yes." She wanted to ask why Ben didn't have to take his turns in the house too, but knew it was not the time for that kind of argument.

And so it was done, with Dorothy pale and objecting and Nat as unblinking as an owl until he left the table. Walking alone to the barn, he smiled with some secret satisfaction. With the whole family involved in the future of the farm, perhaps he should be looking for more land himself.

Floyd Gowler might have saved his own life by renting the thirty acres to Ben, although he could not have foreseen how that would come about. Age was telling on him these days, his back in such pain at times that he could barely bend over. Stubbornly, though, he refused to give in. He only consented to go to Doc Halw, whose office was hardly a block from his house if the distance had been measured that way, because he enjoyed trading insults with him.

"For Chrissakes, Floyd, it's high time for you to quit farming," Dr. Halw said, hardly bothering to examine his old friend's aching back.

"It's high time for you to quit doctorin' too," Floyd snorted. "I suspect you couldn't hear a heartbeat in an elephant through that thing around your neck anymore."

"Heh. I can hear well enough to hear *your* heart, and that's saying something since it sounds like it's hitting on only one cylinder."

"One cylinder's all I need."

"All right, then, go on back out there and try to outwork the hired men and kill yourself. You're only going to hurt your own dear Della, and God knows she's had to take enough of your stubborn ways as it is."

"Huh. This old body is far from dead, and *she'll* tell you that too if you ask her the right question."

So Floyd continued to try to "work the pain out" of his back. After he could no longer hoist the sack of hog feed onto his shoulder for the staggering trip across the lot, he found that he could manage a five-gallon bucket of feed by securing a metal hook to the handle of the bucket and then attaching an old V-belt to the hook and looping the belt over his head. Keeping his back ramrod-straight with both hands around the bucket, stabilizing it against his stomach as if he were pressing a baby to his bosom, he could manage to limp his way along without too much pain.

So encumbered, he was making his way across the hog lot one morning when his foot stepped into a hole rooted out by the hogs. The sudden shifting of his body and its weight sent a blast of pain up his spine so severe that he passed out and fell to the ground.

The hogs, which had been pushing around him as he walked, now swarmed over him, nosing the feed out of the bucket and sniffing at his skin. In only a few minutes they would realize that fresh blood was only the rip of a tusk away. Once tasting blood, they could react with the gluttonous frenzy of lions over a zebra carcass.

But Floyd's fall had been observed. Ben had been worrying over whether it was more seemly for him to go ahead and crop the thirty acres by his own counsel, like a veteran renter would do, or whether he should talk the work over with Floyd. Fortunately for Floyd, Ben decided that it was more prudent, given the circumstances, to seek the older man's advice. That very morning he had called Floyd to set up a meeting, but had not gotten past Gowler's phone operator, Fannie Bay, who ran the exchange out of her front parlor facing the village's main street.

"Yes, Floyd's to home now," she said, after her usual gushing "Number, please" and after recognizing Ben by his voice—as she recognized nearly everyone's voice in the vicinity. "He was down at the general store earlier, but he headed back towards his place about half an hour ago."

"Thanks, Fannie. I expect I'll just drive down to see him. If anyone calls for me, that's where I'll be."

So it was that Ben was just turning into the Gowler driveway when he saw Floyd fall into the welter of hogs. Ben, knowing the danger, reacted instantly, tramping the accelerator of the ancient pickup he had bought only recently and tearing across the lawn, directly toward the hog lot, throwing sod out behind the spinning tires and causing the unknowing Della in the house to almost faint. Turning the key off and letting the truck coast to a stop, Ben jumped from the cab and soared across the fence in one swift motion. Yelling at the hogs to scatter them, he leaped into the middle of the fray, only a last quick shift of his feet keeping him from landing right on Floyd's head. With relief he saw that the hogs had not started in on the body, but he could not tell if Floyd was unconscious or dead. He scooped the limp body into his arms, surprised at how light it was, and somehow managed to open the gate and push through while cradling Floyd's still body in his arms. Then he loped as fast as he could, thus burdened, toward Doc Halw's. Halfway there he was forced to stop for breath, and when he knelt and eased the body to the ground, the manure-smeared face of his burden wrinkled up, and out of it came a shaky but dauntless voice: "Take it easy, Ben, my boy, you're tearin' hell outta my back." Astonished, Ben stared at the old man, and then they both broke into wry smiles. "By God, ain't it a good thing I had that bucket of feed? Otherwise them hogs might've *et* me!"

There was much cursing and swearing on all sides over the incident, and Floyd was ordered to bed indefinitely. This time he did not object, which would have been fruitless because he could not walk.

"Your farming days are over," Doc Halw pronounced grimly.

"Your farming days are over," Della repeated, even more grimly.

Floyd stared at the ceiling through slitted eyes and kept his own counsel.

He was lying there still utterly disconsolate three days later when there was a timid knock on the open door. Floyd turned his head and, seeing who it was, smiled for the first time since the accident.

"Well, bust my britches, Emmet, if you ain't the sight I've been lookin' for," he said.

"We came as soon as we could, Gramps," Emmet said. "You gonna be okay?"

"Oh, hell, yes. I'm just layin' here mostly to humor that goddamn old sawbones down the road. How you doin', anyhow?" And he sat up, despite the pain, and held his arms out to embrace the prodigal grandson.

"You gonna be here long enough so I can get outta this bed and show you what I've been up to?"

"I've been doing a lot of thinking, Gramps. Ginny and I have talked it over. We're coming back to stay."

Floyd sank back on the pillows and let out a long, triumphant sigh. "Fetch me my pants and that goddamn cane hangin' on the bathroom door. We got work to do."

In ten days Floyd was limping around the farm, getting in everyone's way. In twenty days he appeared as good as new, causing Doc Halw to shake his head in wonder. Della looked at Floyd, her hands on her hips, and said: "Sometimes I believe you staged it all on purpose, just to get Emmet back."

EIGHT

Meanwhile, the cardinals burst into song across Killdeer, the soil warmed, and farmers walked in high-stepping agitation and anticipation across their fields, watching the soil dry. Planting time would soon be upon them.

Emmet found himself totally engulfed by new demands. On the farm, Floyd overplayed his hand a little by trying to defer to Emmet in the decisions that had to be made about the farming, even though Emmet had been away and could not make such decisions. Emmet was therefore forced to bounce the decisions back to Floyd. That made Emmet look indecisive in the eyes of the hired help and the renters. In the bank, where the family believed that he needed to gain experience, perhaps to take over when Uncle Cy retired, even the most remedial duties were new to him, making him look indecisive to the other tellers. At home he had to be overly solicitous to Ginny, who, accustomed to Florida, was suffering acute homesickness in what to her appeared the cold, hard landscape of Ohio. Emmet was thankful for the spring coming on now, putting sunshine in Ginny's eyes. "If we'd have come here in the winter, it wouldn't have worked," he told his mother.

On top of all this, he had not yet confronted Nan. In fact, he had gone to considerable effort not to confront her. Once they had passed on the road, but if she recognized him, she did not wave, as everyone did around Gowler. Twice he had seen her in town across the street from the bank, but she never looked his way to nod, although he was sure she noticed him. Once she even came in the bank but pointedly went to the other teller and never once looked Emmet's way. He retreated quickly to the bathroom. He wondered if she thought of him as much as he did of her, or if she thought of him at all.

Ben's thirty acres had not been plowed the preceding fall, which would have made the heavy soil easier to disk down to a seedbed now after winter freezing and thawing. But on the other hand, plowing it himself in the spring meant that he did not have to pay the previous renter for doing the job. In a dry spell in early March, he had begun to plow with his father's team of horses, deliberately avoiding the expense of the tractor. Nat seldom used the horses anymore anyway. The neighbors remarked on this tactic with surprise and something bordering on disapproval—"even though just five years ago they were all doing it," Ben remarked to Emmet with some amusement. But Emmet could not understand his friend's decision either. "Why work that hard to save just a few bucks?" he asked.

"A few bucks is a lotta bucks to me," Ben replied without thinking and suddenly between them rose the barrier of wealth again. Neither said anything, embarrassed, remembering the days when Emmet's Pony was the symbol of their social difference. Now it was Nat's drafters.

All through March Ben kept at the plowing when he had spare time and the weather allowed, able in an hour to turn half an acre. By mid-April he had finished and Nat could not once complain that Ben had been using his tractor when he needed it. Ben had so enjoyed the quiet of plowing with horses that he was half tempted to do the disking with them too, but the heavier tractor disk did a better job of leveling the furrowed surface of the soil and working it to a fine seedbed. Besides, the tractor's lights allowed him to run at night when neither he nor the equipment was needed on the home farm. "Tractors are supposed to be a labor-saving device," Nat said one day, watching Ben at work, "but all they've done is make us work all night, too." At planting time, to head off any possibility of Nat's growling because he needed the tractor himself, Ben resurrected the old horse planter, put a long horse tongue that had been stashed away in the barn on it, and planted his corn with the horses. Although the horses were slow, Ben was beholden to no one and there was no gas and oil bill to pay either. He amused himself with the thought of charging Floyd, who had to pay half the expenses, for half the fuel he didn't use.

"Why you foolin' round with those horses?" Floyd said one day, coming to the field to observe how straight Ben was getting his rows.

Ben grinned. "I'm saving the both of us a gas bill."

"Be careful you don't save a dime and lose a dollar."

"I'm puttin' those savings into nearly twice the fertilizer we generally use," said Ben, figuring that was the perfect time to tell Floyd something the old man would not be inclined to agree with. "I don't expect your renter put much on at all last year."

"Was in soybeans last year and didn't need it," Floyd said testily.

"What about the year before?"

"Was in soybeans then too."

"Well, when was the last time you put any fertilizer on that field?"

Floyd didn't know for sure and decided to change the subject.

The corn crop came up beautifully, as it did all over the county because the weather for once was so good that no one could think of anything to complain about. No hard rain had crusted the soil bad enough to prevent the emergence of the seedlings. No spate of drizzly cold rain had threatened to rot the seed rather than sprout it, and yet there was plenty of moisture to germinate the kernels and send the seedlings skyward.

As the corn peeked through the ground, Ben went over it with the rotary hoe, a tool whose whirling blades pulled by the tractor in road gear neatly destroyed germinating weeds without hurting the tiny corn plants. A few days later, he started regular weed cultivation between the rows with the old horse cultivator to avoid using the tractor and mounted cultivators, which now were in daily and even nightly use on the home farm. He said that he could do a better job with the horses. But by the time he started on the second cultivation, he was falling behind the growing corn, and so he switched to the tractor because it was faster, and again, it enabled him to run at night when he had spare time from the home farm, where haying was now in progress.

"You're going to kill yourself if you don't get more sleep," Dorothy scolded. But Ben only grinned. Never had a local corn crop looked so good, and Ben's thirty acres, fueled by a double dose of fertilizer and its own natural fertility from two years of soybeans preceding it, grew best of all. He walked up and down the rows, talking to the burgeoning stalks.

"You guys just keep growing now and make a hundred bushels per acre. At $2.30 a bushel, ol' Ben'll be on his way." Mentally he conjured up the fantastic vision of 115 dollars an acre for his half of the crop, which, times thirty acres, equaled the unbelievable sum of $4,500 with few expenses to pay out. He hardly dared to think about it.

But as the crop grew luxuriously through the frequent rains of late summer, the price of corn began to fall from its lofty high of $2.30, which had been only 5 cents under the hitherto all-time high.

"Damned if I can understand how that market works," Floyd said, admiring the thirty-acre field with Emmet and Ben one Sunday. "I swear the Board of Trade is crooked. Those sonsabitches sit on that exchange in Chicago and they make money on the up price and make it again on the down price. We're a bunch of dumbasses out here lettin' 'em do it. We should store it all in our own granaries, and let it rot if we don't get our price. Then we'd have 'em by the balls."

"What do you think that field's going to yield, Gramps?" Emmet asked, envy as well as wonder in his voice.

"You're lookin' at hundred-bushel corn, maybe a hundred twenty," he said. "Best corn I've seen in this ground. I was afraid you'd burn those plants up with all that fertilizer, Ben, but I was wrong."

When Ben said nothing, the old man continued. "Now I'm going to show you a trick you might need to know some day. I'm going to make us both a little more money that those goddamn traders don't know about. I'm going to turn the lambs in here. The fence around this field is still good enough to hold them."

Ben and Emmet looked at Floyd in disbelief. Turn lambs in a cornfield in August?

"You'll see. My father did it as a matter of course. They'll eat off the lower leaves and hardly ever get smart enough to reach up for an ear. They eat the weeds that's grown up since cultivation time too. Tides me over the period of short pasture, and I'll pay you for half the gain I get."

So for three weeks a hundred lambs sifted through the cornfield eating weeds and the lower green leaves from the corn, gaining about ten pounds each, or a total of a thousand pounds, which at 20 cents a pound amounted to $200. "That's how a real farmer digs a little money out of corners of the farm that the college boys don't know about," Floyd said, handing Ben a check for his half. "Now if we were *really* trying to squeeze money out of this crop, we'd cut and shock the field like in the old days and feed the fodder to the ewes and horses over winter. But I ain't up to it anymore."

"What's a shock of fodder worth?" Ben asked.

"Well, if you get it cut and shocked while there's still a bit of green in the leaves, a fodder shock is worth maybe a dollar and a half to me. I'd pay you a dollar for your half and your labor."

Ben's mind was racing. An acre of corn made about 25 regular shocks, and once these shocks were husked out, 3 of them made a fodder shock, or about 8 fodder shocks per acre. So in a thirty-acre field there were about 250 fodder shocks. Because his first duty was to his father's farm, Ben knew he would not have time to cut and shock the whole thirty acres, but he could do half and with luck and hard work, make $125 on the fodder he would not have if he used his father's tractor and mechanical corn picker to harvest the grain.

He went home, hauled out the old corn binder, and began putting it in shape for the harvest. Nat shook his head. "You really can use the tractor picker," he said, almost plaintively.

"Floyd will give me a dollar for every good fodder shock," Ben said. "Can't make fodder shocks with a corn picker."

"Lord, boy, you won't finish harvesting that field till March."

That proved to be almost true, but as Ben pointed out, there wasn't much else pressing to do in winter anyway. He began "hearting out" the field on Labor Day, cutting lanes by hand so the binder and horses would not knock down any corn as the machine cut and bundled the stalks. He set the hand-cut stalks around galluses—four uncut stalks tied together with a length of green stalk. Later he would set the tied bundles of stalks that the binder made around the galluses. All through September he worked, running the binder for a while, then, often by moonlight, standing the bundles up into shocks. Bone-weary, he fell into bed after midnight, only to roll out again at six o'clock for chores and then all day in his father's fields, then staggering back to his thirty acres to cut and shock some more in the evening.

Had he not been so continually tired, Ben would have found a certain charm in reliving earlier days, when his parents had harvested all the corn this way, his father shocking up the bundles while his mother drove the horses on the binder. He remembered how she would not allow Nan and him to use the shocks for make-believe Indian teepees when they had lived on the Killdeer farm because she was afraid of rattlesnakes lurking under the shocks. Once, when Nan was a newborn baby, his father had bolted an old wooden beer case on the tongue of the binder for her to sleep in while his mother drove. Dorothy claimed that Nan's contrariness was evident already. The baby slept better on the binder bumping and clattering along that she did in a soft bed in a quiet room.

One evening while he worked, Nan came to visit him, bringing along a new friend, Mary Livingston. Ben had noticed her in Gowler a time or two, but had not met her formally. The Livingstons had moved into a little farm west of Gowler when her father had secured a teaching position at the high school. For that reason and because they were newcomers, the Livingstons were thought to be a bit uppity. Farmers made snide remarks about the schoolteacher's part-time farming efforts. But Nan liked them, especially Mary, probably because their romantic ideas of farming were the opposite of her own. Nan fed on contrariness.

"You mean your mother actually kept Nan in a box on the binder tongue?" Mary asked in astonishment when the Bumps re- told the story. She was home on a college holiday and obviously had never seen a binder before. She kept asking questions, which Ben patiently answered. To his surprise, she soon joined in with the shocking, clumsily at first but then getting the hang of sock- ing each bundle securely into the shock so that the whole would stand solidly.

"They look so pretty standing in rows," she said.

Ben looked up sharply. "I think so, too," he said, pleased that she recognized one of the reasons he liked farming, and one of the rea- sons, in fact, that he had wanted to shock the corn rather than use the picker.

"It's a lotta work, that's what it is," Nan sniffed.

"What are you studying in college?" Ben asked, ignoring his sister.

"I'm majoring in English. I want to be a grade school teacher. Don't know why I need to go to college to do that, but that's the rule."

Ben, dragging a bundle in each hand as he walked toward a shock, stopped, surprised at her remark. That was not the usual outlook he heard from teachers. They all seemed to accept the idea that to be done properly, all activity required higher education. "I surely do agree," he said, and then was embarrassed, realizing that he was demeaning her college studies. "What I mean is that there's things to learn out here, too," he said lamely, trying to smooth over his unintended rudeness. She only laughed, nodding to assure him that she understood both his real intent and his seeming blunder. When she and Nan left in her father's car, Ben stared after them a long time before returning to his work.

For some reason, he was not surprised when the Livingston car pulled off the road the next night and Mary walked out into the field, this time alone. His surprise came in recognizing his own keen pleasure in her return.

"When I got home last night, I realized that I didn't know anything at all about farming even though I live on one," she said, awkwardly. She was afraid her expressed reason for returning might appear, as was the truth, as merely an excuse to become more acquainted with this strange young man. "Why do you put corn in shocks in the first place?"

Ben stared a second and then smiled. He hoped her question was an excuse. He hoped she had come back because she was interested in him, not corn.

"I never asked myself that," he said in reply. "But now that I think about it, the reason is mainly to protect the leaves from the weather so they can dry out without losing nutritional value. The shocks also afford a good, cheap way to dry the ears. Not everyone used to make shocks. You can let the stalks stand until the ears dry and then husk them right off the stalk, doing by hand what the mechanical pickers do today. But then the fodder is not as high quality as animal feed."

"What happens to the shocks?"

"Through the late fall and winter, I'll open them up, husk the ears out, and set the bundles back up in big fodder shocks, which we'll eventually feed to the livestock—in this case I'm selling them to Floyd Gowler and he'll feed them to sheep." He paused. She seemed satisfied with his answer. She started putting bundles in the shock again, which again impressed him powerfully—he did not know any woman except Nan who would be unafraid to join in work that was so new and physically difficult. There was a graceful pertness to the way she moved, tossing her head constantly to keep her loose auburn tresses out of her eyes. Her face knitted in a concentration which emphasized her high cheekbones and almost oriental slant of brown eyes. Her body, under blue jeans and a boy's flannel shirt, seemed possessed of an unlimited vitality. Ben found it hard not to stare at her.

"You should wear gloves," he said, and pulled off his own to hand to her. "The twine on those bundles can tear your skin up."

"But what will you wear?"

"Oh, my hands are toughened up enough to go awhile without 'em."

"Do you work this hard all the time?"

"I hope not. I'm farming this field in my so-called spare time, to make some money so I can buy my own farm."

"You must want to be a farmer awfully bad."

"Oh, yes. It's the only way I could live. Are you happy living in Columbus, going to school?"

"I don't know. I thought I wanted to do that, but I don't know." She was silent a moment and then said words that she had not known were in her. "My life doesn't seem real most of the time." She thought he would think that sounded weird.

"That was how I felt in the army," Ben said. "I guess I feel that way whenever I'm not on the farm, to tell the truth."

"What do you do when you do leave the farm?" she asked. "You ever go dancing or anything?"

"I used to, in high school. I suppose I would go out if I had someone I really wanted to go out with or who really wanted to go out with me."

Their eyes met, but only for an instant. "I suppose you have lots of dates at college, with all those boys around," Ben continued, trying to sound nonchalant. "Must be hard to figure out which one to go with."

"Oh, I'm not very popular. Hardly any of them ask me a second time."

Ben considered her remark and then heard himself say: "Well, when you're home again, maybe I could ask you a first time?"

She smiled. "Maybe you could." And then she deftly steered the conversation to what seemed like safer territory but which she later realized was even more potent with possibility. "How long will it take you to get your own farm?"

"Oh, my. Just depends on how the crops do and how quickly I can round up the down payment. I know what kind of place I want, something that will sell cheap but have good promise." And before he hardly realized it, he was off into his dreams, telling her of plans that he had shared with no one. The next six shocks went up in record time, and suddenly he realized that she was out of breath, trying to keep up with him.

"Oh, my, I'm boring you to death and wearing you out at the same time," he said.

"Oh, no. But I do have to go home. Mother will be worrying about where I have gone."

They were not aware, as they chattered at the far end of the field, that Nan had pulled up along the road and noticed Mary's car parked there. She had smiled, assuming perhaps more than she should, but, she figured, probably not. It was her first smile all day because she and her father had been arguing again about what was fitting work for a woman on a farm. While Nat gave great lip service to the idea of Nan being his partner, sort of, he could not reconcile himself to Nan making decisions about the farming, or doing really nasty farm work, like castrating pigs. His objections infuriated Nan.

"You don't really want me to take over the farm some day," she had said, hotly. "You just want me to be your errand girl."

"I don't know if I can stand being bossed around by *two* women," Nat mumbled.

"Well, you had better listen to us. Mom and I *both* believe you should get another tractor and get rid of those pasture-gobblin' horses."

"Ben needs those horses," Nat said defensively. He didn't believe that any more than Nan did, but the horses were his last connection to the old farming days that he did not want to admit were passing away just as he was.

"You just don't like it because I can fix tractors better than you can," Nan replied primly. Ever since she had figured out why their tractor wouldn't run one day when he couldn't, and replaced the cracked distributor cap, she had put him at a disadvantage, and she used it mercilessly. Distributor caps were almost as foreign to Nat as bathing caps, but he was mortified that his daughter had diagnosed the tractor's ailment before he had.

Nan on first impulse had parked her pickup and started across the field. Then she changed her mind. If she were going to play matchmaker, better to leave the two to themselves. She smiled again and headed back to her truck. Just then, another truck pulled off the road behind her, stopped, and turned off the lights. The person inside opened the door, stepped out, and started to walk into the field, whistling.

Oh, damn, Nan muttered. It was Emmet. She started to run into the standing corn nearby, but it was too late for that. Emmet had stopped abruptly and recognized her in the dusky twilight. He knew the car but had presumed that Nat would have come to the field, not Nan. Both were thankful that the twilight did not reveal the perplexity on their faces.

"'Lo, Nan." Emmet said, trying to sound casual, the way he had practiced for their first meeting.

Nan did not make it easy for him. She remained silent.

"Just thought I'd drop by to see how Ben was doing."

Still no reply.

"I hear you're farming with your Dad."

More silence.

"Look, Nan, I'm sorry. You don't know how sorry I am."

She headed for her truck.

Watching her, reduced now to desperation, Emmet said what he had never planned to say. "You know, I really do still love you."

Nan stopped in her tracks, turned, and looked back at him. If he could have seen her face clearly, he would have seen a hint of hopefulness that her voice did not betray.

"Emmet Gowler, you are the dumbest jackass in the whole world." And with that, she climbed in her truck and spun away.

With fifteen acres of corn and fodder safely out of the weather within their own tent-like shocks, Ben turned his attention to the other half of the crop when time permitted. The stalks and leaves had weathered to a dead brown by now and were of minimal value as feed, and he proceeded to harvest the fat yellow ears directly from the stalks with the mechanical picker hitched to the tractor. It was only now that he could get some idea of how good the crop was, as the gathering chains straddling the corn row stripped the ears off, dropped them on a bed of rollers which caught and pulled the husks from the ears and sent the latter in a yellow stream up the elevator and into the wagon behind the picker.

"We're lookin' at hundred-thirty bushel," Floyd said gleefully.

"This is the best side of the field," Ben said cautiously. "The shocked side isn't as good, I don't think."

Much of the joy of the good crop was taken away, however, by the sliding market, which had dropped to $1.80 a bushel and showed no signs of leveling off.

"Should we sell now on future delivery?" Ben asked Floyd, "before it goes lower?"

"You do what you please with your half," Floyd said, "but I wouldn't. This price slide smells fishy to me. I say we hold. Emmet and I got enough crib space for our corn. If you want to store yours, I know a way you can make yourself some cheap cribs. Then we'll wait for a good price, and if worst comes to worst, we'll feed out a bunch of hogs and sell the damn stuff that way."

Floyd talked the county highway department out of some old snow fence, enough to form two rings of it about fifteen feet in diameter. Then he directed Ben to drag together several small logs originally intended for cutting and splitting into firewood. On the logs they nailed old boards to form a crude platform. They put one of the snow fence rings on the platform. In the middle of the ring Floyd set a rolled up coil of rusty wire fence, which he had rescued from the trash pile in his woods. "We'll fill the ring of snow fence with corn," he explained to Ben, "and the roll of fence in the middle will act as a central shaft for air circulation. And after we fill this section up with corn, we'll set another round of snow fence on top of the first, and do the same thing over. Then you can pile some of the bundles from your shocks on top, like roof shingles, to keep off the rain. You can make as many cribs as you need and it won't cost you much more than your labor. We'll hold the corn until the Chicago Board of Trade freezes over."

Ben shoveled every other wagonload of corn into his makeshift cribs, and Floyd, or usually Emmet, hauled away the alternate loads to their conventional cribs, and thus the crop was divided. The air circulated through the snow fence cribs as well as it would have through the finest cribs ever to come from a factory.

As winter set in, Ben turned to the slow, cold job of husking corn from the shocks, resetting the bundles into fodder shocks, then hauling the ears to the last of his snow fence cribs and shoveling them in. Alternate loads he hauled to Floyd's crib. Some days Nat came to help with the husking, their talk making the hours pass more tolerably. Regularly, Floyd or Emmet came to the field with tractor and mud sled to haul a fodder shock away to their sheep. Ben looked forward keenly to these visits. There was nothing lonelier than a cornfield in January. Constantly he watched the road, looking for Mary's car to approach.

By the end of February, he was finished, and believed that now he could husk fast enough to win any contest. The skin on his fingers even under gloves, had callused, hardened, chapped from the cold, and cracked painfully open. One night when he was applying Bag Balm salve to a cow's teats which were similarly chapped and cracked, he decided to rub some on his hands. His skin rapidly began to heal.

His field had yielded at final count, a whopping 120 bushels per acre—3,600 bushels of corn. Ben thought he might sell, but the market price was awful. So he waited, as Floyd directed. Nothing in farming stays the same for long, Floyd said.

The following year, 1947, the sun forgot how to shine. It began raining in March and wouldn't quit. Ben almost felt lucky that Floyd had taken the thirty-acre field back for Emmet. Corn could not be planted on time, and suddenly the corn price began to advance. "Those buzzards on the Chicago Board of Trade smell a short crop," Floyd said. By July, after it became apparent that some fields had not gotten planted at all and what was in the ground was not going to make much of a crop, the price rose above $2.00 again. To the amazement of all, corn soared past $2.50 a bushel. Ben wanted to sell.

"Wait a bit," Floyd said, "Something tells me that there's some puff left in this rally."

"Yeah, wait a bit," Nat agreed. "Been a lotta sellin' and the price is still not hurtin' for it. People still hungry in Europe."

So Ben waited, his ear glued to the radio, morning and evening. He could not believe the news: $2.60. $2.70. $2.80. He walked on air, afraid the grim reality of market gravity would reassert itself. What goes up must come down. If the price rose much higher, he could make $5,000 on his share of the corn, an impossible fortune to him and enough for a down payment on a small farm.

One morning in December, he got a call from Floyd. "Corn's $2.94, my boy," the old man said, his voice full of glee not just from the fact of the matter but because he had predicted it. "Time to sell, my boy. Farmers always wait too long and sell on a down market."

Ben sold. Since his corn had dried in his own cribs, there was no drying charge, and no storage charge either. Most of his take was pure profit since he didn't have to pay for any labor. After deducting what little cost there had been, he still pocketed $5,012, not counting the fodder shock money or the lamb pasturage rent payment. He was by his standards, rich. He deposited the money in the Gowler bank. Cy Gowler, the banker, part owner of the Gowler land with his brother, looked over his glasses at him. "Well, congratulations, Ben. You've done us all well. I suppose you're going to go out now and buy yourself a car."

"'Spect not," Ben said, smiling. "I'm going to buy a farm if I can."

Cy nodded approvingly. "You'll go far in this world, Mr. Bump. Come talk to me when you find what you are looking for."

Because the market did edge up a little for a few days, to the unbelievable $3.00 a bushel, Emmet talked Floyd into holding one crib of the bonanza corn. But the price started to fall in 1948. Emmet belligerently held. By the fall, corn bottomed out at $1.30 and Emmet said he'd "let the rats eat it." He finally, and very quietly, sold it, or what was left of it, in 1949 for $1.50 a bushel, "rat turds and all."

Pinky Ghent's pink face flushed to a florid red as he elbowed his way with exasperation through the crowd in his store. "How the hell can a man wait on customers with half the town hanging around in here?" he grumbled loudly. If anyone heard, they pretended otherwise. The object of their attention was not groceries, hardware, kitchen utensils, V-belts, overalls, work shoes, cigarettes, fishing licenses, hog rings, sheep wormers, hoof trimmers, or even the wood stove, around which Gowler's patriarchs were wont to gather every morning for coffee, summer or winter. Nor was their attention being drawn to the euchre game at the card table nearby, which Pinky maintained had been going on continuously since 1929. "Same game," he liked to say, "but the players change every few years."

"What's going on in here?" Squeaky Tibbs asked, after he had stomped the snow from his boots and entered the store. From the stockyards where he worked across the street and down the railroad tracks to the north, he had noticed, with the all-encompassing eagle eye of the veteran villager, the unusual number of people coming into the store. He reeked of hog manure, but today Pinky didn't care. Maybe the smell would drive some of the people out.

"Must be shippin' a lot of hogs today," Pinky said, making a great show of sniffing the air.

"Why, that's right, Pinky my friend, but how did you know?"

Pinky stared at Tibbs out of the bottomless well of patience and fortitude that storekeepers maintain to keep from going crazy. He waited for Squeaky to buy something, doubting that the stock-yards manager intended to do so any more than the other people in the store.

"What's going on back there?" Tibbs repeated, stretching his neck. "Did Oak Jonly finally die at the euchre table?"

At that moment, the cluster of people divided a bit, and Pinky silently pointed at the object of their attention: a walnut-stained wood cabinet, something a practical carpenter might fashion using an Art Deco–style radio as a model. It was about the size of a refrigerator, with a ten-inch square window cut into the top half of the front panel. The window glowed with a cool greenish light. It reminded Squeaky of luminous paint. Across the window luminous human figures occasionally flitted, as fleeting as fireflies. The raised letters highlighted in gold under the window spelled "Crosley."

"I'll be damned. It's one of them tellyvisions, ain't it," Squeaky squeaked, and then, as if hypnotized, he let the glowing eye draw him, too, into the cluster of idolaters. No one seemed to notice the smell of pig among them.

"Yeah," Pinky muttered, more or less to himself. "They'll watch that thing okay, but not one of the tight bastards will buy it."

A train rumbled into town and broke Squeaky's trance. He had work to do.

"How much is that tellyvision?" he asked on his way out.

"Three hundred, but for you I'd knock a little off," Pinky said.

"Three hundred. My God, Pinky, it'll break down in a month. Why, look at it. It's blurry as a blizzard right now." And out he went.

Pinky waited three more weeks for someone to buy the set. No luck. He thought about charging admission to the store. A better solution finally came to him. He would raffle the damn thing off at fifty cents a chance.

The raffle brought in $362. Don Fragner had the winning ticket, which irritated nearly everyone because he was from Linner. In 1972, twenty-three years later, he would proudly tell Pinky that the set "still runs good."

But soon after the coming of television to Gowler, things began to change. Infrequently now, and finally not at all, did knots of people gather on front porches or in front of the general store after supper to gossip until the Sportsman highballed through town at 9:03, signaling bedtime. Instead the villagers went from the supper table to the television set and stumbled into bed in a daze at midnight. Eventually even supper was taken in front of the thing, and the quality of home cooking degenerated accordingly. "I can feed the mister hash ever' night and he don't even knowed it," Alice Tarmin said.

This new social order also had the effect of cutting down on the number of people who were up and about at 6:00 a.m. Mike Speckle decided to sell the cow he kept in the shed at the rear of his lot, claiming that now since he had passed sixty-five, he just "felt tuckered out all the time." Granny West decided that advancing age also explained her "tired bone syndrome" as she called it, and sold her chickens. Others trooped into Doc Halw's office complaining of attacks of "nerves" and other vague disorders that revealed themselves in chronic headaches, persistent constipation, and irregular menstrual cycles. Pinky noted a big increase in the number of pairs of five-dollar magnifying eyeglasses he sold. Doc Halw noted a similar demand for variously colored sugar pills he routinely passed out as medicine to people who didn't feel good but in whom he could find no sickness.

"I want some more of them green ones you gave me first, Doc," Granny West said. "The orange ones don't help atall."

Halw nodded solemnly and gave her another bottle of green ones. Later, over a beer at the Blue Room in Linner, he nudged Floyd Gowler next to him at the bar and muttered. "Helluva day, Floyd, but green pills going like the funny papers. We've got a real epidemic on our hands."

"Yeah? What's that?"

"Televisionitis."

That summer, when Pinky scheduled the first of the outdoor movies, which were projected on a screen hung up against the side of the firehouse, with the projector setting on the back seat of Joe Nox's car, sending its beam of light out through the open door, only a few people came. That was strange. Normally, the area between the firehouse and the railroad tracks would be jammed with people on chairs or on straw bales in the back of pickups or sprawled on blankets in the grass. Pinky counted the audience: thirty-two, mostly children. At this rate, it would not justify the advertisements that he and other merchants paid to have run ahead of the movie. Must be that goddamn television.

Ben Bump was present, however, and with him in his mud-splattered pickup was Mary Livingston. Ben enjoyed the outdoor movies immensely. "It's not the show, but the audience," he explained to Mary. "Some real funny things happen." She soon learned what he meant. When a freight train rolled through town, drowning out the sound track, Joe Nox turned off the projector until it passed. Everyone groaned and waved fists at the train. As always, this struck Ben as terribly amusing, and he pounded the steering wheel in glee. Mary wondered about Ben's sense of humor. On the other hand, she could not wait to tell her city friends that there was a place where moviegoers had their show interrupted routinely by passing locomotives.

She snuggled up beside Ben as they sipped chocolate milkshakes from Closson's Bakery and Confectionery across the street and giggled while Hopalong Cassidy blazed away on screen and Lester Cordrey, on a bench in front of it, ducked the bullets. Occasionally, in the thick of a horse chase, Lester would stand up, waving his arms wildly, and yell, "Git them bastards, Hoppy, git 'em!"

Lester's absorption in the film sent Ben into another steering wheel–pounding frenzy. "Everybody thinks Lester is crazy, but I think he's saner than most of us because he's the only one who admits he's crazy," he said. "If he's really crazy, how come he knows every hillbilly song written in the last thirty years by heart?"

Mary, unable to keep her mind on the movie, mentally reviewed the events that had led her to this evening. She and Ben had been going together for almost two years now, and from the first, there had never been the slightest doubt in her mind that they would marry. Armed with the five thousand dollars from his 1947 bonanza corn, Ben had gone farm hunting. By the summer of 1948, Mary, out of college, had joined him. They had courted while visiting farms for sale. Nothing seemed to suit Ben, and Mary found that the education she was getting under Ben's tutelage was at least as interesting as the one she had received at Gwendmere. As her schoolteacher father often said, farming was a very interesting occupation, and it was too bad there wasn't any money in it.

One day, for instance, they found a nice, level farm like she thought he had been looking for. "Nope, don't like the lay of that place," he said. "Too low and too flat. Lot of blue clay on that place."

"Blue?" The world of Gwendmere taught nothing about soils except that they were brown or black and not to be brought into the house.

"Well, yes. Up 'side of really black loam, it's grayish to the point of blue. It's tough, heavy stuff. Makes good bricks and field tile. Used to be a tile factory in Gowler, and there's still a brick factory in Surrey. That blue clay bakes hard as iron, but unlike iron, never rusts. Takes twice as much gas or horsepower to plow blue clay as sandy loam."

"It *does?*" she responded keenly, having never thought in such terms.

"Well, nearly so. It pulls that much harder. Of course that's becoming true of all farmland. As the topsoil washes off and you get down to the subsoil clays, it takes more power to plow. Some people say the tractor came along just in time." She could tell that Ben thought that was amusing.

At another farm he sighed and said in a disappointed tone, "Those yellow clay knobs won't grow nothin' but Canady thistles and white thorns."

"But the house is nice," Mary reminded him, hopefully.

"It was built before all the topsoil washed off, you can bet on it," he said. "Don't worry about a house. We can always bring a house back, but topsoil is another thing."

The place Ben had originally wanted was the eighty acres which encompassed the thirty he had rented from Floyd Gowler. With Emmet back, that was out of the question. Ben pretended outwardly to understand. But inwardly it irritated him. No one in the county could be on better terms with Floyd and no one a closer friend to Emmet, but he could not persuade them to sell the eighty from their thousands of acres. When Ben dropped a broad hint, Floyd pretended not to hear. When Ben tried out the same suggestion on Emmet, his friend shook his head. "Ben, there's a whole family of Gowlers involved in this—aunts and uncles and such, all with a finger in the pie. Great-Great-Grandfather Dave laid down a law our family considers sacred: 'Money glides but land abides.'"

Another train drowned out the movie, and the action had to be stopped just as Hoppy was delivering the final punishing blows to the villain's chin. When Nox stopped the film, groans from the audience once more filled the darkness.

"You have time for farm hunting tomorrow?" Ben asked. Mary nodded, her head against his shoulder. "I heard about one that just might be it," he explained. "It's going to be auctioned off in a few weeks."

The old Higgins place they tramped over next day was actually one of the first farms Ben had looked at, only a couple of miles from his father's land. But earlier, the owner, a widow living now in Surrey, had shown no interest in selling. Recently she had died, and the heirs could hardly wait to get rid of the property and divide up the spoils. Not a one of them had ever worked on the farm nor even set foot on it for years.

As Ben and Mary walked over the fields, feeling, as Mary said, like ghouls, planning the beginning of their lives together so soon upon the ending of the former owner's life, their hearts began to beat faster. It was plain that the farm was everything they had been looking for, and since it contained only a hundred acres, they might be able to afford it if the price per acre didn't go high.

"Not the best land, actually, except for the bottom fields along the crick, but that will work to our advantage," Ben said, more to himself than to Mary. "A little hilly it is, and that means it won't command a top price. But it's not too hilly, and it still retains a lot of topsoil. I can grow corn in the bottom fields. The rest is just rolling enough to drain well and raise good clover."

"Back in ancient Roman times, the poet Virgil sang the virtues of clover in his *Georgics*," Mary said, pleased to make a connection between her classical education and Ben's world of practicality.

"Really?" he exclaimed. "You mean they write about stuff like that in literature? Wow."

After a pause, he continued his previous vein of thought. "But today cash grain farming is pushing clover out of the rotations. Who wants to work hard making hay and being tied to the farm by live-stock when he can get rid of animals altogether and sell corn."

"But you said the price of corn was too low."

"Yeah. That's why I want to go back to the old way."

"But what's really so great about legumes?"

"Clover takes nitrogen out of the air and puts it in the soil. A good stand of clover will add as much as a hundred pounds of ni-trogen per acre per year free. That's a real profit."

They came to a halt on a hilltop, out of breath from climbing and talking at the same time, leaning now on each other for sup-port, or using that as an excuse to edge into an embrace.

"My father says that to get any real profit from farming, you have to feed your crops to animals, and sell the meat, or milk or eggs," Ben continued his lecturing, as if he were trying to ignore the embrace.

"Kiss me," she said. He did, and she went racing off across the field, trailing laughter.

He caught up with her at the creek and they sat on the bank, watching the water flow by. "This is another good thing," Ben said, unable to stop talking about farming even when sexual desire was surging through him. "Water. This creek is fed by springs and doesn't dry up in summer. And there's a good spring up by the house too."

"Kiss me," she said.

"This farm's also got a ten-acre woodlot," he continued, as if to ignore her again. "You don't really pay more for these things but they are worth a fortune to the kind of farming I want to do. A woodlot means furnace fuel and lumber for building."

"But what about the house? It looks poorly," she said, almost giving up on the kiss.

"It's basically sound. That's another advantage for us. The farm will sell lower because of the sad condition of the house. But the roofline is straight and the foundation is solid. I checked. I'll get it fixed up over winter. We've got our whole lives to turn it into a castle." He paused, realizing the most important consideration of all hadn't formally been attended to. He turned to her with that serious look that sometimes meant a joke was coming. But not this time. "Mary, will you marry me?"

She smiled at him. "You know I will, Ben," she said, her eyes shining.

She lay back on the grass, her eyes still fixed on him. Ben looked at her longingly, but as Mary knew, he would not move to touch her without a sure sign of invitation. He was not aggressive by nature, and that was one more reason why she loved him.

"Kiss me," she said again. And this time he smothered her in eager embrace. At first she was surprised at the intensity of his ardor, but then found that she was pleased. There was a wildness under her cool, civilized exterior that was surprising even to her. She surrendered. If this was to be their farm, let the planting begin.

For Ben, the week before the farm sale dragged by with ago-nizing slowness. He could think of nothing else. "Know exactly how high you dare bid before you even go to the sale," Nat told him, as if Ben did not already know that. "I wish I could help you with the money, but—"

"No, no," Ben interjected. "I know you can't, but I wouldn't want you to anyway. What if I failed and couldn't pay you back? That's what happened to folks in the Depression."

Nat stared at him but decided not to pursue the idea. "Don't be too eager at the sale," he continued. "Make the auctioneer beg. If the sellers know you want the farm bad, they might try to bid you up." Ben nodded. He had already gone through every possible situation that could occur and how he would react to it.

All except one.

A farm auction's success is based on the premise that everybody loves a show. The better the show, the more spirited the bidding. An auction is usually conducted at the farm, no matter how run-down, on the shaggy lawn in front of the old farmhouse, or on the porch or in the barnyard, with the barn as scenic backdrop. Such a homey, homely outdoor theater lends not only the prescribed authenticity to the sale, but an ambiance of solid virtue that cultural fantasy ascribes to rusticity. Farm auctions, says the myth, are always honest.

In reality, they can easily be manipulated by every sort of connivance the human mind is capable of, and Sherwood Brady, the auctioneer waiting for the crowd to assemble, knew how to work them all. Sellers hire bidders to run the price up until they are told to stop by some furtive signal. Buyers hire lawyers to bid for them so that other bidders don't know who is trying to buy the farm, especially when rival farmers are apt to bid up the land out of spite when the bidder is a neighbor with whom they don't get along. Auctioneers hire bidders to raise the ante too, but the best auctioneers become adept at pulling bids out of thin air.

Brady prided himself on being not just the prince of showmen, but cunning enough to get worn-out tractors and rundown land sold at a price higher than anyone thought they were worth. "You never lie about the merchandise," he always told his assistants. "But always accentuate the positive, and if there ain't no positive, make one up that will be hard to prove wrong. With a tractor that's near death, you almost whisper that this model is certain to become rare and very popular with collectors. For a land auction, stir up competition among neighboring farmers well before the sale by telling one of them that 'there's talk' to the effect that the farmer across the road is trying to buy the land before it comes to auction, which is nearly always the case. Then you go to that neighbor and tell him the same story. Pretty soon everyone's riled and telling their wives they'll be damned if they'll let the farm go cheap. Sometimes they decide to buy the farm when a few days earlier they never even gave it serious thought." Brady always concluded his lectures with the story of how he got a good price out of barn that had part of the back half of the roof "blowed off." "The barn had a new concrete floor in front and I stood on it and talked new floor so hard that the bidders never looked to the back of the barn to see that part of the roof was gone."

Now he mounted the lectern-like platform from which he conducted his show, a ludicrously large white cowboy hat perched jauntily on his head, a brazen silver buckle on his belt protruding over his bulging belly, his bellows-booming voice warming up with jokes that farm wives in the audience would not have tolerated in any other situation. "You all remember Al Higgins. He kept this place in a very high state of fertility, as he did Mrs. Higgins. He went bald early in life, they say, from his head rubbin' against the bed headboard whilst he kept strivin' for a higher degree of fertility." Snorts from men; pretensions of disapproval from women.

Ben was in agony. He did not like Sherwood Brady to begin with, and now, as the auctioneer expounded for what seemed like hours on how the house and barn were as tight and square as the day they were built, and the land just waiting for "a little upliftment in the fundamentals like the lady who didn't wear a bra."

Ben hoped to get the farm for $13,000. He could then use $4,000 of his corn money for the down payment that Cy Gowler required. The other thousand would go for machinery and to fix up the house a little. If he had to, however, he would bid to $14,000 and worry about machinery and house improvements later.

Brady finally got down to business. "Who'll start at $300 an acre for this fine farm?" he threw out, in case there were any neophytes with more money than brains in the audience. The crowd stared at him derisively. Quickly he came down to $250 and then $200. Still no bids. "Well, okay, I see I've got real, no-nonsense farmers who came here to buy a farm, and by golly, we're going to sell her. Let's quit wastin' time. Who'll start us off at a ridiculously low $90 an acre?"

The first hesitant bid was made, and jumping the price by $5 an acre after every bid, Sherwood Brady worked himself into the kind of frenzy that an orchestra director would envy, waving his megaphone, which he did not need, like a baton. He spotted a mere wink of an eye from a man in the front row—"ninety-five we have, now how about a hundert." He noted a furtive flick of a finger from a man leaning against the chicken coop—"a hundert we have, now a hundert five." He pretended to spy a nodding head way up on the porch of the house from someone who was not even paying attention to the bidding—"a hundert and five, now one-ten, and let's roooollll." Along the way he may have pulled a bid or two out of the sparrows in the barnyard catalpa trees—who could know for sure? The bidding did not slow until it had risen to $125 per acre. That's when Ben made his first bid. It was a long time before there was another raise, and for a wildly hopeful minute Ben thought his $125 bid would stand. Finally, however, someone raised to $130. Ben was ready to raise again, but suddenly he felt a hand squeezing his arm. "Hold on, son, hold on," Nat whispered in his ear. "Brady ain't going to let it go for dat. He's got another act to play. Let him stew."

Sure enough, when no more bids were forthcoming, Brady began to act as if he were totally astounded and bewildered. "Now, folks, you all know this farm is worth more than a hundert thirty an acre. This ain't 1934, you know. The corn this place can grow with a little upliftment is well above average. You know that you can double the value of that house and barn with nothing more than a coat of paint. Tell you what I'm going to do. We'll just take a little time out now, and you folks who want a really great buy on a good farm, talk it over. Don't let an opportunity like this pass. It'll not come again. The Lord ain't makin' no more land, you know." He wiped the sweat from his forehead and retreated back into the house.

Nan had been cruising the crowd, trying to spot who had pitched in the last bid on the farm. She sidled up to Henry Remp, who made no secret among his friends that he was dying to lay her, as he put it, a remark that when Nan heard it secondhand, replied, "and dying is what he'll get if he tries." But now she was all temptress. "Looks like you're going to get the farm," she cooed ever so coyly. He stared at her. "Wisht I was," he said. "No, it's your old sweetie Emmet Gowler who's to have this farm, and his grandfather'll make sure."

Nan's eyes popped wide with astonishment and then narrowed. What the heck did Emmet need with more land? And bidding against his best friend. Damn. Ben had said Emmet had been acting a little offish lately.

She left Remp gaping and sifted through the crowd again. No Emmet. Must have some lawyer bidding for him. But then she spied him, standing a little removed from the others, behind the old corn shredder that went for five dollars. He was using the machine to hide behind. She marched straight at him, her hands clenched into fists, the anger rising in her.

"Emmet Gowler, why are you doing this?"

Emmet shook his head and stared at the ground. "Nan, I didn't make the world the way it is. I've tried to tell you that. You can't set still in business. Gotta grow."

"You've already got more land than you can handle. You know Ben has his heart set on this farm."

Emmet continued to stare at the ground, but his jaw was beginning to thrust slowly forward and set, the kind of set that belonged to men like his great-great-grandfather who for money would drive sheep on horseback all the way to Baltimore, dismounting only to relieve himself. The ardor of competition had laid a cast iron hold on him. "It's a family thing, Nan. The pressure's on me. I'm gonna do what I've gotta do."

"No, you aren't," she shot back fiercely, her face right in his chin.

So locked in each other's eyes, neither realized that Brady had started the bidding again. After a minute that seemed like eternity to Ben, he felt his father squeeze his arm. "Raise it half," Nat muttered. Ben hit his chest with the edge of his hand, palm down. "And now I got 137.50," Brady crowed. "Who'll take her up to $140?" Emmet tried to step around Nan to make a bid. She stepped with him. Emmet's face turned red. "This is Gowler country," he growled at her, "and by God it is going to stay Gowler country." He raised his hand, and for a second Nan thought he was going to strike her. "One forty we got," Brady shrieked, like a backcountry Methodist preacher whipping the crowd into a frenzy. Who will make it $145?" Ben was trembling now. He was at the end of his rope. Again he halved the bid. "And now we got 142.50, and let's hear 145." Emmet, swept away now by the lust of aggrandizement, and enraged by Nan's eyes boring into him, jumped the bid loud and clear: "One *fifty*." A sigh swept through the collective crowd, and the air was so still that the chirping sparrows in the catalpa tree could be heard distinctly trying to raise the bid.

Ben's head dropped. He dared not bid over $150. He thought he was going to faint. It was Emmet who was taking the farm away from him and Emmet could go on bidding no matter what it took. Ben sank slowly to a stooping position, as totally defeated by the realization that he was being outbid by his best friend as by losing the farm. Mary knelt beside him, trying to comfort him. "It's okay, Ben. We'll find another place." Sherwood Brady tried Ben for one more bid but when it did not come after five pleading minutes, he quit. "Okay, folks, we've got a bid of $150 an acre on this farm. Are you all through?" And again with great pomp and ceremony, he repeated. "Are you all through at one fifty?" Silence. "Going once, going twice, going . . . "

"*One fifty-one,*" a shrill, high voice wavered over the crowd. All eyes turned in wonderment. Lordy. It was that Nan Bump, that hussy. The nerve. Women did not bid on land sales. Just like her. In the stillness, Nat's voice could be heard muttering as clearly over the crowd as the Angelus bell from the church tower in Linner. "Gott in Himmel."

Then Nan turned back at Emmet. Instead of the rage and belligerence that had radiated from her before, her face softened to a sudden loveliness. Abject pleading was not in her vocabulary, but she would do whatever she had to do. Too low for anyone else to hear, she said: "Please, Emmet, for whatever we still have between us, let it go." Emmet looked at her, dumbfounded, and knew in that awful second that there was no one in the world he cared for more, and that he was bound—cursed—by that realization. He wheeled and walked abruptly away. Floyd Gowler, looking on, was for once frozen like a statue and could not bring himself to move or to speak. And as much as he wanted the land, he suddenly saw another possibility. He did not raise the bid.

While Brady tried to beseech the crowd for one more go at it, his eye on Floyd Gowler, Ben made his way to Nan, confusion on his face. "I can't swing that much money," he told her frantically.

"Don't worry about it," she said. "I can make up the difference from my savings and you can pay me back when you can. Remember the Fruit Juice."

Even though Emmet had capitulated in the bidding, Ben knew with a dreadful certainty that the old easy friendship between them was not going to be the same again. He stopped by Emmet's house the next day, drove under the carport that had really been built for buggies, and pounded on the door. He was thinking about the first time as a child that he had been in that house, when in awe he had viewed its walnut and cherry paneling, its Vermont slate entranceway, its field rock fireplaces, and especially its faux-marble bathtub and mother-of-pearl toilet seats. Even back then, the money had been between them. Now when Emmet came to the door, sheepish grin and all, Ben let it all go.

"I just want you to know what I think of you. You bid me up even though you don't need more land," he said. "If I can't make my payments now, it's your greedy fault. I thought you were my friend. I've a mind this minute to take you out in the woods and beat the crap out of you."

Emmet was aghast. Could this be the quiet, humble, modest Ben Bump he thought he knew? Had it been anyone else, he would have led the way to the woods and done his own share of beating. Ben's seeming saintliness was evidently just a disguise. When farmland was at stake, he was just as hard and driven as the rest of men.

Out loud, he only said, "It's just business, Ben. You know that."

"Just business for you because it doesn't really matter to you. It's bloodletting for the likes of me. Dad is right. The only difference between Gowlers and Bumps is not brains or hard work but because you got here a hundred years before we did. An accident of history. You have no idea what different worlds we move in. And from now on you stay out of mine." Ben turned and stalked back to his truck. Emmet watched him go, a heaviness settling over him.

Nan might have had as much reason as her brother to feel angry at Emmet, but instead she seemed to have gained an inner peace. When Emmet's name came up in her presence now, the usual hostility did not flare up. She would just stare pensively into the distance, and Ben thought surely he could discern a bit of satisfaction creep over her face. He could not know that she had done something more than outbid Emmet for the farm. She had forced him to admit that he loved her. She could go through life now apart from him if she had to, because she knew that in spirit they were not apart.

Emmet was thrown into a state of enormous confusion and guilt by the events at the sale. He feared that he had lost Ben's friendship for good, but perhaps had regained Nan's. Nan's friendship only worsened his predicament, however. How was he going to make it through life knowing he was more in love with Nan than with Ginny? Ginny would know even if he remained perfectly faithful to her. Women always know. He kept trying to dismiss Nan from his mind, but the harder he tried, the more his sweet Ginny appeared as lacking in spirit as a dishrag, while tempestuous Nan towered in his eye like the Statue of Liberty come alive. The more he tried to be angry at the way she had taken advantage of him, the more he admired her for it, and the more he was inwardly glad to know that she still had feelings for him too.

Emmet had other grave problems with which to contend. The task he faced in taking over the Gowler lands, as his grandfather was now so hell-bent on him doing, was awesome beyond anything he had foreseen. He tried to work in the bank, as both Floyd and Uncle Cy desired, so that he would get a sense of the patriarchal responsibility he was supposed to feel toward the community. But he could not stand being inside all day. His uncle's tedious devotion to duty was beyond Emmet's comprehension or patience. Every night Uncle Cy went through every canceled check. Every single one. Cy Gowler said that he had made only one bad loan— for a mere $225—in forty years. And he always seemed to know, as if by divine inspiration, when the bank examiners were coming. Not that it mattered. Everything was always in order. When Emmet told him that farming, not banking, was his life's desire, Cy looked at him a long time and sighed. "Well, then I'll back you in starting a farm equipment business to help support your farming habit." He paused and then added softly: "Nobody ever made much money from the farm, Emmet, but from the farmer."

Despite Floyd's desire for Emmet to take over the farm, he balked a little when he realized that it meant giving Emmet a say-so in important decisions. But that problem solved itself ever so slowly. As Floyd's vitality began to fail, Della brought Emmet into the decision-making process so tactfully that her husband was hardly aware of it.

When Emmet looked closely into the ledger books, he realized that the farm's finances were in disarray. What meager accounting Floyd had kept showed that the sharecroppers were not nearly efficient enough to make a profit. Production per acre had increased on the home farm, under Floyd's direct control, but many of the other farms were decreasing in yields steadily. Floyd was carrying some of the sharecroppers, paying their share of expenses occasionally or allowing them to claim more than half the crop. The underlying problem was that hired help rarely ever had the dedication for the fine little touches and the constant attention that successful farming required. Sharecroppers almost always misused the land. "A borrowed horse never tires," is the way Floyd liked to put it.

Also, Emmet knew that the heavy Killdeer soils were decreasing in productivity because the tile drainage systems crucial to the jackwaxy soils had deteriorated or sealed over. Not properly drained, Killdeer soils were next to worthless for anything but permanent pasture, and often not that. Compaction from the increase in annual cultivation, often because of plowing or fitting the soil when it was too wet, only made matters worse. Floyd had made a killing with soybeans during the war years, but environmental reality would not long be thwarted, and the wetlands were moving back to claim their rightful place on the prairie. His grandfather had not been joking when he said most of the land should never have been plowed in the first place.

One night, bent over the records, Emmet began to laugh almost dementedly. Ginny, playing with the two boys, looked up in mild alarm. She never knew what to expect from Emmet and was a little afraid of him.

"Everybody thinks I'm going to inherit a fortune," he said, hollowly, almost bitterly. "What we've got coming to us is just what the Farnold boys say it is, a big chunk of real good huntin' ground."

It was apparent to him that the Gowler holdings would survive only if they were consolidated into one operation, managed by enlightened and caring farm and business methods, with modern machinery replacing the inefficient and slothful work that characterized most of the twenty renters. They had become a drag on the business, like ragtag family that his grandfather felt obliged to take care of.

"They've got to go," Emmet sighed.

Ginny stared at him, not understanding his devotion to the farm. "Why doesn't your family just sell the whole thing? We'll take the money and all live happily ever after on the beaches of Florida."

Emmet grinned ruefully at her. Ginny was a good person in her own way, and as appealing to him now as she had been when he had awoken in the Navy hospital and found her staring at him. But sometimes he wondered how they had ever married. They were so different in outlook. She did not have a snippet of farmer gene in her. He could not expect her to feel or understand a farmer's love for the land, bred into him almost genetically by four generations of a family's connection to it. What she was saying surely made more sense from any other perspective.

"I'm gonna go talk to Floyd tomorrow," he said. "Maybe he knows some graceful way I can get rid of twenty tenants."

Pulling into the Gowler homestead the next morning, he spotted his grandfather sitting under the white oak tree on the edge of the barnyard, facing away. Snoozing as usual, Emmet thought, with one eye on his beloved farmstead. Pulling a timothy stem from the lawn's edge, Emmet crept up behind Floyd and lightly touched the old man's ear with the fuzzy seed head, just as Floyd had done to him when he was a boy. He hoped his grandfather would think it was a fly in his ear and slapt at it. No response. Again. Still no response. Suddenly a sickening fear slammed through Emmet. His grandfather was much too still. He jumped around in front of Floyd, knelt, and knew. The old man's skin was stone cold.

The eyes, staring stubbornly at the sheep in the shade of the barn wall, saw nothing.

Letting out a cry of protest, Emmet turned away, walked, then ran towards the woods, towards the Killdeer swamp beyond, towards the embrace of wilderness he blindly hoped would blot the nightmare from his mind. The dead face looming before his mind's eye now was not his grandfather's but his copilot's. Once again, as he had relived it so many sweaty nights, he was returning from a bombing raid, joking with his copilot in hysterical glee about having made their torpedo run and survived once more. But when the copilot did not respond to his radioed chattering, Emmet had jockeyed himself around in the cockpit to see behind him a face cast in death, leering crazily at him through the bloodied, pierced cockpit glass, sagging above a breast torn to hamburger. Emmet screamed all the way back to the aircraft carrier.

But he overcame his horror and flew more missions. And then it happened again. It was after that, after the second copilot died behind him, that Emmet did not speak a word for three months.

Now he felt himself edging into that same black world of silence again, as if he could not help himself. He fought the sliding-down feeling, fought the vacuum of grief and horror that wanted to suck him in. Why should he be so shocked now—he who had seen two copilots die behind him—that a grandfather should not live forever? He crashed on through the swamps, sobbing as he had sobbed in the cockpit before he had succumbed to total silence.

He must not now surrender to the luxury of crawling back within himself and letting Ginny take care of him again. There were the two boys now, as well as Ginny, depending on him. There were aunts and uncles and all those tenants. He had to take the cards life dealt him and he had to play them himself. Or as his grandfather would say: "You go up to the plate with a ball bat in your hands, you gotta swing the damned thing."

Eventually, he found that he had entered a heavy stand of second-growth woodland, a bit of upslope rising out of the wetland grass. Easy stuff to get lost in. A queer memory inserted itself into his consciousness—the night he and Ben had gotten lost while coon-hunting. Swiftly upon that recollection came the realization that he was looking at, through his tearful eyes, the very same apparition that had loomed into their lantern light that night. Miser Meincer was emerging from the brush, looking remarkably like he had looked that night ten years earlier. The patched pants could not have been the same pair, but Emmet was willing to bet that it was the same hat on his head. Miser had seemed old that night. Now he appeared ancient. Emmet tried to turn away and swiftly wipe any sign of tears from his eyes. Twenty-seven-year-old men do not cry.

"I do believe it's Emmet Gowler," Miser said in his customary quavering voice. They eyed each other. "What's botherin' you, boy?"

Something in the strange man's curious stare drew the words from Emmet, and in the drawing, though he did not realize it, Emmet escaped the all-consuming depression that was threatening to overtake him. "My grandfather's dead. Floyd's dead." Emmet was surprised that he could speak the words. "I found him dead and I didn't even have the guts to tend to it. I just ran off. I just ran off to let someone else find him in the barnyard, sittin' there, deader than a doornail." He wanted to go on and explain that he had run because of the dead faces in the cockpit, but he could not. "And my friend Ben Bump hates me."

Miser's face showed no emotion. For a minute he said nothing. Then: "Your grandfather was a giant of a man. I expect you be wondering if you can fill his shoes?"

Emmet glanced at him, surprised that his real fears, which he thought he kept hidden behind an exterior of daredevil boldness, could be so transparent to a man he seldom saw or talked to. He nodded, but instead of responding directly, he replied, "Why can't I just go off into the swamp and live like you do? I never asked to be born in a rich family."

"Nor I to be a swamp fox," said Miser. "You be wrong if you think there's no strife in my world. Not even the varmints escape it. There's allus somethin' after them, man or beast. Nature is a chain of fear. Of worrying about finding something to eat on one hand and of being eaten on the other. The only difference is that the animals don't know it like we do. Every time farmers drain another part of Killdeer, my life is threatened a little bit more. The varmints don't know that. The only place security sleeps in peace is in the coffin."

"If you don't like the way you live, why do you do it?" Emmet asked.

"Not a matter of liking. Everything else I can think of I dislike more." He paused. "Though there is some satisfaction in being able to piss just about anywhere and anytime I feel like it."

Emmet grinned in spite of his grief.

"But I expect I'm one of the luckier ones," Miser continued. "I figure my world will come to an end 'bout the same time my life does. Lots of folks have to live on into a changed world they never chose or foresaw. Like the Indians. Like maybe farmers someday."

Emmet shook his head at such a queer notion. "Somebody's always going to have to raise the food," he said.

"The cowboys, like your great-great-grandfather, thought there were always going to be cattle drives too," Miser said.

Emmet considered the idea for a few silent moments. "Remember that night we were lost, when you said Gowler might disappear as surely as Bowsherville did?" he finally asked. "Do you still think that?

"It's started already," Miser said with a sigh. "The hotel's torn down, isn't it? The stockyards is closin' down. Your uncle's going to quit grinding flour at the elevator, I hear. Everybody gets their bread from the Omar Bakery man."

By the time Emmet walked back to Gowler, there was a new kind of resolve in his step. It was nothing Miser had said, and yet it was everything he had said. It was as if his grandfather's dead face was canceling out the dread of the copilot memories and healing him. "History be damned," he repeated. "I'm gonna make Gowler the center of the universe."

The first thing he did after the funeral was sell off the last of the sheep, symbolically letting the neighborhood know that the old era was over and a new one had begun. The fact that Nat Bump bought them surprised him from a monetary point of view—there was no money in sheep, he believed. What could be the significance in the transaction? Next he opened a John Deere dealership in partnership with his uncle. He hired two long-time tenants to work in the dealership. That conveniently solved the problem of relieving them of their rented farms. Two other promising tenants he hired to help with the farming. Seven tenants quit when they learned they had to pay up past debts if they wanted to continue. Several, past retirement, Emmet allowed to continue for the time, knowing that old age would soon solve the problem. That left only four families he had to fire outright, and two of them nodded with fatalistic meekness when he explained that if he did not consolidate, the whole operation would go under. Only the Remps and the Chafers remained to be confronted. He knew that was not going to be pleasant.

As he pulled into the Remp driveway, Emmet could tell by the hostile look on the faces of Lem's two boys, Henry and Louie, both about Emmet's age, that they already knew why he was there. Emmet spoke as humbly as he knew how, grinding out the fateful words.

"I gotta consolidate the land into one farm to make it go."

Lem looked away, but Henry sneered. "You be bitin' off more than you can chew."

"I hate this as much as you do," Emmet replied. "But you do have land of your own. It's not like I'm ending your farming."

"No, and by God, I'll tell you something," Henry said, bitterly. "Maybe we'll farm four thousand acres too one day."

Emmet's attempted diplomacy left him. Like his grandfather, he could not back away graciously from confrontation and the neighborhood might as well know it right now. He might have been born with a silver spoon in his mouth, but he was going to have to chew his food just as hard as the rest of them. "And by God by that time I'll have six thousand," he said dryly.

The Chafers reacted with the same kind of surliness, although they too had land of their own to fall back on. They nodded at Emmet's news but did not comment on it until he drove away.

"Little rich boy's gonna play big farmer," Jubel Chafer said, and his father laughed.

"Might be we'll be playin' that game too," he said.

The Remps and the Chafers and Emmet Gowler knew the shape of the future and its horrible battle cry. It was 1951 now; time to get big or get out.

THIRTEEN

Meanwhile, Ben faced problems at the opposite end of the economic scale. Since he had been forced to use the money he had budgeted for machinery along with Nan's loan to cover the unexpected increase in down payment for the farm, he was in a quandary. He could always borrow his father's equipment, but his stubborn independence rebelled against doing so. For one thing, he would be working less on the home farm and so could not justify using the machinery on his own place as much as a trade for his labor. Nan was making it very obvious that she could handle the home place without his help. Borrowing machinery would also mean that there would be occasions when he might not be able to perform a cropping procedure exactly at the right time because his father or Nan would be using the equipment. Timing was everything in farming.

One day while he and Mary were driving around, talking about their upcoming wedding day, they passed a farm where two men were trying to load a team of horses onto a truck. Ben slowed. "Those are *very* nice horses," he said. Mary, who knew something about horseflesh too, at least the riding horse kind, agreed. Seized by an impulse, Ben wheeled into the driveway. He had seen the farmer many times but did not know him personally.

"That's a mighty nice team of horses, Mr. Laarnen," Ben said. He noticed then, that the farmer appeared to be in some kind of anguish.

" I hate to get rid of them," Laarnen said quietly. "But what's a man to do these days? I'm gettin' old and everybody's gettin' tractors and I gotta get one to stay in competition." He gazed at his horses. "But God, this team is too good to make dog food out of."

"I would be most obliged to buy 'em," Ben said, as if he had planned all of his life to stop at this farm on this day for this purpose. "I'm wanting a team to farm with."

Laarnen looked at him sharply and recognition came over him. "Oh, you're the Bump boy that was farmin' on Gowler's with a team last year. You turned Amish?"

"No, sir. Just partial to horses."

"A young man wanting to farm with horses?" Laarnen laughed.

"Horses might be the only way I can afford it right now."

Something in the sincerity of Ben's voice moved the old farmer. "By heaven, if you like horses enough to want to farm with them, by heaven, I'll *give* 'em to you. And the harness too. All I ask is that you let me come over and work them a little on occasion."

The other man tried to object that Laarnen had already agreed to his sale, but the farmer would not not hear of it, no money having passed hands.

"Well, at least I can haul 'em to your farm," the trader suggested to Ben, hoping to cut his losses. "Only charge you five dollars."

"Oh, I think not," Ben said. "These horses don't act like they've ever been on a truck, and it would scare them too much. They might never get over it. It's only about three miles back to my place. I'll just walk them back, and by that time we'll be acquainted with each other." Laarnen smiled. He had made the right decision.

Ben talked his father, who had finally sold his horses, out of all the horse-drawn machinery still stored in his barn, and before long he had the required minimum set of equipment: plow, disk, harrow, planter, hay mower, hay rake, hay wagon, and corn binder. He had fully equipped his farm without spending a cent except for minor repairs on the machinery. He could hire custom harvesters to cut his oats and wheat.

Ben and Mary bent to the task of getting their home ready for their life together. While Ben stretched new fences and put in his first crop, Mary made a garden, pruned back or replaced overgrown bushes, and made curtains for the windows. She filled the house with secondhand furniture purchased cheaply at farm sales. While she painted the inside of the house, Ben painted the outside. Standing back and gazing at their humble but prim little white frame house, and with their wedding day only a week away, she watched Ben clean out and brick up the spring near the house and knew that none of her classmates, setting up housekeeping in the finest homes in Columbus, could be any happier than she.

The wedding itself was another matter. Dorothy, with heavy pressure from her side of the family, was bent on having a church wedding, even though that presented a seemingly insurmountable problem. Mary was not a baptized Christian. It was hard enough getting church approval for marriage to a non-Catholic. Marriage to an unbaptized person was, in Catholic tradition, null and void without a special dispensation from a bishop, and such dispensation was hardly ever granted.

"You're kidding," Mary said. She and her mother had gathered with Dorothy and Nan to plan the wedding.

"And you have to go to classes in advance, too. That's the law," Dorothy replied peevishly. She had seldom questioned her religion because never before had her agenda run counter to Church doctrine. She was glad that Nat was not in the house. He would have been delighted by her irritation. "No offense, Mary. I know you're not a heathen really, but the Church has this law."

"But I really am a heathen," Mary replied, amused. "What am I supposed to do, pretend I'm not?"

"Well, that *would* be nice. At least get baptized."

"But the only reason I'd be doing that would be so we could have a church wedding. It would be lying."

"What they want mostly is for you to promise to bring up your kids as Catholic," Nan said. "The rest is a breeze." She knew. She had checked it out when she thought she would be marrying Emmet. He had been baptized but was not a Catholic and not likely to ever become one. And not likely to promise to bring children up Catholic either.

"Well, I don't want my children joining anything that compels them to think there's something bad about people just because they don't get water sprinkled on their heads," Mary replied.

Nan giggled, then giggled louder, having thought of something that had never crossed her mind before. "I think you're the first heathen I've ever met, Mary. Are they all as nice as you?"

Mary smiled. "Let's ask around the neighborhood and find out how many unbaptized pagans there are in Gowler. Are you a heathen, Mother?"

Margaret Livingston smiled. She had said little up to now, not knowing whether she dared air her true feelings in front of Dorothy. But it seemed Dorothy was open-minded on the subject. "My family is full of disbelievers. I don't really know about your father's people. I think he may have been baptized. I'll have to look it up. It was never important to us. Did you know that the word 'heathen' was first used in reference to 'people of the heath' in ancient England? The country people on the heath were suspicious of the gods they saw as being rooted in urban society."

"Really?" Nan said. "Well, then I'm a heathen too."

"I bet Miser Meincer is a heathen," Dorothy said. "And if Floyd Gowler wasn't, he should have been." All four joined in laughter.

Mary turned to Nan. "You won't mind being bridesmaid to a heathen?"

Nan hugged her. "I think we should have the wedding in the barn like the Amish do. They aren't heathens, are they?"

Dorothy sighed. "My mother and aunts are going to have cat fits." Her family had all come to America ahead of Dorothy. It was in fact because they were established in Jergin County that Dorothy and Nat had come there in the first place.

"They'll get over it," Nan said. And then she switched oars. "Who's going to be best man?"

"Ben wants Emmet, but he can't bring himself to ask," Mary said.

"Emmet's the right choice," Nan said, minding her own agenda. The others nodded agreement.

It took all his moral strength, but Ben finally worked up the humility to ask Emmet to be best man. Emmet was so pleased that Ben seemed to be getting over his anger about the farm sale that he readily agreed before he realized the consequences. He would be partnered with Nan, the bridesmaid, and that might be most embarrassing. Somehow he knew Nan was behind this. But he wanted to be on at least speaking terms with Ben again. And the idea of being at the altar next to Nan involved some delicious possibilities.

But it was not down altar steps that they marched, his arm in Nan's, but down the sloping bank of Dorothy and Nat's bank barn entrance. The new young Methodist minister in Gowler, who had not been shy about remarking that a good way to bring heathens into the church was to marry them, officiated at the ceremony. Dick Farnold played his fiddle and Thrankie sang, loud and clear and surprisingly sweet. Cy Gowler was there, which both Emmet and Ben took special note of. Mary's family and urban friends were well represented, obviously enjoying the novelty of a barn wedding, although their stylish clothes and well-tinctured faces looked as out of place there as a flock of sheep in a beauty salon. "You may be starting a trend, getting married in a barn," Nan whispered to Mary.

Nan was almost as radiant as Mary, the calluses on her hands covered with white gloves, her eyelashes as long and fluttering as those of any of Mary's college friends and her waist trimmer. When she met Emmet's eyes at various times during the ceremony, ever so momentarily, of course, she looked away and smiled with a brightness that made his own uncomfortable countenance look more uncomfortable still. She was enjoying herself at his expense, he knew, and there was nothing he could do about it except roll his eyes and stare dourly into space.

Dorothy was crying, and she did not know for sure if it was because her boy was getting married, or because of Nan hand in hand with Emmet, or because none of her family, not even her mother, not even Aunt Matilda, her favorite sister, attended.

FOURTEEN

Mary was going over the farm accounts on the kitchen table when Ben came in from the barn. She had a flyswatter in her right hand and only one eye on the accounts as she waited for another fly to land within striking distance. Ben stopped whistling when he saw the account ledger. He didn't like for her to look at the books. The books were not telling a very promising story.

"Here it is the second half of the century under way, and that prosperity that's supposed to be just around the corner still hasn't come into view," she said, sarcastically. Swat! One more dead fly.

"I still have the hogs to sell," Ben replied. "That'll give us enough so we can make the land payment."

"We're not getting ahead, Ben." Swat! "You've got to buy a tractor so you can farm more land."

"As long as we're paying off the debt, we're getting ahead. A tractor would just get us deeper in debt. Anyway, you need a new washing machine worse."

"No, I can get by." Swat!

"So can I."

What he really wanted to do was milk a few more cows. But that would mean getting a milking machine. And if he bought a milking machine, then he would have to buy even more cows than he really wanted to justify it. Then he would spend just as much time milking by machine as he did now milking by hand. And he was averse to buying more cows. Raising his own heifers was a far cheaper way to increase herd size. But it took so long.

"Maybe I should teach a while," Mary said. She knew he would balk at that. He would see a wife having to earn money away from the farm as a sign of his failure as a farmer.

"I know something better that you could do and in the long run make better money."

"Yes?"

"Learn how to milk. If we were both milking, I could start increasing the herd, and before long we'd have enough heifers coming into the milking string that I could justify a milking machine."

"Why is it that women always end up milking the cows?" she asked. Swat!

"They're better at it." Ben knew he was lying. So did Mary.

"Men just say that to get out of doing it."

Ben laughed ruefully. That was probably true. "Well, I don't intend to quit milking. I just need some help until I get enough cows to justify a machine."

"And I'll sure enough need a new washer then so I have time to help with the milking. No matter how we work it, there's always something has to be bought. I see why farmers want children. They want a free labor force."

Ben shrugged. "Having babies costs money, too," he said glumly.

Mary was glad he did not seem disappointed that she was not pregnant yet. Most farmers viewed children in somewhat the same way they viewed cattle: the more the merrier. Not to have a bunch was another kind of failure.

"Just do the arithmetic on it," Ben continued, his head back into the prospects for increasing the herd. "If you go to teaching, what'll you make? Forty dollars a week, maybe? Fifty? But if we milk more cows, you'd be making more than that. Three cents a pound for milk, and a cow giving sixty pounds a day is a dollar eighty, times twenty cows comes to a $252 a week, half of it from your labor. Course the cows won't give that much every week. But that's good money if you don't have big expenses. And as the herd improves, the cows become valuable property, and we can sell the calves that we don't need for a good price. More cows is a cheaper way to expand than more acres."

Mary stared at him. Her wish to teach had no more to do with making money than his desire to farm. But she decided not to try to explain. "All right, I'll learn how to milk," she said in a resigned tone of voice.

She started taking lessons that very night. "You have to squeeze from the top of the teat to the bottom, while pulling gently," Ben instructed her. "Start squeezing with your top finger, and sort of let the pressure of squeezing move from that finger down to the next, to the next, to the next, all so fast that after a while you feel like you're squeezing all the fingers at the same time. Then do the same with the other hand on another teat, in a rhythm, first one and then the other, back and forth. When you catch on to it, the milk just seems to gush continuously into the bucket. You should be able to milk a cow in five minutes when you get good at it, and you'll have three inches of foam on top of the milk from the forceful, rapid squirts."

Mary tried, holding her head back from the cow as far as she could.

"Don't be afraid of the cow," Ben said. "Put your head right into her flank. Move in close. When everything is as it should be, a cow wants to be milked. But in case she doesn't, you're safer up against her if she should kick, and you can feel when she's thinking about kicking and get the bucket out of the way."

"Oh, sure."

"Really. If you're in close, she can't get a good whack at you."

"How come you always milk from the cow's right side?"

"No special reason. If the cow was used to it, you could milk her from either side."

"How do you keep dirt off the cow from falling into the milk?"

"Well, sometimes you don't," Ben replied with a wry grin. "That's why we strain the milk as it goes into the milk can. Furthermore, *we* keep *our* cows very clean—clean off their flanks before milking. And *we* milk into buckets that have a cover over half the top to cut down on the possibility of dirt falling into the bucket. *We* aren't going to get a reputation for dirty milk at the creamery."

For the first month, Mary's hands and arms ached excruciatingly when she milked. She was grateful for the time between cows, when she poured the contents of her bucket into the strainer and watched it go down through the cloth strainer pad. The specks of dirt on the pad made her wonder just how clean the milk really was. She started inserting two pads into the strainer. The milk strained more slowly, but at least that meant more rest time between cows.

Eventually her grip and her forearm muscles hardened to the task. Ben said milking was excellent exercise for a ballplayer—it would put more force and snap into his swing and therefore improve his batting average. Oh, sure. She was going to play a lot of baseball. Finally, however, milking became a relaxing job, almost restful, a good time to talk over with Ben the events of the day.

Ben showed her how the cats would readily lap a stream of milk squirted at their mouths directly from a teat. He himself liked to drink milk still warm with a head of foam on it, drawn directly from the cow into a glass. She tried it. It tasted like cows smelled to her, and she didn't like it. "I'll take mine chilled from in the refrigerator, thank you," she said.

Ben had named his highest-producing cow Old Sideswiper because she had developed the most lethal kick that he had ever been on the wrong end of. If she hadn't given so much milk, he would have sold her. Her kicking had become habitual because she came into the stable with an udder nearly bursting, and milking always began in some discomfort for her. Most cows kicked more or less straight ahead, upsetting the bucket or, as often as not, ending up with the hoof in the bucket. That meant throwing the milk away, cleaning the bucket, and starting over again, although some farmers would strain what milk they could save even after a cow's dirty hoof had stepped in it. Old Sideswiper, however, had her own patented kick: forward in the characteristic manner, but on the return she reached out sideways in a vicious arc capable of knocking a grown man flat on his back. Ben had tried to cure her by putting hobbles around her back legs, chaining them together so she couldn't kick. For most cows that was effective, but Old Sideswiper would then hop up and down, her back legs like a piledriver. Or she would lose her balance and sag over on Ben, who had no other choice but to use all his strength to prop her up again or be squished beneath over a half ton of cow. So he quit using the chains. And he never let Mary milk Old Sideswiper.

But there came an evening when Ben was so late from the fields that Mary decided to start the milking alone. When her husband did not return after she had milked all the cows except Old Sideswiper, she decided to go ahead and finish the job, thinking how pleased Ben would be. Besides, Old Sideswiper had been behaving herself of late, Ben said.

Mary plopped down on her three-legged stool at the proper distance from the cow, set the bucket, slightly tipped, between her legs, and gingerly reached under the ponderous udder for the teats. Old Sideswiper was already wary. Only Ben had ever milked her. Moreover, she was peeved that she had been left standing in her stanchion so long, her corn and oat meal already eaten, her udder aching. Someone had to pay. Lightning-swift, her near leg came forward, bypassing the milk bucket miraculously, and then executed its out-flung swipe. Fortunately for Mary, she did not react as fast as a veteran milker might have to get out of harm's way, or Old Sideswiper's hoof would have struck her with its extended full force. Instead, the leg caught her on its return while she was still up close to the cow and threw her backward. Mary landed on her backside several feet away from the cow and, as luck would have it, in fresh manure, courtesy of the cow next to Old Sideswiper, who was impatient to get back to the pasture field.

Surprising transformations occur to even the most civilized people when they have been kicked by a cow. "You bitch," Mary muttered, a word she had not known was in her vocabulary. She checked herself for injury, the anger in her still rising. Her ribcage throbbed. Maybe cracked one. She repeated with more emphasis, "Bitch."

She waited until she could breathe evenly again, then grabbed the milk stool and swung it in the general direction of Old Sideswiper's backside. Up came the hoof in a blur of motion, deflecting the stool as neatly as a prizefighter might and sending it back into Mary's face. She reeled against the stable wall, narrowly missing a pitchfork leaning there. Grabbing the fork, she advanced and jabbed the tines into the hapless cow's flank. The cow retaliated with another haymaker, but Mary was ready for it now. She dodged the blow and jabbed the fork into the cow's flank again, hard enough to draw blood. Every kick brought another jab, until finally Old Sideswiper had had enough and stood there trembling. The rest of the cows were taking turns urinating and defecating in nervous fear.

Mary's anger passed, replaced by a wave of remorse. How could she have done such a savage thing? What would Ben think, he who preached patience with animals at all costs? What would her friends say. Summa cum laude, out of Gwendmere College. Yeah. Now transformed into an avenging Amazon, spattered with cow-shit, and a rib burning like it was on fire. She put the fork down and broke out sobbing.

Just then Ben appeared at the stable door. He took in the scene and rushed to her. She was crying uncontrollably. He tried to hug her.

"Don't," she bawled, "I think I got a cracked rib."

"You tried to milk Old Sideswiper?"

She nodded, still whimpering. She knew she dared not ever tell him what she had done.

"You tried to milk Old Sideswiper," he repeated, full of admiring disbelief but also great guilt. "Man, oh, man, you are the most wonderful wife that ever lived." He gently put his arm around her shoulders and ushered her to the house. Mary refused to go to a doctor. Her rib was not broken, only bruised, she said. Ben went back to the barn. Why had he been so greedy for more cows that he would submit so fine and gentle a person to the rigors of the cow stable? He was no better than Emmet, or any of the other farmers whose greed he had condemned. He was in fact worse, because instead of trying to satisfy his greed with machines, he took advantage of human flesh, of a human being willing to do anything he asked of her. He went back to the house, begging her forgiveness, hoping somehow to wipe away his terrible greed. "There's not another woman in the world who would put up with me and what I make you do," he said out loud. "You coulda been killed."

Mary nodded, almost savoring his remorse. She wasn't the only thing that had been in danger of death, but she decided not to get into the details. After a pause, Ben continued. "We're up to ten cows now and two more heifers to freshen soon. I think maybe you should start teaching, at least as a substitute, and then we can go ahead and get a milking machine."

Mary scarcely believed her ears. This was a departure from the tradition that Ben so stubbornly clung to. "I can teach and still help with the milking when you really need me," she said, encouraging his new way of looking at life. "I really don't mind the milking. I'd just like to do some teaching because I *like* to." Ben nodded. He understood. It was most difficult for him to admit, but the old days really were gone.

Several months later, after the coming of the milking machine, Ben came in for supper and allowed as how he thought the cows actually seemed to prefer it to hand-milking. "Especially Old Sideswiper. You know something? That cow hasn't kicked once since that night she nailed you," he said. "Can't quite understand it."

Mary busied herself at the stove, hiding a wicked little smile from him.

FIFTEEN

When Nan faced Emmet down at the land sale, she did not know that she was on her way to becoming the most despised farmer in the county. It was bad enough that she was a woman who was proving that she could be just as successful at farming as any man. It didn't help that some farmers still suspected her father of being a German spy during the war, or at least a German sympathizer. But now she was doing something that made the more ambitious farmers livid with frustration. She was going to farm auctions and bidding up the price on land, apparently with no intention of buying but only wanting to bedevil those who wanted to buy. There was nothing the other bidders could do about it except quit bidding and stick her with a farm she might not be able to pay for. But that would mean curbing their own insatiable desire for more land. Nor were they positively sure that she was only tormenting them. What did they know about the Bumps, anyway? How did that wily old bastard of a Nat Bump buy his farm when he was nothing but Killdeer trash? Maybe he'd inherited money from the old country. Maybe he got a bunch of cash from the Germans for spying. Maybe his bitch daughter was somebody's secret and highly paid whore. It was for damn sure no *woman* could be successful enough at farming to bid up values like that.

Actually, Nan's intentions were innocent enough at first. She went to auctions to try to buy another farm. She had convinced her father that they needed to expand by buying land, not just renting it. Nat at first disagreed, remembering how so many farmers went bankrupt in the Great Depression after getting too ambitious with borrowed money. He liked to tell Nan the story of Lars Shipman. Lars had a nice eighty-acre farm paid for and going along just fine. But he decided that the only way he could keep his son in farming was to buy another eighty, which he could only do by mortgaging his paid-for farm. The Depression hit and he lost them both.

Nan scoffed. "That Depression isn't going to come again," she said, "And what's the difference? If you buy more and lose it all, how's that different from not buying any and losing it all anyway because you aren't big enough?"

Eventually, Nat gave in or rather gave up. Arguing with Nan was about like disputing a course of action with a cat. And he had come to depend on her and admired her ability to get things done. It was a wonder how few people could do that. She was a smart one, for a woman. Maybe she was right. Maybe he was just getting too old for modern farming. But he would not mortgage his farm. He had money enough squirreled away for a down payment on another farm, and that would be his contribution to the partnership. The rest she would have to get from a bank on her own if she were so smart, or from someone as foolish as she was.

Nan went directly to Cy Gowler. He stared at her with unfeigned awe that registered as a silly grin. He had never talked over a farm loan with a woman before. He paused a while after she had finished her pitch. She sure was no dummy. "Tell you what," he finally said. "I'll lend up to $380 an acre. That's what land's selling for, Lord have mercy. No more, because there's no way you could pay it back even with the hefty down payment your father can throw in."

Thus armed, Nan jubilantly started bidding at auctions. She would bid to $380 an acre, only to see wealthier farmers or farmers with more "credit potential" outbid her. Slowly it dawned on her what really was going on.

"You know, Ben," she said to her brother after one auction. "The good old American free enterprise system is only free and good if you've got the money to elbow poorer people out of the way. There's no way I can outbid the big boys." On the third try she lost her temper and bid to $400, and still someone bid higher. Afterwards, her father and Cy Gowler remonstrated with her severely. She was playing a dangerous game that could end in bankruptcy.

She glared at them. "Didn't you notice? I didn't buy the farm. Bedsheet Remp did, and he'd have gone higher." She was sure of it. "Bedsheet" had become Henry Remp's nickname ever since the Ku Klux Klan incident, but no one used it where he could hear it. And she could see the same desire in his eyes for the farm as she saw there for her body.

The next auction, she stopped at $400 an acre, but then, when Jubel Chafer and Bob Tarmin took the bid to $450 an acre and Bob Tarmin refused to go on, she spontaneously bid $460, enjoying the way Chafer's jaw worked convulsively as he stared across the crowd at her. By God, if the groundhogs were going to take it all, she muttered under her breath, they were going to have to pay for it. Auctioneer Brady whooped. Every nod made his bank account rise. "How about 470," he roared.

Chafer bid $500 an acre. No goddamn woman was going to outbid *him*. Nan smiled sweetly and declined to vote again. "I was going to quit at 460," she said to her outraged father, loud enough so Chafer could hear as she passed him on the way to her truck. Chafer's fists clenched. But a certain craftiness had entered into his thinking. There might come a time he'd get a chance, like Henry Remp declared he would, to screw the saucy little, butt-swayin' bitch.

Nat and Dorothy held a war conference with her.

"You must not do that ever again," Dorothy remonstrated.

"I forbid you to go to any more sales until you can control yourself," Nat said.

"Forbid till the cows come home," she shot back. "I'm a grown woman and I will do as I damn well please."

"You leave me no choice," Nat wailed. "I'll have to put a notice in the paper that I am not responsible for any debts other than my own."

"Good idea," Nan said, knowing her father could never bring himself to such public humiliation.

But she did discontinue going to sales for a while because she noticed that whenever she started bidding, Emmet left the crowd and drove away. Since her intention was to raise the bids on him more than anyone else, his withdrawal took some of the fun out of her risky behavior. Emmet, realizing what she was up to, told Ben, knowing the message would get back to her, that he had decided that buying more land presently was foolish, that the four thousand acres he operated was enough. Ben nodded, still not comfortable around Emmet. To him a hundred acres was enough.

Finally, an eighty came up for sale that even Nat thought they could afford. It was close to the home place, not the best land, and not kept up. Surely it would sell below $400 an acre. Or if it went a little higher, maybe they should buy it anyhow. But he could not bring himself to do the bidding. Thinking that Nan was over her brash behavior, he told her to do it, but to watch him closely. He would signal her when to stop.

The bids came fast, and the price shot up past $400 before Nan even made a bid. So surprised was her father that he forgot to signal her not to bid higher. But she made no attempt to do so anyway, and before long, the price was edging over $500 an acre, higher than Nan had ever risked in her taunting gambles.

That's when she noticed who was upping the bid. "Look at that," she muttered. "Dob Hornley wants that farm, Dad." They both smirked. "Dob's bitin' off more than he could chaw and his teeth aren't gettin' any younger," Nat said to Nan. She laughed loudly. Both of them were remembering Dob Hornley playing Ku Kluxer. Brady, always with one eye on Nan anyway, since her bidding was making him a richer man, turned to her expectantly.

"$510," she cried.

"Gott in Himmel."

"Five ten we got," boomed Brady, smiling graciously in Nan's direction. He had begun to entertain a fantasy about her. She must be infatuated with him. She was bidding to gain his attention.

Nan stared back at him, her lip curling in disgust. "I think maybe I will make that ape share his commission with me," she said to her father out of the side of her mouth. When Hornley raised to $525, she came back with $550. She remembered the look on his face when she had leveled the shotgun at him. When that look returned, she would know it was time to quit bidding.

"Five fifty we got, how about six hundred?" Brady said, quiet now, looking directly at Hornley as if the bidder were a king about to make a major announcement to the world. Brady knew he should have asked for only $560, but maybe Hornley was as flighty as they said he was, and would swallow 600 whole in the heat of the bidding. Hornley did, nodding and glaring at Nan. The look Nan was waiting for crept across his face. She turned and walked away. It was the first farm ever to sell for $600 an acre in Jergin County. It would be enough, Nan figured, to bankrupt the dumb ass.

SIXTEEN

The high-stepping farmers around Gowler were becoming more "efficient," as the farm magazines observed, and production began to rise dramatically. The "efficient" farmers increased yields not only on their own land, but on the land they rented from less ambitious farmers, the kind who thought of farming as something to bring in enough cash for necessities while they spent most of their time at hunting, fishing, and other rural pleasures. When modern life suddenly demanded more cash than these leftovers of an older culture had ever dreamed it would, they sold out or rented and slowly drifted away to factory jobs or to welfare. Thus all the farmland came under the control of the new "efficiency," and the result was a growing surplus of grain. The Gowler land under Emmet's management now produced an average of 110 bushels of corn per acre, while in his grandfather's day the tenants were doing good to average 80. The more "efficient" the ambitious farmers became, the lower the prices fell. The lower the prices fell, the more farmers were pressed to even greater "efficiencies." They had no choice: Either keep on increasing production, or turn for help to a source they all despised: the government. They did both.

"Every one of us hates taking subsidies, but not a damn one of us will refuse them," Emmet was snarling at Ben.

"And the ones that get the most, need it the least," Ben said, accusingly.

"You can get just as much per acre as I do."

"I'm not in the subsidy program," Ben said proudly. "It doesn't pay enough. The only way I can keep up the farm payments is to feed my grain through the cows, not sell it outright. You have your land paid for, so you can afford to take a bribe for pulling land out of grain production. Especially since you know you are going to raise just as much as you ever did by taking your worst ground out of production and pouring more fertilizer on the land not in the program."

"Damnit, Ben, I gotta make ends meet too."

Ben did not reply. He and Emmet were beginning to get along again, and he didn't want to stand in the way of that. Besides, Emmet couldn't even imagine what it was like to pinch pennies the way he and Mary did, so why try to point that out to him. Emmet would only say again, "Jeeeze, it's not my fault I was born rich."

Emmet had actually stopped by Ben's place to feel him out on the government's latest strategy. "We just got the notification at the elevator," he said. "Listen to this. Uncle Sam is gonna pay us to store grain in sealed bins to keep it off the market. It still belongs to us, but the bureaucrats will tell us when we can sell it. They think they can keep the grain coming to market in an orderly fashion that will keep the price up but allow for something they call 'ever normal granary,' so in a bad year there's enough grain to go around." Emmet watched Ben closely, wondering if his compatriot was smart enough to see the stupidity in this move. Ben was milking, was used to having grain farmers stop by to complain about low corn prices. Like the blacksmith of old, he was a captive audience always sure to be in the cow stable at chore time, morning and evening. He was only half listening to Emmet and said nothing.

"It's a bunch of crap," Emmet continued. "The buyers know the corn's still out there. It's not like it doesn't exist just because it's in a sealed bin. This is just another way to keep the price of food too low for us to make a living. The way to raise the price is to dump all that corn and wheat in the ocean."

Ben laughed at the irony of the situation. Emmet, realizing what he had said, had to laugh too.

"Why don't you guys just quit raising grain for a year?" Ben asked, trying to sound innocent.

"Hey, if everyone did it, I would too. By God, I would. But you know farmers can't stop producing. We gotta come up with land and machinery payments every year."

"But if you raised less, the price would go up and you'd make more. It's really very simple."

"Oh, sure, easy enough for you to say, willing to milk cows every day."

"You could at least be feeding steers or hogs with that corn."

"There's too many farmers already trying to beat the grain market by feeding livestock. Meat prices are going down too. And so is milk, for that matter, so don't tell me you aren't hurtin'."

Ben said nothing. He was only staying afloat because he continued to farm with horses, with an overhead so low Emmet would not have believed it possible. He bought nothing he could make the farm provide, and carried debt only on his land.

Emmet went home and did some heavy thinking. He had learned that the government grain storage payments were high enough to cover the cost of the newly designed steel bins coming on the market, with a little left over. That little left over he could turn into profit. By storing very large quantities of grain, he could make some real money. "Now you're thinking right, Em," said Cy. "You make money from the farm*er* or the government, not from farm*ing*."

When the market prices did not rise in response to grain being marketed "in an orderly fashion," the government determined to hold it off the market until they did rise. Emmet laughed. National and international grain buyers had to be laughing their asses off, he thought. He built another big bin. The government was making grain storage a very profitable business. New crop grain was going to flood in before the old crop could be sold "in an orderly fashion," and it too would have to be stored under government seal.

Ton upon ton of surplus corn and wheat poured into Emmet's government grain bins again that fall. The profit was not quite what he had expected, but enough to persuade him to try feeding cattle after all. He built a feedlot and bought a hundred head of young steers to feed out on cheap, surplus corn.

The first time Emmet broke the law seemed wholly justifiable to him. His foreman at the elevator, Jake Lavendar, came into his office one morning with an uneasy look on his face.

"Boss, we fairly well got a problem."

Emmet looked up. He had plenty of problems. His wife wanted to spend a month back home in Florida as he had promised her, and his steers were standing knee-deep in shit and not gaining worth a damn. He waited for Jake to explain.

"That corn in bin no. 2 don't look so good, boss. I fairly think you gotta move it now. There's a hot pocket up on the left side that looks fairly bad. Gonna rot. Or catch on fire. I think maybe grain-drying technology isn't keeping up with bin-building technology."

Emmet turned to his secretary. "Get that goddamn CCC office on the phone," he barked. He hardly waited for the man on the other end to identify himself.

"Tom, we've got some corn that needs to be moved out like I told you two weeks ago. You know corn isn't plastic. It deteriorates. If we don't get this stuff sold, it isn't even going to be worth giving away to India."

"Now, Mr. Gowler, just rest easy. This is the responsibility of the Commodities Credit Corporation. Be assured that we will move that grain in due time. The information we have on your bins indicates that there's nothing to worry about just yet—"

"*My* information says otherwise," Emmet said, anger rising in his voice.

"I'll look into it and get back to you."

Emmet slammed the phone down. "Jake, can you get to that hot pocket in no. 2 easily?"

"I fairly think so."

"Take a load or two out and we'll feed it to the steers."

"But boss, I'm fairly certain that bin's sealed."

"You just fairly pretend you don't know that and fairly keep your mouth shut."

"Okay, boss."

It took Emmet only a week to find some new crop corn not under seal on a farm in the next county, pay the farmer enough to convince him to sell it, and replenish the grain he had taken from bin 2. He actually made a couple of pennies a bushel on the transaction, and no one was the wiser.

Except himself. The maneuver had been too easy. Now temptation reared its head. Marketing news constantly flowed in and out of his elevator office, and frequently he had felt compelled to pass up opportunities to make a profitable sale on a spot market because he couldn't move the grain in sealed bins. Now it occurred to him that he could sell sealed grain with only minimal risk, sort of like lending out money in the bank. Take some out and then put some back in before the government knew it, and make a profit on the switch. No losers. He called it the "switcheroo."

The first big switcheroo was a sure thing. He heard about a large southern Ohio feedlot needing a couple semi-loads of grain in a hurry and willing to pay a nickel above guaranteed government price. He filled the order. A week later, he was able to buy grain three cents a bushel under the going price to replenish what he had taken out of the sealed bin. He had barely completed the switcheroo when Tom Laffin, the inspector from CCC, finally showed up. "I don't see why you're concerned," he told Emmet. "Bin no. 2 looks fine to me."

"It's bin no. 1 that I was concerned about," Emmet was not really lying. He needed to get the inspector's attention away from no. 2, where he had solved the problem, of course, and now it really was no. 1 that was looking bad.

"You're near the top of the list, Mr. Gowler. We'll start emptying that bin soon."

"Soon" was a word that meant only "sometime" to the CCC. Two months followed while Emmet chafed. Finally he could be patient no longer. To hell with it. The market took a little upward bump and he sold a hundred thousand dollars' worth. That got rid of the deteriorating grain in bin no. 1, and he soon could buy new corn and fill the bin again. No one was hurt, and grain that might have spoiled was saved while he made a little money.

He started to speculate on a grander scale. Eventually he was dealing in millions of dollars' worth of grain that was supposed to be sealed, always getting grain back into the bins before the inspectors visited. Once when he could not get a bin of corn filled before a Laffin visit, he dumped two feet of corn on top of a bin full of wheat and told the CCC the bin was full of corn. Never dreaming that anyone would try such a ruse, Laffin believed him. But it was a stressful business and was taking its toll on Emmet.

Ginny began noticing changes in his manner. Relations between them had not been all that warm for several years, but he had always stayed cordial and caring for her, if in a reserved sort of way that somehow seemed fake to her. Even during sex he seemed preoccupied. Now he would come into the house at day's end, turn on the radio to grain market news, and hardly acknowledge her. Sometimes he gulped down his food, rushed to the bathroom, and vomited.

"Emmet, what's wrong?"

"Nothing, dear. Just a pressing day."

"Emmet, please talk to me. What's ailing you? You know you've been going back to the office every night this week. You don't even play with the kids much anymore."

"I know. It's just the press of business, I tell you. I finally got rid of the last sharecropper, Ed Black. Hardest thing I ever did. You know what he said? He would stay on taking care of the place for nothing if I just let him live there. He really doesn't care if he has anything much. I told him he could go ahead and live there but I wasn't going to keep the house up. He was happy then. Can you believe it?"

Ginny stared at him. She realized suddenly that her real feeling for him had always been pity. She had not understood him in his mental breakdown in the war, and she did not understand him now. He just seemed so vulnerable under his bold front, and that was endearing to her. She had thought it was love.

She suddenly wished she had never seen Emmet lying so abjectly depressed in that hospital bed. What was it about her that constantly needed something to feel sorry for? That was why she had become a nurse in the first place, she realized. Maybe she had rebelled against her own do-nothing family, wealthy almost entirely from the accident of owning land in Florida that kept doubling in price as northerners with money kept streaming southward to flee winter. All her father had to do was take money made in selling property and reinvest it in other property that in turn spiraled in price as the population wave from the North rolled on. Let the realtors take care of the details.

What a fool she had been. Her sisters now lived in comfort on old beachfront land that was worth more money than the whole of Gowler Farms. They whiled away their afternoons playing canasta, their backs often to the ocean that made them wealthy. Between games they planned their evening outings. Ginny had made a terrible mistake, she now thought. She wanted to be part of that life. And it would be so easy. Emmet could sell out of the farming game, which was going to kill him, and they could live in utter luxury where none of that hateful snow ever came.

She was sure it was not Ed Black that was bothering him. Getting another 140 acres to work into his consolidated farm was ice cream on apple pie to him. Something else was going on.

"It's that Bump woman, isn't it?"

He looked at her in astonishment. Ginny never mentioned Nan. He snorted. For once he could talk honestly. "For God's sake, no, Ginny. Why in the world would you say something stupid like that when I am having a really hard time in the business?"

"Why should you be having a really hard time in the business? You're the richest farmer around, aren't you?"

"Yeah. That's the problem." But he did not explain.

"If the business is giving you a hard time, why don't you sell it? Get out of it. With the money, we can go to Florida, like I keep saying."

Emmet got up and turned on the television. "So that's what you think. It's not nice here?"

Silence.

Maybe he should tell her about the switcheroo. But she wouldn't even understand the arithmetic.

"Tell you what. Give me a few more weeks to clear things up, and we'll go to Florida for a long vacation."

SEVENTEEN

The switcheroo was making money, but the feedlot was losing it. Just as his shrewd old Uncle Cy had predicted, Emmet admitted to Ben. Beef prices were dropping too low for cattle to be profitable, even if they were fed on cheap corn. Furthermore, the winter had been warmish and the ground had not frozen deeply. "I would not have believed that steers could churn up that much mud and shit," he grumbled. He had brought Ben to the feedlot to take a look at his problem. The animals were caked with manure halfway up their sides, as if they'd been swimming in it. Without the truckload after truckload of crushed stone that Emmet dumped around the feed bunks at considerable expense, the steers would surely have become helplessly immobilized in the quagmire. He had heard of it happening. "Now I know why big feedlots are located out west where it's dry," he added.

Ben was horrified at the quicksand of mud and reeking manure. Feeding steers under such conditions was cruelty to animals to him. And he, for one, did not want to eat meat that for nearly a year in a feedlot was shielded from this soup of runny manure by only a thin coating of skin and hair. There was no solution to the mess, either. Concrete would have helped, but the cows would still have been standing knee-deep in liquid manure. There was no way to get rid of it at the moment: the fields were too soft to allow for spreading. It would require an unimaginable tonnage of bedding to soak it all up. Ben did not want to get into another disagreement with Emmet, so he tried to ignore the latter's persistent questions about what to do. "Quantity always kills quality," he mumbled through his fingers as he leaned his elbows on the top rail of the fence and pressed his hands to his face.

"What's that?" Emmet was eyeing him keenly.

"Better get some more stone in there."

"That's not what you said."

"Yeah, it was."

"No, it wasn't. I heard the word 'quantity.' You don't much approve of this, do you?"

"Do you?"

"How the hell did I know it wasn't going to freeze up this winter? Remember, it was you said you have to market corn through animals to make any money. I'm doing the best I can. I got all this land to take care of, all this production, and a goddamn payroll to meet every week."

"Well, you could sell it all except for a nice little farm, and—"

"Cy would die before he'd see the farm broken up."

"You couldn't do it anyway. Too much like your grandfather."

"Well, what's wrong with that?"

"Nothing, nothing." Ben knew it was no use to argue.

Emmet wondered if he should tell Ben about the switcheroo, which was weighing so heavily on his mind that he could think of little else. He had promised himself that as soon as he replaced the grain he had sold out of bin no. 3, he was through with this kind of illegal gambling idiocy. But just as he opened his mouth to talk about his dilemma, a pickup came bouncing into view up the lane. They stared at it until it stopped beside them.

"I fairly got some news for you, Emmet," Jake Lavendar said, His face was even whiter than it usually looked under its daily pallor of grain dust. "That Laffin feller is pokin' around the bins."

Emmet blanched. "Take Ben back to his farm," he said, and with hardly a word of farewell, he jumped into his own truck and wheeled away.

Laffin was waiting in Emmet's office, his investigation complete. The look of satisfied bureaucratic arrogance wreathed his face. He wasted no time. "Mr. Gowler, we have a problem. I don't need to explain, do I?"

Emmet wanted to wipe away the man's gloating little smile with a fist. He declined to answer.

"Your bin no. 3 is empty, Mr. Gowler."

Emmet would not give him the satisfaction of asking how he had become suspicious. "I can have that bin full again in three days," he said. "No one would get hurt or lose a thing. I did us all a favor by selling the grain before it went bad." Then he added sarcastically, "I wonder how much half-rotten corn the government has been marketing 'in an orderly fashion.'"

"You have broken the law, sir, and the penalties, as I'm sure you know, are severe. And then you have to deal with the farmers whose grain is gone."

"They needn't worry. I'm probably making them more money than the government would have."

"I would not like to be in your shoes."

"Nor I in yours."

"Is that a threat?"

"No, just a philosophical observation. There will come a day when all this governmental pissing around with the market system is going to backfire."

"Don't bet on that," Laffin replied. "As long as human beings are going to piss around with the market, the government will have to piss around trying to stop them."

Cy Gowler's dewlaps quivered convulsively when Emmet confessed his waywardness. Emmet was afraid his uncle was going to have a stroke right there in front of him. Instead, Cy started scribbling numbers on the tablet always at his side. No use berating the boy; the milk was already spilled. "We've got some cash in the estate, but not near enough. We're talking several hundred thousand dollars in fines, you understand. We are going to have to sell land to cover that." He lapsed into silence, staring out the window. "We have to figure out a way to eat our cake and have it too." Emmet, mystified, could only stare at him. "I can buy a couple hundred acres," Cy continued. "My sisters will take a couple hundred. Your mother will too. But they're the only relatives who can be relied on to sell the land back to the estate when you get on your feet again." Emmet was full of awe. Uncle Cy was way ahead of him, trying desperately to figure out how to raise the cash to pay off the government and still keep Gowler Farms intact for the future. "You need to find someone who will buy another hundred or so with the promise of selling it back in the future. Know anyone you can trust that much?"

Emmet started to say no, but then what seemed like a brilliant thought occurred to him. "Maybe. Give me some time."

"You haven't got any time. We're going to have to work hard just to keep you out of jail. Get busy. I'll get Doc to say you're too sick to come to that meeting in Columbus right now. Maybe we can persuade the judge to give us time to liquefy some assets. We need a month, anyway. The bureaucrats may not right off know how much we're worth if we cashed in, and when they find out, they're going to turn into vultures."

As Emmet exited through the front door of the bank, he stopped abruptly. A small knot of men and one woman blocked his way. Like a lynch mob, Emmet thought. But dangerously quiet. Before him stood the farmers whose grain was supposed to be stored in his elevator. The news had already gotten out. Jake had, fairly for sure, made the rounds. Emmet met each one's gaze in turn, Chafers, Remps, Tarmins, Farnolds, and held on one: Nan Bump. She looked less hostile than the others.

"I promise you, each and every one of you, that you will not lose a penny over this. You will get the government's guaranteed price and probably more. You have my word backed by Gowler Farms and Gowler Elevators. We have never let you down and we won't now." He stood his ground. His gritty manner arrested their anger. They turned over the facts of the matter in their heads as they angrily eyed Emmet. The government would stand behind the deal, even if Emmet couldn't. In truth, they all—even the Chafers and the Remps—despised the government more than they de-spised Emmet. And maybe Emmet would sell out, and they all could get a crack at buying his land. One by one they turned away, got into their pickups and left. For now.

Back home Nan was almost surprised at herself. Now that Emmet Gowler was getting just what he deserved, she should have been pleased, or at least angry, since some of her corn and wheat were involved. But she was not. Emmet would make good on the grain, she was sure. That conniving old Cy Gowler would get him off the hook. So why wasn't she enjoying his dilemma? As she watched her hogs eating contentedly from the self-feeder, she re-membered the look on Emmet's face as he stood in front of the bank. It was the same look that she had seen when, so long ago, they went after the Burk boys and Gitchell with Roman candles.

Emmet Gowler had his faults, but he had more guts than any of them. She had gone with the other farmers to wreak some kind of humiliation on him. But if the Chafers and the Remps had attacked him, verbally or physically, she would have switched sides. It irritated her to know that.

"Those hogs look like they shoulda gone to market last week," a voice behind her spoke. She whirled, knowing almost immediately that it was Emmet, knowing he had to start a conversation by belittling her because he felt so insecure.

"A lot better shape than those shit-caked steers of yours," she shot back. Emmet had to laugh. Her fire was what made him love her, damnit anyway. But then he turned grave.

"I need help, Nan." There was a softness in his plea that she had not heard since before he went away to war.

"You sure do."

"I need your help, Nan."

Nan's mouth opened, but nothing came out. She had lost hope of ever hearing those words from him.

"I gotta raise some cash. Desperate, if you know what I mean. I think you can help me if you want to."

"What on earth can I do, Emmet? You know I don't have that kind of money."

"What if I offered to sell you the Ed Black place? It's just down the road from you. And I'd sell it to you reasonable."

Nan tried to make her tongue work. "R-r-r-reasonable?"

"Six hundred an acre. You know it would bring more at auction, especially if you were there. Uncle Cy can arrange to lend you all the money. No down payment."

Nan's mind was now moving fast as lightning, even if her tongue was not cooperating very well. Having her very own farm under those terms was more than she could have ever hoped for, but her mind was racing far beyond that thought to other possibilities even more delicious to contemplate.

"There is a catch," Emmet said, taking a deep breath.

"Yeah?"

"You gotta promise to sell it back when I get out of this mess. At the price you pay for it plus interest at six percent. You can't beat that." He waited for her refusal. Nan Bump might buy the land, but she would never promise to sell it back. Unless she saw that other possibility that he was afraid to put into words.

Nan deliberated. She had already thought of the other possibility. There was a chance that Emmet would get so bad off financially that he would never be able to buy the farm back. In which case maybe she could acquire him too, along with the farm. On the other hand, if he could buy the farm back eventually, maybe she could work it so that she came along in the bargain. In place of six percent interest.

She stared intently at him, wondering if he were smart enough to be thinking along the same lines, wondering if he had divined the real reason why she might accept the deal. Did they both know there was a possibility that neither of them could lose on this proposal, no matter what happened?

"Okay, I'll do it," she said, "but I think you're too damn smart for your own good, Emmet Gowler." She tried very hard to keep a straight face.

"I think you are, too," he replied, matching her grin.

Driving home from court days in Columbus, Emmet felt some relief. Influential politicians, friends of his uncle, had interceded on his behalf. He at least would not have to go to jail. He wondered if he would ever recover from the fines he had to pay. But the shame and public embarrassment over what he had done was easier to bear than the tension that he had endured while breaking the law. Also, his money problems made him feel justified in delaying the trip to Florida with Ginny and the kids. Ginny had seemed to accept his announcement that they could not go now, but she had lapsed into silence. He dared to believe things would get better now. He would take Ginny out to Surrey's most expensive restaurant, the Red Barn, when he got home and cheer her out of her doldrums.

With that thought in mind, he waltzed into the house in a great show of cheeriness, announcing his arrival by shouting for the boys. No answer came to his call. The kitchen was quiet, with that uncanny kind of dead silence that only an empty house can achieve. There was a note on the table. Emmet read it, and twice more.

Dear Em,

I am leaving you and taking the children to Florida to mother's. I would like to say that we will be gone for only a visit, but if I continue in my present way of thinking, I will be seeking a divorce. The shame of that grain elevator thing, whatever it was all about, is bad enough. But when you sold land to that Bump woman and didn't tell me, I knew that there was something going on. I don't belong in your life anymore. I think maybe I never did.

Ginny

Emmet sank into a chair. He felt that he had suddenly been thrust into a spinning tank whose centrifugal force was pulling the blood out of his body like an extractor pulling honey out of hive frames. He had not ever been unfaithful to her. Surely she had to know that. He had never done a mean thing to Ginny or the kids. He liked Ginny. Not the way he liked Nan, but he had never seriously contemplated divorce or adultery. Ginny was a sight easier to live with than that damn Nan would be. Or had he in the deep, dark side of his mind contemplated leaving her for Nan but not been able to admit it in the glaring light of consciousness? If that were true, did Ginny sense it? Or was she just using Nan as an excuse to do what she wanted to do anyway? She had never liked Ohio. Damn it all. Women were always one step ahead of him.

The old temptation to despair began once more to creep into his spirit. The bloody cockpit coated with the hamburgery flesh of copilots loomed up again in his mind. Then in the cockpit appeared his grandfather dead under the pear tree. Ginny was leaving him when he needed her support the most. Why could he not be like Ben, seemingly so forgiving, but as dangerous as a wasp on its papery little nest? Why the hell did he have to be born rich? Why the double hell did he care so much about farming? Farmers were the looniest, stupidest idiots in society, willing to live in constant tension from the unpredictable whims of the weather and conniving, self-serving politicians.

Headlights flashing in the window roused him. Who would be coming to see him this time of night? He went to the door and found two men emerging from the darkness onto the porch. He recognized them and beckoned them inside.

"Did the school burn down or something?" he said, trying for humor. Never had the superintendent and the head of the school board graced his house before. Surely there could be no connection between their visit and his problems with the government. What was going on?

Larry Luvre had worked himself up from science teacher to superintendent by making sure he never told the whole truth in public, and so he proceeded now very carefully, first discussing the weather in time-honored rural fashion, but then not moving on, as was also customary, to formal expressions of interest in "the Missus" and the children. Emmet was wary. Could Luvre, by the mysterious passage of gossip in small towns, have known more about Ginny's leaving than Emmet did? Emmet waited patiently, and in due time, after the ritual exchange of observations about farm prices, Luvre finally got down to business.

"We have heard about your, ah, unfortunate episode with the government," he said, "and I just wanted you to know that we have considerable sympathy for your dilemma. We all know you didn't do anything really wrong."

Emmet's mental antenna hummed on high alert. Larry Luvre did not give a rat's ass about his dilemma, and Jack Cughes, head of the school board, was no doubt hoping Emmet's financial situation would deteriorate to where the Cughes family might get a crack at buying some of his land. Emmet did not reply.

"You are a leader of this community, Emmet, as the Gowlers have always been."

Now it's coming, thought Emmet. The school must need money that isn't forthcoming from taxes. The Gowlers had always seen to that need.

"We, ah, have a delicate situation on our hands," the superintendent continued. "We need your help but hope for the time being that you will keep this between us."

Emmet leaned forward. What the hell—

"You know that the State of Ohio has been following the policy of consolidating schools when and where the consolidation will improve the quality of education," Luvre said, educational righteousness puffing up the tone of his voice. "The state has deemed that it is our turn to join in the progress." He paused, looking for some reaction from Emmet. Nothing. He continued: "We have been told to close Gowler High, consolidating into the high school in Surrey. This is never an easy process, and it will take time to educate the people into realizing the benefits of consolidation." The head of the school board nodded vigorously. He seldom had anything to say, but he was always a good nodder.

"And," Emmet finished for him, "you want me to take a lead in pushing consolidation."

Luvre beamed. "Precisely."

"In return for the school community's support in my crisis," Emmet said. He was almost amused. But under the burden of his personal problems, he was out of what little patience he possessed.

"Well, sort of," Luvre said, but before he could go on, Emmet cut him short.

"I'll tell you right now, Larry, if you and the State of Ohio try to close Gowler School, you have no idea what a fight you are in for. And I don't need your support for my business, either. Now if you're finished, I've got work to do tonight yet."

As soon as his visitors left, Emmet drove to Ben's farm. The threat of school consolidation at least gave him something more than Ginny to be angry about. And it gave him an excuse to talk over his personal dilemma with Ben.

He was surprised at the forcefulness of Ben's reaction to consolidation.

"I don't think so! This is not their school to close."

"Course not," said Emmet, "but we gotta get some strategy going. I don't know any place that's stopped consolidation yet."

Ben believed, as he did in all such matters, that the world was headed in the wrong direction. But no one was obliged to follow that direction, in his view. "I don't accept consolidation in farming, and I won't accept it in education," he said. They could consolidate the whole rest of the world if they wanted to, but not Gowler Village, if Gowler Village did not want to consolidate.

Mary eyed him. What would this stubborn man of hers do if he found out that he might be wrong? But she held her tongue. In the silence that followed, Emmet spoke again.

"I got bigger problems," he said.

"I thought you got straight with the government," Ben said.

"Bigger problem than that."

"The feedlot?"

"Bigger than that. *Much* bigger."

Now Ben and Mary turned to study him intently. What could be going on?

"Ginny's left me."

Both his listeners stared at him, stunned to silence.

"Just up and left while I was in Columbus. Took the kids to Florida to her mother's. Wants a divorce." All his usual toughness left him and he stared at the floor to hide his tears.

"I am so sorry, so very sorry," Ben said, but knew that as sincere as he was, he probably sounded hollow. He could not keep himself from thinking that Nan might yet find her happiness, and he knew that such a thought was turning his supposed sorrow into hypocrisy. He didn't fool Emmet, anyway.

"One thing about you, Ben Bump, you can't lie worth a damn." Now Ben stared at the floor.

"What are you going to do?" Mary asked.

"I'm going to try to get her back, of course. For the boys' sake if nothing else."

"And if you can't?" Ben asked quickly.

Again they stared at each other. They both knew exactly what he would do in that case, but neither dared to say it.

Mary could hardly wait for Emmet to leave before she rushed to the phone to call Nan. Some intuition told her that Emmet was on his way to see her, and she wanted her sister-in-law to be prepared. She was glad now, more than ever, that they were no longer hooked to a party line where someone was always apt to be listening in, especially when Nan Bump's three-ring signal was heard. Listening in on Nan Bump's conversations almost always yielded material for further conversation.

When Nan answered, her parents having much earlier gone to bed, Mary hesitated. Wasn't her business. Oh, well.

"Nan?"

"Mary?"

"Got something you need to know."

"Juicy gossip?"

"Well, yessss, but more than that."

"Spit it out, for heaven's sake."

"Ginny left Emmet."

Mary could hear measured breathing. Nothing else.

"Went back to Florida."

Still no response. Not like Nan to have nothing to say.

"Emmet was just here. He's pretty broken up."

Finally an answer. "Serves him right. Better not come bellyachin' around me."

"I thought you should know."

"Yeah. Thanks. I'll call you back when I get this digested." Actually she had seen headlights in the window, and knew it was going to be Emmet. He had his nerve.

He stood on the porch when she opened the door, waving a paper in front of him. His excuse. "You gotta sign this agreement, Uncle Cy says. About promising to sell the farm back." Emmet tried to look calm and businesslike.

"My word isn't good enough?" She pretended to be insulted.

"Is to me," he said lamely, "but business is business."

Had it not been for Mary's phone call, Nan might have balked. Might have refused out of sheer orneriness. But now she held the door and beckoned him inside. She wondered if he could work up the guts to tell her.

"Too late for paper signing. The farm's mine," she said, trying to squeeze every bit of satisfaction out of him that she could.

"Cy holds the mortgage, don't forget. He's got you wired down so tight you better never be one second late on a payment."

"Conniving old goat. Sort of glad he's on my side now whether he wants to be or not. All right, I'll sign your stupid piece of paper."

He waited in silence while she hunted for a pen. She hunted longer than she would have needed to, giving him time to tell her about Ginny. She thought he took a deep breath more than once, but he did not speak.

She signed the paper. The room was so quiet, she could hear the pen scratching. Was he going to be able to tell her? He picked up the paper, stood there, fingered it.

"You oughta read what you sign, dumb bunny," he said to her, still trying to play at belligerence.

"You oughta have witnesses, dumb bunny. I could swear I never saw that paper, and how would you prove otherwise? I didn't even use my usual handwriting."

He could only shake his head. Women. Always a step ahead of him. He headed for the door. She'd soon know about Ginny from someone else. Damned if he would tell her.

"Emmet?"

He turned. There was that old softness in her voice now.

"I truly am sad about Ginny."

Goddamn. Mary had already called. Women. Jeeesussss. Out loud he said nothing.

"But don't you come hangin' around here. I'm not playing second team for anyone."

"It isn't a second team sort of thing, and you damn well know it."

"You come to see me again, the paper you be wavin' at me better be your divorce."

Even as Nan stared out the dark window at Emmet's retreating headlights, so was Ginny staring out the dark windshield into the darkness that her car's headlights pierced. She was crying. Chris and Jimmy sat in the front seat beside her, staring at her.

"Why isn't Daddy coming, too?" Chris, seven years old, wanted to know. Mommy had said that they were only going for a visit. And why she crying? She should be happy. His brother, though a year younger, sensed something tragic in the air even if he could not put words to it. With that instinct that children so often feel, that older people have lost, he just kept saying over and over again, "I just knew this was going to happen. I just knew this was going to happen." But when he blurted it out, Ginny had no strength left. She could not see the road because of the tears. She pulled off and stopped. And hugged her children and kept saying over and over again, "I am so sorry. I am so sorry," until they too were weeping with her.

"I promise. You will get to see your Daddy and play with him. About as much as you do now."

"We're not coming back?" Chris was now in panic.

"We'll see." She could not tell him the truth.

NINETEEN

Because she was teaching, Mary constantly heard the rumors about consolidation but did not understand the tempest that the idea was creating. It took less than a year after the school officials' unsuccessful attempt to get support from Emmet for matters to come to a head. Tempers flared. Teachers refused to speak to each other. Administrators hinted that if the teachers did not present a united front—in favor of consolidation, of course— they just might get in trouble. Clarabelle Jenkins, who had been teaching for forty years and could retire at half her salary, which was twice what it had been when she started teaching, did not care whether she got in trouble or not. She was tired of the timid attitude of the new teachers anyway. She marched into Superintendent Luvre's office and informed him that the teaching at Gowler was better than it was at Surrey and everyone knew it and that if he had been in the county system even half as long as she had, he'd know it too. It would be better, from the standpoint of good teaching, to move Surrey to Gowler. "And furthermore, my good man," she intoned, shaking a bony finger at him, "if consolidation goes through, you just might as well go back to Cleveland where you came from, because everyone would hate you." But before she huffed out, daring him to fire her, the superintendent had something to say. "How much money are you making as a teacher?"

"Well, I guess you know."

"A whole lot more than when you started, right?"

"Well, I guess so."

"And just how do you think we can keep giving raises so that teachers will go on being teachers?"

"What are you driving at?"

"I'm saying that a lot of us don't like consolidation, but it is a way, when taxpayers vote down tax levies, to go on making pay raises."

Clarabelle huffed again and left the room.

Mary decided that it was because she was not born and raised in Gowler that the notion of consolidating the high school into Surrey did not particularly bother her. What difference did it make where she taught? She would not be a worse or better teacher in Surrey than in Gowler.

"Well, if it doesn't make any difference, why consolidate?" Ben asked her, sharply. "They keep saying that consolidation will improve education, and you just pointed out why that's ridiculous."

She sighed. She had been surprised that Ben, the calm one, would react so emotionally to the debate.

"Why does consolidation irk you so much?" she asked. "You never seemed to care about education before."

"Consolidation is going on in everything, and the real reason is to consolidate wealth and power. You jam more cows in the barn for the same reason you jam more kids in a school building. Lowers cost of production. Who benefits from it? Not the cows. Not the children. If I had my way, I'd never send my kids to any school." He immediately regretted his last statement, not because of what he said, but because Mary would feel that he did not appreciate her work as a teacher. That was part of the problem of consolidation. It got mixed up with other problems that had nothing to do with it, like the bus drivers who were favoring consolidation because it would mean more buses and more opportunities for bus drivers.

"You mean you think teaching is not a necessary profession?" she challenged him archly.

"People are teaching other people all the time," Ben said as if his words were too apparent to argue about. "Everybody is learning from everybody else all the time. Teaching and learning are as natural as breathing. You don't have to pen children up in classrooms for them to learn. That might be the worst place of all to learn."

"Why, Ben Bump, I never knew you to be so anti-intellectual. Without schools, half the kids in the world would never get exposed to the advances in knowledge. They'd never get farther along than what their parents know."

"They don't anyway. Teachers teach what parents want taught. You don't think so, just try to teach kids that Christianity doesn't have all the answers. Besides it just ain't so anymore that they would be held back without classrooms. Radio and television and books and magazines and newspapers are doing the real teaching."

"Well, in school they might at least learn that 'ain't' isn't a word."

"Oh, yes, it is. And a good word. Who put schools in charge of what is proper language and what ain't?"

"I hope you don't use that argument at the meeting tonight," Mary said, staring up at the ceiling.

Waiting for the school officials to open the meeting, Superintendent Luvre searched the audience before him, noting where the probable troublemakers were sitting so that during the meeting he could never look directly at them and thus could hopefully discourage them from speaking out. Toward the front of the auditorium, in the middle, sat teachers firm in the faith of consolidation, their faces beaming support at him. At the rear sat a clot of older Linner residents whom he knew he could also depend on. Linner's school had been closed, along with all the other one-room schools, in a much earlier consolidation into township schools like Gowler, and Linner still wanted revenge. Gowler supported consolidation then, so now, by God, let Gowler get a taste of its own medicine.

While the superintendent sized up the audience and planned what he called his "crowd manipulation," Ben Bump was also taking stock of the situation. The tension in the air, the very public nature of the affair, so different from the somnolence of his barn, was creating a different Ben Bump, a coldly calculating character that he hardly recognized himself. He leaned over to whisper in Mary's ear. "Ever notice that whenever there's a school meeting, the officials sit up front, elevated above us on the stage? They've taken the high ground. Sort of like herding cows. You have to stay right at that certain point a little in front of them where they can't get ahead of you, but not so far ahead that they double back behind you. Some of us should be up there on that stage if we really want to outmaneuver them."

Nan, next to Mary, nodded in agreement. Dorothy, who had stretched her neck from the seat behind Nan to hear what her son was saying, made her usual comment where Ben was involved. "You will go far in this world, Ben Bump. Why don't you take your chair and go on up there?"

"Aaach, no-no-no," spluttered Nat, next to Dorothy, in more than a whisper. "Don't make a scene." His caution was actually directed at Nan, not Ben. He doubted that Ben would get up in front of a crowd even if his life depended on it. But Nan, well, you could never tell about Nan.

The meeting began with the usual discussions of school business which the board members needed to vote on. A new teacher had been found to take the place of another who had resigned. A new assistant coach was needed for basketball. Payment of the coal bill, which seemed excessively high, needed approval. Several windows had had to be recaulked at an estimated cost of $17.50. The library fund had to be approved. The janitor had not had a pay increase since he had been hired ten years ago. The voting on the multitudinous details of running a school was always the same: five yeas, no nays, measure carries. A couple of times the vote was four to one, when Sarah Barth, the only anticonsolidation board member, refused, just to be contrary, to make the vote unanimous. There seemed to be an extraordinary amount of business that evening, and the crowd began to squirm and mutter. Few of them had ever been to a school board meeting before, and they were amazed that such trivial and obvious matters had to be carried off with such *Robert's Rules* pomp and ceremony. They also did not know that when controversial matters were to be discussed, school board meetings were choreographed in this manner in the vain hope of boring the troublemakers to numbness and so taking the edge off of their tempers.

Finally the meeting got down to the real reason the auditorium was jammed with people. But, still hoping to becalm the spirit of rebellion against consolidation, various school officials now gave strung-out commentaries on why consolidation was necessary to the survival of the school district. Often various charts were unwound dramatically and pinned to a large bulletin board set on a tripod, the information so displayed purporting to show how much money consolidation would save and how it would improve the quality of education. One chart demonstrated that the population of the school district was declining and so there would soon not be enough students in the Gowler school system to use teachers efficiently. A set of fuzzy photographs appeared as proof that the Gowler building was beginning to deteriorate. One chart indicated projections of how money could be saved busing the students all to a centrally located school.

The longer the officials talked, the more rapid became the tap of Ben's shoe against the floor. And when Superintendent Luvre delivered his most compelling argument to win the people over to consolidation, that it would provide for a bigger pool of students for the sports teams, the tapping of Ben's foot increased to an almost machine-gun staccato. Nan had seen his foot tap like that in the seconds before he attacked Wayne Gitchell in front of the theater. Mary saw it every time Ben recalled the Ku Klux Klan encounter. When Ben tapped his foot that way, and then started expelling air in huffs rather than in an even flow, both women knew that some kind of explosion was likely. Both women shivered in anticipation—with apprehension on Mary's part, with glee on Nan's.

Finally the speeches were over and Larry Luvre stepped to the lectern. "We will now open the meeting for public comment. You will please limit your remarks to no more than five minutes each in the interest of ending the meeting at a reasonable time."

The crowd muttered disagreement. Ben's foot quit tapping and he let out one last, very audible huff. He stood, picked up his folding chair, and strode toward the stage.

"Gott in Himmel."

Ben climbed the three steps to the stage, walked over next to the superintendent, plopped his chair down, and deliberately seated himself. He said nothing. All the officials and school board members on the stage stared at him curiously. The audience was momentarily taken aback. In his chair, Ben loomed a head above the superintendent and exuded an air of controlled outrage. After he was sure he was not going to faint from the inner terror he felt, he stood again, hoping his shaking legs did not show through his jeans. Taking a deep breath, in which he seemed to grow in stature several more inches, he spoke in a voice resonating with ominous resolve, clearly audible to the farthest reaches of the auditorium without benefit of loudspeaker: "Whoever wants to speak can take as long as the previous speakers did if they wish." Then he sat back down, looking at the superintendent, daring him to disagree.

Superintendent Luvre's head swayed crazily from side to side. He had not planned for this. Principal Girth seemed to turn to stone. Neither of them nor the school board members could find the nerve to challenge Ben's seemingly uncharacteristic behavior. But if any of them had objected, they would not have been heard, because, after a moment of stunned silence, the audience roared approval. Luvre knew this was not the best moment to invoke *Robert's Rules of Order*. What he needed now was Sheriff Mogan's rules of order, and he was grateful to see the lawman standing in the aisle.

The first speaker to rise and be acknowledged was Lester Cordrey, as Luvre had hoped. Whatever the old idiot said against consolidation, it would cast the hue of extremism over the opposition. But Luvre became alarmed because, perhaps taking a cue from Ben, Lester walked up on the stage to deliver his oration, taking his good old time to get there. For a few long seconds he was silent, just staring at the audience. Finally he drew a deep breath and in measured syllables, thundered.

"God*damn* consolidation."

And in the silence he descended the stage steps with great aplomb. A titter slipped away into the tense air from way in the back, then another from closer to the front, then an outbreak of giggling from Nan Bump, and then deafening applause from all over. Later everyone agreed that they should all have just gotten up and left right then.

During the pandemonium two figures edged toward the stage. One was the sheriff up the left aisle, easy-like, just letting everyone know that he was there. The other was Emmet Gowler with what appeared to be a rolled-up chart or two under his arm. He stopped next to where Nan Bump sat, whether by design or happenstance it was hard to say. Nan looked up and studied him.

"I wish those were giant Roman candles," she said wickedly, loud enough for him to hear.

"How do you know they're not?" he replied. They looked at each other, unable to hide expressions of mutual memories, the good old days of what seemed like long ago perhaps coming alive again.

Mayor Jallup next rose to be recognized, and he too stepped up on the stage, perhaps by now thinking that was proper protocol.

"If you look into the legal arrangements that public education is based upon," he intoned, "it is an incontestable fact that the public school districts belong to the people of the districts, not to a bunch of state and federal bureaucrats, NOR," and here he paused for emphasis, "NOR to the school administrators. What we have here is a failure of the democratic process. We don't want consolidation, and we voted for school board members who had given us to believe that they would represent our wishes, not the State of Ohio's wishes. The political power structure that wants an educational system not for the people or the students but for the increased financial welfare of the education profession."

More applause, but also objection. A teacher in the proconsolidation camp shouted out without benefit of *Robert's Rules,* "The state pays $1,186 for every student in the district, so it ought to have a say!"

"The state does not pay one penny for anything," the mayor shot back. "The state makes no money to spend. The money you talk about is tax money from the taxpayers, and the biggest mistake we ever made was to allow Columbus to take it from us and give it back at the state's discretion."

Shouts and murmurs from all sides. Luvre called for silence and tried to catch the sheriff's eye. "We will maintain order in here tonight," he warned, "as I am sure Mr. Bump here beside me would want to do." That was clever, he thought. If Bump wanted to be part of officialdom, they could accommodate him and suck him into the righteousness of the system, just like they did school board members.

Miser Meincer tottered toward the stage, then had second thoughts and decided to speak from the floor. "We've had to deal with rattlesnakes afore, and I guess we kin again," he said, jerking his thumb toward the stage. Those close enough to hear his frail voice laughed, except the teachers. Some of them had never seen Miser before and were astonished that such a strange-looking creature in tattered clothes and furs had survived into modern times. "I saw the farmers come into this country and the last of the Wyandots leave," he continued, his tremulous voice ascending into almost a wail, "and now I am living to see the factories come in and push the farmers out. I've a notion that the Injuns will come back after the factories have destroyed theirselves. But none of you will believe that, anymore'n if I had told you when they built this school in nineteen and twenty that in just forty years it would be closed." The auditorium was quiet now, taking in his words. Remarkably, it *was* just forty some years since the local people had funded and built the school. Everyone over forty realized for the first time how quickly forty years had passed. Everyone under forty was surprised that the school was no older than that. To them it seemed to have existed forever.

"Over in Europe they got buildings three, four hundred years old that they're still usin'," Miser continued, almost as if he read their thoughts. "We are the most wasteful bunch of Yankees that ever lived, and there will be hell to pay some day."

Meincer shuffled back to his chair. There was no applause; there were no jeers.

When no one else rose to speak, Emmet walked up the aisle and mounted the stage steps. Even though he was still a bit young for the part, he was the patriarch of Gowler and knew it. He bore the name of the town that his great-great-grandfather had founded and the Gowlers had ruled for so many years. Emmet was the heir to that throne. It was up to him to stop the closing.

Emmet went directly to the chart stand, unrolled the first of his charts, and pinned it over the last one that Superintendent Luvre had left there. Emmet's chart showed a map of the county, with the Surrey school district in one color, the Crarey district in another, and the Hackmore district in a third.

"We have been given to understand that it is only natural for us all to consolidate into Surrey because of its central location in the county," Emmet began. "But as you see here, Surrey Village may lie close to the center of the county, but it does not lie in the center of the Surrey school district. If you consider this issue geo-graphically, Gowler is more centrally located than Surrey is." He waited for that to sink in, then pinned up a second chart which showed in bold letters all the villages of the county.

"We have also been given to understand that it is only natural that consolidation should center in Surrey because it is the most populous village. But if you count in the villages of Negrada on the east side of the county, Margales on the southwest, Linner and Dedota on the southeast, and Scarby on the west side, all of which have allowed themselves to be consolidated already into Surrey, these villages are actually closer to Gowler or not any farther away from Gowler than they are from Surrey. In other words, there's more total population in the county closer to Gowler than to Surrey. Whatever figure you care to believe as to the amount of money saved by consolidating into Surrey, there will be greater savings by consolidating into Gowler."

Again he paused, and then pinned a third chart up that showed an area in red in the farmland just north of Gowler. "I now suggest to the school board and the State of Ohio that we do just that. We will consolidate our schools into this area in red, which, geo-graphically and population-wise, is nearer to the center of the school district being affected than Surrey is. This forty acres shaded in red are part of Gowler Farms, and Gowler Farms will donate it to build there the most advanced consolidated school district in the state."

A hush fell over the audience. Superintendent Luvre knew he had been outmaneuvered. Emmet stared at him, wondering how he would worm out of the situation. The school officials had expected passionate pleas for keeping small local schools, which Emmet knew was a waste of time before a bureaucracy whose mind was already made up. Proposing consolidation to Gowler instead of Surrey would guarantee, however, that the whole county would be thrown into concern. Up to now, Surrey had been able to be smug, believing that consolidation would not mean the loss of *its* local schools. Not even the president of the United States could engineer a closure of Surrey's schools into Gowler without a riot or at least a vote that would go against consolidation.

"This is all, ah, rather precipitous, Mr. Gowler," the superintendent said, frowning, stalling for time to gather his wits. "We have no plans for such a colossal undertaking as that."

"Oh, yes, you do. There are plans for new schools out in the middle of the countryside all over the state. I wouldn't wonder if the oil companies and bus manufacturers aren't engineering the whole damn thing."

"We must stick to the topic at hand," the superintendent said, trying by smiling to indicate how ridiculous Emmet's proposal was.

"You mean you won't take under serious study an offer of land worth thousands of dollars as a gift for a new school?"

The superintended was flustered. This was one turn neither he nor anyone in Columbus or Washington, DC, had anticipated. While he hesitated, Ben again stood up.

"I move that consolidation be tabled and this meeting adjourned until we can take Mr. Gowler's wonderful offer under consideration. Do I have a second?"

"I second the motion," Lester Cordrey shouted immediately.

"Just one moment here!" the superintended thundered. "You people can't do this!"

An ominous murmur moved through the crowd. The tensions of the last few weeks now boiled up in Emmet, and his control popped like a cork off a bottle of champagne. He let it all out.

"Everyone in favor of allowing Ben Bump's motion to stand, say 'Aye,'" he shouted, and a roar of ayes filled the auditorium.

"Everyone in favor of Lester Cordrey seconding the motion, say 'Aye,'" Emmet shouted again, caught up now in a near-frenzy of sudden power. Again the auditorium rocked with ayes.

"This meeting is adjourned!"

"Like the living hell it is!" Sheriff Mogan boomed as he sprang quickly up on the stage. He secretly delighted in what Emmet and Ben were doing, but by God he was the law and he by God would maintain law and order because by God that is what sheriffs were for. Besides, if the people started questioning the school board, how long would it be before they questioned the police?

"You will remove yourself from this stage, Mr. Bump. And you too, Mr. Gowler. And you will sit down quietly, or I will sit you down quietly."

Whatever it was in Ben that had made him want to take Emmet to the woods and beat the crap out of him after the sale now rose in him again, almost against his will.

"What are you going to do, sheriff, shoot me?"

Mogan was thoroughly provoked now. He moved firmly toward Ben, and when Ben didn't budge, the sheriff's momentum knocked the husbandman off balance. That looked to Lester Cordrey's wild mind like an attack on Lester's favorite farmer. He sprang from his chair and up the steps. The sheriff was looking at Ben, patiently giving him every chance to come to his senses, which Ben was about to do, grinning in fact at the ludicrousness of the situation. That's when Lester jumped the sheriff. Two board members came to the lawman's aid, although he wouldn't have needed it. They grappled with Cordrey, carrying him back down off the stage to his chair. The Farnold brothers, in the front row, could no longer contain themselves and flew at the board members. The Farnolds were not particularly alarmed by consolidation; they just didn't like the board members. Several teachers sprang up to defend the board, and before Superintendent Luvre could decide on a safe escape route, a full-blown fight was in progress.

"REMEMBER THE FRUIT JUICE!" yelled Nan, seeming to float over the crowd to stand beside Ben and Emmet.

"Gott in Himmel."

Since there were not enough consolidation supporters to muster a real battle, the melee soon dissolved into a settlement of other matters. Dob Hornley, who had been forced to sell the farm Nan had bid him up on, had only been waiting for a chance to settle a few scores. The Chafers had their own agenda. They beat Emmet to the floor. Bob Tarmin remembered that the Farnolds had rented a farm away from him and attacked them. Bedsheet Remp went after Emmet, but Nan jumped on his back, her fists pounding his head on both sides. Remp shook her loose and paused only a second: "Okay, little girl, you asked for it. I've wanted a piece of you for a long time."

Emmet, who, for all his boldness, was not a man who sought serious violence, had been trying to get away from the Chafers. But when he heard Henry Remp, he erupted in a way that scared even Nan.

"You so much as touch her and you're dog meat," he snarled.

Remp took one look at Emmet's angry face and decided that retreat was a wise alternative at the moment. Nan beamed. It was all she could do to refrain from hugging Emmet right in the middle of the madness. Ben, towering above the crowd, had scared Hornley into retreat, and with nothing better to do, he grabbed Henry Remp and threw him in the same general direction as he had thrown

Hornley. By the time Emmet turned his attention back to the Chafers, they had decided to disappear, especially since the sheriff, and now a couple of deputies, were bearing down on them.

Just as fast as the crowd had erupted into violence, it quieted again. The stage was entirely empty of officialdom, and no one was quite sure where they had disappeared to. Emmet and Ben stood sheepishly in front of the sheriff, heads bowed. Only Nan seemed to be in high good spirits.

"Handcuff me, Mr. Mogan," she said, holding out her arms and smiling evilly. "I've never been handcuffed before."

"Young lady, you mind your tongue," growled the sheriff, biting away a grin. "I am very much tempted to do just that and throw the lot of you in jail till you cool off."

"Gott in Himmel," Nat once more remarked, still rooted to his chair in the audience.

In the embarrassed silence of the numbed crowd, the sheriff did the kind of thing that kept getting him elected. He looked balefully around the empty stage. "All the people who know how to handle *Robert's Rules* have done flew the coop," he announced loudly. "So as sheriff of this here county, I do hereby table this whole damn meeting until a future date."

TWENTY

Emmet's offer of land for a new county-wide school saved Gowler from consolidation for the moment. Another year passed in relative educational peace. Surrey residents were not about to move their schools to the outskirts of Gowler, no matter how much they had favored consolidation when they thought it was coming into their town. Surrey had the clout to vote down consolidation, and the school authorities did not want to give them the chance. No proposal was put on the ballot. The county's school officials, after consulting at length with state officials, who in turn consulted at length with federal officials, declared that a "new study" was underway. It indicated that delaying consolidation for a while would save more money than accepting free land for a new complex of buildings. But there was a condition. If Gowler wanted to continue to avoid consolidation, its chances would be greatly increased if it built a gymnasium for the enhancement of "physical education."

To the surprise of nearly everyone, farmers in the Gowler district did just that, waging a fierce campaign that brought in enough money to add a basketball gymnasium to the school within a year. Ben, Mary, Nan, and Emmet sat discussing the matter in Herb's

Diner, sipping coffee as they happily watched the August drizzle outside that was keeping them from farm work. August drizzles meant good corn crops.

Herb's Diner did not start out to be a restaurant. Like so many early buildings in rural villages, it was built as a quick, temporary domicile, something to be torn down or added to when the occupants could afford something more substantial. Instead, it was abandoned, most likely because of the noise of the railroad locomotives rumbling by, then bought by Herb's father, who believed that if he had the verve, or lack thereof, to stand over a hot griddle nine hours a day, he could make a fairly decent living frying hamburgers. Knock out a wall, fill the space gained with five tables plus as many booths along one side, with a counter added along the other side, and he was in business.

There was nothing, absolutely nothing, in the diner that was attractive except the hamburgers. Herb had added a jukebox, which helped, only at the moment it was out of order. The floor was linoleum, worn through to the original wood floor where foot traffic was the heaviest. The plate-glass window in front of the diner was its only saving grace, providing almost all the light available inside. Herb said it was not good to have too much light in a restaurant. It would encourage people to examine their food too closely, he said. The tables and chairs were of wood, rescued from a café that had gone out of business in Linner, the next village to the east. The booths had high backs stained a dark walnut, and hard bench seats. The high backs were much beloved by young people who could steal a kiss or hold hands or stare longingly at each other and not be seen by other customers unless they were passing directly past them. Ben could remember, as a teenager, using the old crank telephone that still hung on the wall, but was no longer in service.

Emmet had made history of sorts as a child by riding his pony, called Pony, directly into the diner and refusing to leave until Herb gave them each a Tootsie Roll.

"What the hell is physical education?" Nan snorted, knowing full well what it was. "Country kids get plenty of exercise working on the farm. They don't need any stupid fizz ed."

"But someday there won't be any real country kids," Ben replied quietly.

"You're both being naive," Emmet growled. "Sports is the thing that generates school loyalty. School loyalty wins approval of new tax levies. New tax levies allow increases in salaries. Most of the parents like it that way. That's why we got the gym funded. If it weren't for sports, many parents wouldn't care if the kids went to school at all."

Herb approached the table. "Anyone want another sweet roll? Got two left. And you better enjoy 'em while you can, because I'm going to ree-tire next year."

The four were stunned. Denial and disapproval showed on their faces. "Well, look," Herb continued defensively, "I'm gettin' old. None of the kids want to be tied down with this. This is damn neared an eighteen-hour-a-day job. Any of you want to take it on? I'll sell the place real reasonable."

"But where are we gonna get something to eat?" Nan lamented. "The bakery's closed, and now you."

Herb shrugged and walked away.

"It's happening," Ben said, looking across the table at Emmet. "The egg market, the bakery, and now the diner." Emmet knew what he meant.

"Could be worse. School coulda been closed."

"I'm not sure it won't be."

"What do you mean, 'It's happening'?" Mary asked.

"Miser Meincer told us once that Gowler would disappear just like Bowsherville did."

A silence. Then Nan spoke. Silences made her nervous. "Not the same as Bowsherville," she said. "We've got the railroad."

"It'll be a cold day in hell before the elevator, the bank, and the general store go," Emmet added stoutly.

"Your great-great-grandfather got his start in the general store at Bowsherville," said Mary, who had been reading Jergin County history. "I bet he said the same thing about Bowsherville."

Voices rising from a nearby booth caught their attention. Dick and Franklin Farnold, Doc Halw, and Lester Cordrey were deep into debate.

"Nothin' smells worser than skunk spray up close. Not only makes you puke but it'll burn your eyes out," declared Dick, as solemn as a judge delivering a death sentence.

"That ain't bad at all compared to a really rotten egg," Franklin countered. "The egg has to be so old there's nothing left inside it but a kind of rubbery skin. Now that *will* make you throw up."

"Speaking of which," Doc Halw offered, "have you ever smelled blood puke from a patient who had had his tonsils removed using ether as an anesthetic?"

"A rotten potato smells worse than a rotten egg," Dick said, unable to address an odor as strange as ether puke.

"Fresh manure from a nursing calf will drown out a whole bin full of rotten potatoes," Franklin countered.

"You boys are mere pups on this subject," Lester Cordrey interjected in his shrill, high-pitched voice. "After you've been puked on by a buzzard protectin' her nest, you know that skunks smell like French purr-fume."

"Hey, Lester, we're trying to eat over here, " Emmet said, pretending to be offended.

"Calf shit reminds me, " Nan said. "The farm magazines are saying manure is hardly worth hauling anymore."

"Farm magazines want to sell fertilizer," Ben replied.

"According to organic farmers, manure is about the only fertilizer you need," Mary said. "*Organic Gardening and Farming* tells all about it."

"Tells all about what?" Emmet asked.

"How farmers are wrecking the soil with chemical fertilizers and spraying stuff that causes cancer."

"You believe that shit?" Nan asked.

"Well, maybe. Surely better to use manure and compost."

"What's compost?"

"Rotten tree leaves, old manure. Stuff like that."

"There aren't enough leaves and manure in this whole county to fertilize even my land," Emmet declared.

Ben stirred uncomfortably. He'd read some of Mary's magazines. "I don't see anything so different about organic farming," he said, coming to her rescue. "I'm using very little fertilizer because I've got lots of manure. And clover plowdown after hay. I can control weeds by cultivating. Like we always did before weed killers came along."

"You couldn't do it if you were farming four thousand acres."

"Which is why you shouldn't."

"Gotta get big or get out," Emmet said, needling Ben. "Can't go on like Gramps did."

"Maybe a farmer can't go on like you do, either."

They stared at each other. The humor of the situation dropped away. The Maginot Line of wealth that separated them once more reared up before their minds' eyes.

Ben remembered that he really should be cleaning out the manure gutters behind the cow stanchions in the barn at this very moment. He looked at Mary and said as much. They rose awkwardly and headed toward the cash register. Emmet was alone at the table with Nan. Hadn't planned on that. People at other booths were taking note.

"You don't need to talk to Ben that way," Nan scolded. "Did it ever occur to you that putting on all that chemical fertilizer increases yields only to drive the price of corn down? We're just playing right into agribusiness's hand."

"I was just kidding and he knows it."

"And you don't farm four thousand acres anymore. I farm 140 of it, and don't you forget it."

Emmet grinned. The more belligerently she treated him, the better he liked it.

"And that reminds me, isn't it about time you sold that land back to me?"

"You couldn't afford to buy it if I did want to sell, which I don't."

"What do you mean? You've only made two payments on it."

Any other two people in their situation would have been uncomfortable, but Emmet and Nan were obviously enjoying themselves.

"Yeah, and you couldn't come up with even that much."

"We've got an agreement, you know," he said.

"I never agreed to be the *first* to sell back. You buy back from your relatives first, and by that time we'll both be in the old folks home."

Emmet laughed. "Well, can I at least come over and see if you're ruining my land?"

"Better corn than you ever grew."

"Show me."

Her eyes narrowed. "I told you the next time you came around, you better be waving a divorce settlement."

Instead of embarrassment as she had expected, Emmet reached into the inside pocket of his jacket, pulled out a sheaf of papers, and plopped them triumphantly beside her cup of coffee. Now it was Nan who was embarrassed, though she tried to look cool. She had to get the damned redness out of her face. "Don't think I'm going to be a pushover," she said. The words came out in a fonder tone than she had wished.

"Let's go look at your corn."

He paid for her coffee and followed her out the door. Nan was grateful that no one was on the street at the moment. She got into her truck. Emmet waited on the sidewalk.

She eyed him. Oh, what the hell. "Get in," she said, out the open window.

During the fifteen minutes it took to get to the Black farm, the only sound was the windshield wipers slopping back and forth. All the while Nan prayed that they would encounter no one, particularly her parents. Emmet, for his part, was numb with the almighty possibility that she was going to accept him back into her life. She pulled into the driveway, past the deteriorating house and barn, across a pasture field where she was grazing dairy calves, and down a lane alongside the cornfield. They were now alone and out of sight of any road or farmstead.

"If you've got any corn that's half as good as this on that worthless jackwax of yours, I'll *give* you the farm back," she said.

"Don't brag too much or your luck might change," he replied. "It's just because you got two inches of rain this summer where I've gotten only a half inch."

"It's just because you got more land than you've got time to plant properly. You slop it in, some too early and some too late. You spend more time moving from farm to farm than you do actually farming."

He grinned ruefully. She was about half right. "What if I just plain surrendered?" he said. "What if I admitted right out loud that you are ten times smarter than I am in every respect and always have been?"

She looked at him. Exhilaration swept over her, obliterating the cruel memories of the past. Maybe what she dared not dream was going to happen. "What if I admitted right out loud that I love you anyway." she replied.

He turned to her, stunned. He knew that what she said was true but never thought she'd admit it. He started to say something. Once. Twice. She waited for the three magic words. I. Love. You. They did not come. Instead, Emmet dropped his head.

"Nan, I miss my kids so much I can't stand it. I miss them so much that . . ." He started to cry.

Oh, God, Emmet Gowler actually crying.

" . . . I miss them so much I'm not sure I can handle it. Those two little boogers are the only thing I have left, you know. I tried to get them, but I just couldn't break Ginny's heart. I just couldn't have that fight. Especially after she was willing to sign papers renouncing all financial interest in the farms. You know, she coulda broke me. Real easy. But all she said was that if she got custody of the boys, she didn't care about anything else." The tears were rolling down his cheeks now. "The hell of it is, I don't care about anything else either. But I just couldn't fight her. Even if I could win. I just couldn't do it. And so I gotta travel eight hundred miles just to see my boys. And pay through the nose to support them."

"Well, at least you've got children, " Nan said, and immediately knew she was still being cruel. God. Quickly, hoping to cover up, she added, "Maybe when they grow up they'll come back to farm with you."

Emmet only shook his still-bowed head. Nan realized that she had only made matters worse. In her practicality, she had bared the awful tragedy. Except for brief visits, Emmet would not enjoy his children growing up. What an idiot she was. She slid over next to him and put her arm over his shoulder. He turned eagerly to her and hugged her. Both of them were sobbing now. Emmet for himself, Nan for Emmet and herself, for she understood that there was this whole family thing that she could not share, that was always going to be between them, that was always going to complicate their relationship.

By now their embrace had turned unwittingly from compassion to passion. Both realized what was happening, but it was happening to two people they hardly knew. They were kissing. With increasing excitation. What the hell, if the only solace left was sex, so be it. They tumbled out of the cramped cab into the rain and, still kissing, eased to the wet grass, clumsily stripping away clothes as they fell.

Ben knew his neighbors thought him odd. Here it was, going on 1958, when modernism was supposed to finally triumph over tradition, and he still farmed with horses, still shocked his corn and husked it by hand, still made haystacks, still milked only twenty cows, still farmed only 120 acres while most farmers were following the drumbeat of "get big or get out" and borrowing heavily to expand. "Your place looks like the Ford Museum," Emmet said to him one day. "You ought to charge admission and make some real money." He meant it for a joke, but his tone was also complimentary, for, in truth, Emmet was beginning to admire Ben's stubborn ways. Ben only smiled, a little painfully. When he looked at his account book, he understood that he was not making much money. But he also understood that he was not losing any either. That was evidently not the case with so many other farmers who complained loudly around the tables in the Blue Room. They *said* they were losing money, anyway. And although Ben never believed farmers who claimed to be losing money—the ones who said they were making money were usually the ones who were lying—farmers were going out of business in alarming numbers. Most of them were just tired, Ben believed, like Herb in his diner, and didn't have children willing to be "tied down" to husbandry.

But in any event, part of the problem was low prices combined with all the high expenses of tractor farming. Farmers complaining to Ben, still the captive audience in his cow barn during morning and evening milking, did not seem to be interested in examining the reasons why Ben was not losing money. He wanted to tell them, for example, that while he was working and earning money at milking they were just standing in his cow stable doing nothing. If he had said that, they would have felt insulted and replied, as usual, that it was all the government's fault, encouraging overproduction so that consumers could get cheap food.

"You and Mary can get by because you're livin' like the Amish," Jack Cughes said once. "Most of us believe we have the right to live like our urban counterparts." He really believed that Ben and Mary were operating on money that old Nat Bump had made from moonshine.

"I can't think of anything worse than living like our urban counterparts," Ben said.

Cughes stared at Ben strangely and suddenly remembered that there was a discussion going on that evening in Blue Room about organizing a labor union.

Since Ben rarely sat in the Blue Room and discussed such ideas, did not in fact belong to any farm organizations, he did not pay much attention to all the political rhetoric about the Farm Problem, as it was commonly referred to. So he was wholly unprepared for what happened one evening when he was finishing up milking. As he poured milk through the strainer into cans, he was suddenly aware of a knot of men standing in the darkness right outside the milkhouse. Most of them he knew.

"'Lo, Ben," Dick Farnold said. "Looks like we got here just in time not to have to help with the milking." He meant to be funny, but his voice sounded strained.

"Well, hi, Dick. Oh, there's plenty to do yet. You can crawl up in the mow and throw down a little hay." Everyone laughed, but nervously, the way they would at a preacher's joke. When no one spoke, Ben asked, "What's up?" He was eyeing the man wearing a tie, whom he did not know. He was not surprised when the others turned to the tie for an answer. The spokesmen always wear ties.

"We're here on behalf of all the farmers who are joining the National Farmer's Organization," the man said, extending his hand. Ben kept both of his hands occupied with the milk bucket. "My name is Jim Lebberer and I'm your district representative of NFO. We're hoping that you'll join us in our national effort to save the family farm."

Ben studied the milk strainer. He was not a joiner. Nan had already remonstrated with him for not becoming an NFO member. "You can't get anywhere by being nice," she had scolded him. "The middlemen aren't ever going to give us our share of the profits unless they're forced to." But Ben only shook his head, even though he agreed with her. It was not his way, at least not as long as he could see other more peaceful ways. Cheap as milk was, he could still make a little. If the big-spending farmers couldn't, that was their problem.

He said as much now.

"That's just why we will eventually be forced out of business," Jack Cughes said to him. As head of the school board, he was expected to say something. "We won't unite."

Ben wanted to say that he would not unite behind Jack Cughes for any reason. Jack was one of those guys who liked to be in the limelight as long as nothing special was demanded of him. Ben knew that Jack Cughes wouldn't make any money farming if milk prices doubled. He'd be off somewhere delivering speeches when he should be delivering calves.

"I don't see how uniting can help us make more money," Ben said. "The only way to cut production is to go back to farming sanely, not going out there and seeing how many acres you can run a tractor over in a day or how many cows you can cram into a barn. You think the owners of those big California dairies are willing to cut production? They've got investors who wouldn't let them if they tried."

"You'd think different if you had kids to raise and put through school," Cughes replied.

Now Ben bristled. Cughes was not smart enough to know how that remark cut into him. Or maybe he was. "When our children come along, I don't think I want them in schools that turn out people who make stupid-ass remarks like that," Ben said evenly.

"I apologize for my colleague," said the tie quickly. "We are hard-pressed and don't always say the right thing. We want to demonstrate to farmers and consumers the power we have to raise farm prices. We want to know, when the right time comes, if you will unite with us and go on strike."

"Go on strike?" The idea almost frightened Ben. "A farmer can't go on strike. How do you make your corn go on strike?"

"You hold it off the market."

"How long? They'll know you've got it. They know you have to sell it sometime."

"At our price."

"Won't matter to me. I'll be feeding it to my cows and hogs."

"Hold them off the market."

"Won't work and you know it. They've got to go to market sometime. Gonna let 'em die on the farm? Anyway, I got payments to make."

"So do we all."

The farmers waited. Ben held his silence. He thought their talk was foolish. But he also knew the dangers of not complying with local community pressure. If he didn't cooperate, would he find dead cows in the pasture some morning or his barn set afire, shades of the KKK? Would he be physically attacked the way unions attacked factory workers who wouldn't honor strikes? Men in fear of losing their livelihoods do not fear the law.

"I'll think about it," he finally said. "I don't think it's come to that yet."

He watched them climb into their cars and drive away. He was afraid this would not be the end of it.

When he entered the house, Mary knew by the way he kept staring at the floor that something was amiss. This night of all nights. She had fixed thick T-bone steaks from their own steer, homemade French fries from their own potatoes, and a mince pie from their own mincemeat. She had something special to celebrate and did not want him in one of his withdrawn, sulky moods. She finally pried the reason for his dour face out of him.

"Well, you could dump milk once," she said brightly, somewhat to his surprise. She was obviously in too good a mood to be disturbed by the news. "We could make a bunch of butter out of it and freeze it up."

He smiled then. "But that just shows how impossible the whole idea is. If we did that, we wouldn't be buying butter. And we'd be encouraging people to buy oleo."

"Well, I've been thinking of starting to churn butter anyway. You know we could live pretty good without making any money at all once we got the farm paid for."

Ben mulled over her particularly playful mood. Maybe he could tell her the part of the meeting with the farmers that was really upsetting him.

"That Jack Cughes is an ass," he said. "He had the nerve to tell me that we'd be more inclined to dump milk if we had the expense of children to raise. I like to busted him in the jaw."

Instead of the hurt, worried look that usually came over her face at the mention of children, Mary smiled. Without a word, she lit the candles she had kept out of sight in the pantry and set them on the table before Ben's mystified eyes. Then she poured some of her homemade dandelion wine in their glasses. Ben followed her every move, wonderment overwhelming him. She lifted her glass and beckoned him to do the same.

"Here's to that ass Jack Cughes," she said. "You tell him we for sure will start dumping milk at his every command, for we are going to have a baby and couldn't afford to do otherwise."

Ben's eyes shone bright in the candle flames. "You mean, you mean . . ."

"Yep."

Each threw an arm around the other, and they danced around the room so vigorously that the cat on the windowsill outside became alarmed and scurried back to the barn.

Nan was in such a bitchy mood that Mary almost changed her mind about telling her about the baby. Nan had been out of sorts for a long time. It had something to do with Emmet, Mary was sure, but what, she could not divine. Now that Emmet and Ginny's divorce was public knowledge, Mary had assumed that he and Nan would arrive at a more peaceable relationship. But if that had happened, it was not apparent. Mary feared that telling Nan about her pregnancy might only make her sister-in-law feel more alone. But if she didn't tell before the pregnancy became obvious, Nan would be irritated too.

Mary knocked on the kitchen door, yoo-hooed, and went on in as was her habit. Dorothy was peeling potatoes, an arduous task now that arthritis had warped her hands. Mary had not seen her for a few weeks, and noted sadly how much she was aging even in that short length of time. Nan was reading the paper, evidently having just come in from the barn. Her long-sleeved shirt hung out over her manure-speckled jeans. Her hair was covered by a large blue bandanna tied in the back. Even in work clothes carelessly worn, Nan looked pretty. In fact Mary often thought that careless dress accentuated Nan's beauty.

"Look what the cat drug in, Mom," Nan said by way of greeting. "It's been a while." She put the paper down, took a knife from the drawer, and began helping her mother with the potatoes. Mary found a knife and joined them.

She remarked on the nice size of the potatoes. That led to the usual exchange of information about how much their gardens had produced that year, as if they lived a hundred miles apart instead of in the same neighborhood. But Nan seemed tense. Noncommittal, too. Mind on something else. After a pause, Mary gathered herself in her chair and smiled.

"Well, I've some good news. We're going to have a baby."

Dorothy threw her hands in the air, jumped up, and hugged her daughter-in-law. Nan reacted with a certain reluctance, a sort of combination of joy and reserve, the way Ben looked when desperately needed rain fell to help the corn just after he had mowed hay.

"I thought you'd been looking extra glowy," Dorothy said. "When's it due? I bet Ben hasn't come down out of the sky since you told him."

"An April baby, it appears," Mary said. She was watching Nan closely. Something wasn't right.

"Spring babies always get off to a good start, like spring lambs," Dorothy said. Nan finally hugged Mary too, but there was a detachment in her manner that she could not hide. "Whatcha gonna name him?"

"Well, it might be a girl. I was actually thinking of naming her Nan."

Instead of looking pleased, Nan objected. "Oh, you shouldn't do that. I'm just a wayward crank of a bitch, not a name to saddle your child with." Both Mary and Dorothy stared at her. If she had laughed as she spoke, they would have understood, but there was more conviction in her voice than she had meant to put there. Now Mary knew for sure that something was wrong.

"Nan, what's the matter?"

Nan got up and walked out the door. Mary stared at Dorothy, who shrugged, inured to her daughter's fits and starts. Mary caught up with Nan halfway to the barn.

"What *is* the matter," she asked again. "I tell you good news and you stomp out the door."

Nan whirled, embraced Mary, and sobbed uncontrollably. "Oh, Mary, I'm pregnant too."

Minutes passed before either of them could speak again. By then, they had walked to the springhouse.

"Does Emmet know yet?" Mary asked.

"Huh. He's not the only man around, you know," Nan snapped, spunky even in her desperation.

Mary could not repress a smile. "Have you told him?"

"Hell, no, and I won't, either." And she broke into tears again.

"Nan, come on. You know he loves you and you love him. And he's free to marry now. It's really good news, not bad."

"Oh, you don't know my family. Mom's sisters will have conniptions. Those old-time Catholics don't believe in marrying a divorced person. You don't know how I'll be chewed up and spit back out again. And besides, he won't say it."

"Who won't say what?"

"Emmet won't. He can't bring himself to say those words. I. Love. You. I don't think he really does."

"Yes, he really does. Emmet just doesn't know his own mind and hardly ever has. He's so full of trying to live up to being a Gowler that he doesn't know his true self."

"Well, ever since, ah, ever since it happened, he hasn't said a word to me. He got what he wanted and then off to see his boys in Florida again."

"No, no, Nan. He's just ashamed. He figures he took advantage of you, I bet. He's too ashamed to talk to you."

"Yeah, ashamed all right. Ashamed of me. Thinks Gowlers are way high up above Bumps. He'll say I did it on purpose, to force him to marry me. And that would be the end of anything between us."

"No, Nan. Ashamed of himself."

"Why isn't he man enough to say so?"

"Give him time. And give yourself time. You have a hard question to answer too, you know, and it isn't about your being pregnant. If it's gonna work out, you have to be able to be a real mother to his boys. Emmet isn't stupid. He's wondering about that, you know. He thinks he can get his kids back at least half the time if he could show a stable home life. He would like that. My mom says that once you have children, life is never your own again. Never. Till the day you die."

Nan had stopped crying. It was true. She would never be able to love Emmet's boys as if they were her own.

"But you could love them plenty enough to make a marriage work." Mary was reading her mind again. "You know what your problem is, Nan? You think everything should work out perfect. That everybody should measure up. Life isn't that way. Everyone's imperfect. Accept it. See the good side. What if neither of us ever had a baby? That happens to women who want children, you know. They learn to bear it. Wouldn't you rather have a baby under any circumstances than not?"

Nan wouldn't answer.

"I thought so," Mary continued. "C'mon, cheer up. If your family throws a fit, let them. You know Ben and I will stand by you. And so will Emmet if you stand by him."

Nan stared at Mary. "You're a good person, Mary Bump."

"Go tell Emmet. Now."

"To hell with Emmet."

But she told him anyway. It took all the humility she could muster, and humility was not her strong point. If he said one word, even gave one look that said one word about her taking advantage of him to force a marriage, she would find a way to bankrupt the whole damn Gowler family and see him end up in a shack in Killdeer. She found him in his office, catching up on grain elevator paperwork. He smiled at the sight of her. He had not been sure she would ever speak to him again.

"Gotta talk," she said, and went back out to her truck.

He followed, puzzled and unsuspecting. She beckoned him to get in the truck, which he did, and she spun out of the parking lot and onto the road, heading south out of Gowler.

"Sure is good to see you," he said clumsily, remembering the last time they had occupied the cab together. "I've missed you."

"Yeah. Missed the heck out of me down there in Florida." She realized that she wasn't acting the way Mary had advised.

He took her jab submissively. What else could he do? "Well, I'm back now and I'm glad to see you."

"Emmet, I'm pregnant."

He did not so much as move an eyelid for the next mile. Just stared out the windshield, as if stone-deaf or stone-dead. What surprised him was how glad he was to hear it. Now they would *have* to go forward together.

She in turn took his silence negatively—the bastard was going to say that it was my fault, that I did it on purpose, her mind was saying. The more the apprehension grew in her, the harder her foot pressed on the accelerator. Then she had an even more outrageous thought. The idiot thinks maybe that poor Henry Remp finally got to me. That thought pushed her foot down on the accelerator even farther. The longer Emmet remained silent, the more furious she became. If he said the wrong thing—and almost anything he said would be the wrong thing at this juncture—it would be the end of their relationship.

"Nan, would you please slow down. I can hear a rod about to go slammin' out right through the hood."

For once he had totally baffled her. And he had done so without intending to gain some advantage, but solely out of fear of dying. The speedometer needle of the rickety old truck was bouncing up against eighty. Nan was not used to hearing the totally unexpected. She not only slowed down but jammed on the breaks and skidded to a stop.

"Just what the hell does that mean?" she barked at him.

"It means that I don't want our *child* killed before it's born."

Nan stared at him, totally disarmed. The hostility drained from her face. By God, when things got right up to the edge of the cliff, the idiot wasn't so dumb after all. "Say it," she ordered. And when he looked puzzled, she repeated: "Goddamnit, say it!" And in truth when Emmet Gowler was really standing on the edge of the cliff, all pretense and worry and calculation stripped away, when life was just there before him beyond all artifice, he did know what was required of him.

"I love you, Nan. But goddamnit, you know that."

Emmet's admission was still not enough. Nor was it enough that he stood by her through the tense days that followed, when Nan felt the brunt of righteous indignation from her parents and her mother's entire family. It did not even help when Emmet's mother and those ancient grandaunts of his, Iva and Ironia, supported her, grudgingly, or at least accepted her pregnancy without religious prejudice. They had their own brand of prejudice to come to terms with. "Might be what you'd expect from Killdeer trash," Ironia said, as if the almighty pure blood of the Gowlers had had no part in conceiving the baby. Nan, aware of that kind of prejudice too, became convinced that Emmet was only making a show of loyalty and responsibility because it was the honorable thing for a Gowler to do. After another big fight with her mother about marrying divorced men and Dorothy's insistence that the baby had to be "brought up Catholic," she told Emmet she couldn't marry him.

"I by God don't need your sympathy," was the way she put it instead of admitting that the family opposition was too much for her to endure.

"Well, by God, then don't marry me. Do whatever you goddamn please because you will anyway. But just remember, that's my baby too and I aim to help raise it."

"You only got my word for that," she said, tormenting him.

"Jeez. You are too much." And away he stomped. Nan started after him to apologize, then caught herself. Started again, stopped, waited for him to turn back to her. He did not. "You are one stupid woman," she muttered to herself, and then went to the barn to start evening chores.

Her father had already brought the steers in off the scanty late fall pasture, and broken a few bales of hay in their mangers. His disappointment and disgust over his daughter showed whenever he had to look at her, so he avoided her eyes as much as possible. Out of her hearing, he was punctuating almost every mumbled sentence with "Gott in Himmel." When he saw Nan come into the barn now, he turned abruptly away. Nan had tried to act contrite, hoping to gain his forgiveness. But now that Mary knew of her shame, now that the secret was out, she did not feel shame. Just anger.

"You know something, Dad," she addressed his back. "I'll bet you and Mom had sex before you were married."

His body stiffened, but he did not turn around.

"I'm right, right?"

"Mind your manners, young lady." Then he stomped out of the barn. He had suddenly decided that he should go back and check a floodgate. He never brought up the subject again.

Trying to keep his mind from fussing and fuming over Nan, Emmet had taken up golf that fall, and that led him to another brainstorm. He was sitting in his pickup, staring disgustedly at a field of soybeans that he had not been able to harvest because of wet weather. And here it was almost Thanksgiving. It had been wet all summer, and in the heavy clay soil the beans had fared poorly and were hardly worth harvesting.

"There isn't twenty pods on most of those plants," he said. "I could make more money off this farm if I turned it into a golf course."

He meant it as a joke, and Jake Lavendar, in the cab beside him, took it as such. "Aye, and the fairways would fairly be half under water after every big rain," he said. They looked at each other and laughed, but Emmet stopped laughing almost immediately. On second thought, why not a golf course? His lightning-quick mind had in that instant made the decision. Crazy as it sounded, he knew he was going to do it. Knew it before he even ran the numbers. Knew it even when the numbers did not hold up very well. He went straightaway to talk to his uncle.

Cyrus Gowler was in no mood to entertain any more crazy notions from his nephew and dismissed him out of hand. Emmet appealed to his mother and to his aunts. They held the purse strings. "But look here, Mother, I'm the one who's going to do the work." He knew he could play on her sympathy. Her poor fatherless son and all that. "I'm all you got to keep this farm together, and I can keep it together with golf. I can make more money selling golf balls than I can selling beans." He pulled records, mostly out of his hat, to show that the land in Swamp Poodle had never made any money since during the war.

"Even if a golf course breaks even, it will be better'n beans."

"What's a golf course cost?"

"Depends. We could go at it gradual. Don't have to try to shape it all up in one year. Can do nine holes instead of eighteen."

"There's not a dozen people around here who play golf."

"Oh, you'd be surprised. And we can pull in people from as far away as Delaware and Columbus now that the new highway is in."

"What do you know about making a golf course?"

"Oh, there's companies lay out courses for you. And if I can grow wheat, I can darn well grow golf course grass."

Eventually he beat her down. And the rest of the reigning family members. They grew tired of being bothered. At the very worst, the money would not exactly be wasted. They could refer to the golf course as their very own country club in conversation with their urban friends.

"Well," his mother said, as her final word, "I guess if it doesn't work out we can always plow it up and plant it to beans again."

Uncle Cy almost relented: "If you can get Ben Bump to say he'll play golf, I'll go along with it." Uncle Cy was sure that Ben Bump would never play golf.

That evening, in from the barn, Ben had pulled off his boots and was relaxing while listening to the radio news. The phone rang. He tried to outwait Mary because he hated to talk on the phone. But she was busy at the stove. Resignedly, he lifted the receiver and said hello.

"Ben, this is Emmet. I have a favor to ask of you." Emmet was the only farmer Ben knew who never small-talked before he got down to the business at hand.

"What's up."

"If you were to be asked in the near future if you liked to play golf, would you say yes?"

Ben was baffled. He had not thought that Emmet could ever surprise him again. Must be a joke. He'd play along.

"Play golf? I've never played golf and you know it."

"Well, you might like to play golf if you tried it."

"Emmet, whatever are you up to? You want me to play golf with you?"

The disbelief in his voice was plainly evident.

"Just curious. You like to play baseball and football. I'm just sure you'd like golf if you once tried it."

"What *are* you up to?"

"C'mon, will you just say, if someone should ask, that you wouldn't mind playing a little golf some day. You don't ever really have to play. Just say you'd like to."

"Not unless you tell me what you're up to."

"Oh, all right. I'm thinking about building a golf course on Swamp Poodle. By God, if it won't grow beans maybe it'll grow greens." It came out in a rhyme. Emmet thought it sounded clever so he repeated it. "Won't grow beans, why not greens."

Ben laughed. "I think you found some of Miser Meincer's hooch."

"Uncle Cy said that if you would play golf, he'd go along with the finances."

"Oh, I see. And when it goes broke, it'll be my fault."

"Jeez. Will you just tell Cy you wouldn't mind playing a little golf if he asks?"

"I've got a feeling I'm going to regret this."

A couple of weeks later, Ben was in the bank making his farm payment. It was kind of a milestone. Only ten more years and he'd be out of debt if he could keep up the rate of repayment he had bound himself to, which was five hundred dollars more per year than the repayment schedule actually called for. Ten more years and then he'd be free and no one could ever take his land away from him.

"I see you're paying off faster than you need to," Cy Gowler said, pleased. As a banker he was not pleased, but as a businessman he was. "There's a chance, however, that you could be investing that extra five hundred into something that would increase your income by a thousand. Have you thought of that?"

"There's also a chance I could invest that five hundred in something that would lose a thousand."

Cy smiled. It wasn't often he heard young men talk the way that he had figured things when he was climbing up the ladder. "You'll go far in this world, Ben, my boy," he said, echoing Ben's mother.

"Only as far as I want to go."

"And that will be farther than the richest people go," Gowler said with approval. Then, as if the thought had just then occurred to him, he added:

"Say, do you like golf?

"Don't rightly know." Ben replied, keeping his face straight only with effort. "Never tried it." He waited while Cy nodded understandingly.

"But you know, I wouldn't mind taking a crack at it some time."

"Oh, really?" Cy showed surprise.

"If there was a course around here someplace. I wouldn't drive all the way to Delaware or Columbus, that's for sure."

And so the people of Gowler Village had something really crazy to gossip about. A golf course? "I thought I had imagined everything possible for Killdeer," Miser Meincer said whenever he had the chance to talk to anyone. "To think that where that boy's great-great-grandfather made history by becoming the Wool King of the World, grazing sheep and trail-herding them to Philadelphia and Baltimore, is now going to be a city slicker's playground. Might as well tell me that Bowsherville will be reborn."

The first money the golf course produced, however, went to Ben Bump. He volunteered to make hay from the grass and weeds that in a second year would hopefully turn into fairways. Emmet let him have the hay for free, remarking wryly that Ben's profit from the golf course was the last profit anyone made from it.

While Emmet fussed over the golf course, Nan and Mary grew big with child. Ben could think of nothing else but the birthing, so much so that on several occasions he would come into the house of an evening and only then remember that he had forgotten to slop the hogs, or gather the eggs, or turn the cows out of the stable. Then he had to go back to the barn, embarrassed, to finish up properly.

But despite his and Mary's feelings of happy anticipation, the war between Nan and Emmet continued. Just about when they seemed to be patching things up, Emmet would feel the need to go visit his boys in Florida, which would put Nan in a vile mood. She grew particularly intransigent when he spent Christmas in Florida, "abandoning me," she complained querulously to Mary, pretending more travail than she actually felt, hoping for sympathy. "And all he wants to talk about is that stupid golf course."

Nan, perhaps as a way to compete with the golf course, had also received a financial vision from on high. If cows and sheep and pigs wouldn't make a decent profit on her farm, maybe horses would. She would raise fancy horses, which she would sell for fancy prices to fancy people. She decided on Arabians for no particular reason that she could explain, and bought two mares and a stallion, which cost her seventy-five hundred dollars.

"Gott in Himmel!" Nat mumbled when he heard, but he did not outwardly oppose her decision. In her situation, the poor girl needed all the encouragement she could get. Nat had in fact disobeyed his rule about "not making trouble" in the community by telling Dorothy's two sisters, forever quaking about Nan's "condition," to mind their own business. Nan hugged him for that, the first hug in a year or so. Dorothy got the message too, and began to take Nan's side when relatives dared to start their incessant hand-wringing in her presence. Some semblance of peace and understanding returned to the Bump homestead.

But with Emmet, not so, except to the extent that Nan quit pretending to be displeased with his visits. She had found another way to make him suffer. Whenever, in desperation for something to talk about other than the coming birth, he brought up the subject of his golf course, she would talk horses. Conversation would follow a certain predictable pattern.

"Been too wet to do much work on laying out the greens, but the course is all surveyed and planned out on paper."

"I shoulda got horses sooner. Why raise an animal that sells for three hundred dollars when I can raise one that sells for fifteen hundred dollars on the same hay and grain?"

"I'm going to put a couple of ponds on the course. A nice touch, don't you think?"

"I think the real money is going to be in getting some of those rich bitches in Columbus to board their horses with me."

"And they can play golf while they're up here."

"And if the golf doesn't work out, you can use the course for polo and I'll furnish the horses. What do you call a place where you play polo? A polo course?"

It was a long winter.

Came an unseasonably warm week in late February with the snowdrop flowers popping up and blooming on southern exposures as fast as the snow melted. Nan was tired of carrying the baby. Choring was difficult now, especially when she had to bend over, but she was too stubborn to let her father take over completely for her. Less than two more months. It would be such a relief and a release. And she was itching to ride her horses. She wondered sometimes whether she was meant to be a mother. Why couldn't you just order babies from Sears and Roebuck?

"Think I'll go for a little horseback ride," she said to her mother, teasing.

"No, you will not, young lady," Dorothy retorted hotly.

"Oh, c'mon, Mom. Just a little trot around the pasture."

Dorothy would later say that Nan was tempting God with talk like that because of what happened next. Nan would blame it all on a corncob. What a corncob was doing on the steps leading down from the main level of the barn to the cow stanchions on the ground floor no one could explain, unless, according to Dorothy's theology, God had put it there to bring Nan's pride down. At any rate, Nan stepped on the cob, which, as cobs will do, rolled under her boot. Nan lost her balance, her feet shot out from under her, and she bounced halfway down the stairs. That she was able to save herself from falling all the way was, in Dorothy's view again, because God really did care for her, even if, for a moment, He had been inclined to punish her.

Nat, feeding the hogs, heard her yell and then cry out for help. He found her spread-eagled out on the steps, breathing heavily, trying to right herself.

"Mein Gott."

Nan thought she knew immediately of two facts. She had broken no bones. And she was going to lose the baby.

Staggering, Nat carried her to the car, shouting for Dorothy.

"She fell. Call Emmet."

"Emmet, hell. Call the doctor," Nan said.

"We're going to the hospital, " Nat said to her. She did not protest.

Emmet knew something was wrong. Jake had not bothered to stop at the shed they referred to as the clubhouse, but had careened across what they referred to as the fairway, making huge ruts where Emmet had carefully and painstakingly leveled the ground for what would be the green on hole no. 5. But he did not have time to protest.

"Get in, quick. I fairly got some bad news for you. Nan's gone and fell and she's on her way to the hospital."

Emmet could tell from the look on the doctor's face that things were not going well. But not going as bad as they might.

"The baby's delivered. It's in an incubator. There's a chance. A good chance, but I don't want you to hope too much."

Nan was heavily sedated and hardly recognized him, or Dorothy or Mary or Ben, who soon arrived. When she did talk, it was to demand that she see her baby.

Emmet took her hand. "The baby's okay, Nan. It's *okay*. A boy."

"Don't lie to me. Take me to him."

"Oh, no, you don't," the nurse standing by said. "You just lay there and rest. We got to get the bleeding stopped."

"Well, then bring the baby here." Even in her helplessness, Nan could be difficult.

"Just you relax, now," Emmet said. "Everything's being take care of. What happened, anyway?"

"Goddamn corncob," she said. It would have been funny under other circumstances. Then she faded out of full consciousness again.

For a full twenty-four hours, the baby's life hung in the balance. No one would or could say one way or the other. For all that time, Emmet did not eat, would hardly leave Nan's bedside except to check the baby, hooked up to a respirator. Whenever Nan roused enough to know what was going on, it was Emmet's face that met her fuzzy vision, and slowly it seeped into her consciousness that this man really did love her. He would describe the baby to her in minute detail, how its little premature body was totally whole and perfect, every finger, every toenail absolutely perfect.

"What will we name him?" he would ask.

Finally she answered. "How about Floyd?" She knew that would please him.

"You say that because you know I would be pleased."

"Yes," she replied.

When the baby did not show solid signs of recovery, Emmet, in his usual way, grew more belligerent.

"Honey, he's gonna make it, I know," he said. "He's just as stubborn as you are."

"You're really meaning that he's not going to make it," she replied, steely-eyed. But even in that extremity, she noticed that he had called her "honey" for the first time.

"No, he's going to make it. Tough little booger. But I want to do something just in case. Just in case."

"What do you mean, do something," Nan asked, the fear in her increasing.

"I want to get married. Right now. Right this very minute. If Floyd doesn't pull through, I want by God for him to die as our legitimate son."

Although it was not a time for rejoicing, Nan felt a flutter of joy. He really must love her. He wanted to get married even though that "for better or for worse" was decidedly the latter. He wanted to get married even if Floyd did not live. He must love her for her own sake. She nodded consent.

"Get Father O'Brien here pronto," Emmet said to Nat, "and if he can't perform the ceremony right now and fast, I'll get someone who will."

Father O'Brien was summoned, and although he displayed some misgivings about the impromptu nature of the wedding and whether the bride and groom were truly penitent and worthy of the sacrament of matrimony, and the fact that Emmet was a divorced man, he knew this was no time to quibble over canon law. It might mean Gowler money flowing regularly into the church, a possibility that could override a considerable amount of theological doubt. The reverend conjured up a suitable ceremony, half Catholic and half pure inspiration, and brought it off in his usual lordly fashion.

Nan, upright in bed, and Emmet, sitting on the edge of the bed, pronounced their vows in agonizing uncertainty. Never had the old refrain of "in sickness and in health" carried such poignancy. Emmet fished from his pocket his grandmother Della's huge diamond ring, which he had somehow talked his mother into giving him, and put it on her finger.

"Oh, wow, Emmet. I can't wear that to the barn."

"Grandmother did, so I don't see why you can't." Nan did not protest further.

Dorothy would say that what happened after the wedding absolutely proved the existence of a just God, and even Nat would not outwardly dispute her even though he wanted badly to point out that in the depth of the crisis, she had said that her just God was punishing Nan for her wayward ways. As if somehow the aura of matrimonial legitimacy carried with it the power of health, the baby began to show signs of strength. Before Nan's and Emmet's rapt faces, Floyd began to breathe stronger, began to cry, began to smack his lips in anticipation of sucking. By the next day, he could breathe long enough on his own that Nan could nurse him, though, said the doctor, it was another miracle that Nan had any milk. The time that mother and child could be together increased at each session, and three days later, Nan refused to let the nurses take the baby from her.

"I know how to keep him better than that goddamn respirator," Nan said, and everyone feared to dispute her. In ten days Floyd was on his own, out of danger. And his parents could sit together, holding hands, and not argue. No need to talk at all.

Three weeks later, Mary and Ben were parents too, but as Mary would say, the event was almost anticlimactic, after Floyd's birth.

"In case you haven't noticed, Nan and Emmet have a way of eclipsing us in everything," Ben said, only a little ruefully, only a little enviously. He could only view the tempestuous relationship between his sister and his friend with apprehension, if not downright sorrow. He never understood how people could make life so difficult for themselves.

Ben and Mary's baby, a boy too, they named Nathaniel, after his grandfather. Mary decreed that the boy would be called Natty but did not explain that she was thinking of Natty Bumppo in the classic *The Last of the Mohicans*. Natty just might someday be the last of the husbandmen. Nat was pleased more than any earthly or unearthly reward that he could imagine. He now had two grandsons: one to be a wealthy Gowler someday, the other to be the smartest farmer in the county. How could life be so good? Or, as he would say when filled with emotion, how could life be so *gut*?

Henry Remp, with the cunning that comes from being a constant underdog in the struggle for money, decided that Emmet Gowler's golf course was an opportunity that he could take advantage of. The Gowlers must not be making much money farming, he concluded, or they would never have plowed up good soybean land. He and his father were moving forward, but that was different. Remps could squeeze nickels into dollars, something no Gowler, accustomed to having plenty, understood. Despite low farm prices, the Remps were expanding acreage, concentrating on small additions. Forty acres here, sixty acres there, never getting in over their heads, but by slow accretions they had already put together six hundred acres and were headed for more. Much of their land was Killdeer jackwax and so sold for less than the going rate, but they knew how to farm it. Now Henry wondered if the golf course just might be the undoing of fancypants Emmet Gowler. If he worked it right, the Remps just might get their hands on some Gowler land.

His scheme involved Nan Bump, now Nan Gowler, whom he'd like to get his hands on too. He was convinced that she desired him as much as he desired her, and so a plan that he would have considered stupid under any other circumstance seemed plausible. He waited until he knew Emmet was occupied at the Gowler holdings farthest from his home, and then boldly drove up to the Gowler mansion and knocked on the door.

Had Nan known who was knocking, she would not have opened, or if she had, would have prettied up a bit just to taunt him. In her new role as mistress of the manor, she was living in what was for her a dream world. She and Emmet had not gotten into a single argument since they married. Well, maybe a couple of little ones. Although she had at first been leery of moving into his big house, where surely the presence of Ginny would weigh heavily on Emmet's subconscious, she had finally agreed. Fixing up the old house on her farm had been her first plan, but between Arabian horses and golf greens there was no ready money for doing the remodeling. But, even discounting the finances, it would have been perfectly stupid not to move into Em's house. At first she felt awkward there, but soon adapted and found herself glorying in the faux-marble bathtub, mother-of-pearl toilet seats, solid walnut and cherry wall paneling, green Vermont slate entryways, and fieldstone fireplaces that so many years ago Ben had described to her in awed tones. And, most astounding of all, a whole huge third floor, empty and forlorn, that had once been, in Victorian times, a ballroom. A ballroom, for godsakes. In Gowler, Ohio. A huge room whose only purpose was partying and putting on airs. That a kid from Killdeer could end up in a marble bathtub was so preposterous to her that she found herself giggling every time she sat down in it.

As it was, she opened the door with baby Floyd in one arm, her hair a mess, her jeans showing stains of recent visits to the barn. Seeing Henry Remp standing there was almost frightening, or would have been if she were not overwhelmed with curiosity. She quickly recovered from her surprise and struck a lofty, queenly pose, at least as much as possible with a baby in one arm. Queenly as in Madonna and Child, she thought. She did not greet him but waited, the way she figured the mistress of the manor would wait for a servant to speak.

Remp, for his part, had rehearsed just how he would present himself, affecting great humility, not even daring to raise his eyes to her.

"I beg your pardon, Mrs. Gowler. I was just passing by and thought I would stop to congrat—"

"What do you want?" she cut him off.

"I was looking for Emmet."

"You know where Emmet is as well as I do. Maybe better."

"Well, I thought he was in the fields over Blackstown way, but couldn't find him there," Henry lied.

"Well, then I don't know where he is either."

"Well, what I wanted to ask him about might be better spoke to you, come to think of it."

Floyd started to fuss. "Better spoken," she corrected Henry's grammar.

Henry forged ahead, ignoring her retort, which he did not understand anyway. "Meanin' no presumption about anything, you know, but if a fella don't ask, a fella can't find out."

Nan jiggled the restless baby. This better be good.

"My father and I, uh, we're lookin' for land, like everyone is, and I just wanted to ask, just ask, mind you, if with all the work you have with your young'un now and those horses and buildin' the golf course, if maybe you'd be thinkin of rentin' out some of your land. Or maybe even if you ever gave any thought to sellin' the Black farm." And he shot a quick smile in her direction, hoping it suggested a little more than a business inquiry—maybe, just maybe, a fleeting allusion to the sexual interest he was sure she felt toward him.

Nan did not laugh as she wanted to. Actually, she could appreciate his request. Everything was fair in war, especially the kind of war waged to get more land. She wouldn't have thought that he'd have the guts to ask. But it was the little smile, his oozing male arrogance, that galled her.

"*Mister* Remp, I have no idea what kind of daydreams your teeny mind has cooked up, but as far as the Black farm goes, it would have to snow ten feet deep in hell and freeze the devil's ass to solid brass before I'd sell you, or rent you, one clod of dirt. If you have any other business, you take it up with Emmet. But I wouldn't advise it."

Remp headed back to his car, cowed but not altogether dismayed. He hadn't really expected any more or less from her, the bitch, but at least he'd conveyed a furtive notion that he was still interested in her, which is what he was so sure she wanted to know. That was the main thing. And the next time he asked about renting or buying land, it wouldn't be so difficult. One day, when he was as rich as any Gowler, and goddamn Emmet had been brought down, she'd come crawling.

Meantime, he had some other notions of how to get Gowler land. He was not sure if old Floyd Gowler's empire was back under one partnership after it had been split up, so folks said, to get Emmet the money to pay his government fines. But if Ironia and Iva Gowler still owned parts of it independently, at least on paper, maybe he could rent their parts. He'd heard that the old bitches loved money above all. Then, too, asking might at least reveal the current status of the farm ownership. He'd offer them more than they could refuse. Even if they still refused, maybe they would then insist that Emmet pay more. If Emmet had to pay more, maybe he'd go broke quicker.

Renting land had only recently become a burning issue in the neighborhood. As Cy Gowler liked to remind the staff at the bank, as long as everyone had been content to produce both livestock and grain, marketing their crops more profitably through their animals than selling them direct, the need to expand to more land was not as intense. But as more farmers abandoned husbandry and embraced machinery—"new-iron disease," as Ben called it— the equipment costs started to climb and grain overproduction caused prices to fall. The more that situation dominated economics, the hotter grew the demand for more land to farm. Iva and Ironia, among other elderly widows, loved the attention their land ownership attracted. There was something a bit devilish about hosting young farmers in their drawing rooms. And to sedate old ladies, all farmers were young.

Iva had come home from New York to live with her sister Ironia in their waning years, and both found Henry Remp especially entertaining and quite handsome in a rough sort of way. Although they had no intention of renting to him at any price, and couldn't anyway without Cyrus's concurrence, they plied him with cookies and tea until he had upped his first offer of sixty dollars an acre to sixty-five, an outrageous sum in 1961. When neither responded favorably, but still seemed interested in him, he changed his strategy. He would rent on the halves. He would supply the labor and machinery, they the land. Other costs, and the profit of course, would be split between them. He figured he could cheat the old bitches and they'd never know.

Ironia glanced at Iva knowingly. She would lead the poor boy on. It would be interesting to see just how far he would go.

"My la-a-a-nds sake," she exclaimed, liking the sound of a phrase she had never used before in her life, "you make a most generous offer, young man. But you see, our land is, well, some of it requires better drainage, and I wonder how you think about that."

"Well, yes, ma'am. All the land around here needs better drainage, and I would encourage you to put in more tile. It will repay you a hundredfold. I have always urged my landlor—uh, clients—to spend money on tile. Best investment you can make."

"Well, it would repay *you* a hundredfold too," Ironia said, batting her eyes like she figured Betty Grable would do in the act of exposing a long stretch of leg. "I would only rent under the condition that you help pay for any new tiling or other improvements. Have another cookie."

Henry Remp thought rapidly. Renters never had to pay for long-term improvements since they could lose the land the next year. But perhaps he could make an exception. It would be worth it just to hurt Emmet Gowler.

"I suppose I might agree to that. This one time."

The man's a fool, Ironia thought. Or he's up to something else. She could hardly wait to tell Emmet. Out loud she practiced her "la-a-a-nds sake" again and said she'd "think about it."

When Henry told his father of his possible success, Lem scowled at him. "Boy, ain't you got no sense atall? You'll lose your ass renting land that way. And that old bitch would take it away from you the minute you paid your share of the tiling. Ain't I taught you nothin'?"

"But Pa, it's a way to get our foot in the door."

"It's a way to get your foot in your mouth."

Iva and Ironia went right down to the bank and told Cyrus, and Cyrus went right over to the grain elevator to tell Emmet, and

Emmet picked up the phone and told Nan, who immediately called her mother, and very soon the whole neighborhood was laughing heartily over the news that a Remp had tried to rent Gowler land. But amid the laughter, Ironia did point out, glancing narrowly at Emmet, that the poor Remp boy had been willing to pay sixty-five-dollars-an-acre rent. Perhaps Emmet might as well? "Oh, sure," Emmet replied. "Or perhaps the really smart thing to do would be to rent out all our land to lunatics like Henry Remp until they went broke."

But in the end the aunts caused Emmet a financial problem, not Henry Remp. They died within three months of each other, dropping a bomb of inheritance tax on the farm partnership. Cy Gowler kept staring at the figures and growling, as if threatening them would make them fall in line the way he wanted them to. He was trying to figure out how to pay the tax without selling land or borrowing money. The Gowlers had become "land-poor"—rich in evaluated holdings but short on cash. The partners had spent the reserves to pay Emmet's fines and build the golf course.

"We can either borrow about a hundred thousand dollars or sell some land," he said to Emmet, seated on the other side of the desk. "The government'll give us a little leeway, a plan to pay off the tax over time, but the sonsabitches want a nice chunk up front too."

"I can't believe we owe that much, " Emmet said.

"Well, there's four thousand acres of land, all told, valued at five hundred dollars an acre at least, and that comes to over two million dollars, counting in the value of the machinery and houses. Iva and Ironia were full partners in this, and you're inheriting their parts, and you gotta pay that tax one way or another. And you are borrowed up to your chin at the bank what with that golf course and all."

"Well, there must be considerable cash I'm inheriting too," Emmet said. "That oughta cover it."

"I thought so too, but they don't have all that much. And they willed most of it to your boys in Florida. I tried to talk them out of that. Always a dumb idea to skip a generation in passing on inheritance."

"I won't sell, hell or high water," Emmet said with finality. "You can lend me the money privately if the bank can't. You owe it to the farm. That's where your money came from."

Cy smiled. He liked that kind of spunk, even though most of his money came from investing in stocks.

"Don't think I'm going to be your sugar daddy. You're going to have to pay me back regular, and you're going to have to cut back unnecessary spending to the bone."

Emmet was barely listening. When things got tough, he thought offensively, not defensively. The State of Ohio had been buying up Killdeer land to make a wildlife refuge. Although farmers who lived in the area didn't think the wildlife needed any help, the government could always pay more for land than a farmer would. Selling Killdeer land to the state of Ohio had saved more than one landowner's mortgaged hide.

"Cy, I know that money glides while land abides, but don't you think this is a good time to unload that three hundred down in the swamps to the wildlife people? The wildlife owns it anyway, so why shouldn't we get paid for feeding them all these years?"

"They aren't buying any more, I hear."

"Bet they are."

Cy hesitated.

"They just don't want to appear eager," Emmet continued, seeing he had his uncle's attention. "Maybe we can sell and then talk them into paying us to grow wildlife food on it. That's about what we're doing now anyway."

Cy smiled. The boy might yet get somewhere in business. "See what they've got to say."

And so it eventually came to pass. Emmet could pay his inheritance taxes to the state by getting the state to pay him for land that was not making him any money anyway. And there was money left over to pay the last of his debt to Cy. "Money never goes away, just 'round and 'round," he told Ben gleefully.

"You got that right," Ben replied, in more or less good humor. "It goes 'round and 'round from one rich person to another."

But before the sale went through, Emmet had another problem to deal with. When he pulled into his driveway one evening a few weeks later, Miser Meincer was leaning on his mailbox.

"Heerd you're selling to the state," Miser said.

Emmet nodded. He could not tell Miser's mood.

"That's where my pappy lived, you know. Way back. He owned some of that ground at one time, and it ain't rightly ever been decided whether he actually sold all of it to your grandfather. I don't recollect anybody actually knowed just how they worked that out. Property lines are hard to keep up in the swamp."

"What are you saying?"

"T'ain't no bother to me, as all the land belongs to the Delawares and Wyandots far as I'm concerned, but the Remps have grazin' rights on some of my land and they say also on some of the land you're fixin' to sell. Something about a long-ago understandin' that they had with my pap and your grandpap. I allus went along with it, not carin' one way or t'other so long as they took care of the fence like the agreement called for. Now Henry Remp's been stormin' at me and says he has rights to that ground, that they been using it for forty years without any protest and so have legal right of way there and you can't sell it 'less he releases it, and he by God ain't going to release it. He thinks he can void your sale."

Emmet laughed. "What a lot of crap."

"Says the title ain't free."

"What a lot of crap," Emmet said again.

"Says he can tie it up in court for a long time."

"We'll see about that."

After Miser left, Emmet stormed into the house, his neck glowing red. He'd had it with the Remps. He said as much to Nan, who stared at him, weighing in her mind whether to tell about Henry Remp's visit. She had been afraid to tell him before because of his temper. Now she decided she must.

"Son of a bitch," Emmet said and stormed out of the house. He jumped into his pickup, wheeled around, and headed for the Remp farm. Nan watched him, wondering if maybe she should leave the baby with her mother and follow in the car.

Emmet fumed as he drove. The Remps hadn't had livestock on that little bit of swamp pasture for years. It was underwater till June. They were just making trouble. The Gowlers had let them use it, way back when they sharecropped with his grandfather. Didn't seem important. Good public relations. The farther he drove, the angrier he got. But it was Henry's visit with Nan that was really firing him up. If the asshole wanted a fight, by God, he'd get one.

Only Mrs. Remp was at home. The men of the family were gone, she said, eyeing Emmet fearfully. They were fixing fence, she added nervously.

"Fencing?" Emmet didn't think the Remps had any livestock left.

"Over at the old Caleb Meincer place," she said, a shakiness coming into her voice.

Realization slowly came to Emmet. The "old Caleb Meincer place" was Gowler land, as everyone knew, including the Remps. If they were repairing the fence there, that meant that Miser was correct—they had a loony idea of harassing him with some fantasy about grazing rights, legitimized by longstanding word of mouth. Down the road Emmet roared again.

Getting to the wetland pasture, back off the road and hidden by brush and native prairie weeds, was not easy. The old lane back to the property didn't look negotiable by truck, but sure enough there were fresh tractor tracks to follow. On foot, Emmet could shortly hear the Remps, quarreling as usual. Obviously there was a difference of opinion on the wisdom of fixing fence on Gowler property. If he had not been so angry, Emmet might have found the whole scene comical. As he came into view, the Remps quieted and watched him intently as he approached.

"What in the hell do you think you're doing?" he demanded.

Lem and Louie shifted their gaze to Henry, giving away whose idea the grazing-rights scheme had been.

"Pretty obvious, I'd say," said Henry, hammering in a staple, trying to look nonchalant. "Need to put the cattle back here again. Running outta pasture by the barn."

Emmet laughed in spite of himself. "Again? You haven't run cattle anywhere for five years. And if you don't do any better than you did the last time, you won't even get your fence fixin' paid for."

"Make a whole lot more than that little-white-ball lawn you're tryin' to grow."

"I'll tell you once, nice. Pack up and get your trespassing hides out of here." Even if Emmet had noted that he was facing three-to-one odds, he would still have said the same thing.

"Not trespassin', little rich boy," Henry replied, lip curling in derision. "We been comin' back here without one objection from any Gowler for forty years. We been usin' this pasture by right of previous agreement, and no Gowler has disputed that either."

"You know that's bullshit," Emmet said. "Get out of here before I lose my temper."

"Can't for fact do that," Henry said. "Got them calves over yonder to look after."

Sure enough, across the pasture, emerging from high weeds were a dozen of the sorriest feeder calves that Emmet had ever seen. Henry must have gone to the stockyards and bought the cheapest things going through the sale barn. Lem, the father, seeing Emmet's rising anger, shook his head, knowing the whole idea was stupid, and started shuffling toward the tractor nearby. He'd always known that Henry would get him in trouble, and now trouble was coming. He wanted none of it. Louie stayed with his brother. He didn't mind trouble as long as it was headed towards Emmet Gowler.

"You coulda sold me the land instead of to the state," Henry said, bitterly. "Given us a chance. You almighty rich bastards don't want anyone else gettin' ahead, do you?"

Emmet laughed incredulously. "I was doing you a favor. You know damn well this land won't make a profit by farming it."

"Just because Gowlers don't know how to farm in Killdeer don't mean Remps can't. Money don't make you smarter'n us."

"If you had a billion dollars you'd still be a Killdeer swamp-jumper."

"Like that little bitch you married."

Emmet tore into his adversary, heedless of the fact that Henry was bigger and brawnier and with a brother standing by, just in case. They went at it clumsily, two men not used to physical combat, fists flying wildly, feet wobbly, stumbling, falling, rolling on the ground almost like a parody of fighting. When it looked like Emmet was getting the upper hand, Louie jumped into the fray too. Their father, overcome with anxiety, came back from the tractor to try to stop the fight. Emmet, breaking free momentarily, lit into the old man too, doubling him over in pain. That was enough to push Henry beyond any civilized sensibility. He grabbed the hammer he had been using and charged Emmet, now held tightly by Louie's arms. But as Henry swung, a blow that could have been mortal, a human wildcat hurtled onto the scene seemingly from out of nowhere, partially deflecting the blow to Emmet's head. It took all three Remps to subdue her.

She sobbed in defeat, struggling to free herself to get to Emmet, who lay unconscious on the ground.

"I think you kilt him," Lem said, standing over the body. "Oh my God, I think you kilt him."

Nan screamed and sunk her teeth deep into Henry's arm, holding her. He yelled in pain and jammed his knee into her chest to hold her down. The bloodlust shone in his eyes.

"What are you gonna do?" Louie said fearfully.

"I'm gonna screw the bitch and then kill her. Hold her down and you can get some too."

He started to loosen his belt. Suddenly he jerked upright, stood there momentarily as still as a statue, a puzzled look on his face, then crumpled to the ground. He had not even heard the report of the bullet that brought him down. His brother looked off into the brush from where the shot seemed to have come, saw nothing except the wrath of God, and, trying to keep up with his father, dragged his motionless brother to the wagon and hoisted it aboard. Lem gunned the tractor motor and tore back down the lane and out of sight.

Nan, struggling in Louie's grip, had not heard the shot either, and watched, completely baffled, as Henry fell to the ground. Even after the Remps disappeared down the lane, she did not know what had happened, but went straight to Emmet, holding his bleeding head in her arms, sobbing and moaning. "They killed him. They killed my Emmet. Oh God, oh God, oh God!"

Slowly she was aware that there was someone standing over her. Her eyes followed up the deerskin-clad legs to the dirty flannel shirt and sheepskin vest, to a pair of patient old eyes peering down at her from a grizzled face. It was surely God, straight out of the Old Testament.

"*Miser!* Miser. He's dead. Em's dead."

The old man bent his head against Emmet's breast, raised up and patted Nan. "I don't hardly think so," he smiled. "Gowlers is much too hardheaded to let a little thing like a hammer blow kill 'em. Get your truck back here. We gotta get him to a doctor."

The Remps at home knew Henry was dead but called a doctor anyway while they waited in cowering fear for the sheriff. They used the time to concoct a story. The Gowlers had attacked Henry while the Remps were peacefully at work. In self-defense, Henry had hit Emmet with a hammer, but then either Nan shot Henry or a stray bullet from some hunter had accidentally killed him. For all they knew, the latter case was the truth.

But the sheriff did not come. An ambulance bore away Henry's body, and the tearful, fearful Remps, still waiting for Nan's vengeance, finally decided that a stray bullet really had found Henry, preposterous as that was. Nan, arriving at the hospital, was wholly absorbed with Emmet, who had not yet regained consciousness. The news of Henry Remp's death was all over the hospital hallways, but no details. She knew she would protect Miser any way she could, but had not yet figured out how she might do that. When in doubt, stall. Remain silent. Let the Remps make the first move. Louie would surely put his foot in his mouth.

Strangely enough, no one was ever brought to trial for Henry Remp's death. When Sheriff Mogan questioned the Remps, they claimed that it must have been a stray bullet but did not elaborate, astonished that Nan Bump hadn't brought charges yet.

"Well, that's bullshit, for sure," Mogan growled, but being unable to find the bullet, he had nothing to go on. When he questioned Nan, who was still waiting for the Remps to commit themselves, she said that Emmet had rushed out of the house, in a hurry as usual, and had tripped and fallen, bashing his head on the brick corner of the breezeway. She dared not show any curiosity about what the Remps were saying, and affected great surprise that Henry was dead. The Remps waited. When Emmet regained consciousness, all hell would break loose. If he didn't, all hell would break loose anyway.

The situation was exceedingly curious. The Remps in truth did not know how Henry ended up with a bullet through his chest, and Nan could argue with herself that she could not prove absolutely that Miser had been the killer, since she was a bit preoccupied at the time. So there the matter lay, and though Sheriff Mogan kept his own counsel, he seemed uninterested in pursuing the matter. Perhaps it was a stray bullet. Perhaps it was proof of the God that he did not really believe in finally doing something worthwhile in Jergin County. But he would hold off judgment until he could question Emmet.

Emmet lay in a fitful coma for two weeks, coming in and out of consciousness while Nan hovered over him, attentive to his every breath. As she said once, dryly, she was able to love him unconditionally when he was unconscious. Then one morning when she came into his hospital room, he was suddenly aware of her, suddenly cognitive, wanting to find out, as he put it, "what the hell happened." To her amazement, he did not remember anything of that fateful day's events. She told him what she had told the sheriff. If Emmet's memory returned, well, she'd deal with that when it happened. For now, Henry Remp was dead and it served him right. The surviving Remps could tell whatever lies they cared to, so long as her savior, Miser, remained free from prosecution. She in fact realized that now she held the loutish Remp clan in her power, a kind of blackmail—veto power—over any attempt on their part to stand in her way. Maybe that would pay off someday.

But the concussion left Emmet somewhat changed. He was not quite so nettlesome. Nor would he challenge Nan over differences that came up between them as he was wont to do before. He became, in a word, a bit *meek,* a little more pliable to Nan's suggestions. Their marriage gained in solidarity and steadiness. Nan sometimes mused, in her private mind, about whether it had taken a blow to the head to save their marriage. Marriage counselors might want to consider that, she thought.

Miser and Nan necessarily entered into an alliance of silence. For Miser's protection, they had to keep a discreet distance, but they had never kept anything else anyway. Occasionally now Nan would bake him a rhubarb pie, which he said he was uncommonly fond of, and he would in turn bring her roasted snapping turtle, which Nan considered a delicacy more tasty than the best fried chicken. When they did meet, he remained steadfastly unrepentant about the whole episode, only a little chagrined that his shot had not struck Henry in the shoulder as he intended but square in the heart. "Aim's not as good as it use to be," he said, as if he were discussing some varmint. In public, when Henry Remp's death came up in conversation, he would say, "Good riddance." Occasionally he might become more expansive. "People been killin' each other ever since Cain and Abel and they ain't never gonna stop. Fact is, mark my words, when farmers really get to competing for the land that's left, there'll be more killin'. Mark my words." And then he would shamble off to his swampy home grounds, which now belonged to the government and so, belonging to no one in particular, belonged to everyone as it once had.

About a year later, Miser died in his cabin, the body undiscovered until it was mostly decomposed. There were no relatives to mourn his death, but Emmet, at Nan's insistence, furnished a headstone and all of Gowler turned out for the funeral. For years, a bouquet of flowers appeared mysteriously on his grave in the old Bowsherville cemetery. No donor was ever discovered. Nan made sure of that.

By the middle sixties, both Emmet and Ben felt that they could breathe a little easier about the future. They had, each in his own way in two entirely different worlds of farming, maneuvered the human forces that seemed to be eternally arrayed against them. Both, again each in his own way, began to walk and to talk with a jauntier air. A little too much so. As Nat put it: "Never get uppity about farming. Old man weather makes the crops grow, not you."

The golf course was beginning to draw a steady flow of clients from the burgeoning suburbs beyond rural Jergin County, and Emmet saw success within his grasp. Seeing Franklin Farnold play in his barnyard gum boots, sometimes with a not-so-faint residue of cow manure still on them, was the sort of fringe benefit that kept the big-city golfers coming, eager to carry tales back to Columbus. Even local people found fringe benefits in the game they had never thought they would play. Jake Lavendar, always Emmet's main assistant in all the latter's endeavors, admitted plaintively that he once walked clear across a fairway to pick a fresh white meadow mushroom, only to find when he got close that it was a golf ball. Jubel Chafer got so taken up with the game that he fashioned his own driver the traditional way—out of persimmon wood.

Only Ben resisted. Golf just did not seem a proper pastime for a husbandman.

Mary and Ben's second child, Amelia, had been born a year after Natty, and the two children, now seven and eight years old, were the couple's glory. Nat, over on a visit, looked at Ben, who was watching the children play, and remarked: "The way you're beaming, that's all the light you need to do barn chores at night." Ben and Mary were over forty now, and they felt the first inklings of that middle-aged satisfaction referred to in Jergin County as "getting over the hump." They did not have to shape every action of their lives around their grim budget of never spending more in a month than they made in a week. Occasionally, they would even dine out at the Dairy Barn, pricy as that might be. Before the meal, they might order a sip of bourbon, which Ben always referred to, with that impish smile of his, as "the Fruit Juice." Often Emmet and Nan came along, with Dorothy babysitting all the children—Floyd, Natty, and Amelia—at the home place. Sometimes the whole family went to the restaurant, even Dorothy and Nat. While the children worked crayons over coloring books to while away the time waiting for their food to arrive, the adults, no doubt aided by the sipping, would embark on eloquent discussions about everything, but especially the war. The war talk could be heard at almost every table. Ben could feel the enmity in the stares that sometimes came his way. He was the one who had avoided combat in World War II by ways never fully explained and in a community that prided itself on the number of flags it could raise to God and country. People didn't forget, never mind that most of them had not seen combat either. It rankled Ben. Men who did not have to go to war simply because of the accident of birth that made them a couple of years too young or too old ought to keep their mouths shut about who was patriotic and who was not. But before the public eye, he was silent. To question the real intentions behind fervent patriotism was as dangerous as questioning the real intentions behind fervent religion.

It was dangerous to talk about the war around Nat anyway. He was too old to care what anyone thought of him, and he could speak loud enough for the whole restaurant to hear. He found it difficult to believe that Emmet, who had nearly lost his sanity if not his life in World War II, would not now condemn altogether what Nat referred to as the "Veetnam idiocy." He would draw himself up into a state of shaky malevolence, his loose jowls quivering, but then lose heart and shrink back toward silence. Then he'd have a change of mind, draw himself back up, and speak out anyway. "If your little Floyd was old enough to go, or your boys in Florida, you'd change your tune, Emmet Gowler."

"I didn't say I was for the war," Emmet responded, almost in hushed tones so people at other tables couldn't hear. "I just said we have to take a stand or else communism will take over."

"Ja, ja, you believe that horsedreck," Nat exploded. "Remember, I fought on the German side in the First World War and then became an American. I can see both sides. As a German soldier I was told we must stop American imperialism. We didn't even know what imperialism meant. I don't think Americans know today what communism means either. Just big words to get people stirred up." He pounded the table, excited enough now to lapse into a bit of immigrant English. "Dat Johnson and his car dealer McNamara just want to chuice up the economy."

Dorothy rolled her eyes. She had come to America unwillingly, but once there she had embraced her new country completely and could barely abide her husband's lapses into what she called pidgin

English. She had studiously scraped German off of her own tongue, and she scolded her children if she heard them imitating their father's lapses. Sometimes Ben did it anyway, just for fun, another quirk that had inspired his nickname of "Amish Bump."

"Quit saying *chuice,* for heaven's sake," she whispered now. "You want the grandchildren to grow up talking that way too?"

Nat scowled. The others smiled. Emmet decided not to answer his father-in-law. He didn't really have an answer. He realized he did not know what imperialism really meant and didn't understand much about communism either. And what use was it to argue with an old man set in his ways? It wasn't good for Nat's heart to get him stirred up anyway. Ben on his part knew it was time to change the subject. He chose farm subsidies, which was only a little safer. They could all start at different positions about government handouts and argue themselves into a semblance of agreement. That wasn't going to happen with the war.

"Well, the little guy gets subsidies at the same percentage rate that the big boys get," Emmet said, teasingly, answering Ben's opening sally about rich farmers getting too much help from the government.

"Ten percent of a hundred thousand is a whole more money than 10 percent of ten thousand," Ben replied.

"Well, it helps the small farmer more. He's the one who needs the help."

"Not so. Take away subsidies, it's the big farmers who would go broke. Not you, maybe, but all those who are borrowed up to their eyebrows. Wouldn't affect us little farmers much at all because the piddlin' amount we get hardly makes any difference."

"The government keeps saying that subsidies are there to help the family farmer," Nat opined. "'T'ain't so. It's to help the greedyguts."

"Doesn't help them, either," Emmet said. "That money just passes on through to the suppliers."

"And the price of land just keeps going up to where the small farmers can't afford to expand," Ben added.

"Big ones can't either, really. They're just kiddin' themselves," said Emmet. "My God, if I didn't have my land paid for by inheritance, there's no way I could afford to buy it or rent it at the prices today. I don't know how the Remps and the Chafers and such do it. They must believe that malarkey in the farm magazines about the advantages of perpetual debt."

Nan intervened. "Can't you guys ever be happy? Heavens, things are going pretty good."

"We've got a four-inch deficit in rainfall going into summer, my dear. That's enough to put any farmer in a contrary mood."

Mary looked knowingly at Nan. "This is what happens when men and liquor meet," she said.

But Emmet's dour appraisal of the weather was more prophetic than any of them realized. Not a drop of rain had fallen near Gowler since mid-April, and while the crops had shown little stress through May, feeding on the ground water of early spring, by June the farmers fell into the habit of scanning the sky almost constantly, trying, by sheer willpower, to draw a shower out of every dark cloud that appeared on the horizon.

June passed with only one sprinkle that barely measured two-tenths of an inch. That brought a chorus of the wry remarks, as farmers tried to wring humor out of what might turn into tragedy.

"Not even a grass-greener."

"Gave the ants a drink."

"Honeybees could lick drops off the grass and not have to fly clear to the creek."

"Creek? Ours has dried up."

"Amish Bump says he managed to get a hundred bales off his first cuttin' of hay, about half, but will be lucky to get ten from the second."

"What drives me up the wall is that over t'other side of Linner, it rained two inches last Thursday."

"They must all go to church regular over there."

"Did you hear about the congregation over beyond Mansfield somewheres that organized a pray-in for rain? It rained all right. A four-inch downpour with hail that shredded the corn to ribbons."

"My dad always said, 'Be careful what you pray for.'"

" A guy west of us says his neighborhood got a nice shower last week but he learned not to talk about it in Gowler 'cause it pissed people off so."

"I hear Lester Cordrey has taken to parking his car outside all night with the windows rolled down."

"Mabel Lavendar left her wash out on the line for three days trying to invite a shower, and the dust got it so dirty she had to run it all through the washer again."

"We've had red sky in the morning and whirlwinds moving toward the sun, and mackerel skies, and sun dogs, and it still doesn't rain."

"You know what Mom always said: 'All signs fail in dry weather.'"

The air, lacking moisture, filled with bizarre theories.

"I tell you, it's all because Gowler sets on the old Sandusky Plains. 'Tweren't any trees here when the settlers first came because in the old days it didn't rain during the summer. Weather's going back to the old days."

"Well, that's bull-loney. It rained like hell west of Marion, and that's Sandusky Plains country too."

"I don't know about that, but I've lived here for seventy-five years and I tell you there are regular summer rain trails through these parts that summer storms usually take. There's one between Delaware and Marion, going west to east, and one from Crarey across the northern part of the county too, passing just above Bucyrus and on to Mansfield. And there sure as hell is more rain in summer around Toledo to the north and below Columbus to the south."

"Horse manure. The rainfall records don't show it."

"That's because they don't measure the rain in July and August apart from the annual amount. The annual amount is about the same."

"I read somewhere that tornadoes follow certain alleys, so why not summer showers?"

"Adrian Farnold says that it has never hailed on his place because this area is located between two rivers, the Sandusky and the Tymochtee. The Indians said that, he claims. And, you know, it never has hailed bad here like it has up around Crarey, far as I can recollect."

"You guys are all addled by the drouth. Crarey is between two rivers too, like everywhere else."

By Independence Day the grass was brown, the corn stunted—"looks like pineapple plants," Nat said—and the soybeans hardly six inches tall with a pallor more white than green when the sun beat down on them. Farmers fell to silence and either stayed home, making life miserable for their wives, or attended too many classes at Blue Room University. A fight broke out there when someone from Surrey, out of his element, walked in, surveyed the scene of disconsolate farmers lined up at the bar, hunched over beers, and remarked cheerily, "I thought the rain this morning would have made you guys happy."

Heads swiveled in unison to stare at him.

"You dummkopf," Nat Bump growled. "That sprinkle wasn't enough to float a flea."

"Rained fairly well up our way."

That's all it took. It wasn't much of a fight, however. Jubel Chafer lifted the intruder off the floor by the seat of his pants and tossed him out the door.

When that story got around, Pinky Ghent decided to call off the Independence Day fireworks celebration. Too much bad feeling in the neighborhood. Besides, he was looking for an excuse to stop the festival. He was getting old and people weren't coming anymore like in the old days.

"But maybe the skyrockets would jostle some rain out of the clouds," Jack Cughes suggested.

"Well, then, you buy some and see," Pinky replied.

Possibly because he was so intimately attuned to the biological life of his farm, Ben took the drouth more personally than other farmers he knew. As he watched the plants wither, it seemed to him that his own bones were shrinking. As the cracks widened in the ground, it was as if the pores of his skin cracked open too, parched for moisture. Mary tried to cheer him up.

"There's some good in those cracks in the soil," she pointed out. "They're breaking up the hardpan layer from too much plowing."

Ben managed a little smile. Mary was right, and he had never thought of that. But about that time, the weather forecaster on the radio crowed that folks could look forward to another lovely, sunny weekend. He switched off the radio and stomped out the door. Natty and Amelia were in the garden engaged in an experiment that should have amused him. They had stuck a garden hose down a crack in the soil and were watching intently as the water ran down the crack. Amelia was holding the alarm clock she had brought from the house. They smiled as their father approached.

"It's been on for six minutes now, and the water's still going down," Amelia announced proudly.

"It's probably coming out in China," Ben said. Both of the children giggled. He was forever amazed at them. Any child might think of running water down a crack in the ground, but he doubted that many would keep track of the time it took before the water welled up to the surface again.

"I think it's spreading out under the whole garden," Natty said, solemnly. "That would be better than sprinkling, you know. In this weather, sprinkle drops might dry up before they hit the ground."

Even Ben laughed at the joke, although in his depression laughing came hard. Natty was always coming up with humorous observations far beyond his age. Ben had a theory about it. Given the chance, given the freedom to say and think what came to their minds without the constant pressure from adults to conform, children might express a level of intelligence higher than that of their parents, who had not been encouraged to think independently. He tried to raise his children to think on their own, but he was about to see an example of it that he did not think so amusing.

To distract his mind from the drouth, he had been driving himself to the kind of work that in calmer times he probably would not have done. Now, for the fourth day in a row, he led Natty and Amelia, all armed with hoes, to the cornfield. He had decided that the dry weather might be weakening the weeds as much as the corn, although there was little evidence to that effect, and so it would be a good time to cut the Canada thistles in the corn. He knew from experience that cutting this pest, which spread by root and by seed, only seemed to make them grow better. Only many years of uncultivated sod and mowing would get rid of the devils. They loved to be cultivated, he always said, and so had taught the children. But now he needed desperately to find some way to fight the drouth and decided that maybe in a dry year, hoeing the thistles would be effective. And anyway, it was good training for the children. They needed to learn that life as not one long, continuous good time.

But both Natty and Amelia were in open revolt as they each walked the space between two cornrows, hoes flailing at the weeds in imitation of their father. Natty cut off a stalk of corn and pretended that it was an accident. Ben pretended not to notice. Amelia began to beg dramatically for water.

"Is the sweat running down your belly yet?" Ben asked by way of reply.

"Down my back," she hissed.

"Until it runs down your belly, you haven't worked up a real sweat."

Both children started to whimper. The temperature had to be over 90 degrees, and they could barely see the far end of the field. They both had passed into what society officially prescribes as the "age of reason," and this was not reasonable to them.

"Daddy, why are you doing this?" Natty said when they had finally reached the end of the field and were starting back. "You said this corn wasn't going to make a crop anyway. You also said once that hoeing just makes Canady thistles grow faster."

Ben was afraid to look directly at him. "Sometimes you just gotta keep on going even when there's no hope," he said. "'Specially in farming. You can't quit just because things aren't going right."

"Like those slaves picking cotton in *Gone with the Wind?*" Natty asked. Actually, it was not a question.

Ben kept hoeing. He'd been bested and knew it. "We'll take a rest when we get back to the other end."

Mary was waiting for them with lemonade, but realizing just how hot it was in the field, she insisted they all go back to the house and sit in the shade. She glared at Ben. He offered no resistance. He was feeling ashamed. When the children were out of hearing range, she turned on him.

"Ben Bump, I know you think you are doing the right thing, but you might consider something. If you want the kids to stay in farming, you're going about it all wrong. You're teaching them to leave."

Trying to sleep that night, Ben rolled from side to side, knowing that he had done the wrong thing. He hadn't been trying to teach his children the merits of hard work. He just wanted them to feel as miserable as he felt. He was acting out of spite against the weather, about as foolish a thing as a man could do. Would he ever learn that other people did not have his kind of fervor for farming and that there was no way to force the nonfervent to it? Then he had a thought that was also uncomfortable. In the secrecy of his mind, he ridiculed other humans for what he called their religions of make-believe magic. But it was plain that he held magical beliefs about his religion too, the religion of farming.

He was suddenly aware of a sound that made him hold his breath. A pattering spattering on the tin roof. Raindrops? Was he dreaming? Showers had not been forecast. He listened not daring to move lest the magic end. The pattering increased. Became louder. Turned to a steady drumming. Continued, louder yet.

"Mary, wake up. Mary. It's raining."

"Shhh. You'll spook it away."

He lay there, listening in rapture. Surely there was no sound so sweet as a gentle rain drumming steadily on a metal roof after months of drought. Finally he drifted off, his first sound sleep in two months.

TWENTY-SEVEN

With Herb's Diner closed in Gowler, the only place in the county south of Surrey for farmers to gather and complain was two miles away, at the Blue Room in Linner. Griping had taken on a particularly plaintive tone by 1969 because after all the wondrous new farm technology that had emerged in the sixties, the long-promised prosperity still had not quite made it around the corner, or had for only a few. As yields of corn and soybeans increased, prices fell. The group drinking coffee in the Blue Room on this particular fall day after corn harvest was having a difficult time accepting what logic was telling them. Mary Bump was having trouble accepting the fact that they were not accepting the facts that were plain enough to see. She thought she might make the point by backing into it.

"You're bragging about how well weedkillers are working, but there's another side to it," she said, her gaze taking in not only Ben, Emmet, and Nan, but Jake Lavendar, Jack Cughes, and the Farnold boys, who were hardly boys anymore, but growing a little stouter around the middle and a little grayer around the ears. "First they cost money, lowering your profit potential, and secondly, they increase yields, causing overproduction, which means lower prices."

Ben looked at her, a little taken aback. It was not like Mary to speak out like that, and with an edge in her voice too.

"Well, I don't care how much weedkillers cost," Franklin replied. "There wasn't enough bindweed to plug up the cornpicker once this year. It was just thantastic."

'I suppose you're gonna say you raised 300-bushel corn," Emmet said sarcastically.

"Well, that field over by you went 190 to the acre, and that's the truth," Franklin countered. "We narrowed the rows down to thirty inches apart and didn't plow weeds even once."

"Yeah, but it cost so much more in chemicals and fertilizer that it didn't net any more'n the 150-bushel stuff," his brother, Dick, said with his customary long face. "And what really hurt was where we paid for 200-bushel corn and only got 120-bushel average."

"Somebody will fairly hit 300 bushels again one of these days," Jake Lavendar said. "Just a matter of time."

"Hasn't happened since nineteen and fifty-five, and I doubt the truth of that."

"Think of it, though. Three-hundred-bushel times three dollar a bushel. Nine hundert dollar an acre." They were all silent, contemplating their holy grail.

"We'd be so rich we could afford to buy ice cream cones when we went to town like we did when we were poor."

"You ain't never gonna see three-dollar corn again in your life."

"Would if we'd all cut back on how much we plant, like Mary says."

"Oh, sure. Who's gonna go first."

"Nevertheless, as long as you grow more than the market can handle, you're gonna get less. Every car manufacturer in the world knows that."

"We ain't raisin' cars. People starvin' all over the world. They need all the grain we can grow."

"Well, they can't afford to buy it for what we gotta have to grow it."

"They can afford guns, by God, they can afford food."

"The world's got us comin' and goin'. The government pays us just enough to stay in business. And then they get cheap food so consumers can pay out their asses for cars and houses. If a car costs eight thousand dollars, then a bushel of corn ought to be three dollars, maybe four."

"Well, they know better than stick us with acreage controls like they tried in '61."

"Haw. They just turned around and acreage-controlled us from another direction. You can't hardly take a shit without the Department of Agriculture's approval. The government found out we'd take bribes, and that was the end of our freedom."

Ben did not comment. He knew everyone around the table was doing fairly well whether they admitted it or not. Maybe not great, but okay. He was beginning to wonder if he were the one who had made the wrong choice, staying old-fashioned and milking cows. He and Mary just barely got by while the others rode high on big tractors, making more than he did in half the time. Some of them were starting to go to Florida in the winter like Emmet and Nan always did. Nan appeared to be even making money on those weird horses of hers. Said she could raise them for fifty bucks a year and in two or three years sell them for fifteen hundred dollars apiece to people around Columbus who had more money than brains.

On the subject of corn, Ben had plenty to say but was inclined not to talk. The others would just laugh at him. He had long been interested in open-pollinated corn. When he started farming on his own, he had bought some seed of a strain of Reid's Yellow Dent that occasionally sported uncommonly long ears. Nat had warned him not to grow the stuff because it was prone to lodging in strong winds. Nevertheless, Ben, in his contrary way, put out a plot of it every year, hopefully far enough away from his hybrid corn so that the two wouldn't cross-pollinate. Actually, he didn't care if it did cross a little. That might put some stalk strength into his corn. He called his experiment "recreation farming"—seeing how big the ears might get, and how strong the stalks, if he selected seed for those traits and kept replanting it. To his surprise, after nearly twenty years of selective breeding, about half of the ears achieved a length of twelve inches, with some up to fourteen inches long, and one even sixteen inches. There was a problem, though, as Mary pointed out to him with a smile. Every time he bred in a little more stalk strength, the ears got bigger and some of the plants still fell over.

Now Emmet forced him to talk. "You should take a look at those big ears on Ben's open-pollinated corn. Good thing he husks it by hand. Those ears are so big they'd tear the hell right out of a combine's cylinder bars."

"Might be worth the risk," Ben countered. "Ears twelve to fourteen inches long and fat enough to have at least twenty-two rows of kernels, weigh out to nearly a pound of grain per cob. If I plant 20,000 stalks per acre and each stalk bears a pound of grain, that means 333 bushels per acre, figuring corn at sixty pounds per bushel."

The others all laughed. "Amish Bump," as they often called him, might not be as backward as he pretended to be. Matter of fact, Franklin pointed out, "the Amish are the only farmers making any real money these days." Ben nodded with the others, but declined further comment.

But Mary, sitting beside him, decided, after her first bold remark, that she had stayed in the background in family and neighborhood discussions about farm issues long enough. She had learned a thing or two. And coffee loosened her tongue as much as alcohol did others'. Over the years she had discovered something she found amusing. Farmers might know a lot about what went on in a piston engine, but not much about what went on in the soil. They were generally illiterate about the biological basis of their business. She knew because of what she had learned expanding her gardens, orchard, and herb beds. As her knowledge of horticulture deepened, so did her curiosity about agronomy. So she started reading up on it. To her amazement, she learned that there were some six billion soil microbes of one kind or another in a teaspoon of soil—more than the entire human population of the earth. When she first brought up facts like that at Blue Room University, the others fell silent. Trying to engage them in discussions about soil pH, cation exchange capacity, organic matter content, and microbial life in the soil only made them nod silently and look out the window. However, when she tried to explain to them how pesticides and chemical fertilizers might be disrupting the complicated life of the soil, they sneered. "Can't be hurting the ground too much," Nan said. "Our yield's been going up nearly every year."

Now Mary mused out loud. "I wonder if organically grown corn might outyield corn grown with artificial fertilizers?"

Hoots all around. "Before fertilizers, farmers were lucky to get 70 bushel to the acre," Nan said. "Now we get 120 without hardly trying."

Mary knew, from reading agricultural history, that yields of over 200 bushels per acre had been reported in virgin soils even before hybrids, but she did not say so. She knew better than to try to sound learned in Blue Room University. Ben came to her aid. "Well, be careful, Nan. That kid in Mississippi who grew 300-bushel corn in '55 used a lot of manure."

"You couldn't raise 300-bushel corn around here on a whole Rocky Mountain range of manure," Emmet said.

"Probably not on that blue Killdeer clay of yours," Mary replied. "But I kind of think I've already done that in my garden. Hard to figure, though, with small plots, what the equivalent of yield per acre is. Especially when I double- or triple-crop. But I bet I could grow more my way than you can with artificial fertilizers on that pancake clay of yours. Even if I used open-pollinated corn."

It was like someone had raised the bid a hundred dollars in a Blue Room poker game. They all looked sharply at her. It was not like Mary to talk uppity.

"Why don't we find out?" Nan replied coyly. "Let's have a contest. I'll plant an acre of corn my way and you plant one your way. Could be interesting."

"Well, it would hardly be fair. My garden plots are so rich I know they'd outyield a similar-sized plot in any of your fields."

"Ba-loney."

"No ba-loney."

And so it was agreed, Nan and Mary making a big show of shaking hands while the men made jokes and urged them on.

Through the winter the community argued out the conditions under which the contest would go forward. It was finally agreed upon that the plots had to be right next to each other, to grow under exactly the same weather conditions and soil types, if the contest was going to mean anything. But this presented a problem for Mary. To be truly organic, she pointed out, her plot had to be on soil that had not been "poisoned and compacted half to death."

"Well, if you're on new ground and I'm not, that would be an unfair advantage for you," Nan protested.

"Which proves my point," Mary replied. "You guys are ruining the land."

"Oh, I'll still beat you with hybrids."

"Maybe. Maybe not."

Where in the whole county might they find two plots side by side that met the proper qualifications? Emmet, sensing greater possibilities in the contest than the others as yet foresaw, suggested that Mary's plot could be right at the edge of his large lawn, which had never been cultivated as far as he knew, with Nan's plot in the field right next to it. That this location also happened to be almost directly across the road from the golf course entrance did not at first seem of any significance to the others.

Nan insisted that Mary could use only purely natural fertilizers and soil conditioners, and no pesticides at all, and that the plots had to be farmed by farm machine methods, not hand methods. That would mean that Mary could not cultivate weeds by hand and therefore could not plant as densely as Nan could, using herbicides to control weeds rather than row cultivators. Mary, on her part, insisted that Nan not use any natural organic fertilizers, no manure, no compost at all—only manufactured chemical powders. Nan promised not to sneak any manure into her plot, and Mary, no 10-10-10 chemical fertilizer on hers. Irrigation of any kind was disallowed.

Local farmers around Gowler, and especially at Blue Room University, were captivated by the contest. Not only were the contestants female, which was eyebrow-raising enough, but these were two women who merited more than passing eyebrow-raising. Both were quite pleasing to the eye, that is to say, and if a man were to observe them while they worked their corn plots a little longer than propriety dictated, he could just say that he was studying the corn. But more than that, everyone was curious to know more about that Nan Gowler, the Bump bitch who had played havoc with farm auctions and whose father, Nat Bump, had been a bootlegger and maybe a Nazi sympathizer. Oddly enough, these details did not deter them from rooting for her rather than Mary Bump. When life got down to the really important issues, farmers knew where they had to stand.

"That Mary Bump is a Livingston, you know. *Schoolteachers.*"

"And *not from the farm.*"

"They say she's one of those environmentalists what wants us to lose our asses farming without fertilizer."

"Damn blue-eyed liberal."

And even more disconcerting, she was married to Amish Bump, whose very methods of farming were an open slap in the face to modern agribusiness. He seemed not to be going broke yet, as most of them had predicted.

They had to side with Nan even if she was a bitch. She was, at least, their bitch.

Nan and Mary had little inkling of the stir they were causing. But it soon became obvious that they had touched many seemingly disparate agendas. That two women rather than two men were involved was no doubt the first item of interest. What did women know about growing corn? When the home economics agent at the courthouse in Surrey heard about the contest, she immediately called the head of the Home Economics department at Ohio State University's College of Agriculture, and she immediately called the editor of *Ohio Today* and strongly urged her to look into what was surely a great human interest farm story, featuring the woman's angle for a change.

The article that followed pitted "Nature's Acre" against "Chemical Acre," which aroused at least three seemingly unrelated groups to put their own spin on the contest. The New Feminist League trumpeted the role of women in agriculture. *Organic Farming Today* saluted farmers for finally recognizing the role that organic practices could play on the modern farm. And the World Fertilizer Institute pointed out that without manufactured fertilizers, mankind would starve to death—even if, heaven forbid, Nature's Acre won the contest.

Never were two plantings of corn attended with so much pomp and ceremony, so much pride and prejudice. Earnest discussion took place at Blue Room University over whether the signs of the zodiac should be considered, seeing as how, according to old Nat Bump anyway, Scorpio was the best for corn planting. It was finally agreed that whatever the right or wrong of astrology, the corn in both plots had to be planted on the same day to ensure equal footing with the weather gods and the moon goddess. That led to a heated argument over which day, weather permitting, would be ideal. All the younger farmers voted for a day in the last week in April, when, so the universities had taught them, chances were best for a high yield. All the old farmers protested, said that was too early, too risky, too cold yet. They all finally agreed on May 10 or when beech tree leaves were as big as squirrel ears, whichever came first. In a compromise, it was decided that whatever the precise day, depending on weather, they would plant no earlier than May 7. There was also lively debate over how the ground ought to be worked, over the number of kernels per acre to plant, and especially over how deep to plant the corn.

"An inch deep is about right, especially if the ground's a little cold like it sure as hell will be in Killdeer."

"Oh, shit no. Two inches to be safe, to be sure of enough moisture. Those plots aren't in real Killdeer dirt anyway."

"An inch and a half is about perfect in my experience."

"Depends. I always go for an inch and three quarter."

"An inch and a quarter is better for May 7."

Finally it was decided that these decisions should be left to the contestants because such considerations were part of the whole idea of which method, chemical or organic, was better.

Both Ben and Emmet offered to do the actual planting for their wives, but Nan sneered in reply. Mary had never planted corn with the horses before, but she said if Ben could do it, so could she. If her rows were a little crooked, she pointed out, there might mean more corn plants in them.

As it turned out, rain fell on May 7 and so both plots were planted on May 9—just as well, Ben said. "This o-p corn won't germinate in cool soil as fast as hybrids." Nan used the highest fertilizer rate ever heard for corn in Jergin County—five hundred pounds of NPK along with a generous dash of every micronutrient recognized by agronomy as critical to healthy plant growth. Then she came back with a side dressing of liquid nitrogen in June.

Mary plowed under ten tons of composted cow manure and then applied ten tons of chicken manure, which she said contained all those micronutrients that Nan was paying big bucks for. She applied two hundred pounds of expensive bonemeal and rock phosphate on the surface after the corn was planted. Then she side-dressed in July with every bit of mature leaf compost she had on hand, soaked in fish oil nitrogen supplement. "Broomsticks would root in that soil, it's so rich," Ben claimed. Both Emmet and Ben complained, good-naturedly, that if they tried to plant a whole

commercial field the way their wives were planting their plots, they would go broke before harvest.

The corn grew vigorously, of course, and so identical did the plots look that Emmet put up two signs to identify them: "Nature's Acre" in front of Mary's corn and "Chemical Acre" in front of Nan's. Soon another sign went up, at a discreet distance, but not too discreet, from Nan's plot. "Arabian Horses. Reasonable. Inquire at the golf course." Then a fourth sign appeared next to Mary's corn: "Mary's Herbal Home Remedies. Watch for sign two miles east on Twp Rd 59." Someone was then moved to put yet another sign right under "Nature's Acre" which read "God's Acre." The general speculation was that this sign was the work of members of the Country Fundamental Baptist Church of Linner, whose pastor took a dim view of chemical farming. Although he never admitted being the author, Emmet then added a sign under "Chemical Acre" that read "Mammon's Acre." He figured that injecting a little religious controversy into the contest could only heat up the general interest. The six signs inspired a whole volley of inscriptions. "Superstition Farming" sprouted overnight in front of Mary's plot, followed within days, or nights, by "Advanced Scientific Farming" in front of Nan's. When neither the county highway department nor the two women objected, signs started popping up like mushrooms. "Coon Hounds, 497-2300." "Fresh Eggs, Deman Farm." "Join The NFO." "Homemade Bread and Jams, Mabel Fridley." "Gun Repair Jack Olsen." "Prepare to Meet Your God." "Killdeer Jerky at the Blue Room." "Chemical Acre's Seed Corn Donated by DeKalb." That last sign inspired Ben, who was finding the whole development increasingly amusing. In front of Mary's plot, he put up a proclamation: "Amish Bump's Old Fashioned Braggin' Corn. Foot Long Ears for Seed, fifty cents each. 14-inchers, a dollar."

When Lester Cordrey realized that if Ben Bump could sell his corn for a dollar an ear, he might make $20,000 from the plot, he began to tremble—"like I got the chilblains," he tried to explain.

Cy Gowler, who was getting too old to read written signs but was still able to comprehend cultural signs very well, could barely contain his enthusiasm as he watched the proceedings. After lunch with business associates in Surrey, he insisted that they accompany him down to Gowler. He parked in front of the army of signs and beamed. None of his guests were impressed.

"Did you drive me all the way down here to look at a damn cornfield?" one of them asked.

"Not the damn corn, damnit. Don't you see? You guys think rural areas are losing business to consolidation. Look at that. Lots of business. It's just gone underground. We gotta figure out a way to encourage this."

"Doesn't look to me like it needs any encouraging."

Traffic did indeed increase on the Gowler road, not just because of the corn contest but from the hunters and birdwatchers whom the new Killdeer Wildlife Area attracted. Traffic also increased at the golf course, not to mention at Blue Room University. Jerky sales boomed. The general store, which had been getting out of groceries after Pinky died in favor of crafts and antiques, started selling Mabel Fridley's homemade bread, Deman Farm's brown eggs, and Katie Long's handmade woolen items. With Closson's Bakery long gone, as well as Ramsey's Egg and Poultry Market and Mrs. Smith's Dry Goods, it seemed the smart thing to do. Then a newcomer to the area, seeing that there was no grocery and who did not suffer from the fading hope that had infected the native retailers in the village, decided to open one in the building that formerly held Herb's Diner. Johnny's son, also Johnny, decided to keep Johnny's Filling Station and Auto Repair open a while yet. Yet.

The corn in both plots was knee-high by the Fourth of July, was in fact every bit of twenty inches tall by then. By August, a clear difference in the two plots of corn became evident, even if the view was somewhat obscured by a still growing number of signs. Mary's open-pollinated corn was up to twelve feet tall and still reaching for the sun, while Nan's hybrids topped out and tasseled at about ten feet. As the ears began to form on both plots, it was evident that there were many more on Nan's corn, but those on Mary's were going to be huge things, at least some of them. Speculation, which from the beginning had favored hybrid corn, wavered.

But clouds were gathering on the horizon, both in reality and figuratively. A thunderstorm bent Mary's corn at an angle severe enough to put even an average yield in doubt. Mary wanted to stake up every stalk, but the terms of the contest did not allow handwork.

"Don't despair just yet," old Nat told her. "That corn'll straighten up some. The stalks will look like sled runners, but the ears will develop."

The wind did not faze Nan's hybrid corn, and she began to celebrate victory. Too soon. One morning she realized that something strange was affecting her corn. It started turning a sickly yellow, changing to a brownish pallor. At first she thought someone had sneaked into her plot at night and sprayed it with some weedkiller that the corn could not tolerate. But when the pallor of death spread through the cornfields all over the county, and then all over the Midwest, it was obvious that the whole crop had been stricken with some disease. The phones jammed at the agronomy departments of all the land grant colleges, and at every herbicide company and seed dealer in the nation. Plant geneticists scrambled to find an answer. Corn on the Chicago Board of Trade shot up the limit every day, as traders—"the parasites who feed on our blood and sweat," Emmet said—saw a short crop coming.

Strangely, Mary's corn was unaffected. Indeed open-pollinated corn all over the nation was unaffected. Although that was not much relief to the corn industry because so few farmers grew open-pollinated corn, it was a key to the mystery. So was that fact that some hybrids, especially older ones, were also unaffected. Hardest hit were the newest hybrid strains.

Emmet, at the elevator, first heard what had happened and rushed down to Blue Room University to spread the news.

"We're in deep trouble, boys," he intoned. "It's a fungus. Causes southern corn leaf blight. Almost all the hybrid corn breeders have been using Texas male-sterile cytoplasm, whatever the hell that is, to develop the new single cross-hybrids we're all using. A new strain of the disease, Race T they call it, really plays hell in hybrids with that cytoplasm in them. It's killing almost the whole corn crop."

There was silence around the room. A Cornbelt without corn was not something easily imagined.

"Jesus. The whole country could fairly starve," Jake Lavendar said.

"What they gonna do?"

"The breeders have gone to Argentina to plant seed that contains other germ plasms not affected by the disease. They figure they can grow a crop over winter down there and have seed in time for next year. Until then, boys, it's a damn good thing we got a lot of carryover corn from last year."

Mary, of course, won the contest, sled-runner stalks and all. The Natural Farmers Society and the Organic Farming Association had a field day, and the Country Fundamental Baptist Church in Linner held a victory celebration with a fried-chicken supper for anyone who wanted to come. DeKalb, although its corn had fared no worse than other corn, was never again the preferred hybrid in the county. And never again did the farmers of Jergin County possess unbounded faith in agribusiness.

But the big winner was Ben. Because southern corn leaf blight put the fear of the Lord in farmers, as he put it, everyone wanted seed from his corn, never mind the sled-runner stalks. He saved enough seed to plant twenty acres of his own and sold the rest: forty fourteen-inch ears for forty dollars; three thousand twelve-inchers for fifteen hundred dollars, and the rest, by the bushel, for a hundred dollars a bushel.

During milking, Ben told Natty about his latest brainstorm, feeling sure that his son would be intrigued. "We've been thinking too much in the old ways to succeed in farming," he said, after they had shared a laugh over selling corn for so high a price. "But the new ideas about getting bigger are not at all new ideas. Just adding on to the present thinking. Now here's a really new idea. Let's grow this open-pollinated corn, call it 'Amish Bump's Famous Old-Fashioned Corn.' Get some cute little burlap bags that hold five pounds and have that name printed on them and sell the corn for five dollars a bag. People would buy it, I just know. Just think, if we could sell twenty acres' worth, at a yield of a hundred bushels per acre, that would be a hundred and twenty thousand dollars!"

To his surprise, his son did not respond positively. He seemed to be only half listening, a teenager now, a little sullen in the face of the parental world. "That would be a lot of work sacking that many bags up. Every bushel would make twelve bags and a hundred bushels twelve hundred bags and twenty acres twenty four thousand bags."

Ben stared at him. Natty, like Amelia, had quit homeschooling and was now in public school. He was tired of being ridiculed by other students because of his father's way of farming, and had fallen under the influence of a science teacher, Robert Lux, who made sarcastic remarks about organic farming or any other notions about agriculture that were at odds with the get-big ideals of agribusiness. Mr. Lux had been very much on the side of Chemical Acre during the contest. Natty had first been angered by his teacher's opinions, then embarrassed. The scientific facts assembled by university experts supported the teacher's contentions. So, quietly, Natty began to doubt his father's traditional way of thinking. When he tried to defend Ben by pointing out to his teacher that it was the old-fashioned corn that had survived southern corn blight, the teacher sneered and said that the corn "industry"—everything in farming was an "industry" now—would, by next planting season, have new hybrids to take care of the problem.

So now Natty, too young to have a frame of reference of his own on which to form an opinion, wavered in his loyalty. He did not know which side was right, but Mr. Lux's way certainly meant much less physical work.

"If I really could make a hundred and twenty thousand dollars by sacking up corn, I would sack for as long as it took," Ben said sourly.

"But that's just you, Dad. You will work yourself to death and think it's fun."

Back in the house, Ben repeated the conversation to Mary when the children had gone to bed.

"Amelia's talking the same way," she replied. "She said the other day she didn't want to be a farmer's wife. She wants to be a nurse."

"A nurse," Ben snorted. "For heaven's sake, that's ten times more stressful and low-paying than farming."

"Now, hon, you know what you've always said. They should go out and get a taste of the world before they go into farming, or they will always think they missed out on something."

"It's your schools that are doing it," Ben said coldly. "The rich want a large supply of factory workers, not independent farmers. The government wants to get rid of us too. Some years we don't even have to pay any income tax."

Mary did not answer. She was not sure he was wrong, for one thing. But she wanted both children to go to college, and now that she was teaching full time, they could afford to send them. If they did go, however, that would mean a quarrel with Ben. But there was no helping it. The way the world was turning, there was a great possibility that neither Amelia nor Natty might come back to farming. But she could not say that to Ben just yet. It would hurt him too deeply. He would have to get used to the idea slowly, over time. She felt a great sorrow for him. His world was passing away. And it seemed that whenever something did turn out favorably for him, like the corn contest, something else immediately followed to knock the legs out from under him. It was a shame, too, because she knew that his ideas were not really old-fashioned but far ahead of what was considered modern at the moment.

Ben leaned over the bottom half of the Dutch cow stable door, listening to the hum of the milking machine vacuum motor and the measured, repeated click of the pulsator. At each click, the teat cups on the front quarters of the cow being milked tugged downward and the cups on the back quarters let up, back and forth, gently pulling the milk in alternating tugs from the teats into the milker bucket. He did not consciously hear the gentle noises, but if the least hesitation or irregularity had occurred in the steady clicking, he would have sprung quickly to the machine to find out what was wrong.

Natty, home from college, listened to his father chattering on about a new idea that was gripping his imagination. Ben did not notice how Natty was shifting uncomfortably from foot to foot, evidently waiting for an opportune moment to say something. Quiet by nature, his son often seemed, in all his early years working with Ben, to be his father's shadow, hovering near him, anticipating unerringly what needed to be done. Ben spoke proudly of him as the perfect farmer's son, seeming to grasp instinctively, without the kind of instruction most young people required, what and how farm work needed to be done.

"We've been farming all wrong," Ben was saying. "We don't need to be plowing up all the fields every year to grow grains. Look how expensive that's become. The cows can do most of the work themselves, simply by grazing. It's so obvious that we've overlooked it. Keep the land in improved pastures that will provide grazing for at least ten months. Farm animals will produce plenty of meat, milk, and eggs without all that expense of annual grain production."

"Dad, there's something we need to—"

"Do you have any idea how much money would be saved in machinery, fuel, and fertilizer costs?" Ben went on. "And the animals would eat the weeds too, could be all the herbicides we need. It is just such a great—"

"Dad, I've been offered a good job in the oil fields in Texas."

Ben, deep in his thoughts of farming revolution, stopped short, whirled around, and stared at his son. He could think of nothing to say. He could almost hear his plans for the future with Natty at his side crashing down around him.

"It pays very well," Natty continued, looking in vain for some sign of congratulations in his father's expression. He added, desperately, "I'll save enough money so I can maybe come back to farming as your equal partner.

"I thought I'd try it. See what it's like."

Ben managed not to say, as he so wanted to, that Natty could save money working on the farm too. Nor did he repeat what his father had always insisted, that it took three dedicated generations to make a financially successful farm. He knew he needed, instead, to show approval. He tried, but his words sounded hollow. "Well, if you don't try something else, you'll always wonder if farming was the right thing. I guess."

"Yes, that's what I was thinking, too," Natty said, seizing on Ben's words, trying to squeeze some sign of approval out of them.

Ben needed to get away. He didn't trust his emotions. "You finish up here," he said. "I forgot to close the back pasture gate."

Stumbling along in the dark, full of foreboding now about the future, Ben glumly reviewed what suddenly seemed like the fruitlessness of his life. Natty's decision made it so apparent. Here it was 1978, and he was over a half century old already. He could remember when his father was that age and seemed, to a boy's eyes, an old man. But what held his attention now, thinking of Natty, thinking of time's relentlessly continuing change, was not how quickly he had grown older, but how quickly the kind of farming he was following had gone out of mainstream agriculture. His father had come to America bearing with him an agriculture that was more like that of the Middle Ages than that of modern times. In hardly two generations, the old ways had been swallowed up by the piston engine. While most of the offspring of the farmers who came to America before the turn of the twentieth century remained in farming, most of their offspring drifted away to the towns and cities. A tidal wave of change had passed over the landscape with hardly a whimper of public acknowledgment, let alone protest. The husbandmen who understood what had happened limped silently off into the gloaming of old age, or wrote sentimental recollections of a past that only other old husbandmen honored. Very few people cared for a real farming life tied to animals and the natural world, and now his own son, his beloved Natty, born to farming, possessing the physical and mental knack that could make farming successful, was proving the cruelty of it all. Most people were glad to be shut of real farming. Husbandry was not a song that the modern ear could hear. Ben wondered if the few who could not deny the song were somehow cursed.

He did not feel cursed himself—just cheated by what had become the economics of the situation. Now even his son, as his daughter had already done, was declaring for the new life. The money gods had smiled on the piston engine and the farmers who swore allegiance to it, a seeming fact that he had chosen to ignore. In his devotion to husbandry he had selfishly ignored any other possible future for his family. Perhaps if he had embraced modern farming more avidly, Natty and Amelia, wanting to live more like their "urban counterparts," would be enjoying the fruits of the new flow of money that seemed to line other farmers' pockets these days. Perhaps then they would have chosen to stay on the farm. But a husbandman could hardly live like his urban counterparts, money or no money. He hated that phrase. What was the urban counterpart of husbandry? Apartment dwellers taking their dogs out on leashes so the poor animals could shit on the public grass?

He knew that Mary would like to travel, perhaps to the ocean beaches of Florida and the ski slopes of Colorado, surely a trip to Europe to visit the places that her study of history had enshrined in her mind. That's what "successful" farmers were doing. But if she pined for such diversions, she never said so, and in fact seemed of one vision with him. She seemed to enjoy diversions at home, like hunting Indian relics and morel mushrooms, fishing and swimming in farm ponds, sledding and skating in winter, bird watching and wild flower collecting, all the many activities that he found more exciting than faraway travel. Not that they had much choice in the matter. If they did want to go on a trip, who would take care of and milk the cows properly? Dairy farming surely suited him, if for no other reason than that he dreaded the whole idea of traveling afar. He had no interest in fat, nude angels painted on church ceilings or skyscrapers thrusting ridiculously into the clouds. A couple of hours away from the farm and he began to get nervous.

He did know that Mary shared his interest in the farm. If that had not been so, he could not have succeeded, if indeed he was succeeding. It took two people, at least, to make husbandry work. But had his chosen way of life cheated his children out of theirs? He and Mary had both insisted on homeschooling them, restricting their involvement in activities at school that other children were being immersed in, growing up without the so-called proper integration into social life. Had they been wrong, as the critics of homeschooling said? His children had surely seemed happy enough. But the homeschooling was the reason Mary had encouraged them to go to college, to get out on their own for a while, and she insisted on it when Ben resisted.

Damned college. He remembered suddenly the words of an old Grange song: "How you gonna keep them down on the farm after they've seen Paree?" But Mary had a good answer. "I went to college, Ben. It didn't keep me from seeing the good opportunities in farming. You've got to let the children see the rest of the world. You've always said that. If they don't come to farming after seeing the other alternatives, they won't last in it anyway. You've always said that too."

Staring out at the moon, he contemplated the possible results of all the changes. If farmers quit raising livestock, who would do that work? Did the wise men of economics really believe that huge animal factories, manned by poorly paid laborers who lacked the art of and devotion to husbandry, would produce enough meat, milk, and eggs to feed the world? Ben had seen what happened when Emmet tried to operate a big feedlot: mountains of manure and steady ministrations of antibiotics to keep the animals from getting sick. Would subsidies keep corn cheap enough so that the animal factories could afford to buy huge quantities of it shipped in by train and truck?

Mary had fixed Natty's favorite meal that night, but there was not much talk around the table about how tender and juicy was the pork roast, nor how crispy the fried potatoes. Natty gulped his food down, guiltily keeping his eyes on his plate. Ben was stony silent. Mary thought she might have to leave the room to cry. She wanted to ply Natty with questions, wanted him to know how proud she was of him for the incentive he was showing, but was afraid to say so in the face of Ben's belligerence. Natty finally left the table.

Ben, in utter desperation, started talking about pasture farming again, loud enough for Natty in the living room to hear. He was hoping against hope that he could convince his son of a future more promising than hustling vanishing reserves of oil.

"We don't really need to be planting and harvesting and storing and drying and transporting all that grain," he said. "Don't need plows, disks, combines."

Mary was not used to her husband making grandiose remarks. Nor did she feel like humoring him. "Have you been into the hard cider again?"

"Think about it. A cow has four legs, teeth, and four stomachs adapted to making efficient use of forages. Why are we penning her up and hauling food to her? She's perfectly capable of feeding herself and saving farmers a lot of time and money."

"You've been reading *Front Porch Farmer* again, haven't you?"

"Well, like that book says, why can't I just sit on the porch and watch my animals graze for their food instead of beating myself to death feeding them machine-produced grains? Or maybe I could buy up oil stocks while they grazed." The latter of course was for Natty's ears.

"You said that the guy who wrote that book farmed in Georgia where it's warm year-round, and he was probably rich enough to quit farming anyway."

"Well, maybe I was wrong. Maybe winter weather is not as much of a hindrance to pasture farming after all. We could graze corn and stuff that sticks above the snow in winter like the buffalo did. Dad brags about the year he fattened a bunch of steers on corn in the shock. Worked fine and he didn't have to husk all that corn. He could have just left the corn standing in the field and turned the steers in. He wouldn't have had to work at harvesting at all."

"He'd still have to plow and plant."

"Still be a big savings. And you can sow clover, wheat, rye, and oats right on top of the ground with a twenty-dollar broadcast planter over your shoulder, and they'll make a fair stand. Look how Emmet's wheat fields grow up in volunteer wheat after harvest. "

Mary nodded. Emmet's volunteer wheat coming up in the stubble of the harvested crop was a little joke in the neighborhood. Emmet, always in a hurry, tended to overlook details of farming, like adjusting the combine so all the grain going through it went into the bin, not back out on the ground with the straw. Losing just two bushels per acre was enough to grow a nice stand of volunteer wheat, and didn't worry Emmet like it would Ben.

"All I'm saying is that most seeds will sprout naturally right on top of the ground if it rains, and then you could graze them. So why till soil?"

Natty re-entered the kitchen. "If it's such a good idea, why haven't farmers been doing it?" His voice quavered. He had never challenged his father before.

Ben took the challenge in stride. Maybe Natty was listening to him. "Well, for one thing, the government subsidizes grain, not grass. All of agricultural policy is framed to favor grain. Easier to ship grain overseas than hay to balance trade."

"Then why not take advantage of subsidies, if that's where the money is?"

That was too much for Ben. He pushed away from the table and stalked out of the house. He didn't come back in until he knew Natty had gone to bed. Then he was up at four in the morning and didn't come back to the house until his son had left for college. Mary kept to herself all day, crying.

Ben had to talk to someone. Over at Emmet's, he started out by talking about pasture farming.

"You are out of your mind, Ben Bump," Emmet said even before Ben could lay out the whole notion.

"You wouldn't say that to your great-grandfather. He was a pasture farmer, you know. He ran sheep and cattle all over this country, and he made money."

"Economics changes things. This ground is too expensive to keep in pasture."

"It's too expensive for grain, too. That's why the government has to subsidize you to grow it."

Emmet smiled, looking off into the distance. Ben could make backward farming sound logical while being unaware that he was a dying breed, a husbandman. His kind would disappear in another generation. "You're the Last of the Mohicans," he said.

"Natty isn't going to farm with me," Ben said.

Emmet could hear the disappointment in his brother-in-law's voice. He knew how Ben had counted on Natty. It had seemed a foregone conclusion. The irony was that Emmet's own young Floyd, who had showed more interest in golf than farming, was now eager to stay in farming, at least the kind Emmet practiced.

"I truly am sad for you," Emmet said, and he meant it. He had two sons in Florida whom he dearly missed. In fact, he had been calling them nearly every night lately, just to talk. They were old enough now to handle phone conversations, but acted polite and hesitant, as if they were talking to an uncle, not their father. But when he did get them talking, he was surprised that they often asked questions about the farm. They remembered. They seemed more interested, in a way, than Floyd was. Time after time, he was on the verge of just outright asking them if they ever thought of coming back to be part of the golf course/farming enterprise, to be part of Gowler Enterprises. But with Ginny surely listening to every word, he dared not. And he was afraid their answers would be negative. "But you know, you have to let young people make their choices. You just have to."

Ben nodded but did not answer. He wasn't going to get any sympathy here.

In an effort to change the subject, Emmet brought up a new rumor in the neighborhood. "There's one of those big chicken factories coming in here."

Ben looked stunned. "Here?"

"Yeah, here."

"Here as in Gowler?"

"The Remps are going to sell them the land. And then Louie gets to be what they call a manure broker. Think of that, you old grasslander. A manure broker, for shit's sake."

"What does a manure broker do?" Ben had to smile.

"You just gotta start thinkin', Ben ol' boy. When you put ten million chickens in one place, you got a lot of manure on your hands."

"No one would be crazy enough to try to raise ten million chickens in one place."

"You just don't think big enough, my friend." Emmet was enjoying himself. "Know how much manure that makes?" And before Ben could figure it out, Emmet answered his own question. He'd already run the math. "If a chicken eats a hundred pounds a year, about what it does, it will shit about forty pounds. Forty pounds times ten million is four hundred million pounds, or two hundred thousand tons." He waited for Ben to be properly impressed. "That's over five hundred tons *every day*. How's that for a chickenshit operation? "

"I don't want to live within twenty miles of it."

"Hey, we could all quit buying fertilizer and use chickenshit."

"I don't buy any now."

"I keep forgetting. But the rest of us could really use that manure."

"What do you think they'll charge for it?"

"See, that's the beauty. They think they can make money on it, but if we won't buy it, they'll have to give it away to get rid of it. They haven't thought that far, I guess."

"Who is 'they,' anyway?"

"Rumor says someone from out of the country. Some Dutchman. Must be rollin' in dough."

"What do you do with ten million eggs every day? They'll have to have a steady stream of semis hauling feed in and eggs out."

"Eggs and manure."

"This'll never happen. There's not that many eggs laid daily in the whole state, is there?"

"You're lookin' at the future, Ben."

"Don't tell me you think it's a good idea."

"Hey, all that manure for cheap fertilizer and a ready-made corn and soybean market right here."

"And then we'll get a million-head hog factory, and then there won't be anybody left around here 'cause the smell will run everyone into the next county. And your house won't be worth two cents."

Ben climbed back into his pickup and drove angrily away. The end of the world must be coming. He'd talk to his father. Surely old Nat would have something sympathetic to say.

Nat listened to Ben's revolutionary pasture farming ideas, then smiled. "Well, you're going right back to how we did in the old country!" he exclaimed. "We couldn't raise crops on those mountainsides. It was *all* grazing and hay. Drove the cows and sheep up the mountains in spring and back down again before snow flew. And stacked hay for winter." His face glowed with the memories. "That was a good time. War wrecked it all."

Do you think it would work here?

"I never gave it the thought," he said. "Don't know why not."

"Natty's taking a job away from the farm." Ben eyed his father intently. Nat's face grew somber. He did something he had never done before. He embraced his son.

"I can't say I know how you feel," he said, the pain visible in his face. "You stayed with me, sort of. But it hurt when you decided to go on your own, even just down the road. Sometimes I think the second-hardest thing in life is to do your best to raise your children, and then they leave you. But they have to leave you, one way or another, you know. That's life."

Ben nodded, then turned away. He did not want his father to see his tears.

After years of assuring himself that four thousand acres was enough farm for anyone, Emmet Gowler changed his mind. If the Remps and Chafers were moving up to four thousand acres, then he, by God, would move up to five thousand. Land prices had been going up dizzily since the late seventies, and as 1982 approached, there was little sign of the boom slowing down. Well, actually, as he would recall later, there were a few economists warning that in an economy based on money interest, what goes up precipitously will in all likelihood come down precipitously. But Emmet was listening to the optimists. Buy now and avoid the higher prices of tomorrow. The good Lord wasn't making any more land.

Emmet believed because Emmet wanted to believe. He didn't really care about making more money. He just wanted to walk among the high-rollers and get that nod of recognition reserved for princes of capitalism. The golf course, although not particularly profitable, did bring the proper esteem he longed for. But he wanted more. He wanted to have a tombstone in Oak Hill cemetery bigger than that of his great-great-grandfather David. David's monument was nearly three stories tall. The old sheep-and-cattle farmer had paid for it in 1897 by selling the farm he had bought in Iowa years earlier, which had risen in value since the frontier land sales. He had planned in his early years to drive cattle and sheep from all over the Midwest to urban markets, as he was doing already from Ohio to Detroit and Philadelphia before the Civil War. At that time, he could not foresee the railroads.

Emmet liked to say that his ancestor's buying land in Iowa and Illinois was no different that his decision now to buy land in Mississippi. David Gowler came to be called the Wool King of the World, and Emmet dreamed of being hailed as the Soybean King of the World.

He told Ben about the land scheme, knowing that Ben would be against it, but curious as to how his friend would express his opposition.

"I've got three partners," Emmet explained. "Two big farmers I know in Illinois and an agricultural economist. We bought four thousand acres down there. We're calling our partnership the Vulcan Venture. You know, after that old god. We're gonna vulcanize farming. Make it better."

"Sounds to me like Killdeer all over again." Ben had never heard of Vulcan and doubted Emmet had either. A name an economist might think up.

"What do you mean?"

"Remember when farmers, including my Dad, thought Killdeer looked like rich, black, level land and couldn't understand why it was selling so cheap? They thought the locals were ignorant. You could be making the same mistake."

"Well, this economist fella, Dr. McLoden, has looked into the deal and says it's a winner. He's well respected, you know. And the two farmers. I know 'em. Smart cookies. They say we can't lose. I looked the place over. Level, black land and—"

"Just like Killdeer? "

"No, no. Lighter. Lays right along the Mississippi. Good for cotton, and we think it will raise hellacious soybeans. They grow thirty-acre beans down there, so we figure we can easily get fifty. We've got more know-how." No reply from Ben.

"We've got to diversify, you know," Emmet continued. "If it doesn't rain here one year, maybe it'll rain in Mississippi. If the corn market's down, maybe the bean market will be up. Or cotton. We might rent out the cotton. None of us knows how to grow it firsthand. Anyway, the government will take care of us. There's so few farmers left, it can't afford not to."

"So that's the way capitalists think these days."

"A capitalist has to take opportunity where he finds it."

"Why don't you relax and take up a hobby, like golf?" Ben asked, sarcastically.

"That's what farming is. A hobby. My business is golf."

"You said golf wasn't very profitable either."

"Well, it's diversification. You can make a whole lot more money from a bushel of golf balls than a bushel of soybeans. And if I have to, I can always plow the whole thing up and crop it again." He smiled. "That's what Mother always says."

"Does Nan go along with this?"

"I tell her that we gotta think about our son. If I need four thousand acres to stay in farming, he'll need eight thousand. And we gotta think about Chris and Timmy down in Florida. They might want to farm some day too."

"So Nan doesn't go along with the idea."

Emmet grinned, sheepishly this time. "She says so long as she has her own farm, and can't lose it to any harebrained Gowler scheme, she doesn't care."

Ben laughed. That sounded like Nan, all right.

"One thing I don't understand about that farm down there," Emmet went on. "It comes with eight bulldozers. Kind of strange. They've got levees to keep up, sure, but *eight* bulldozers? I guess that's part of thinking big."

The collapse in land prices came suddenly. One day farms in central Illinois were selling upwards of three thousand dollars an acre, and the next day the vitality just squished out of the demand, like a tire when the valve pops out of it. Economists would later say they could date the beginning of the drop almost to the day. General realization of the sudden change, however, came slowly because the harbingers of market news, as always, played down the negative figures, hoping that they would go away. Instead, the situation got worse. Land purchased for three thousand dollars an acre in 1981 would not bring one thousand dollars an acre by 1983. It spelled ruin for high-rollers who had financed expansion with borrowed money.

"People are talking just like they did in 1933," Nat Bump observed dryly. "Only they don't know it because none of them were farming in 1933."

The land bust dealt the Vulcan Venture a double blow. The investors had paid "only" nineteen hundred dollars an acre for the Mississippi land, but its value by 1985 had wilted to eight hundred dollars an acre, and even then no one was buying. But that was only part of the dilemma.

As it turned out, four of the bulldozers needed major repairs.

As it turned out, 1982 was extra-rainy along portions of the Mississippi Valley, and even eight bulldozers could not keep up with washed-out levees.

As it turned out, the three thousand acres were more like twenty-five hundred, with a five-hundred-acre lake lapping at the dead furrows when high water occurred.

As it turned out, the Vulcan Venture did not vulcanize anything except the bank accounts of the party who had sold the land.

"Good fishin' hole," Emmet joked sourly, in the same tone of voice he used when referring to the Gowler holdings in Killdeer as "good huntin' territory."

But the situation was not a joking matter. With upwards of five million dollars invested in the land alone, and with crop prices languishing, the Vulcan Venture lost its sparkle overnight and lost money consistently. When the three farmers learned that their expert economist was trying to divest himself of his share in the venture, Emmet became alarmed.

"What's this about you trying to sell out of the partnership?" he asked McLoden on the phone.

"The university is beginning to question the prudence of professors being in business while drawing full-time salaries from teaching," McLoden said, clearing his voice.

"Bullshit," Emmet replied, and hung up. He'd been a fool, he could see now.

Somehow he had to think of a way out without losing everything. But what?

Meanwhile, Ben was busy turning his little farm into what he liked to call a paradise of grass and clover. He had to move slowly, trial and error, changing only one field at a time, as he learned what was required to make milk profitably with only a minimum of grain and the soil cultivation that grain required. By 1985, he had worked out most of the problems. He had established fields of permanent cool-season grasses for spring and fall pasture, and fields of legumes and clovers for hay and for dry midsummer grazing. The permanent pastures reseeded themselves naturally with bluegrass and Little Dutch white clover and increased in vigor every year from the manure and urine the cows dropped. The rest of the acres, thirty, he divided into three rotated plots, one of corn and the other two red clover. Only the ten acres in corn had to be cultivated, which meant that a plot in the rotation was cultivated only once every three years. He found he could renew the red clover by broadcasting more seed into the existing clover in its third, declining, year, or, in the aftermath of the bared corn field, eliminating machinery for seedbed preparation. With only ten acres of corn, he could use his horse machinery for both planting and harvesting. If only Natty were here to share his sense of victory.

He tried strange new ideas, like growing oats in corn for grazing both crops in December and January. That worked but had some disadvantages. Fall oats were prone to fungal disease in the shade of the corn. Grazing corn in winter worked better, and he learned by accident that the animals favored sweet corn. They ate the stalks right down to the ground. And he could use some of the sweet corn to sell at the local farmer's market which was starting in Surrey.

The real problem with winter grazing was that it was practical only on frozen ground. During thaws, the cows tramped six-inch holes in the soft soil surface and had to be kept in the barn and fed hay along with a little corn. He could disk a pugged field for cropping the next year, but in the long run he wanted to avoid all cultivation. The mud problem prompted him to an experiment that made even Mary wonder about his enthusiasm for what he constantly called "a new way to farm." He decided to buy some sheep. Not just any sheep. Dairy sheep—crosses with East Friesians, which were touted for their ability to produce milk.

"Milking *sheep?*" was Mary's reaction. "What's come over you, Ben Bump?"

"There are sheep dairies all over Europe," he replied patiently. "I've been reading. The United States imports almost all of its Roquefort cheese, you know."

"How do you milk a sheep?"

"Just like you milk goats."

"Well, wouldn't goats be better, then?"

"I may try goats too. But I know sheep better than I know goats. And I keep thinking that sheep produce wool too, not to mention lamb chops."

"Where are you going to get them?"

"There's sheep dairies around. In New England, anyway. I've already contacted one."

"Are dairy sheep expensive?"

"Yes. I can't afford them really. But I'm only going to buy a ram and breed up from there. I'll look for high-producing ewes around here, whatever the breed. We had one when I was a kid that gave as much milk as a goat."

"But why, Ben? What's wrong with cows? "

"Sheep and goats can run on pastures in winter thaws without ruining them. Cows are too heavy."

"You are really something else." And she kissed him.

Mary was easier to convince than Nan because Mary had not grown up in agriculture and so had not inherited the prejudices of the Midwestern farmer. Nan just howled at the sheep dairy idea. "Don't sell your cows just yet, brother dear. Milk sheep? You're getting as daffy as that husband of mine. He's hauling his tractors and equipment on semi-trucks to Mississippi, and you're going to milk sheep. God help us."

"Well, what about those weird horses of yours?" he replied defensively.

She ignored that. "And you know what he says? He says because he uses that equipment twice a year now, once here and once down there, it actually pays to haul it around like that. I tell you, men can find a reason to make anything sound sane."

"Producing sheep cheese is not foolish," Nat said from the corner where he was dozing in his old rocker. They had not thought he was listening. Mostly he slept these days. "We milked sheep in the old country," he continued. "Actually it tastes just as good as cow's milk. Ask your mother."

Ben beamed. He was getting the kind of support he needed from a source he had least expected. His father had never seemed fond of new ideas. But, as he was pointing out, this was not a new idea.

"What you've been doing is bringing to America an ancient pastoral kind of farming from the old country. And you didn't even know it."

Dorothy, frail now and almost as bent as Nat, smiled and said once more what she had said so often through the years. "You will go far in this old world, my boy."

That reminded Ben of the first time she had said that, when he had hidden the Fruit Juice in the park pool. His eyes filled suddenly with tears. All of them had come far since those days. Maybe they would go all the way back to the beloved land of her youth that she never really wanted to leave. Maybe he could bring it to her.

"We have all come a long way," he spoke his thoughts out loud.

"Ja, and I'm about at the end of the trail," Nat said, looking furtively at the others and then looking away again.

"Now don't you go talking that way," Dorothy remonstrated. "You're doing just fine."

"Not long for this old world," Nat said again.

"Have you been feeling poorly?" Ben wanted to know.

"Not really, but I got some discussion I want to have with all of you. I've been waiting till we were all four here together, alone."

Dorothy and Ben stared at him, not knowing what to say or where Nat was headed in the conversation. Nan looked out the window, rolling her eyes.

"I don't want all that funeral stuff. I don't want people staring at my dead body. I want you to take me out on the hill behind the barn and bury me there, soon as I'm dead." He was out with it now, and felt a great relief.

"What are you telling us?" Ben asked.

"I'm just saying I don't want a church funeral."

"You are going to pain me over religion even after you're dead," Dorothy said. "I just don't see why you have to be so stubborn."

"Why does the unbeliever always have to be the bad guy?" Nat replied. "Why can't my beliefs be respected? I don't want people staring and praying over my dead body. They by Gott called me a Nazi and a traitor all my life and I say to hell with them."

"Humph. You don't believe in hell either. You should try to make it a little easier on the people who love you," she replied. "What do you care about the ceremony if you're dead?"

Ben cleared his throat. Why was everything so difficult? "Mother, it's all right with me if Dad wants to be buried on the hill. That he doesn't want all that churchy stuff." He was looking at Nan, looking for help.

Nan had obviously not given death much thought so far. The realization that her parents were approaching that time unnerved her. For once, she had nothing to say. But Ben was insistent.

"I guess I don't care much one way or the other," she finally said. "Do we have to talk like this?"

"So the truth is, Mom, neither Nan nor I oppose our father's wish. As for me, when the time comes, I'd just as soon be cremated and the ashes spread over the farm."

Dorothy, aghast, sucked in her breath. "But that's against the church," she said.

"Now, Mother, you know I don't care what the church says any more than Dad does." Nat's rocker was thudding and knocking away rapidly now. He was enjoying the turn that the conversation had taken.

"Actually, lots of folks are getting cremated," Nan said, emboldened by Ben now. "Aunt Matilda says she's for it."

"Matilda's just trying to get attention," Dorothy sniffed. A pause. She'd take another tack. "I thought it would be nice if Pa and I would remain side by side in blessed ground when it was all over. Can't a wife get her way on one thing in life?"

Silence. Nat wanted to repeat back to her about what she had said earlier about his selfishness, but decided not to push his luck. More silence.

That fall, Ben and Mary drove their pickup to Vermont to get a Friesian ram, leaving Nan and young Floyd to look after the cows. Ben wished he could call on Natty and Amelia, but they were off in their own worlds, making money. Ben and Mary drove through the golden days of autumn basking in a sort of second honeymoon, confident in their love for each other and that they were on the road to success, even if the sheep-milking experiment didn't work out. While grain farmers struggled, the Bumps were starting to make real profits from their dairy. Milk prices were increasing a little, and surplus young heifers were selling at very good prices. With grass farming, milk production was holding steady, while costs were coming down. It would be at least five more years before they had enough sheep for a dairy flock, but in the meantime cows would surely continue to be profitable. That also gave them time to learn cheese-making, time to build a neat little store from which to sell cheese, eggs, even lamb chops, a way to enlarge the business so that Natty and Amelia could be a part of it if they ever decided to come home. Lamb prices were on the rise too, as immigrants from eastern and Asian countries flooded into the United States. Mary thought she might learn how to spin and weave their own wool into rugs and shawls and sell those too.

"Why, I declare, Ben Bump, what are we going to do with all that money?"

He smiled and squeezed her hand so hard it almost hurt.

Emmet had been right about one thing. As he put it suc-
cinctly, the government saved the Vulcan Venture's ass. In
order to stop the hemorrhage of money out of farming, the U.S.
Department of Agriculture came up with a program called
PIK—payment-in-kind. The fundamental idea, the theory, was
to decrease production to where supply was more in line with
demand.

Emmet, drinking coffee with a knot of farmers in Blue Room
University, could not repress his smiles at how the program was
unfolding. As far as he could figure, PIK would be the biggest give-
away program yet, and maybe profitable in ways the government
had not foreseen.

"This is like giving poor people food and food stamps both, only
poor people can't buy and sell their stamps," Emmet said to no one
in particular.

"What do you fairly mean by that?" Jake Lavendar asked. He was
listening to Franklin and Dick Farnold discussing tractors at the
other end of the table, a subject much more interesting to him than
the government's latest farm program scheme.

"I cannot for the life of me understand why some of the Amish
and Mennonites switch to tractors sometimes, but only steel-

wheeled ones," Franklin was saying. "Like there's something evil about riding on air."

"For one thing," Ben Bump replied, "steel wheels will last a whole lot longer than riding on air, and you don't get flat tires."

"Might get your teeth jarred out instead," Dick answered. "What you save in flat tires, you lose in dental expenses."

"There's one respect in which rubber tires are not an advantage over steel lugs," Lester Cordrey said officiously. "In the early days in Killdeer, the rattlesnakes were so thick they'd strike at the tractor tires rollin' past 'em, and their fangs would get stuck in the rubber. All of a sudden you got a rattler comin' up on the tire and maybe landin' in your lap, and that's not the kind of excitement anyone appreciates."

"You're thull of shit," Franklin said. "That couldn't happen."

"The hell I am!" Lester roared. "You go talk to old Bob Myers. By God, it happened to him. He says if it weren't for fenders on the tractors, he'd be dead by now."

"Dad says that old Bob's dad could smell rattlers when he got close to them," Dick recalled. "He could smell them hidin' under wheat shocks, and he'd turn over those shocks real easy before he forked them on the wagon."

Franklin started to tell about his latest stroke of genius. He had acquired seven older tractors and fixed them all to run for about the price of two newer ones. "I got tired of hitching and unhitching implements, not havin' kids around to help," he explained. "Now I just keep each tractor hitched to a particular implement permanently. Never have to get on and off the tractor seven times or so to get hitched up proper. Worth the extra cost, and the tractors don't wear out so fast because you don't use them as much as when you got only one or two."

Emmet was waiting for a proper moment to get Lavendar's full attention. Now he broke in. "Well, instead of giving us money out-right, Uncle Sam is going to give us certificates that stand for so many bushels of grain we produce, or actually," and here he chuck-led, "for what we don't produce." He kept smiling because of what he believed was going to happen. "They will give you certificates, depending on how much land you don't plant, that stand for so much of the grain in CCC storage that it has already bought from us once, and then we can sell it again but not to the government. You can redeem the certs whenever you think their value will allow a little profit beyond and above subsidy floor prices. Right?"

"I guess so. To be honest, I don't fairly understand it."

"Well, here's what farmers will do. They'll start betting with those certificates. So will investors. They'll start trading in them instead of in real crops. It'll be just like the stock market. Pretty soon those certificates won't represent the real grain situation, but just another way to gamble. Farmers love to gamble. A whole lot more of them are signing up for the program than the gov-ernment figured because, hell, you can't hardly lose. Uncle Sam thought this kind of subsidy wouldn't cost so much, but because it has to buy grain to cover the certificates now, the program is cost-ing more."

"Well, what's fairly wrong with that? Sounds like it will get rid of surplus."

"Only temporarily. PIK is still a set-aside program not all that different than the one in the sixties. Every set-aside program ever made has the purpose of carrying farmers over a period of hard times so they can continue to farm exactly the same market-glutting way they were farming before the crisis. Set-asides guarantee noth-ing will change, so there'll always be another round of surpluses.

The government and John Q. Public want surpluses so food stays cheap. Only this PIK thing goes one even better. Not only do you get paid in certificates not to plant crops, but the real juicy part is that big farms have a special compensation. In effect they get paid *more per acre* in certificates than small farmers do."

"Oh, come on."

"Hey, says so here right in the *Farm Journal*."

"You mean the richer the farmer, the more he gets paid?" Ben asked. "How's that for democracy?"

"Well, sure," Emmet said, feigning self-righteousness to needle Ben. "Since we're bigger, we should get more."

"And that's not all," chimed in Franklin. "You can put your whole thucking tharm in the program and that's what rich landowners will do."

"And then if you're sharp at buying and selling certificates, you just *really* might make some money by not farming," Emmet concluded triumphantly.

That's how he got out of the Vulcan Venture. He and his fellow entrepreneurs put every acre of their Mississippi holdings that the government allowed, especially the five-hundred-acre temporary lake, into the program. The PIK certificates saved the three large-scale farmers from disaster, and so the government agencies considered the money well spent. The farmers eventually sold their certificates during brief spikes in grain prices, which allowed them to break even on overall annual production, more or less. Hardest hit was McLoden, whose fee for giving speeches telling farmers how to make more money declined significantly.

The Vulcan partners sold the farm in 1987 for twelve hundred dollars an acre, seven hundred less than they had paid, and felt lucky, since in addition to the PIK money that had kept them afloat, they could also take a huge deduction on income taxes for the losses they had been incurring. When Emmet did the accounting, he figured he lost outright only about a "hunderd-thou" but "a quarter million for tax purposes." When he said that, his accountant looked thoughtfully toward the horizon and did not respond. The other farmers claimed similar losses.

The company that bought the land from the Vulcans, so insiders in Mississippi were fond of saying, included people who had been in the partnership that had sold it to them in the first place. The running joke along the lower Mississippi Delta was that the buyers were now looking around for another northerner who thought he was way ahead of southern agriculture.

THIRTY-ONE

Dorothy called Ben one day to say that Nat had not come back from the barn at dinnertime and she could not find him puttering around anywhere. Expecting the worst, Ben drove over to his father's farm, checked the barn and barnyard, but could not find him. He called out and, to his relief, heard a faint answer up the hill behind the barn. He spotted Nat's stooped figure, and as he approached, could hardly believe what his father was trying to do. He was leaning on a shovel, looking peeved. Beside him was the beginning of an excavation, about four by eight feet in size—big enough for a coffin. But the old man had removed barely a few inches of dirt off the top of the rectangle.

"Dad? What are you doing?"

"Diggin' a grave, but I got all tuckered out. Not worth a damn anymore."

Ben stared from the dirt to the man and back again. "I said I'd do it when the time comes, Dad."

"The time has come."

"Have you talked to a doctor?"

"I don't need to pay money to know that I'm headed west."

"Headed west?"

"Old saying. Setting sun."

"Are you hurting?"

"Not much. That's the good thing. I guess that's good."

"How do you know, then?"

"I'm just givin' out. I can tell. Heart hurts just from diggin' up ten shovels full of dirt. Took all I had to walk up the hill."

Ben stared at him.

"It's okay, son. It's not worth living when you don't feel like living anymore. I used to dread dying, but when you're there it ain't so bad. Then you just want the relief of it. The only bad part is feeling like I'm letting you and Nan and Mother and the grandchildren down. Like I'm failing the family. It helps to try to find ways to take care of my dying that don't bother you."

"But we *want* to be bothered," Ben said softly. "You're our *father,* for heaven's sake." He took the shovel gently from Nat's hands and started digging. What a crazy thing. Digging his father's grave while his father watched.

"Did you ever hear the one about the gravedigger who had to quit his job because of age?" Nat asked. "He could still dig 'em, but he couldn't get out of the hole no more."

Ben laughed, harder than the joke deserved. It encouraged him to ask something that had been gnawing at him.

"You know, Dad, when I think hard on it, death seems as natural as birth. At least death from old age. So why does it upset us so? When a child is born, we rejoice at nature's miracle even though we know it will mean problems and heartaches as well as happiness. Why shouldn't we rejoice when someone dies who needs to die? That's a sort of miracle too, isn't it? If people didn't die, we'd be in an awful fix."

"Ah, Ben, the times I've thought about that, over and over. We crave to keep on living, even when we know the arithmetic of not dying won't add up."

"Yeah. What if everyone who ever was born was still alive?" Ben was shoveling furiously now.

"Used to be people would make sure there was a keg of beer at the wake, just like at weddings. A celebration of a life well lived and death a relief. Dat's the way to go." He could not stop himself, when overtaken with emotion, from slipping back into his immigrant English.

"How about some Fruit Juice instead of beer?" Ben said, mischievously.

"Your mother would have a hemorrhage."

"I bet not. Why don't you run off a batch for the funeral? They can't throw you in jail if you're dead."

A huge smile broke over Nat's face. Even in death he would have the last laugh at what he called government of the wealthy, by the wealthy, and for the wealthy. He grabbed Ben's hand and almost fell into the hole, shaking it. "By Gott, *dat's* what I'll do."

After that, Nat's health took a turn for the better. There was a certain spring in his step that Dorothy had not seen for months. He was humming again as he went about his daily routine. The habit had once driven her to distraction, but now it came as a welcome respite. As he took a new interest in life, he quit hanging around the house, which had always made her nervous. That he would disappear for hours at a time did seem a little strange, but that was preferable to standing around, shadowing her.

"What's gotten into you lately?" she asked. "You're acting like you're up to something."

"Just feeling better," he said. "I think it's all that asparagus and dandelion salad we've been eating. Old pisser's workin' better."

She glanced at him sharply. "You mind your language, old man. You'll be talking like that around the children one of these days, and I won't tolerate it."

Nat only half heard her. His mind was busy figuring out a way to build a whiskey still while keeping the project from her watchful eyes. He had first decided to go into Killdeer and dig up the still he had buried so long ago, but after a preliminary jaunt trying to find the old landmarks in what was now mostly brush, he was so exhausted that he decided the better course was to build a new still. That meant acquiring copper coils and something to use as a boiler, among other things. He had to depend on Ben more than he liked, but there was a benefit to that: it was high time Ben learned how to make good whiskey. Never know when the government might get smart enough to make bootleg legal. His humming grew louder. Life had taken on meaning again.

Ben ranked wooden fenceposts over the burial hole he had dug and told no one about it, except Natty, whom he pledged to secrecy. Natty, on the phone, seemed distant, hesitant, noncommittal. If only his son were there to share the conspiracy, Ben thought. He decided to use the old potato storage shed behind the corncrib to set up shop. It had a dirt floor, so a fire under the boiler would not set the building ablaze. Though completely hidden from view of house, road, or main barn, it was close enough to the water tap in the milk house to run a hose to the condenser for the constant water supply needed to keep the condenser cool. Also, handy to the still was a pile of stovewood which they had worked up the preceding year for winter fuel. No one would be likely to notice if they used some of it to fire the still. For a boiler, Nat spirited Dorothy's old pressure canner out of the cellar when she was away visiting Nan. It no longer sealed well enough for pressure canning, but as an evaporator it would not require pressure. Ben removed the valve on top and soldered an adapter to connect to the copper piping, using silver solder, not lead, as Nat directed him. Lead solder could adulterate the finished product. Next, again with Nat in command, he soldered together a little copper tank into which the copper pipe from the evaporator would run. Nat filled the cannister with ceramic electric fence insulators. "Most bootleggers use marbles," Nat said, enjoying the mystification on Ben's face. "Insulators work 'bout as well. You can even skip this part and go right from the evaporator to the condenser—if you don't mind your whiskey tasting like battery acid. The experts call this tank a stripping column. They'll use fancy plates that do the same thing insulators do. The liquor steam rises up through them, and what's called the low wines, the poorer stuff, condenses and drip back into the evaporator while the good alcohol goes on to the condenser." He paused, staring at his son. "Didn't know I was so smart, did you?" he quipped. "Early bootleggers skipped this step and just ran the vapors through a tank of water called a thumper or doubler, which helped to distill a finer spirit, but not much."

Next Nat turned his attention to the final step in the process, the condenser. This required another length of copper pipe, formed into a spiral. Ben filled the pipe with sand, as his father directed, so that bending it into a spiral would not crimp the passageway closed. Ben started humming under his breath as he worked, like his father. He was becoming intoxicated with making moonshine, and hadn't even tasted it yet. The spiral piping was then positioned in a five-gallon bucket of water, exiting out the bottom of the bucket through a hole sealed tight around the pipe so the water could not leak out. A hose bringing cool water for condensing from the milk house completed the assemblage.

Now it was time for action. Into a fifty-five-gallon barrel half full of boiling water Nat poured fifty gallons of cornmeal and let the mash soak for eight hours. When it had cooled to 80 degrees, he prepared the malt and yeast mix, the malt from barley, sprouted a little, dried, and milled. Ten pounds of barley malt, two pounds of rye mash, and a half pound of yeast. "Do not add sugar to the mash," he said, as if lecturing students. "Sugar is the easy way to get fermentation started, but bad moonshining. Makes the whiskey burn the throat. You want it to go down as smooth as plum juice." Ben nodded, suppressing a smile. He did not intend to make whiskey himself and did not even think they would actually make a batch now, but anything to keep that light in his father's eyes.

"Using malt to start your yeast instead of sugar is another secret to good moonshine. Then if you could get a really good yeast from a distillery, you'd be in business. But distilleries guard their yeast like it was gold. We'll just have to use regular kitchen yeast."

"Really?"

"Now go home and do your chores. We'll lay low and let this ferment for a couple of weeks." He winked. He was having fun.

It took special willpower for Ben not to tell Mary what they were doing. Next to milking sheep, this moonshining business was the most amazing idea he had ever observed. This was how his father had gotten the money to pay for his farm. Now he understood. His father had it right. The government of the wealthy by the wealthy and for the wealthy did not want poor people making whiskey, because they just might make enough money to buy land.

In about two weeks, the phone rang. Mary answered it as usual. She listened, nodded, said, "I'll tell him," and hung up, a perplexed look on her face.

"That was your father. He said to tell you that he thinks there's a change of weather coming on and that you should be sure to take a look at the sky tonight. Is he all right? Could he be getting maybe, you know, a little senile? He's seemed so vigorous lately."

"Oh, we were arguing about whether it was going to rain," Ben lied. "I said it wasn't, so now he's teasing me because it's supposed to shower tonight. Believe me, there's nothing wrong with his mind."

After chores and supper, Ben said he had to check the electric fence at the back of the farm. There was a short in the line somewhere along the road, he said. He sped away in the truck, headed straight for his father's farm.

"It's ready," Nat said. "See how it bubbles up. Frothy. Take a taste of that froth. The fountain of youth, the old-timers claimed."

"Smells and tastes like beer," Ben said.

"That's sort of what it is. Tomorrow we gotta start distillin', okay?"

"I think I'll have another taste of that froth," Ben said, winking.

When he parked the pickup back at his own barn, he picked a sprig of mint from the garden to chew on. Mary could smell beer a mile away. He tried to think of a time when he was as excited and amused and also as apprehensive as he was now. Maybe after the Roman candle fight so long ago.

The next day Nat started a fire under the evaporator, the converted pressure cooker, held up above the fire by a few fire bricks. As the mash began to cook, he kept a sharp eye on the thermometer on the lid of the pressure cooker. "The closer you can keep the heat steady just under 180 degrees—about 175 degrees—the better for the taste, and better for avoiding a hangover when you drink the stuff," he said. "The old-timers didn't have thermometers. They dripped hot wax on the copper tubing coming out of the evaporator. When that wax started melting, the liquor was coming and it was time to cut back on the fire. The whole point is that alcohol boils quicker than water, and that's how you get the two separated."

Soon he turned on the water from the milk house hose to the condenser, and shortly the first drippings dribbled out of the condenser. To Ben's surprise, his father let the alcohol fall on the ground for a short time before setting a container under the spigot. "The first whiskey is harsh, contains too much poison stuff," he explained.

"And you have to know when to stop collecting the condensation, too," he explained an hour later. You want to stop when the alcohol content falls below 110 proof. Or a higher content if you want really good stuff." He caught a spoonful of liquor out of the condenser and lighted it with a match. It burned readily and stayed burning for a few minutes. "That means the alcohol is over 140 proof—seventy percent alcohol," he said. "When the liquor won't burn beyond a sputter, it's time to stop collecting the drippings."

When the first run was completed, he cleaned out the sour mash and poured the whiskey back into the evaporator to repeat the whole process. "It would pay to do it a third time," he said, "but I might be dead by then."

Next Nat turned his attention to aging the distilled liquor. "We should age the whiskey in oak barrels, but I don't know how long I got," he said once again. "We'll let it soak in charred oak chips for awhile. If I don't die for another six months, that'll make a pretty good whiskey with a good amber color."

"I don't think you're going to die so quick," Ben said, almost smiling.

"Well, why take chances. Let's try some now," Nat said, and both of them did smile.

He sipped and smacked his lips. Ben followed, hesitantly. To his surprise, the clear liquid did just as his father had described—went down as smooth as plum juice. He took a long swig.

"Whoa, young man. Dat stuff'll creep up on you," Nat said, still smiling. "Sip. Tossing down whiskey like you see on TV won't take you very far down the road." Nevertheless, he did a bit of tossing himself. "Want another go at it?"

Ben nodded. He decided that the effects of alcohol were greatly exaggerated. He felt no different than if they were drinking water.

"I don't know that we have enough for the funeral," Nat said after they had sipped a while. "We should do another batch."

"We can hide it in the grave under the fenceposts," Ben said. For some reason that suggestion struck him as deserving of a hearty laugh.

"Well, don't bury any of it with me. Be too dark in there to find the bottle." They both cackled at that. Neither had thought old Nat could be so funny.

Ben stood up, stretched, took a step, and sat back down again. "Wow. Guess I got up too fast. Dizzy."

"That's what happens when you get old, my boy. You ain't old yet."

"Well, I feel old."

"Whatever you do, don't blame the Fruit Juice," Nat said sarcastically. Now they both chuckled, although they still couldn't figure out what was so funny.

So occupied had they become, as they tried ever so solemnly to pour a little more of the Fruit Juice into their glasses, that they did not notice the appearance of visitors.

"What in the world are you two doing?" The voice was coming from someone leaning against the corncrib. A bit of focusing on the figure revealed that it was Nan.

Could have been a lot worse. As she moved toward them and repeated her question, the situation did get worse. A second figure came around the corncrib. Gott in Himmel! It was Dorothy.

The two women took in the scene. Although it surpassed all belief, Dorothy knew she was looking at a whiskey still, and if she had any doubt, it vanished as she studied the two men, swaying unsteadily in front of it.

"Oh, my luffly," Nat said, waving his glass at her. "Seeing you here is indeed a cause for celebration."

So ludicrous a sight did the two men make that Dorothy could not suppress a smile, especially when she remembered that he had often called her "luffly" in the old days when they quarreled about the Fruit Juice. Nevertheless, she knew her duty.

"If you two don't look as foolish as two flies swimming in a bucket of milk. What on earth has gotten into you?"

Nat was only very slowly comprehending the scene. Ben cleared it up for her. "You really ought to try some," he said. "Goes down like plum juice. You don't feel a thing." And then both men broke into laughter again.

Dorothy shook her head. "I don't believe it. My men turning into boys. I've a mind to—" she broke off, too exasperated to talk.

"I want some," said Nan.

"Young lady, you are sixty years old, for heaven's sake. You just follow me on back to the house. Someone in this family has to—"

"I want some."

"Be my guest," her brother said, weaving toward her, holding out his glass magnanimously. "You won't feel a thing." Again his words struck him as enormously funny.

While Dorothy sputtered, Nan sipped. A very wee sip. She swallowed, as if expecting lightning to strike her. Nothing. She sipped some more. Exactly. Like plum juice. Boring. She sipped some more. "It really does taste like fruit juice. Sort of."

"I will not put up with this one second more." Dorothy was blazing now.

"Mother, I think you should take a sip," Nan said. "Really."

"Yes, Mom, I think you might be surprised, " Ben said.

"Look at that. I never thought I'd see the day when my son, of all people—"

Nat had managed to slip up beside Dorothy. He put one arm around her and lifted the glass of Fruit Juice to her mouth. "Come on, my luffly," he said, imitating the broken English of his early immigrant days. "Remember the meadows of Tamsweg. Remember that day when first we met. I believe it was wine that day."

Dorothy looked at his wizened old face and saw the young man who had courted her in the Alpine hills, saw those days of shepherd and shepherdess that they had assumed would go on forever. Her resistance to his embrace relaxed. That look was in his eye that she could not resist, that look that compelled her to follow him across a terrible sea and halfway across a hostile country.

"Don't you trifle with me, old man," she said, but fondly now. It wasn't like she didn't know a thing or two about alcohol or any other forbidden fruit. She smiled. She sipped. She smiled again, a little wickedly this time.

"Well, I think I'm going to crap," Nan said, watching her mother.

Ben sat down on an overturned bucket. Otherwise he might have fallen down. His creamy glance went from one family member to the next and back again. This was just too totally luffly. If only Mary, Natty, and Amelia were there.

"Just the four of us again," Nat was saying, also studying the other three. "Like in the beginning. That was the best time. I thought those days would go on forever. I thought that nobody would grow older for a long, long time. Ha. How dumb I was."

Dorothy nodded. "Strange, how a person thinks. Those were days I thought were bad, but they weren't. I'd take you two little tykes to the pool in the park on those long, hot afternoons and we had the whole place to ourselves, like we were rich and the park was our backyard. We *were* rich. I thought that time of life would go on for years and years. That things would get better financially but everything else would stay the same. Yes, how dumb I was too."

"Remember how that one jar of Fruit Juice started floating towards the surface?" Nan recalled. "I kept one jar underwater by holding it between my legs. I never told, but I peed right on that jar in the water." All of them whooped. But Nan sort of sobered again. "You seemed to have lots of time to play with us in those days, Mom. I could never seem to manage that when Floyd was little. There's no tranquility today."

"I hardly called it tranquil with that damn Fruit Juice always around." Dorothy didn't seem to realize that she had said "damn." Maybe for the first time. "Well, it was different in the old days when your Pa and I were tending sheep and cattle on the mountain slopes. There was so much time then, it seemed. And in the evening we all went back into the village and sat around and talked and visited till it was time to go to bed."

"Like Gowler used to do," Ben said. Long pause. "Maybe we'll get back to that."

As they reminisced, Nat sat down on the ground, his back against the wall of the shed, and just listened. He felt a great weariness and had to force himself to keep his eyes open. Finally he gave in to sleep and slumped over sideways.

"Hey, Dad, I think you've had enough," Ben said.

Nat opened his eyes, straightened up momentarily, and stared into eternity. "There's a box I nailed together for a coffin in the old granary," he said. Then, after a pause, he heaved a sigh. "And I don't mind saying, you are the best family a man could ever have, and *this* is the best wake I ever went to." He closed his eyes and slumped over again. Ben stepped to his side, straightened him, patted him gently on the head. No response. He held his ear to his father's chest. Nothing.

"I think he just died." he said in awe. "Just like that."

Nan bent beside her brother. She wished she knew how to take her father's pulse, like they did so deftly on television, but she didn't need to. This was not the first dead face she had peered into; she knew what death looked like. Dorothy toddled over, stooped down, gathered her two offspring in her arms, one on each side of her husband, and looked into his vacant eyes. No one moved for what seemed like several minutes.

"You were a good man, Nat Bump, and I'll be coming along shortly," she finally said. "If I could make it across the ocean, don't you worry, I'll make it to wherever you're going this time, too."

lthough Nat might have been surprised, a goodly crowd attended his funeral, mostly out of curiosity, and walked up the hill behind his barn to say good-bye. Their curiosity was not just over the fact that his grave was so unorthodox. They had heard that the refreshments just might include a special fruit juice punch that, rumor said, old Nat had made himself. Dorothy's relatives, after talking over the propriety of attending a funeral at which no religious rites would be observed, and at which they would not be allowed to view the corpse, decided finally that it was their duty to comfort their kinfolk. Their tight lips and curt nods of hello were not much comfort, but Dorothy was beyond caring, no doubt partly because of a wee sip of the punch. She even thought that her relatives might provide a little comic relief before the funeral was over. As staunch teetotalers, they might not become aware of the alcoholic basis of their "refreshment" until it was too late. "Papa is comforting me even in death" was how she put it, whispering to Nan. There was that look on her face that reminded Nan of the night her mother stared down the barrel of Old Blunderbuss at the hapless Dob Hornley playing Ku Klux Klan.

Ben did not appear to be exactly overcome with grief either. He was moving through the gathering crowd, offering glasses of punch from pitchers sitting on a makeshift table of plywood over saw-horses and opining that when an honorable man dies a natural death from old age, a joyful celebration is at least as appropriate as a sorrowful one. That was what his father had asked him to say, and so he did. The mourners sipped their refreshment, gingerly at first, then thoughtfully, then steadily, and finally decided that Ben was correct. Arms that had at first been folded protestingly across chests opened up and eased to the task of pouring more punch. Both the flow and volume of conversation increased noticeably. One mourner after another felt moved to voice a declamation or two on the life of "old Nat." Finally, most of them found that they could peer down at the crude coffin in the grave without embarrassment, could even remark that the patchwork quilt draped over it was one of Dorothy's finest.

"Are you going to bury that quilt?" Dorothy's sister Matilda asked, meaning to stress the preciousness of the quilt, but once more seeming to imply disapproval. Nan was quick to reply.

"You think we should take his suit off too and save it?" she said acidly. "Bury him naked maybe."

Matilda's husband tried to smooth over his wife's remark. "Remember the day Nat slammed Dob Hornley up against the grain elevator wall and damn near broke Dob's teeth out?"

"Nobody ever said anything about profiting from war after that, leastways not when old Nat was around."

"But it was the night he marched old Dob and those KKK fellars nekkid right up to the courthouse that I remember best."

"By God, that took some real balls."

"Wonder if he ever did spy for the Germans?"

"Oh, shit, what would he have told them? That we had a good corn year in '44?"

"Well, he wouldn't honor the flag. That ain't Christian."

"If you were a North Vietnamese Christian, whose flag would you honor?"

"Now don't get started on Vietnam, for God's sake."

"I really do think that he was moonshinin', like they said. Had to get some money from somewheres. Sure didn't make it farmin' Killdeer."

"He might have. He was a good farmer. In the old way."

"Didn't do too bad in the new way, either."

Before long, people who had hardly spoken to each other for years were remembering stories. Billy Burks, graying and potbellied beyond any memory of his early years, found it almost easy to mention the runaway of old Nat's horses that he and his brother and Wayne Gitchell had started with firecrackers, and could even smile as Emmet recalled how the trio ended up in a Killdeer wet hole during the Roman candle fight that had been their punishment. Betty Torman, whose presence at the funeral no one could explain, had married Gitchell after all, but was now widowed. "Truth is," she explained, although no one had asked her, "he just blundered from one wet hole to another." And when Nan mischievously brought up the Fight at the OK Dorral, Betty even smiled, as if she were seeking closure on that unpleasant memory. But then she started crying, and Nan impulsively reached out a hand and patted her arm soothingly.

Dorothy's relatives, with a little urging from the punch, were trying to find something nice to say about old Nat, but it was hard going.

"I think he really did believe in the God of our forefathers."

"Yep. He just liked being contrary."

"Maybe, but I don't know how many times I heard him say he didn't believe in the hereafter and didn't think anyone else really did, either."

"He meant well."

"How do you know he wasn't right?" This from Nan, who could not resist being the flash point of any argument she encountered. But no one rebuked her.

"Dad said that dying wasn't as awful as we make it out to be," Ben said. "He said he was just disappearing back into the life force that he had come from. If we rejoice at a birth emerging from the life force, he said, we should rejoice when death takes us back into it. Keeping the life force replenished is the only eternity there is."

People eyed him queerly, and he immediately regretted his words. Was his father speaking from the life force? Or was it the Fruit Juice? Maybe the Fruit Juice was the life force.

"What's 'life force'?" someone asked.

"Just another way of saying God," said another.

"I think God is sort of like a huge electromagnetic coil in the sky," remarked Herman Shackleberger, the community electrician. "Everything's plugged into it, "

"That's a shocking idea," someone else said, feeling the Fruit Juice. Those within earshot started snickering.

"I don't believe in life after death either," declared Jack Cughes. Never before that moment had he admitted such heresy. "But I keep goin' to church just in case I'm wrong."

Snickers turned into chuckles.

"Perhaps it is time for a silent prayer, whatever be our various gods or lack thereof," said Father John O'Brien, who had come to the funeral out of duty to the churchgoing members of the family. But the Fruit Juice made that remark seem somehow humorous, even to him. As they all bowed their heads to pray, nearly everyone was suppressing nervous little grins.

A voice from the crowd announced: "I just want you to know, Nat, if you can hear me, that I cheated you a little one time. Those bales I sold you for two dollars each didn't weigh enough for that price."

"Oh, hell, Fred, he knowed that."

Again a murmuring of suppressed laughter. And then another voice. "I stole a pocketknife out of your toolbox when I was a kid, Nat. It's bothered me all these years."

"I bet even money he knowed that, too."

Those who had been refreshed the most by the Fruit Juice punch now began to laugh outright, and as often happens when laughter seems out of place, it quickly crescendoed out of control. And the harder the people laughed, the more they shed tears too. And the looser became their tongues.

"I coveted some of your goods, neighbor Nat, but that's all." How hilarious that sounded.

"I ain't proud of it, Nat, but we'uns used to make fun of your English."

That was too much for Mary, the schoolteacher, and even she gave in to giggling.

Suddenly, overcome, Matilda wrapped her arms around Dorothy. Instead of saying how she prayed that Nat would escape the fires of hell, as Dorothy expected her to say, her sister was asking for forgiveness. "I was wrong not to come to Ben's wedding," she wailed.

Dorothy was so affected that she turned to Nan in confusion. She had not favored Nan equally with Ben, and now her guilt over that, feeding on Matilda's, caused her to hug her daughter fiercely. If Nan understood, she did not say so. She was way beyond all that.

"Don't go too soft on me, Mom," she said in Dorothy's embrace. "When Mattie sobers up tomorrow, she'll be as contrary as ever. And so will I."

"I was watchin' your father that day when you kept topping the bid," Sherwood Brady felt compelled to tell Nan. "I never saw an old sunburned farmer look so pale. When he said 'Gott in Himmel' while I was trying to pull another raise out of you, that's as close as I ever came to losing track of a bid." He paused. "You notice, though, that he never really did stop you. I bet anything he was proud of you, deep down."

Nan had never thought of that. Suddenly she believed that Brady was right. She wanted to believe it, anyway.

"This is fairly the best punch I've ever tasted," Jake Lavendar roared, uneasy at the silence that followed Brady's remark.

"Yep, thairly it is," chimed in Franklin Farnold, who was obviously going to take his confused consonants to the grave with him. "Just what's in this thruit juice anyway, Ben?"

"You'd have to ask Dad," Ben replied, "and unthortunately, that's not possible now." He found his cheeriness embarrassing but could not suppress it.

He had a plan for the burial, but only another sip of the punch gave him the boldness to proceed. Then he walked slowly to the edge of the grave, pulled loose one of the several shovels he had stuck into the burden of dirt that had come from the hole, and started shoveling. The crunch of clods hitting coffin echoed dully over the hushed crowd. What was Amish Bump up to now? It might be traditional to throw a handful of dirt on the coffin, but he just kept shoveling. In the silence of the spectators, his son, Natty, stepped forward, picked up another shovel, and did as his father was doing. Then Nan. And then her son, Floyd.

"Jeesus," Emmet muttered almost audibly, "they're going to bury him right now, right in front of everybody." But he immediately decided that it was a good idea. It would at least keep people from feeling that they had to make asinine remarks. He took up a shovel and joined in. After a few minutes, two more people grabbed the two remaining shovels and earth thudded steadily into the hole. That was the only sound except for the sobbing from Dorothy and Matilda. When one of the shovelers tired, another stepped forward to take up the work. Soon people were standing in line, waiting their turn. The most energetic shoveler was Louis Remp, and not even Nan knew for sure why. Humans were so unpredictable, she thought. They could prove themselves despicable beyond words and then turn around and show that they might have been something else in a different environment.

Mary, watching, hanging back, could hardly believe what she was seeing. A community burying one of its own. *Literally* burying one of its own. She trembled, holding tightly to Amelia with one hand and with the other hand to a book containing a poem she had found that she particularly liked. She had thought she might read the poem, but did not know if she would have the nerve, or if there would be a moment when a poem might be acceptable to this mostly unread audience. Now, as the soil mounted over her father-in-law's grave, she knew she had to do it. She stepped between the onlookers and the shovelers, opened the book, and cleared her throat. "I would like to read this poem, by Wendell Berry, titled 'At a Country Funeral.'" Her voice quavered at first, then, gaining confidence, increased in clarity and volume.

> *Now the old ways that have brought us*
> *farther than we remember sink out of sight*

as under the treading of many strangers
ignorant of landmarks. Only once in a while
they are cast clear again upon the mind
as at a country funeral. . . .

On she read, her voice growing louder where she thought the words more fitting—

Friends and kinsmen come and stand and speak,
knowing the extremity they have come to,
one of their own bearing to the earth the last
of his light. . . .

She gave particular pause at the phrase "when even the gods were different," wondering if these people would understand. Then on she read in an even voice, emphasizing only certain words so that the people would connect them to the present moment— *this* naked hillside, *this* open grave, *this* organ music, which in this case was really coming from Dick Farnold, who had pulled his harmonica from his pocket and was softly playing "O Bury Me Not on the Lone Prairie," as if he and Mary had planned the whole performance.

Approaching the end of the poem, Mary paused and seemed to rise above the ground a little as she gathered breath and volume for what she thought the saddest and yet most exalting lines of any poem ever written.

. . . And so as the old die and the young
depart, where shall a man go who keeps
the memories of the dead, except home

> *again, as one would go back after a burial,*
> *faithful to the fields, lest the dead die*
> *a second and more final death.*

"The end."

Dick Farnold quit playing, embarrassed now, not able to explain even to himself why he had started. Such a stillness hung over the grave site that the murmuring water of the creek at the foot of the hill could be distinctly heard, like a chorus to the falling tears. Ben had paused to lean on his shovel, no longer able to keep from weeping. Now, in spite of the tears, he resumed the work. Other shovelers followed. The pile of soil that had stood beside the grave disappeared back into the hole. The shovelers mounded over the last of it, patting the earth down smooth with the backs of their shovels, reluctant now to quit. Finally they filed down the hill and to their cars, or, if kinfolk, into the house, most of them with something of an unsteady step. Only Ben remained. He crawled wearily on the tractor nearby. In its manure scoop was a huge rock from the creek bed. His father had directed him to use it for his stone. He drove slowly to the mound of earth, lowered the rock down gently on top of it, and backed the tractor away.

THIRTY-THREE

Ben could sense that something peculiar was in the air. Emmet was acting out of character. Or at least he was acting sub-dued, a state that was hardly characteristic of him. For one thing, he was wearing a strange, rumpled old cowboy hat. He didn't have anything to say, either, not even about the hat. He just stood around in Ben's barnyard, as if waiting for Ben to start a conversation. Emmet had never shown much interest, at least not directly, in what Ben was doing, so Ben decided that his brother-in-law was just trying to comfort him over his father's death. Now, for the first time, they had something so hurtful in common that it could heal the money rift between them. Both had lost their fathers.

"So you actually made moonshine, right? For the funeral?"

Ben smiled and nodded. "It kind of turned out that way, didn't it?"

"Got any left?"

While they sampled the last bottle of the Fruit Juice, Emmet asked about how it was distilled. Ben thought he was just mak-ing conversation. But Emmet kept asking for more details. So Ben dragged the still out from behind hay bales in the mow, where he had hidden it, and did a dry run through the process. "Surely you aren't thinking about getting into the business, are you?" he finally asked.

Emmet shrugged disarmingly. "You know making whiskey is the same as making ethanol. Might we could make our own tractor fuel and drink the surplus." Both laughed.

Then Emmet changed the subject. He wanted Ben to show him over his farm and explain to him more about what this newfangled pasture farming was all about. Now Ben knew his brother-in-law was trying to comfort him. Emmet had always declared that pasture farming was an idiot's pipe dream. But since Emmet insisted, Ben obliged. He loved talking about his work. Hardly anyone ever showed interest.

"What I've done is split up the farm into ten fields each ten acres in size," Ben said. "There's eight fields of various grasses and clovers, another in corn and another for testing new plants for grazing. But you don't care about all that."

"What's this grass, where we're walking?"

"You know what it is. Bluegrass. It's an improved variety. That's why it looks a little different. It's a little growthier than most bluegrass. This variety comes from eastern Europe. Actually, no bluegrass is native to America."

"It's *not?*"

"Nope. I didn't know that either. It came from Europe and swept across America in less than a century. And then Little Dutch white clover grew with it, all without any help from anyone. If you don't do anything except mow it regularly, like our lawns, the land around here will end up being mostly bluegrass and white clover permanently, if it's drained properly. But you aren't interested in that."

"Well, that is amazing. But the way I hear it, ryegrass is better than bluegrass for grazing."

"That's what they're saying. Nobody's pushing bluegrass, because it's permanent and free. That's the way humans are. Something can't be worth anything unless you have to buy it. Bluegrass is not something seed companies can make much money on like they can on ryegrass, so they push ryegrass. Bluegrass is more palatable, persists much longer, and holds up in drought about as well as ryegrass. It just doesn't yield as much forage as ryegrass, and in farming, as you well know, quantity is everything."

"You don't agree."

"Nope. If it rains, a bluegrass-and-white-clover pasture is better, seems to me. If it doesn't rain, you're in trouble either way."

Emmet stopped and looked out at the next field. "That's red clover," he said. "And that over there is alfalfa."

"Those are for hay, or if it dries up in July and August, for emergency pasture. Red clover and alfalfa go right on growing even in dry weather, as you know."

"So you move the cows and sheep from one pasture to another as necessary, and on the hay stands if you need to and make hay on them otherwise."

"At least first cutting when there's a surplus of pasture. I can graze from April until Christmas. Three-fourths of a year. Don't have to feed but a little grain. Cheap way to make milk. And if I can let a hay stand go, it will pasture into January, if it doesn't snow too much."

"Pretty neat."

Could Emmet actually be complimenting me? Ben asked himself. His friend must be sick. "The trick is learning how long to graze a field before moving the livestock to the next. There's an art to it. You can't go by the calendar. You just gotta feel it. And clipping a field after grazing it also keeps the grass succulent and the weeds down. But not always. It just depends. It's art." Ben waited for an objection, but none came. Normally Emmet would have snorted at the idea of farming being art. Everything was science, by the book, by the chart, by the chemical analysis. No place in modern farming for an Amish Bump. But now Emmet said nothing.

Emmet was staring at Ben's cornfield now. "Those are the longest damn ears I ever saw. Longer than they were even last year, I think." He whipped a tape measure out of his pocket. Ben wondered why he had a tape measure with him. "Holy Kee-risterfer, that ear's fifteen inches long!"

"They dry down to about thirteen inches." Ben tried to sound modest. "And this open-pollinated corn still doesn't yield as well as hybrid. At least not yet. But livestock take to it. It chews better. Must have a better flavor. Does to me."

Emmet did not laugh as he customarily would have. He didn't laugh either when Ben pointed out that if one were husking the corn by hand, as he did, husking one big ear didn't take as much time as husking two small ones. Emmet just nodded. He had always considered Ben smart enough in his own way, but of course since he disagreed with Emmet on farming, he could not be really smart. Now Emmet wondered. Maybe his brother-in-law was some kind of genius husbandman, not out of the past, but living in a land that other farmers in the neighborhood hadn't yet discovered.

"But here's something more interesting," Ben said, leading Emmet on to the field he referred to as "experimental." Emmet's jaw dropped. This was a very strange sight for a farm in Ohio. He remained silent, staring at Ben, not believing what his eyes were telling him.

"Yep, that's what you're lookin' at," Ben said, enjoying his friend's bewilderment. "Sweet corn and oats growing together. Planted in July. That's for winter pasture. That's a way I think I can graze even when the snow's flying. Snow won't cover the corn, won't cover the oats much either. The animals love sweet corn ears and eat the fodder better than regular corn. And the oats boost protein in the cows' diets."

Emmet just stared.

"Only an experiment. Maybe it'll work, maybe not."

"Which takes to pasture farming better, sheep or cows?"

Emmet must really think I need special humoring, Ben thought. He doesn't care about sheep or cows. But if Emmet wanted to humor him, he'd humor right back. "Well, sheep are easier because they can run on the sod without too much damage even when the ground's soft. Also, cows seem to need a very high-protein diet to make all the milk and meat that profits demand, but not sheep. Might be that someday we could raise sheep year-round on pasture alone, no grain at all, even in the north. Maybe not even have to make hay, except enough for weather emergencies. But I don't know whether there's as much money in sheep, unless you milk them."

"*Milk* them?"

"Gonna try it." Again he waited for snide remarks. None.

"How many head can you run per acre?"

"Seems like a cow and calf and two ewes and their lambs. Or five ewes and their lambs. But no telling how carrying capacity might increase if you farmed like this for a hundred years, with the ground getting richer every year from the manure and nitrogen fixation from the clover, and no erosion or compaction from tearing the land up so much for annual grains. I'll tell you what I *really* think. I've a notion that sprinkler irrigation would really pay in this kind of farming. You could spread the cost of the installation out over a lifetime. Then I'd never have to worry about too little rainfall. I could have pastures all the time as slick as a suburban lawn." He paused. "Or like those fairways on your golf course."

Emmet broke into a sudden laugh, startling Ben. But he did not explain what amused him so.

"You have to have water in every field, right?"

"I use the crick for three of the fields. Got tanks for the others. One on the fence line between two fields. I'm thinking about little ponds in each field for water, too. And for fish. Like the ponds on your golf course."

Again Emmet laughed heartily, apparently for no particular reason. Just humoring me, Ben thought.

By the time the two got back to the house, Ben realized that he been talking nonstop for an hour, longer than he had ever talked before at one stretch. He hoped Emmet didn't think he needed comforting very often. Emmet, for his part, thanked him for the time, something else he would normally not do, and drove away. Ben still felt a strangeness in his brother-in-law's manner. Emmet seemed to have something on his mind that he wasn't ready to divulge.

And that was true for sure. Emmet's brain had been boiling over with frustration at the way grain farming was going. He felt that he was becoming a mere lackey of overweening government. Without the thousands of dollars in subsidies he was receiving, corn and soybeans on Killdeer ground would hardly pay at current prices. Meanwhile, fuel, machinery, fertilizer, pesticide, and land costs just kept climbing. There was no fun in farming anymore. Make one little miscalculation, or take one little hit from the weather, and what profit there might have been achieved evaporated into thin air or drowned in floodwater. In keeping with Gowler tradition, he professed being a Republican, and he hated to admit that farming wasn't capitalism anymore, if it ever had been. It was time for change again, as drastic as the golf course had once seemed.

But what change?

It was at that point in his thinking that the Fruit Juice reap-peared at Nat's funeral. After Emmet had helped shovel the dirt into Nat's grave and learned the truth about the punch, he had given a great amount of thought to the Fruit Juice. First he thought about starting a microbrewery, turning his corn into beer. But wouldn't it be better to start a microdistillery and turn his corn into bour-bon? He even went to Kentucky and toured a couple of distilleries. The know-how was all in place. The only drawback was the out-landish fees one had to pay for a license to make the stuff legally. The big distilleries had made sure they didn't have much compe-tition. But maybe he could do something about that. Raise hell in Columbus. It was high time farm-made whiskey got the same kind of breaks that farm-made wine was getting. And if it didn't pan out, he could make ethanol instead.

Then, because the Fruit Juice made him think about Ben, and because he had just paid the bills at the golf course and found that it had cleared only $244.25 the last month, he had a second brain-storm. At first he nurtured it only as a form of amusement, because he could foresee that if he followed through, he would become the target of a mighty blowup of publicity in the neighborhood, maybe in the whole state, maybe in the whole Corn Belt. But the idea kept imposing itself on his consciousness until it possessed him. He would do what his great-great-grandfather had done a century ago. He would become a grass farmer like Ben. A rancher. An eastern cowboy. Or maybe an eastern sheepboy. And he would announce his historical change of heart by making a statement no one would ever forget. Just as the golf course had been his statement to the new era in 1960, so now he would turn the land back into prairie and graze sheep on it. Then he thought of something even more ridiculous. He would graze sheep *and* golfers on it. That's when he dug his great-great-grandfather's old drover's hat out of the attic and started wearing it. Whoopee ti yi yippee yippee aye. It was under the spell of that scheme that he had visited Ben.

Ben was just finishing morning milking a few weeks after Emmet's strange visit when a pickup roared into his barnyard, the tires spitting gravel behind them. It was Jake Lavendar, and as he walked towards the milk house, his agitation was evident. Something very disturbing had evidently occurred.

"You gotta fairly come quick," he gasped at Ben. "Emmet's lost it."

"I can't come now. I've got chores to finish."

"I don't fairly care, you gotta come NOW. Won't take long. You gotta stop him. Get in the truck."

Ben rolled his eyes. Now what? Had Emmet and Nan gotten into a real down-and-out fight? Lordy. Always something. "I'll take my own truck."

Jake led him to the golf course. Even from the road, or especially from the road, the cause of Jake's distress was apparent. Emmet had a crew of groundskeepers doing what groundskeepers had never done before to a golf course. They were stretching woven wire livestock fence along the whole course bordering the road. Another crew was putting in posts to extend the fence along the east side. Emmet was fencing in the golf course. He himself was just standing by, in command, grinning exultantly as Ben approached. Every time a slow-moving pickup passed, its driver peering intently at what was going on, Emmet pulled the cowboy hat off his head and bowed in a grand flourish. Ben looked up into the clouds. He surmised what was going on, but could not quite accept it. Now he realized why Emmet had been so solicitous when he had visited.

"You got it right," Emmet said, enjoying the wonderment on Ben's face. "I am turning this goddamn golf course into a sheep pasture. I'm going back to what my great-great-grandfather always knew. This land's made for sheep, not goddamn cornstalks." And he smiled in supreme pleasure at his words.

"See. What did I fairly tell ya?" Jake said, looking at Ben. "Talk some sense into him."

But before Ben could say anything, another pickup roared up and screeched to a halt. Out piled Nan, and it was easy to see that she was as distressed as Jake. She hadn't known what her husband was up to, but Floyd had finally spilled the beans.

She launched right into him, with no thought at all for the workmen and her brother taking in the scene. "Have you lost your mind entirely?" she yelled. Emmet smiled, not at all displeased. Nan gave him no time to reply.

"You going to throw away a quarter million dollars you got in this golf course? You want I should call 911 and have you put in the loony bin?"

Ben stepped between then, just in case Nan was contemplating physical attack.

"Not getting rid of anything," Emmet said, sounding superior and still wearing the demure smile that he knew infuriated her. "Anybody who wants to can still play the course. Just have to watch out for sheepshit. I might cut the greens fee a little."

That stopped Nan dead in her diatribe and her tracks. Several times she opened her mouth to say something and then closed it without speaking. Her brain was analyzing what her husband had just said, going through all the various objections that could be made to that pronouncement faster than a computer could. She realized, in a rush, that strange as it might seem to the then–known world, people *could* still play golf in that situation.

She started laughing. Couldn't help herself.

"I'll keep the greens in good shape and more or less free of manure," he was saying, undismayed, knowing, as he had known all along, that once she got the whole scheme in her head, she would be just crazy enough to go along with it. That's why they were still married. "Hell, this will make news from sea to shining sea," he went on. "Golfers will come from miles around just so they can say they played on the sheepshit course. Won't be so bad. Sheepshit is kind of clean compared to cowshit. We'll get enough free advertising to build another nine holes, and then we can rotate the sheep from one course to the other, and one of them will be relatively shit-free half the time. You can graze a couple of those worthless nags of yours over here and maybe get free advertising for them too."

Nan had stopped shaking her head but was still grinning. "There's golfers would pay double to rent horse-drawn golf carts, I bet," she said. "All they'd have to do after hitting the ball was whistle and the horse would bring the cart right over to them. Better than a motorized job."

Emmet took off his cowboy hat and bowed to her. "Couldn't have said it better myself, my lovely. You know, in a few more years we just might figure out how to make farming pay after all." They laughed and embraced.

Ben had not thought himself a very demonstrative man, but now he was laughing helplessly, no Fruit Juice necessary. He had a notion that this brainstorm would end up no more successful than Emmet's earlier ones, but for sure there would be no boredom in Gowler in the meantime, and the town would become famous enough to draw in tourists. Even if the enterprise turned out to be only a passing phase, Emmet would think up something else to keep things humming. Ben was almost sure what Emmet's next enterprise would be, too: "Old Fruit Juice Bourbon, from the first modern distillery in Ohio."

But there was more reason for Ben to laugh with such abandon. If Emmet ran out of ideas, he and Nan could join Mary and him in his own crazy enterprises: Killdeer Roquefort Cheese, and something Natty had suggested on the phone recently, not altogether jokingly: "Natty Bump's Leatherstocking Line of Killdeer Woolens."

He could hardly wait to get home to tell Mary.